I0628070

Rose Nanashima

Vampire Democracy

Rose Nanashima is a pseudonym.
Further information is available at
www.knightshillpublishing.com

KNIGHTS
HILL

FIRST KNIGHTS HILL PUBLISHING EDITION, JUNE 2011

Knights Hill Publishing ISBN: 978-1937396008

www.knightshillpublishing.com

Printed in the United States of America

Vampire Democracy

Chapter 1.

I stood on the opposite corner of Broadway and Spring for a while, watching the paparazzi mob each minor celebrity who arrived at the new Hedy Rascal flagship store. I expected The Vampire Of The East to be fashionably late. During eight months of fieldwork, I'd lurked in worse places than a SoHo street corner, but the February wind knifed through my sloppy black peacoat. At nine thirty, I decided that if I had to wait, I'd do it where it was warm and there were free cocktails. I crossed the street. Mercifully, the remaining paparazzi ignored me.

"Name?" The PR boy shivering in the entrance wore one of Hedy Rascal's skinny three-piece suits. I was wearing jeans and Converse, but my peacoat was a Miu Miu original, a castoff from one of my father's assistants. My freshly washed hair gleamed white-blonde, straight and slippery on my shoulders. The PR boy looked right through me. They just keep on raising that bar.

I sighed and said, "Clare Standing. No, I'm not on the guest list. Who do I have to call?"

From behind me came a low howl: "There's a reason they call it *human rights*, Clare!"

The boy held the door for me.

"Clare hey *Clare!* You ask your daddy why he don't wanna protect the *women* and *children* of America!"

I didn't drop my father's name very often. Whatever perks came with being the daughter of a senator were outweighed by being the daughter of Nilson Standing, "the maverick spokesman of the religious left." My father had opposed the war in Iraq, supported the ill-fated Climate Change Prevention bill, and was currently trying to block the reauthorization of the Citizenship Act. My mother, an Englishwoman, had died while my brother and I were still children. Shortly after, my father had found Jesus and transformed himself, Batman-like, from a moderate Democrat into a crusader for social justice. Yeah, Nilson Standing was a maverick, all right. He continued to live his faith by giving away his entire income, keeping only the bare minimum for survival inside the Beltway. So whatever perks trickled down to me and Colin, an aristocratic lifestyle wasn't one of them.

There were *some* perks, though. I was inside the Hedy Rascal store.

A flunky reached out to take my coat, but I shook my head. A passing waiter offered me a flute of champagne. I took that. Sipping it, I wandered through the store. Red spotlights pulsated in time to monotonous house music. Journalists swarmed around models clad in Hedy Rascal's new line of bondage-wear. Minor TV personalities played pranks on the waiters. As I descended the spiral metal stairs to the basement, I spotted below me the beautifully shaped skull, capped with tight knots of black hair, that belonged to Leon Foulkes.

He was talking to a sex columnist from the Village Voice.

"The Vampire Of The East. May I have the pleasure?" Exaggerating the slight British accent I got from my mother, I handed my champagne to the sex columnist's male escort and curtsied, holding out an imaginary skirt.

Leon laughed out loud. "Shit, that's some funky shit. Aiight girl, you get on up – no, wait up, I know how this go. Arise!" He tapped me on the shoulder with the shiny cane that he affected. "Arise, Lady – ?"

"Clare. No title," I said, brushing off my knee. I shook Leon's hand and directed a quick smile at his entourage: a brunette in a trouser suit and a heavyset black man in a black leather jacket. Leon wore Hedy Rascal Homme, pinstriped drainpipes and a coat cut away to reveal a vest in different pinstripes, a broad yellow tie. His skin was the same peanut-butter hue as on TV, but he looked thinner in real life, his six feet two painfully stretched. Naturally, he was drinking red wine. "We had an appointment last Friday," I reminded him.

He hadn't shown. "I understand that your time is valuable, and I won't interrupt…"

"Oh no honey, no problem," the sex columnist said. "It was nice to meet you." They drifted away. Her male escort took my glass with him as if he'd forgotten he was holding it.

"I'd be very grateful if you could spare me a few minutes." I raised my voice over the music. "You're known as the public face of vampirism. That's a risky position to occupy at the present time. But I would like to offer you a chance to correct some of the misperceptions that have been propagated in the media."

"Hold on." The brunette in the trouser suit stepped past Leon as he started to answer. "What publication you with?"

"Actually, I'm not." I pulled my wallet out of my jeans and gave my card to Leon. "Department of sociology at NYU. We're conducting a survey—"

"This is the one that's been stalking you." The other half of Leon's entourage moved up. "You don't owe her nothing."

"—a scientific study to promote cross-cultural under-standing. We hope it will provide a counterweight to the media hysterics," I overrode him. Actually, Leon bore a lot of responsibility for the media hysterics, but I intended to give him a chance to claim that he'd been misrepresented.

"For real? You the one been calling my cell, jamming up my voicemail? You got something for me?"

"Some questions. You can even be anonymous if you prefer."

Leon smiled. "Know what this music is?"

"Wack-ass white folks' beats," said the guy in the black leather jacket. He and the brunette both snickered.

"It's called *crack house.* First they had Detroit house. Then deep house, acid house, what-all, now they got crack house. You wanna know about crack house? I was in one." Leon's eyes fastened on mine. They were a peculiar reddish-brown. I wondered if he was wearing colored contacts. "Until I Turned." He paused to let that sink in. "So what you got for me?"

I said evenly, "It could be a matter of life and death."

I wasn't joking. If the Citizenship Act got through the Senate in its present form, vampires in the United States could find their constitutional freedoms gutted. For the amateur vigilantes who already hounded them in many regions of the country, it would be open season.

"Hoo! Well, you forgot one thing, Clare." Leon moved closer to me. I smelled CK Eternity and something else, a musty smell that made me think of some wild animal, a fox, a stoat. He said, "You forgot I am immortal. I can't die. So for me, ain't no such thing as a matter of life and death."

His voice lacked conviction.

We rode across town in a Hummer with tinted windows driven by the guy in the black leather jacket, whom Leon addressed as Skaze. The stereo pumped dancehall reggae. Leon sat in the back with the balance of his entourage – two sycophantic homeboys in street wear – watching the Lakers game. I sat ahead of them with the brunette, Melia. She said to me in a low voice, "Are you sick?"

"Well, I know a lot of people think it's sick to take an interest in vampires. But I see it as essential that more is known about this subculture. They've been very secretive, and I think that's worked against them. That's why Leon is such an important—"

"I mean are you *sick*? Do you have a cold, a stomach bug, anything?"

"Only graduate-studentitis." She looked angry. I explained, "Chronic sleep deprivation clashing with recurrent caffeine and alcohol deficits."

"Well, you can't be sick if you're going to talk to Leon. I didn't want him to come out tonight. He picks up bugs just like that."

"I see. Well, he needn't worry about catching anything from me." I mentally noted: AIDS? Ingestion of blood = high-risk behavior. If not AIDS? Hepatitis, herpes? If none of the above? Secondary vampiric syndrome. Ammo for Brent

4

et al. Shit shit. I said cautiously, "Is it a chronic condition?"

"That would be like what, *vampiritis?*" Unexpectedly, she smiled. "I know there's people saying it's like a disease. Like you could catch it if you get too close to them, even without sharing blood. But if anyone was going to catch anything off of sharing blood, it would be them, not us. That's just logical."

Us? I glanced at her neck in the semi-darkness of the Hummer. Pale skin gleamed through the overstyled chestnut waves.

"No no, uh uh." She gave a coy shake of her head and held up her left hand. There was a Bandaid at the base of her thumb. "And…" She touched the inside of her trousered thigh. "But I'm clean. Most people aren't. That's why I had to ask you, you know."

"I hope there hasn't been any misunderstanding," I said cautiously.

"Oh, you think he might…" She laughed without mirth. "Don't you worry! He wouldn't hit on you in that way, not when he's got me."

"Per my understanding," I said, "vampires can't take blood from anyone who's not a willing—" I closed my mouth on the word *victim,* unnerved by the strength of the prejudices that had boiled up in my gut. It wasn't exactly fear. I simply felt a strong desire not to be sitting beside Melia, our thighs almost touching. I didn't want be in the same vehicle as this – this *woman.* She was a woman, an individual with a heart and soul, but my instincts were trying to dehumanize her. I'd never experienced anything like this around my other interview subjects. Then again, I hadn't had to go through a layer of aides to get to any of my other interview subjects. Maybe that had allowed me to overlook a problem with the format of our study: I'd never talked at any length with a self-identified victim… donor… "Sharer." It had taken me a second to remember the term they used among themselves. "The vampire has to ask for verbal consent before he or she can take blood, and the sharer has to grant it. That's correct, isn't it?"

Melia smiled. Her teeth gleamed in the livid spillage from the green light over West Broadway. For a single instant, I experienced real fear, the hollowing out of your lower abdomen that you can't mistake for anything else. "That's the *etiquette*," she said. "As you've probably noticed, they're real big on etiquette."

My fear now fading, I said, "I've heard it called *the Lore, the Sanguinarian Way,* and *the Dogma.*"

Melia laughed raucously. "Who you been talking to? Those fucking fanghandlers —" it rhymed with *panhandlers* — "that hang out in Thompson Square Park, trading BJs for blood? The hustlers that work the Upper East Side and the Hamptons like clowns at kiddie birthday parties?"

I let an abashed grin show. She was more or less right.

"They ain't real vampires." I wasn't listening to Melia herself anymore, I realized. She was quoting Leon Foulkes verbatim. "They're just poseurs. Wannabes with plastic fangs."

"I've met several who filed their teeth."

"Yeah, they can go the extra yard and fool them that want to be fooled, but they ain't shit. There's only one real vampire on the East Coast, girlfriend, and that is Leon Foulkes, the conducator of the United States of America."

Conducator?

The Hummer stopped. I'd been keeping track of our progress: we were on West 12th, a dark block of brownstones. Leon plunged his head and shoulders over the seat between me and Melia. His cologne assailed me again. "Clare, my very good *new* friend, you are about to experience a unique privilege. You are about to enter the crib of The Vampire Of The East. Blindfold her!" he suddenly cried. "Tie her hands!"

Everyone laughed.

"Just fucking wit' ya," said one of the aides.

The houses in this neighborhood were constructed on the railroad plan, deeper than they were wide. I knew the layout: my mentor and supervisor, Dr. James Merriwick, lived in a similar house a few blocks south of here. But the similarities stopped at Leon Foulkes's front door. Gilt dado rails ran the length of a black hallway lit by flickering electric sconces. The two junior aides peeled off towards the kitchen, where a female voice greeted them in petulant ghetto tones. The rest of us climbed the stairs in the dark to the third floor. Leon held me back until Skaze and Melia had gone into the room ahead of us. Lights came on, as did another dancehall track. "Now you gonna get the full effect," Leon said.

"Wow," I said, stopping on the threshhold. "Just... wow."

It was a lot more impressive in real life.

The interior walls had been torn down, leaving a tunnel with black walls and a black carpet. Track lighting drew my gaze to the far end of the room, where leopard print throws and cushions covered a sort of dais. In the middle of the dais stood a matching La-Z-Boy. More cushions and beanbags littered the floor in front of the dais. These, too, were leopard print, except for the ones that were zebra or tiger print. On one side of the room below the dais was a wet bar, on the other a home entertainment center.

Melia switched on the 60" flatscreen TV and flopped on-to a snow leopard print beanbag.

Leon stalked the length of the room, climbed onto the dais, and settled on the La-Z-Boy, one slim leg curling over its arm to switch like a cat's tail. "Not many people get to see inside of here," he told me.

"Except the cameramen from *News America* and the whole fucking crew of *Entertainment Tonight*," said Skaze, echoing my thoughts. He was at the bar, mixing drinks.

"Not many people in person, I'm saying." Leon stared at me. "Your daddy's the senator for Massachussetts."

"One of them," I said. "This term, he's the ranking Democrat on the Judiciary Committee."

"I got my own researchers." Leon flapped a languid hand at the floor. "I had you checked out. But I don't need to mix it up with no bullshit Congress committee. What they gonna have for me?"

Good call, Leon, I thought, suppressing a fierce shiver of

amusement at the thought of The Vampire Of The East testifying before the Judiciary Committee, uttering his egotistical
riffs while my father gazed at him with heartfelt pity.

I advanced towards the dais and looked up at Leon.
"Shall I tell you a little about the study we're conducting? As
I said, we want to put together an unbiased picture of the
place vampires occupy in society. Our objective is to gain a
better understanding of your culture, after twenty years of
misperceptions and misunderstandings. Hopefully, our findings will contribute to a positive resolution of the controversy over your legal status. Understanding is *the* condition for
social acceptance. I can't guarantee anything, of course, but I
believe that down the road, you and your people will benefit
from opening up to the scientific community." Leon was all
about his personal image, and I couldn't offer him anything
that would enhance that. But there had to be more to him
than an image, or he couldn't have achieved minor celebrity
status and the corresponding lifestyle, the blinged-out den
and crew of lackeys. "I'm offering you understanding," I repeated. "So I think we share the same goal."

"The same goal. She say we share the same goal."

Skaze and Melia laughed on cue. Skaze came up to me
with a glass of red liquid on a silver tray. "Take your coat?"
As he moved behind me to slip my peacoat off my shoulders,
he whispered under the music, "You best not be trying to
fuck with The Vampire Of The East. That's for your own
good I'm telling you that."

While relinquishing my coat, I held onto my bag. I juggled the drink Skaze had given me as I dug out my digital
recorder and survey documents. Leon said, "Have a seat."
He indicated the floor of the dais.

I hopped up and sat crosslegged on the leopard-print
carpet to the left of his throne. "This is the questionnaire I'd
like to go through with you." The distance between us was
awkward. I ended up going on hands and knees to give it to
him.

He barely glanced at the photocopied sheets. "So you're

a scientist."

"A graduate student. This study is my fieldwork. When it's complete, I'll need to write my dissertation, and if it's approved, I'll get my Ph.D. *Then* I'll be a scientist."

"You're not gonna like me for this " Leon's reddish eyes sparkled with fun. "But ain't you just a little old to be a student?"

I was thirty-one. Thanks to my mother's bone structure, most people took me for mid-twenties. It disconcerted me that Leon had seen something like my real age in my face. Then I remembered that he'd had me checked out. Just how thorough had he been? "There's no fixed period of study for a Ph.D," I said.

"But in your case, it took a longer time than usual. Didn't it? Cause your first project, study, your first *try* went to shit. You were over in Ireland. Investigating those old-time Celtic beliefs. Looking for the roots of the proto-religion known as Magick, that's with a K."

He'd quoted from my original research proposal.

"White folks' voodoo," muttered Skaze. He was leaning on the wall to the side of the dais, behind me, so I couldn't keep both him and Leon in sight at once.

"You spent a year talking to Irish witches and warlocks, or any of them that would talk to you," Leon pressed. "Participating in rituals that utilize. what was it? Proven brainwashing techniques."

"Maybe they brainwashed *her,*" Melia said without taking her eyes off the TV.

"I don't believe so," Leon said. "I believe they *couldn't* brainwash her. It don't work on everyone, after all. And that's why one day, without one word of explanation, they up and slammed the door in your face. Wouldn't talk to you no more. Would they? So you had to come back and start from scratch again. But this time, you learned your lesson. You ain't fucking with them gay-ass devil-worshipping wannabes no more. So you pick a different topic." He looked past me to Skaze. "Girl got it right second time out. She came to where the shit is real."

By now I'd collected myself and quelled the impulse to justify my aborted "Magick: Ritual and Belief" project. I said, "We still have an ongoing research interest in magic, but it's not my responsibility any more." I tried a rueful smile. "You could say I was kicked off the job."

"Now you getting twisty again." Leon shook his head. "*We*? Ain't no *we*. It's just you and your professor."

Sadly, he was right: James and I and a handful of undergrads were the entire department. In sociology, an interest in paranormal studies was seen as a shortcut to career suicide, and even though James was known as the father of the field, he still had to fight for research funding. "Mainstream social science dismisses those who lead paranormal lifestyles as…" I showed empathy by using his phrase, with a smile: "Gay-ass devil-worshipping wannabes. But we believe an understanding of these communities is indispensable to —"

"And the fuck you saying that's got to do with us?" Leon strained towards me, fighting the La-Z-Boy's reclining angle. "You saying vampires are some kind of witches and wizards, like that little gay nigga Harry Potter? Cause if that's what you think, you and your professor better go home and study up some more! *Then* you come back and talk to me." He sank back. "Ain't I been saying this shit all over TV for the last year," he muttered.

Leon hostile to magic. Rejects classification of vampires with witches and wizards. How could I have known? All my other vamp interviewees had displayed a cautious regard for magic, with or without a K. And Leon had gone on *Star Jones* together with a self-identified witch, a wizard, a satanist, and a woman who claimed to speak for an army of aliens from the fourth dimension. Had his smiley-faced TV persona concealed antagonism towards his fellow guests?

"Drink that," Leon snapped. "It ain't blood, if that's what you're thinking. It's just a smoothie that Skaze makes with tomato juice."

I pretended to take a sip of my drink, barely wetting my

10

lips. Clearly, I had to dispel the impression that my field-work formed part of a broader study. "I'm conducting my fieldwork in tandem with a group in Japan," I offered. "They're studying the vampire community in Tokyo. Our methods are slightly different, but we share the same objectives..."

The change in Leon's demeanor silenced me. He planted both feet on the floor and leaned towards me, hands braced on his thin knees.

What had he reacted to? Feeling my way, I said, "As you may know, Japan is facing a much —" On my lips was the media's favored phrase: *a much worse vampire problem.* I just managed to veer around it: "A more visible and numerous community of vampires." What was wrong with me tonight? Why did my mind keep slipping into this bigoted groove? "To an extent, vampires have integrated into mainstream Japanese society. So our colleagues at Aoyama Gakuin are employing slightly different research methods. But this questionnaire is identical to the one they're using. It was actually created by them, by Dr. Tsuyoshi Kamikawa and his assistants. I translated it myself to ensure we wouldn't have any discrepancies in the final survey data." Where was I going with this? I was getting more and more uneasy beneath Leon's stare. Skaze, too, had moved around in front of the dais to stare at me over his folded arms.

"You can speak Japanese?" Leon said.

"Of course I can. Although I'm more fluent at reading it. Ninety percent of the literature on vampires is in Japanese. Anyone engaging in serious research has to learn the language," I said rather sharply.

"But you can speak it?" Skaze.

"You ever been there?" Leon.

"Not yet. But I'm going to Tokyo in June. This is a two-year study. For the second year, I'll be trading places with a Japanese graduate student. The hope is that we'll be able to follow up on each other's fieldwork and expand it in fresh directions...."

11

"You're going to Tokyo," Leon stated. He fell back into his La-Z-Boy, grinning fixedly.

Melia rose from her beanbag and flew to Leon's side. She leaned over him, feverishly unbuttoning her shirt, like a mother about to feed an enormous infant. She fumbled down one cup of her bra. A pale, surprisingly full breast tumbled out. Skaze brushed past me and leaned over Leon from the other side. He grasped Melia's shoulder in one huge hand and jerked the other across the top of her breast, twice, in an X pattern. From my angle, I couldn't see exactly what he was doing, but when drops of blood fell on Leon's vest and necktie as Melia maneuvered her breast towards his mouth, I could guess what he'd had in his hand. An auto-lancet. All the vampires used them, if they didn't use syringes, or if they didn't own a pair of the special razor-sharp ceramic fangs sold for $1,499 and up by a small manufacturer in Ohio.

Leon, I recalled, had pointed canines, but so did plenty of people who didn't call themselves vampires.

Melia pressed her breast against his mouth. A drop of blood trickled down his jaw. His hands rose and clutched the breast. He still looked like a child, but now a slightly older one, eating a giant Chinese steamed bun, trying to cram the whole thing into his mouth at once. He showed no awareness that the breast was attached to a human being. He sat up with the nipple and half of the breast inside his mouth, his wide handsome lips concealing the cut. Melia moved with him, her eyes tightly closed. His eyes met mine. He spat out Melia's breast, took another look at it and pulled her back so he could lick off some more blood, then gave her a gentle shove. He held out his hand without looking. Skaze put a clean white handkerchief into it. Leon wiped his mouth and grimaced briefly as he caught sight of blood spots on his tie.

I was still sitting crosslegged on the floor, trying to imprint the whole scene on my memory. I'd only witnessed a feeding a couple of times before. The vampires tended to be private and mysterious about it. And the times I had seen it, the post-feeding energy boost had been nowhere near so dramatic. Bearing in mind that it might have been staged for my benefit, I watched Melia crossing shakily to the entertainment center and taking a handful of Kleenex from a black lacquered box. *No verbal consent given,* I noted. Maybe it was only required the first time a vampire fed from a victim.

"So you're going to Tokyo." Leon's grin was genuine now. "My sister lives there."

"Really? What does she do in Tokyo?"

"Her name's Dorothy. You ask your friends there about her. They might know her; least, they might know *of* her." Leon nodded and grinned.

"Is she a vampire, too?"

"Is she a vampire! Skaze. Is Dorothy a vampire?"

"She's vampire *nobility,*" Skaze said. "She's a hakooshak."

My brain hitched on the word for an instant, and then I heard *hakushaku.* Skaze had uttered the Japanese word for *Count* or *Countess.* But the way he'd pronounced it, I wasn't sure he knew it was Japanese. *A hakushaku.* Some vampires called themselves by titles – the one in front of me was a case in point – but I'd never heard of vampire *ranks.* Nor had Professor Kamikawa, the leader of the Japanese study, as far as I knew.

"How long has your sister lived in Japan?" I asked.

"Oh, 'bout ten years, off and on. She first went there back in the day, and she still comes home from time to time. If you go to Tokyo, you look her up, hear?"

"I certainly will," I said. "It would help if you gave me her contact information."

"Skaze, you get that off of the computer, blood." Leon jumped off the dais. His fatigue gone, he was moving like a cat again. He turned to look up at me. Perhaps it was just the difference in angle, but I glimpsed something wistful in his smile. "If you find her, you tell her to come back and give me some time. You make sure and tell her that. Aiight? Tell her that Leon said. I need a top-up."

When I got home, I found a message from James in my voicemail. "Any luck with the egregious Mr Foulkes? Call me." I didn't do that, because it was already half past two, but I spent the rest of the night typing up my observations and transcribing Leon's answers from my voice recorder (which he'd eventually agreed I could use). By the time I finished it was Sunday morning. I slept for a couple of hours, then dragged myself to Mass. My father now attended a non-denominational megachurch, but I stuck with the bells and smells of my childhood. Kneeling after communion, I prayed for a breakthrough. The closing hymn was the prayer of St. Francis: "Oh Master grant that I may ever seek / not to be understood, but to understand..." I needed to tattoo that on my arm.

I got home and switched on the TV just in time to catch the start of *The Week With Allen Keene:* today's special guest, Nilson Standing (D-MA). Coffee at hand, I plopped down on the chesterfield and phoned James.

To my disappointment, he reacted coolly to my discovery that Leon was hostile to magic, pointing out that it might simply be a personal prejudice. "He *ranted* about it," I argued. "He said they were out to destroy the vampire race," but eventually I fell silent. So did James.

I picked wool balls off my socks. Behind the ancient brown chesterfield, the radiator clanked, drowning the hum of street noise that filtered up to the ninth floor. Winter sunlight flooded through the south- and east-facing windows of the living-room. Our family house in Boston was now the Nilson D. Standing Kids Center, but Nilson wasn't quite altruistic enough to have sacrificed the pied-a-terre on West 78th and Amsterdam, and I never pretended to be anything less than grateful that I didn't have to live in a cell facing an airshaft, like most grad students. After a long night spent in the library or among vampires, I seemed to need sunlight even more than I needed coffee.

James said, "I suppose I should take it that the circumstances of Leon's Turn remain shrouded in mystery?"

He was right. If I'd extracted any crumbs of information about *that*, I would have told him already. Of all the mysteries that vampires created around themselves, Turning was the greatest – and the most crucial to their ultimate status in the eyes of the law and the public. James used the vampires' own word partly out of respect and partly to avoid the phrase that Dr. Isaac Brent at Cornell – chief proponent of the retrovirus hypothesis – had successfully sold to the media: *transmission mechanism*.

"Nothing," I said. "Just the same old story." I leaned over the coffee table and scrolled through the transcribed notes on my laptop. "Here it is. Leon: 'What you think? I got bit.' Clare: 'And after that, you discovered that you were a vampire?' Leon: 'That's right.' Clare: 'So who bit you? Did you want them to?' Leon: 'You should know I ain't gonna say nothing about that.'"

James laughed, sounding irritated. "He claims to be the only *real* vampire. One might have hoped he would have a unique story. And yet, Clare, doesn't the very fact that they all give the same story suggest something to you?"

"That it might be true. But if biting makes a vampire, why aren't we up to our waists in them? Because biting doesn't *invariably* make a vampire. That's why we're looking for other common factors." I sighed in frustration. "And the only common factor we can find is, 'I got bit!'"

"Doesn't that phrase say anything else to you?"

"The formulation itself is suggestive. They're disclaiming responsibility, refusing to admit that they made the choice to adopt this lifestyle."

"Yes."

"And maybe we don't have the tools to identify why they made that choice. Maybe the common factor is neurochemistry, prenatal exposure to environmental chemicals, even the G-word." I meant *genetics*. "Otherwise, I don't know!"

Footsteps thumped in the hall.

"Clare," James said. "We don't have the tools to prove or

disprove any of the medical hypotheses. Our job is not to look for what everyone else is looking for, but to look for what no one else is looking for... what no one else has the eyes to see."

That was the whole point of paranormal studies, of course. We didn't laugh at the possibility that the "missing factors" in the world's persistent mysteries might transcend the categories of conventional science, maybe even the so-called laws of nature.

"Yes, but seeing is believing," I grumbled.

My brother Colin came into the living-room, sat down at the other end of the sofa, and gobbled cornflakes out of a pyrex mixing bowl.

James and I talked for another couple of minutes. When I hung up, Colin had finished his cornflakes. He was leafing through my notes. "Wow," he said. "This guy last night was an extreme case, huh?"

"He's living a suburban pimp's wet dream," I said, trying to reclaim my notes. We tussled. Colin was left with a page that he scanned, puffing his cheeks out comically.

"Oh shit! Bollocks to Betsy! You *saw* this? Why didn't you let me come?"

"You were working late," I said primly. "And I also reserve the right to decide what may not be fit for your eyes, *little* brother."

Colin was an editorial assistant at the Jaeger H. Kilroy Institute, the private think tank associated with Columbia's School of International Studies that published *The Democratic Review*. It was the third rung, after unpaid intern and fact-checker, of the ladder that Colin planned to climb into power. He was determined to make his own way without riding our father's coattails.

Colin and I tried to make a point of watching Nilson whenever he appeared on the talk shows. In a sense, since our mother's death, this was the closest we ever got to him. But here we were in front of *The Week*, and we weren't even watching it. I was TiVoing it, but still, that said something about our family.

"I thought clinical vampirism was defined as a compulsion to *drink* blood," Colin said.

"Yeah, but the symptoms are so subjective. I mean, *you* could say you had a compulsion to drink blood, and they'd diagnose you."

"Rrrrawr!" He produced a Dracula leer. "But aren't there empirical symptoms, too? Don't they develop something like chronic fatigue syndrome if they don't get their fix?"

"That's how it got accepted as a genuine medical condition. But the trouble is, all the symptoms that make up secondary vampiric syndrome – the fatigue, the mental cloudiness, the low core temperature, and even the sensitivity to sunlight – can be psychosomatic. And to complicate the picture further, a lot of them have AIDS or other blood-borne diseases like hepatitis. *There's no proof.*" For a moment I was talking to myself. "There's no proof!"

"OK, but as I was saying, I thought they *drank* blood." Colin pointed to a paragraph of my notes. "This sounds more like cannibalism!"

"Yeah, it was beyond gross. Now give me that. You're far too easily corrupted."

He leaped over the table. I chased and tackled him. The fun part of living with Colin was getting to act like little kids sometimes.

Falling on hands and knees in front of the TV, Colin froze. "That was—"

I looked up. The show was almost over. Allen and his cohost Jeanne always wound up on a lighter note by getting personal with their guests, providing them with the equivalent of a free campaign spot – or a smear ad. This week it was Jeanne's turn to contribute the clip. On the screen behind them, she was signing off from a street corner in lower Manhattan. With unperturbed grace, my father opined, "A perfect family is like a perfect hamburger: it doesn't exist, and even if it did, it would only raise your blood pressure."

"No, but I saw," Colin said. He started flipping channels.

We found it on Fox: a grainy clip of me coming out of the Hedy Rascal store with Leon Foulkes and getting into his Hummer. At least one of the paparazzi must have stuck around.

"Let's see how Nilson Standing's family values rhetoric holds up to the shocking revelation of his daughter's hijinks with America's most notorious vampire," the commentator gloated.

"Revelation," I said. I grabbed the remote from Colin and switched the TV off. "They just haven't done their research." I threw the remote across the room.

"No hijinks, no story." Colin retrieved the remote and dropped it on top of the TV. "And there weren't any hijinks. Right?"

"Of course there weren't. Still, it looks as if I'd better clear off to Tokyo as soon as possible, hadn't I?"

Colin didn't answer. He picked up his empty mixing bowl and headed for the door.

"What are you doing today?" I said.

"I was going to meet up with the guys and shoot some clays. But we couldn't get a slot at the range. So I'll probably go down to the dojo this afternoon. What about you?"

"I was thinking of taking up karate," I said. "Or ninjitsu."

Colin chortled. "Getting ready for some hijinks with those notorious Tokyo bloodsuckers? No, but *ninjitsu*? Those are hardcore heads. They sweat steroids. They wouldn't even let you in the dojo."

"Ha. Actually, I kind of suspected as much," I said. "So what if I come downtown with you? I promise not to embarrass you."

Colin's face lit up. "Great! I thought you'd never ask."

My brother did aikido. Nowadays, it was just one of his athletic activities, which ranged from target shooting to lacrosse, but in college he'd taken it seriously, coming within a whisker of a national championship. He described it as the only non-violent martial art, and when I watched his tournaments, it had looked like a ritualized kind of gymnastics.

18

But before I'd had on my borrowed dogi for half an hour, I decided that Colin had fudged the truth about aikido. If this was a non-violent martial art, the Patriot missile was a whiffle ball. I panted, sweated, marvelled at the stamina of the woman who'd volunteered to "train" me, and knew I would be a tapestry of bruises tomorrow.

But in the shower afterwards, I realized that the practise had had one unexpected benefit: for more than two hours, I hadn't been thinking about anything.

Chapter 2.

I arrived at Narita Airport on a weekday afternoon in late July. In the last couple of months, I'd begun to feel irritation with Dr. Kamikawa's team at Aoyama Gakuin, who weren't producing (or at any rate weren't sharing) as much data as we were in New York, even though there were three of them to one of me. By extension, my enthusiasm for Japan in general had cooled. But as I navigated the airport, my optimism revived. The cornucopic souvenir shops, the news kiosks, the fast food outlets – everything was dinkier, more brightly lit, and *cleaner* than in America. The crowds flowed smoothly through the concourses, and harmonies floated in the air, a mixture of tuneful PA chimes and chorused greetings from the sales assistants at the souvenir shops. The place made JFK look like a third-world entrepot.

I caught the Narita Express for Shinjuku. The onboard announcements were in English as well as Japanese, but the train travelled through an increasingly urban and exotic landscape of billboards and signs in the three Japanese alphabets: kanji, hiragana, and katakana. I glued my nose to the window, trying to read them before they passed out of sight. The experiment was not a success. I'd learned my Japanese by ploughing through academic journals and university press tomes. Advertising slogans were a whole different beast.

As the train began to reduce speed, the rooftops drew closer and surged up into skyscrapers that butted against the incandescent grey sky. It awed me that the Japanese built forty-storey highrises on top of a tectonic fault, in a region which had already seen many devastating earthquakes, most recently the Tohoku Kanto Earthquake last year, which had also brought a devastating tsunami. In line with my usual habit of arming myself with (too much) information, I'd read up on the antiseismic construction techniques now in use:

friction pendulum bearings, shear walls, viscous fluid dampers, and so forth. It hadn't really put my mind at ease… but if twenty million Japanese could exist in Tokyo without fretting about the Big One, I could, too, I told myself.

Still, my amazement grew as the train shot through a three-dimensional maze of concrete, glass, and steel. When I disembarked at Shinjuku, I let out a little scream. The platform was shuddering from side to side. For an instant I was convinced that the Big One had decided to strike on the very day I arrived. But people were hurrying around me, plainly unconcerned, and I realized that the station was just shaking under the weight of all the trains pulling in and out.

Well, thank God there'd been no one around to see that.

I'd already adopted the working assumption that thousands of strangers were the same thing as *no one*. Of course, arriving from Manhattan, it wasn't that big a step to take.

I dragged my suitcase into the underground labyrinth of the station. The crowds were hellish, and it wasn't even rush hour. Everyone around me was speaking Japanese, and I couldn't understand them. I couldn't even seem to follow the signs. While I backtracked up and down the escalators, the heat sapped my energy. The Japanese rainy season had just ended, and the clingy embrace of the air swiftly grew irksome. Sweat soldered my hair to my neck.

I located the Yamanote line at last, rode it to Shibuya, and changed to the Ginza subway line. Straphanging with my suitcase jammed between my feet, I saw my first Japanese vampire.

He was working the look that I'd seen in photographs from Yurika Hamaguchi, one of Dr. Kamikawa's team: the black hair sprayed into spikes, the tattered black sleeveless t-shirt decorated with cryptic graffiti, the black fatigues and combat boots. The arm that I could see was tattooed with an imaginary beast that looked like a phoenix with a fish's tail. His fresh face suggested he was no more than twenty. I felt a spasm of emotion familiar from my months with the "fanghandlers" in Thompson Square Park, some of whom were still in their teens: not quite pity, more like incomprehension that no one had stopped this from happening.

"What are you looking at?" He broke the martyred hush of the carriage with a soft lisp, and I understood what he'd said. *I'd understood!* Involuntarily, I smiled.

He returned me a smile that flashed his fangs: long, slightly crooked, and discolored, probably cheap.

The salaryman next to him made a tiny moue of disgust and shifted a few millimetres away.

Well, in most towns in America, a vampire who wore his or her fangs on public transport ran the risk of getting them bashed out. With a blunt object, not bare knuckles, because by now everyone "knew" about the risk of contamination. By my standards, this was social acceptance.

At the next stop, Omotesando, I lugged my suitcase up to street level and wheeled it along the sidewalk of "246," otherwise known as Aoyama-dori, past bookstores, boutiques, and glass-fronted fashion emporia. An acrid haze of fumes hung over the traffic. The crowds were a visual riot of diversity: salarymen and salarywomen, fashionistas, bohemians, children in sailor suits, high schoolers in tartan-accented uniforms... and the occasional vampire. Male and female alike, they carried black parasols to ward off the sun. But so did other people. That in itself wasn't a giveaway. I was going by their gothically obvious outfits.

Given that these exhibitionists would represent just a fraction of the total vampire population, the paucity of Professor Kamikawa's team's data looked even less excusable. They'd just have to step off campus to do fieldwork!

These thoughts took me the rest of the way to Aoyama Gakuin, a walled campus of ivied brick buildings interspersed with concrete monstrosities. Students flocked beneath the beeches and ginkgos, indistinguishable from the multiply pierced rascals in the Soc 101 and Elements of Paranormal Studies sections I'd been teaching for the last couple of years.

I easily found Turner Hall, which housed the sociology

and anthropology departments, and took the elevator up to the fourth floor.

"Clare! I'm so sorry I can't come to meet you – but you got here OK!"

Misaki Kubota surprised me in the hall as I deciphered the nameplates. She threw her arms around me.

"I've been walking. I'm utterly gross — "

"You didn't take a taxi? You're so crazy! In this heat." She danced back a step and grinned at me. With a round face and feathery cap of black hair, in a long black t-shirt cinched with a pink scarf over a flounced white skirt, Misaki was as cute as a bunny rabbit. We'd done our master's degrees together at Columbia.

"Long time no see, huh?" she said.

"Long time no see," I agreed in Japanese.

She squealed piercingly. "You speak Japanese now! Oh my God!" Taking my arm, she led me down the hall and continued in English, "As for me, I forget all English. So we can talk together in Japanese! Catch up all news." I did a mental double-take. In the past, and in her recent emails, Misaki had had a near-fluent command of English. Then again, I'd just had an encounter of my own with the gulf between spoken and written language. So maybe her spoken English was rusty, and now that I'd revealed some Japanese ability, she felt that she didn't have to try so hard... Yet her chubby little hand clamped my forearm too tightly. She was tense. "So tell me how you think Japan. It must be culture shock, yeah? I think Yurika also having culture shock. She spend two years at Berkeley, but never go New York before."

"I expect she'll be all right," I said. "She'll probably be horrified at how dirty our subways are. But James is there to look after her."

"Oh yeah, James! I wish I can meet him. Now you meet our professor. Kamikawa-sensei!" She uttered the last words as she opened the door that bore his nameplate. An elderly man rose from behind the wooden desk on the far side of the room.

"Miss Clare Standing. It is my pleasure to meet you in the end."

Japan's top professor of *choshizengaku* – which translated, rather alarmingly, as "supernatural science," but amounted in practice to paranormal studies – came around his desk, out from between the walls of books, with a slight limp, one foot turned inwards in a built-up shoe. A childhood bout of polio had left Tsuyoshi Kamikawa wizened as well as lame. Now he was in his seventies. I'd been looking forward to the elfin grin from the photograph on James's desk, where the two of them flanked a waxwork of Gary Oldman as Dracula. But his smile was polite, cautious, glazed.

We shook hands. Misaki left the room.

I answered the professor's questions about my journey, James's health, and the apathy of the American public towards the Citizenship Act.

"Your father does very well to oppose this law."

In academic settings at home, people tended to refrain from mentioning Nilson in front of me. They seemed to think it would be indelicate, even if they partly agreed with his positions (there were few people who agreed with *all* of Nilson's positions). But Professor Kamikawa displayed no such restraint.

"It is sad that he does not have more support. I fear that where America leads, Japan will follow."

"The Act isn't a done deal yet," I objected. "And isn't it the other way round? I have a theory that Japan is twenty years ahead of the West in many areas. Especially those that concern our field."

The corners of the professor's mouth turned down. "I think you will find that Japanese society is much less liberal than yours."

"I don't mean *more progressive*; I just mean *further down the same road*. Urbanization, for example, and all the trends that go with it. The atomization of society, the shifting meanings of kinship, the complexification of relational networks..." I stopped, aware that I was trying to impress him with jargon.

24

"Perhaps you mean *more extreme*," Professor Kamikawa said after a moment, sourly. "It is true that we Japanese tend to carry social trends to extremes. And these trends may develop momentum faster than in America, due to our homogenous society. However, the ultimate outcome in every case is the creation of psychologically warped casualties, who fill the space reserved by Japanese society for outcasts."

I recognized a thread of argument from his seminal book, *Self-Created Outcasts: Vampires In Japanese Society,* which comprehensively treated the history and social role of vampires in this country, while staying vague on the question of what they *were*. I'd read it from cover to cover with a dictionary, since it hadn't been translated into English. It was now a decade out of date. The plans for a second edition formed part of the impetus for our current study.

I was about to broach that topic when Misaki returned with a tea-tray. "Kamikawa-sensei, don't you think Clare's tired and wants to sit down?" She spoke in Japanese. I understood her. It gave me the same thrill I'd had on the train.

But as soon as I sat down, I realized that I *was* tired. I'd been travelling for eighteen hours, the last part on foot through ninety-degree heat with a heavy suitcase. Wanly, I sipped the green tea Misaki had brought.

"We arrange a room for you, Clare. You stay in Yurika's room. It's very good area. Jingumae! I think very *small* for you, but…"

I blinked. "I thought I would be staying on campus. My funding…"

"It is arranged," Professor Kamikawa said in a tone that made me realize what my first mistake with him had probably been: talking back.

"Yurika like her apartment very much. She don't want to break lease. So we transfer funding, so you stay there! OK?"

Misaki seemed almost to be pleading with me. Oddly, that made me more reluctant to fall in with the plan. All the same, I acquiesced. I hadn't much choice – and it wasn't as if I'd been looking forward to living in a dorm room for the next twelve months.

Professor Kamikawa told me to return at nine o'clock the next morning to meet the other two researchers who were working on the study: Keita Matsudaira, a post-doc, and Seiji Inobe, a Ph.D student. Misaki volunteered to take me to Yurika's, and we left the professor among his books, which I'd been eyeing hopefully, to no effect. I'd even tried, "I would love to see your latest article in *Shakaigaku Journal*," but he'd merely thanked me, as if it were a meaningless compliment. I felt cast down. In academia, lending books was a sign of trust, and not lending them was... well, the opposite.

Out on 246, Misaki hailed a taxi. We glided in the direction that she told me was away from Shibuya. After a quarter of a mile, we swerved into a maze of back streets so narrow that the taxi could barely scrape between the high garden walls. Misaki issued a stream of directions to the driver. I tried to memorize the route. Vending machine, quaint little liquor store, house with morning glories trailing over the gate, vending machine, 7/11, shrine with a stone idol wearing a red bib, vending machine... I gave up. We finally stopped in front of a little block of condominiums. With its streaky grey tiles and ornate iron balconies, the building could have been dropped down in Europe without anyone noticing the difference. I renounced my fantasy of an airy tatami room with shoji doors giving on a Zen garden, while uncomfortably wondering how much the Aoyama Gakuin anthropology department was shelling out to cover the difference between my funding and the rent on this place.

But Yurika's apartment on the third storey restored my spirits. The floor-to-ceiling windows would admit plenty of sunlight. Sure, it was small – just a studio with a kitchenette in the corner and a "unit bath," which Misaki apologized for: the Japanese considered it more civilized to have the toilet and bath in separate rooms. But that didn't bother me, and since the studio was furnished with only a single bed, one chair, and a table that would do double duty as a desk, it felt roomy enough. Yurika must have put her personal items into

26

storage, even her TV. Guess I wouldn't be doing any cooking, unless I bought my own pots and pans.

"Look, here are the closets, we call *oshiire*." Misaki demonstrated how to slide the doors to and fro. The closets were empty. "You can store your clothes," she suggested.

Why were we so awkward with each other? We'd got along well in New York. Was it just that almost five years had elapsed since then? While I was pursuing my doomed "Magick: Ritual & Belief" study, Misaki, too, had had her failures. She'd left academia to get married. Then she'd gotten divorced. Maybe it wasn't a passion for research that had brought her back; maybe she just hadn't known what else to do with herself. In that case, I might simply have walked into the hot zone of a generalized resentment. But we had to work together... we had to trust each other...

I wrestled with the catches of the floor-to-ceiling windows. To slide them all the way open, I had to move the table. The cord of the gooseneck lamp snagged on the chair and it toppled. I caught it and picked up an envelope that had been concealed underneath it. My name was printed on the outside.

I stepped onto the balcony and stood between the potted plants to read the English words on the single sheet of paper the envelope contained.

I am sorry I could not see you this time! I would like to talk with you, but the telephone is not safe. It is not safe at the university, either. Remember what happened to Ryu Abe-san! PLEASE listen to my advice. Do not trust Matsudaira and Inobe. They join a bad agency to get money for their work. They get influence with Kamikawa Sensei. Other people influence him, too. It is not easy for him. The Ministry of Internal Affairs put pressure on him. So I am very sorry, but I think you must be careful when you talk to him. Also, Miss Yokoyama is in difficult situation because of this. But you may trust her.

My apartment is safe. This is good area. Even Jaize 3000 lives near here!!! I have only one request for you (smile):

please water my plants!!

I wish you very good luck with your fieldwork. I leave some of my notes with Miss Yokoyama to give to you. I look forward to "comparing notes" with you soon!!

Lots of love, Yurika Hamaguchi

"I've never even met her," I said aloud.

Misaki came out onto the balcony. There was barely room for the two of us amidst the baby pines and sanseveria. She rested her elbows on the railing and gazed at the distant orange sunset.

"Do you know who Miss Yokoyama is?" I said in Japanese.

Her head whipped around. "It's me."

"I thought it might be. But I thought you'd gone back to your maiden name."

"You speak Japanese so well," she cooed absently. "No, in Japan it's not easy to do that."

So Yurika had told me that I could trust Misaki. But could I trust Yurika? All I knew of her, as a woman rather than as a researcher, was the piece of paper in my hand. I said cautiously, "Yurika left me this, to tell me that she'd left her field notes with you."

"Yeah. They're in the office on campus. I'll give them to you when you come in tomorrow morning." Misaki speaking Japanese was a different woman: less bubbly, more practical. Almost reluctantly, she said, "Did she say anything else?"

The sentences that had jumped out at me, of course, were *Remember what happened to Ryu Abe-san* – who? – and: *They join a bad agency to get money for their work.* Yurika's tortured English made it sound melodramatic. Organized crime? The yakuza? Had Professor Kamikawa and his other two research assistants fallen under the sway of some fringe political faction? Then again, there was a likelier explanation: experience had taught me that whenever a mystery cropped up in academia, funding was usually at the bottom of it. So maybe Yurika had tried to warn me that someone was using financial pressure – or outright bribery – to influence the findings of our study.

The very idea of such a heinous betrayal of science was just -- incredible.

I needed more time to think about all this.

Barely aware that in withholding the meat of Yurika's note, I was acknowledging that I didn't trust Misaki completely, I said, "She mentioned someone named Jaize 3000. Who's that?"

Misaki giggled. "Oh, you haven't heard of him? Well, I guess he isn't famous in America. He's a vampire TV *tarento*. Very egotistical, very funny, you know, and he has his own line of logo goods."

"Oh God. So much for the vampire mystique."

We gazed at the sunset. The orange glow in the western sky had thinned down to a blazing band on the horizon.

"Nice view," Misaki stated.

I murmured that it was. But to me, silhouetted against that dying blaze, the skyscrapers of the Tokyo skyline looked like broken fangs in a dead mouth. A mouth so big that we were already inside it.

The sunlight falling on my face woke me. I stretched luxuriously. Then I remembered where I was.

"Shit!" I hurtled upright and stared at my travel clock.

Half-past three.

I'd been due at Turner Hall at nine.

I'd sweated so heavily in my sleep that I couldn't skip a shower. I washed my hair in cold water and threw on the same clothes as yesterday. Then I lost another twenty minutes finding my way out of the alleys to 246, where I could hail a taxi. I burst into the office on the fourth floor of Turner Hall at ten to five, drenched in sweat all over again, desperately trying to remember the Japanese for *jet lag*.

All the desks in the drab open-plan office were abandoned, but for one. A flash of movement in the far corner drew my eye to Misaki, half-concealed behind a barricade of binders. She looked up from her computer screen and smiled weakly.

"I overslept." Outside the windows, which were half-open in an acknowledgement of the feeble air-conditioning, crows cawed in the crowns of the beeches. Without much hope, I said, "I don't suppose Professor Kamikawa…"

Misaki shook her head.

"Matsudaira and Inobe?"

She blinked rapidly. So there *was* something about those two, I thought. A second later I realized I'd referred to them as Yurika had in her note, without the polite suffix *–san.* Maybe Misaki had only been reacting to that slip.

"They doing fieldwork," she exclaimed in English. "Usually not on the campus. They came this morning… to meet you. What happened?"

"I overslept," I repeated. "I'm very sorry." And I thought: couldn't you have called me? Safe or not, I'd used Yurika's telephone last night to call Colin, James, and Nilson and tell them I'd arrived, so I knew the machine worked. But maybe Misaki had called me, and I'd slept through it. I sighed. "Could I have Yurika's field notes? That way, I'll be well prepared tomorrow, at least."

"Oh, of course! I'll get them now." Misaki headed for a door in the corner. I hovered behind her as she switched on the light, revealing an office supply closet. She squatted on the floor, hauled a stack of Xerox paper off the bottom shelf, and plunged her hand into the space where it had been. Gooseflesh prickled my shoulders. For whatever reason, Misaki had *hidden* the notes… in a place that couldn't be linked directly to her. But now she was kneeling on the floor to peer into the space. "They're not here," she said, voice high.

We searched the closet, sifting the office supplies and pressing our cheeks to the dusty floor to look under the bottom shelves, in vain.

"Someone's taken them," Misaki said through clenched teeth. "And I can guess who!" Then she shook her head. "But no one knew they were here!"

"You didn't make copies?"

She shook her head again. "I didn't. Didn't want… Yurika didn't want me to."

"Well, clearly she had reason to be concerned," I said gloomily.

"Maybe tomorrow I can ask the other grad students if they saw the notes," Misaki said, indicating the empty desks. "We've got one regular employee here, too, the office manager…"

"Do you think it was Matsudaira and Inobe who took them?" This time I left the –*san* off their names on purpose.

Misaki flinched. "If I've got time, I'll come by tonight," she muttered. "Maybe we could go out for dinner."

Misaki was *in a difficult situation,* Yurika had said. Trapped by her loyalty to her colleagues and her obligations to Professor Kamikawa. What chance did I have against that?

Chapter 3.

On my way back to Yurika's apartment, I bought a prepaid cell phone, since my American phone didn't work here. I called Misaki's cell, intending to give her my new number. There was no answer.

Sighing, I went into a little gourmet supermarket and bought a half-baguette, some Brie, a packaged salad, and a bottle of wine. Fine Japanese cuisine could wait. Or, if Misaki did come by, my sandwich and salad could wait. Living on a student's budget, I was no stranger to leftovers.

Back at Yurika's building, I poured myself a mug of wine and paced between the kitchen counter and the window.

Without Yurika's notes, I knew nothing about her field-work except the findings the team had sent to New York, which I'd already memorized. What else could I do to prepare for tomorrow? To repair the bad first impression I'd made on Professor Kamikawa, which I'd certainly compounded with my no-show today? I compiled a mental list of material to review. I even had some of it with me. I settled down to read, but I kept reading the same paragraph over and over.

Eight o'clock. Eight thirty. Misaki obviously wasn't coming.

"All right," I said aloud. "So you don't want to share your sandbox." Now I was thinking of Matsudaira and Inobe, who hadn't even bothered to phone me. "Well, I know a trick worth two of that."

I unpacked my suitcase, transferring clothes and books to the closet until I reached the only after-fiveish outfit I'd brought: a one-shouldered black camisole with funky crochet trim, paired with an ankle-length khaki skirt that had a fan of kick pleats in the back.

When I unfolded the skirt, a toy gun tumbled out, accompanied by a bundle of black nylon straps that untangled into a shoulder holster.

"Oh my God," I gasped. "Colin."

He'd made some mysterious comments on the phone last night about its being "convenient to work for a bunch of neo-cons." He'd even mentioned how the big cheese of the Kilroy Institute, Weston C. Stamforth, could "pull strings" and "put a word in the ear of Homeland Security" for his friends. How puzzled he must have been by my lack of reaction, not knowing I hadn't yet unpacked.

The gun was a good copy: a Glock automatic the size of my hand, heavier than it looked. Real guns weighed about seventeen thousand pounds, as I remembered from the only time I'd ever held one, at the range in Jersey where Colin and his friends shot clays. I'd gone along with them out of curiosity, but the experience hadn't converted me to the joys of target shooting. It was scary watching my little brother fire a gun with such singleminded intensity. I had the same fraught feeling now, although the gun in my hands was only a copy. A 9mm, the weapon preferred by discerning gangstas, illegal in some states – and Colin had thoughtfully packed a shoulder holster with it. There was also an envelope of documents: a firearm license and a license to carry concealed, both in my name.

As I handled it, the truth came to me.

"Oh Colin," I said aloud. Very gently, I replaced the Glock in my suitcase. "Haven't I got my green belt in aikido now? Don't you think that qualifies me to defend myself against the notorious bloodsuckers of Tokyo?"

In a side pocket of the suitcase, I found another little present: a box of 9mm parabellum ammunition labeled *Silver Bullets*. The cartridges didn't look like silver, but Colin had gone to town on the label, decorating it with clip-art gravestones and vampire bats. When I saw that, I finally laughed.

"Someone's got too much time on their hands at work."

I would chew him out as he deserved, but I also owed him. He'd given me my first proper laugh in days.

I changed clothes and applied a touch of brown eyeshadow and mascara. My coloring was too fair to take any more makeup than that. Although I had the same hazel eyes as Colin and Nilson, I had my mother's near-colorless hair and skin. I'd always been told that black didn't suit me, but with one pale shoulder on display, I looked striking, I thought.

In the field, in Ireland as well as in New York, I'd found that being a fragile-looking blonde was an advantage. "Pretty" was the way to go: nonthreatening florals and demure skirts. But here in Tokyo, I couldn't afford to look vulnerable... no matter how I felt.

Roppongi looked and sounded, for the first few seconds, more like home than any other part of Tokyo I'd yet seen. I put that down to all the black and white faces mingling with the Japanese ones. They were USAF personnel from Yokota and Marines from Yokosuka, with a leavening of civilian expats. Hip-hop blasted from cruising lowriders and the doorways of bars. But the unstructured street interactions all around me conveyed a sense of volatility that I'd seldom experienced in the States. Touts and flyer girls latched onto potential customers with a wheedling persistence that my brain labeled *Third World.* Compounding this impression of sub-critical tropical mayhem, glossy sedans here and there disgorged phalanxes of suits with open collars and wristwatches that cost more than my rent in New York.

I walked slowly, scanning the vertical stacks of illuminated bar and club signs.

There.

A white girl stood at the base of the building, handing out flyers. Her listless demeanor contrasted with the aggressive work ethic of the Japanese flyer girls. Thin to the point of scrawniness, she had bottle blonde hair as out-of-condition as her skin. She wore blue eyeshadow and frosted lipstick. Her pale blue shift dress stopped at mid-thigh, leaving bruised bare legs on display above sparkly plastic heels.

I stood in front of her and held out my hand. She put a

flyer into it, then looked me up and down with an expressionless sneer.

"Do you work at Exiles?" I said mildly.

She rolled her eyes. "No, I just hard out these flyers for fun." Her voice was flat, with a trace of Southern vowels. "This is a vamp club, you know."

"I know."

"No, you obviously don't." She waved a hand down the street. "Try Gas Panic or 911. Human clientele, no cover charge."

It always gave me a jolt to hear non-vampires referred to as *human*, the humanity of vampires so casually disposed of. Terminology does matter.

"Or if you really want the vamp experience, I recommend Twilight. Just go up that way, hang a right at Motown, and —"

"I'm looking for Dorothy Foulkes."

"Oh." She gave me a cold, swift, assessing look. I'd taken her for a raddled twenty-five, but now I had to raise my estimate of her age to match the confidence in her grey-blue eyes. "Oh, so that's your story," she said. Then she yelled, "Ryota!" A boy came across the sidewalk, sporting spiky pale purple hair and a brown leather vest over bare pectorals. She shoved her flyers at him and said something in Japanese that I couldn't catch.

The elevator creaked and jerked and spat us out on a drab grey landing. The single door bore a red stained-glass inset in the shape of a spider.

"Wait here." My guide pushed through the door, letting out a bassy blast of music. The door fell shut again. After several moments, she reemerged. "What's your name?"

"Clare."

She vanished again.

I speculated about what might lie beyond the door. Back home, I'd talked my way into a couple of "blood bars," the tightly guarded underground clubs where donors and vampires could pick each other up. I'd never seen a vampire feed off a living person at such a place, although various concoctions of decanted "blood" were available. The dominant aesthetic of black leather and heavy makeup evoked the S&M scene. There was a lot of overlap.

Tokyo's vamp clubs, *vamukura* in Japanese, had barely existed when Tsuyoshi Kamikawa published his definitive book, but from subsequent articles by other scholars, and from the Aoyama Gakuin team's more recent data, I'd learned that the clubs had since proliferated. They attracted a broad spectrum of customers, ethnographically indistinguishable from the clientele of the average snack bar or hostess club. Vamukura, it seemed, had become simply one more flavor in Tokyo's eternally evolving smorgasbord of nightlife options. It offered the vampires a way to make a living without hiding their identities, and it offered the customers, I supposed, a safe thrill. But what exactly did that consist of? And how safe was safe?

"All right," said the blonde, reappearing. "She'll see you."

I followed her into the music – a reggae track with Japanese vocals. On the stage at one end of the room, a redhead writhed around a pole in front of a curtain, down to a filmy camisole and G-string. The customers nearest her watched in silence. On the other side of the room, another group of men rocked with laughter.

At the head of the pushed-together tables sat a light-skinned black woman with an elongated skull and delicate features. The resemblance was unmistakable. This was Leon's Foulkes's sister, Dorothy.

The scrawny blonde placed a cold hand on my arm, holding me back.

Dorothy spoke in Japanese, drawling slightly. "This gentleman just tried to educate me," she declared with a finely done note of incredulity. "He don't know that I *am* an educated woman. Yeah. I got my degree in Japanese male psychology."

The men roared. Dorothy smiled, not enough for me to see whether she had fangs, and topped up their drinks from a bottle that rested in an icebucket. Even that movement was graceful. Further down the tables, two other women served beer.

"Dorothy, this is Clare. You want her to wait in the office?"

"No. You take my place here, Ruth. I need a break from y'all," she told the men. "You know what this is here?" Languid fingers indicated me. "This is another educated woman. Name is Clare. She's from the USA. Say hello to her now."

"Hello, Clare!" — "Howdy!"

"*Hajimemashite*," I said with a bow of what I judged to be the correct angle. "*Yoroshiku onegai shimasu.*"

"*Yoroshiku!*" — "How are you, very well?" — "Clare-san, kissu please!" The greetings came at me in English and Japanese.

"That's right," said Dorothy. She rose, a complicated mass of black skirt falling past her knees. "You better be nice to her, otherwise she might psychoanalyze you. And I don't even wanna think about what she would find out. Now Ruth's gonna play with you for a little while. You gentlemen know our Ruth; she loves to play."

Dorothy swept past me. I followed her to the bar. Like many vampires, she wore way too much perfume. It occurred to me that Ruth, the scrawny blonde, hadn't smelled of anything.

We ducked under the bar and edged past a stocky Asian man in a chef's coat. I just missed burning my arm on the griddle where he was cooking something that looked like lumpy pancakes. At the end of the bar, Dorothy preceded me into a cramped office where a young white man lay sideways across a leather armchair. Staring vacantly at the ceiling, he didn't even turn to see who'd come in. A spotty Japanese youth sat at a desk, counting receipts. He wore a sort of maître-d' uniform: a shiny black vest and bowtie.

"Ogino-kun, get out there," Dorothy said in Japanese. "Ruth is busy. There's no one outside, no one on the door…"

The maître d' went, casting a sour glance at me.

"And you, Aleksey," Dorothy continued in English. "You can't be hanging out in here all night. I don't know if you're in a trance, you're composing a symphony or what, but go and do it in the dressing-room."

"Angela kicked me out," the man – Aleksey – said with an accent that I guessed to be Russian, given his name. As if making an enormous physical effort, he swung his legs around and sat up. He massaged his face with hands that seemed to belong to a different person, so large and finely muscled were they in contrast to his slight physique. "She said that she can't concentrate on her *toilette* when I am there."

"I ain't surprised," Dorothy said. "Can't nobody concentrate with you mooning off in a trance the way you do. But I need this room now, so you and Angela are just gonna have to play nice."

"She said that it's embarrassing for her —" Aleksey coughed delicately — "In front of a man."

Dorothy laughed, a rich burst of amusement that reminded me vividly of The Vampire Of The East. "If that don't take the cake! That girl, she's gonna drive me so far up the wall I go through the ceiling." To me, she added, "Angela, that's our tarento, she *is* a man. Biologically, anyway. A new half is what they call it. She's a Filipina. She's saving up for her operation, but she already convinced herself... I'm saying, she done gone too far with that shit. I don't see any of the *real* girls blink an eyelash at changing in the room in front of Aleksey. Hell, would you?" She gave me a mischievous little smile. "I mean, he is pretty, ain't he?"

The word that came to my mind was *undernourished*. Aleksey had hair the color of wet sand and cheekbones sharp enough to open a letter with. Greenish-grey eyes burned with anger or irritation. His lips were sensuously formed, but pressed together in a tight line. He stood up: five eight, five nine, in a white t-shirt over tuxedo pants.

"Aleksey is a refugee," Dorothy said. "From the new democratic Russia." She emphasized the adjectives sarcastically.

"A defector. Dorothy, please learn this word."

"A political refugee, then. To be a defector, you got to have served your government first, and you ain't never served anyone willingly in your whole life. *Have* you? All you done is run away. Until you got caught." Aleksey went rigid, flattening his hands on his thighs as if to stop them from forming fists. Dorothy chuckled and stepped up to him. In her stiletto heels, she was the taller. She kissed him gently on the cheek and stepped back. "We love you anyway. Now go and tell Angela, no diva tantrums, because I said. Oh and by the way, this is Clare."

"How are you," Aleksey said, not looking at me as he passed out of the office.

Dorothy sighed. "You see what I got to contend with," she said, seating herself behind the desk. "But I never say no to talent. Even if it comes in a high-maintenance package like our Russian *de*fector, there." She indicated a folding chair at the corner of the deck. I sat down. Shaking a cigarette out of a pack of Marlboro Lights, she held out a Zippo to me.

"No, thank you," I said.

"Take the lighter."

I took it.

"Now light my cigarette."

I spun the wheel and extended the lighter towards her. She inhaled and leant back.

"Very good. That was the first thing you gotta learn."

I thought back to the way she'd introduced me to her customers. "I assume you've heard about me from your brother?"

"Yeah. But don't look so scared. He ain't told me very much. Just that you're here to do some research. You wanna fill in the blanks on that?"

I started to give my standard spiel: mutual understanding essential for social acceptance, cooperation with science benefiting one and all, blah blah blah. Now that I was sitting in the manager's office of a thriving vamp club, speaking to the manager herself, who didn't visibly lack for any benefit that greater social acceptance could confer, I felt and sounded less persuasive. *Damn.* I shouldn't have been in such a hurry to come here. I should have waited until I'd had the chance to tag along for a few days with Matsudaira and Inobe, so I could adopt whatever interview technique they were using. Dorothy might be a gaijin, but she was operating in a Japanese environment, and she didn't look as if anything I said was impressing her.

She resembled Leon very closely, though she was slender, not emaciated. Dark freckles sprinkled her peanut-butter skin. She wore her lightly straightened hair in a single French braid, fastened at the nape of her neck with a silver barrette in the shape of a spider. Smaller silver spiders clung to her earlobes, and another one hung from a chain in her cleavage. Her dress was a complicated confection of heavy black fabric and unnecessary zippers, some of which were open, flashing a slim fishnetted thigh when she recrossed her legs.

"Seems to me," she said when I finished my spiel. "Seems to me that the only person gonna profit from this is the professor that's gonna publish his book. And your professor in the States, I guess he's gonna write a book, too?"

"You must have heard the saying, 'Publish or perish,'" I said.

"What about you, I'm saying. How is this gonna pay for you?"

I remembered Leon saying, What they gonna have for me?

"This study could jumpstart my academic career," I said. "It'll look good on my resumé when I start my job hunt, and that's just the beginning. Paranormal studies is dismissed as the lunatic fringe right now, but that's going to change. I'll be one of about five credentialed vampire experts in the United States. And I'm young and female. I'll be able to write my own ticket."

"That do sound nice. Although it's gonna crimp your plans if they make vampires illegal in the States."

My surprise must have shown on my face. She laughed softly.

"Oh yeah, I follow the news. But putting that aside. How you financing your stay here?"

"I've got funding from NYU, and from one or two private sources. It's being paid into an account at the Aoyama Gakuin bursar's office. I shouldn't be revealing these details to you," I said, chagrined.

"They won't go no further. But listen. As you will have noticed, Tokyo is an expensive city. And I know they keep you students on a shoestring. I don't think your funding is gonna cover everything you want to do here. You know how much them gentlemen outside are paying? Six thousand an hour. That's drinks on top of that. Anywhere you go to talk to vampires, you gonna have to pay in that range." Her long nails, manicured silver with a cluster of little gems at the tip of each, moved among the receipts, shuffling them so I glimpsed figures that backed up her words.

"My Japanese colleagues have been conducting street interviews and participatory observation in Shinjuku and Harajuku, among other locations," I said.

"And that's why they ain't got shit."

Once again, I couldn't keep the surprise off my face.

"You think I'm reading your mind? If you was a customer, I'd let you go on thinking that. But you just gave it away yourself. They wouldn't have brought you over here if they wasn't hitting a dead wall without enough *data* to wipe their asses on. That's how the Japanese are, they make out like they're doing you a favor, but all the time, they're setting up the hoops for you to jump through." She moved the receipts into two piles on the far side of the computer keyboard. "But on this, they could be right. Because I got a deal for you."

"I'm all ears." I was thinking: She's wrong about that. They didn't push for me to come over here. They just couldn't get out of it.

"You work for me," Dorothy said. "You can be part-time if you like. Say four nights a week. That way, you get to do your observations. This is a high-class club. You'll get *data* in here that nobody else is gonna match. Also, you won't have to worry about money. I'll pay you my regular starting rate, that's two thousand five hundred an hour, and tips you get to keep. How's that sit with you?"

"Dorothy," I said. "In case you haven't noticed, I'm not a vampire." I drew my lips back from my teeth.

She mirrored the gesture, leaning forward with something between a smile and a snarl. I stopped myself from flinching. Her fangs were longer than those of the vampire I'd seen in the subway. How had she concealed them? Why didn't she lisp when she talked? She closed her lips, and I seemed to see the fangs shrinking into line with her other teeth, until they were just pointed canines. *Have the Japanese invented retractable fangs? Why nothing about this in the Aoyama Gakuin team's observations?*

"This is a vamp club. That don't mean all of my girls are vamps," she said. "I got five vamps at the moment, two humans." Her voice hardened. "And I'm about to have *one* human."

"Ruth," I said. "The girl who was handing out flyers."

"You thought she was a vamp?" Abruptly, Dorothy giggled. "I'm gonna have fun telling her that!"

I'd actually meant to suggest Ruth as one of the two "humans" on staff. I said, "Is she quitting?"

"Her! Quitting!" Dorothy laughed. Her eyes actually teared up. "Oh, I ain't heard anything so funny all day. No," she sobered. "It's my other human girl. Irina. No reason you need to know this, but you honored me with the truth about your financial situation, so I'm gonna tell you the truth, too. She's been stealing from me. Dipping her little hand right into the register. And she thinks if she can get behind Oginokun's back and take a handful of receipts, I won't *know...* Honestly. I am sick to God of these fucking Russians. You feel for them on account of they're so desperate, you give them a chance, and they turn around and bite the hand that feeds them." Dorothy lit a fresh cigarette. She seemed genuinely distraught.

"Aleksey," I said. *"He* doesn't..."

"Oh no. Aleksey, he's basically all right. Apart from he got his personal problems. But I am not hiring another Russian for the front of the house Trouble is, it's hard to get white girls for this kind of place. Black girls, too. They got their prejudices... But anyway, that's how you can help *me* out."

"I'm not sure this is what your brother had in mind," I said.

"My little brother." She sighed. *Little* brother; yet Dorothy looked younger than Leon. I would have said she was his junior by several years. Perhaps that was just because she was healthy. She said, "How's he doing? Tell me."

"He gave me a message for you. It was, 'Tell her to come back and see me.'" I didn't have to search my memory for the exact words, because they'd been puzzling me ever since. "'Tell her to come back and give me some time. I need a top-up.'"

Dorothy winced. "Poor little Leon! He's got the anemia, you know. The sickle-cell. Well, he *had* it. And then he went on the pipe, like as if to damp his pain. He been off that shit, and he's cured now, but I guess it's still troubling him. And he keeps on trying to do too much. Trying to be everything to so many people."

"Maybe that's something you have in common," I said, flattering her.

"Well, I'm a take care of him." Dorothy put out her cigarette. "And I think he'd be happy to see you working for me. He do love for people to get along in a win-win situation." Briskly, she stood up. "Now we got to see about your clothes. That what you got on, that ain't gonna work."

I looked down at myself. So much for *striking.* "What's wrong with it?"

"Girl!" Dorothy grinned, and the canines were pointed, but they weren't fangs. "Where do I start? OK, this neckline. Asymmetrical. That's a no, no, no. Haven't you ever heard that men are attracted to symmetry? Wear an asymmetrical neckline and that sound you can hear is your tips shrinking away to nothing. Secondly, black. At Exiles, the vamps wear black, the humans do not. That's my rule. Helps the customers to feel comfortable knowing what's what. Thirdly, you got nice legs, why ain't you showing them off? How do I know you got nice legs? Because that's the other thing my brother told me about you." She grinned wider. "I wouldn't have known otherwise, in that skirt. So you want to lose that. You're skinny, that is a good thing: means you can wear miniskirts. And lastly, shoes. Three-inch heels, minimum. I let Jessica and Shinobu have some leeway on that, because they're tall girls, and you don't wanna be taller than the customer..."

I did my best imitation of Ruth's assessing gaze on her.

"OK, unless you're me, you don't wanna be taller than the customer." She laughed. "But you won't have no problem there. How tall are you, five two, three?"

"Five four," I said. "And since I arrived in Japan, for the first time in my life, I haven't felt short. I enjoy it."

"Well, you get yourself some heels, and you gonna enjoy it more. In fact, the best thing you could do is take a look at Ruth. Ask her where she bought her shit. She might even take you shopping." Dorothy laughed. Everything connected with Ruth seemed to amuse her for some reason. "If you want to start right now – that might be a plan, since Irina's still here and you can learn from her, she's good with the customers, anyway – I bet one of them has a spare outfit in the dressing-room. Now I gotta get back out front. You hear that? That's Angela doing her thing. I got to be there and make sure they don't harass her."

Caught up in the conversation, I hadn't noticed the muffled music changing from reggae to what sounded like a jazz standard sung in Japanese.

Dorothy locked the door of the office behind us. The cook and the maître d', Ogino, stood behind the bar with folded arms. Dorothy shook Ogino's elbow. "Get over to table fifteen, can't you see they finished their bottle?"

How *she* could see that from here was a mystery. But I could understand why Ogino had been distracted.

The bar gave an unimpeded view of the stage on the far side of the club. Emoting into a microphone, one of the most beautiful women I'd ever seen swayed on the stage, olive-skinned, voluptuous, with sleek red waves falling to the waist of her skintight silver evening gown. I had to remind myself that she was a man. Her alto voice carried a pronounced vibrato that turned the melody into a lament.

Behind her, the curtain had been drawn back to reveal a baby grand piano. Aleksey sat at the keyboard, accompanying her with a passion that was almost embarrassing. Of course, those hands: they were a pianist's hands.

Something about the music reminded me of Ireland. I nudged the cook. "What's this music?"

He looked at me and answered in English. I saw that he wasn't Japanese but Southeast Asian, probably Filipino like Angela. "Enka. They call enka. Traditional Japanese music."

Traditional music. That explained it. Traditional music always seemed to be full of grief compounded by nostalgia. I couldn't understand the lyrics, but I could feel the yearning for the fishermen lost at sea, the boys lost in battle, the girls dead at sixteen, an age of short lives intensely lived when every road led to heaven or to hell, and every decision was a matter of life and death. Once in Ireland I'd sat among the young members of the Skibbereen Coven, tears pouring down all of our faces, as an ancient warlock tapped on the bodhran and sang in Gaelic. Here, I watched the customers of Exiles staring silently at the stage, and I empathized with these salarymen who longed in some part of their hearts for a life outside the ordinary. I was like them. I, too, had needed to have my sense of loss expressed for me by a Russian pianist and a Filipina transsexual.

Then they started to heckle Angela. They called out comments that I vaguely understood to have to do with breast implants.

"Shit," sighed Dorothy. "They just can't leave her alone! It's because they love her so much, but..." She ducked out from under the bar and moved among them, bending to murmur into ears.

Ruth approached with a tray of empty glasses. I leaned over the bar. "Dorothy said you might have an outfit I could borrow."

"Oh, you got the job?"

"I'm going to try out," I said. "Just one night."

"I don't know what's to try out. You're blonde, you've got natural boobs, you speak English; she couldn't stop salivating from the minute you walked in the door." Ruth put down her tray. "I'll show you the dressing-room."

Hostessing at Exiles was the easiest job I'd ever done. All I had to do was chat with the customers, pour their drinks, light their cigarettes, and surreptitiously tug my dress down over my thighs. Ruth's spare outfit had turned out to be a shift identical to the one she was wearing, except that it was pale green instead of pale blue. We took the same size, but she was a couple of inches shorter, so the hem rode up to my crotch when I sat down. As the customers grew inebriated, some of them tried to grope me, but by that time, their brains and hands were moving so slowly that I had little difficulty fending them off.

"She's sending you the easiest customers," Ruth hissed in my ear. "The newbies."

"Well, I'm a newbie," I said. "So that seems fair."

I'd learned that most of the customers were salesmen and executives who entertained their own clients here. They tended to request particular girls... usually Shinobu, Eloise, or Jessica. Eloise was the redheaded vampire who'd been stripping when I first came in. Shinobu and Jessica also stripped. The law required that they keep at least a G-string on. But they also performed private dances in cubicles behind the stage, where the law had no way of knowing what went on... or came off. Their stock in trade seemed to be a

46

kind of smouldering ennui that they could turn up or down at will. The other two vampires – Beth and Natasha – had no such power, as far as I could see, to subdue or tantalize. Lacking vivacity, giving a bedraggled impression even in their evening gowns, their only attraction seemed to lie in the fact that they *were* vampires.

Ruth and Irina, the "humans," occupied a definite place in the hierarchy of the club, above Beth and Natasha but below the trio of "top hostesses." Most groups of customers included a couple of "cherry boys" – newbies. Ruth and Irina – and I, in my role as trainee – had the task of soothing their nerves and easing them into the world of vamukura with the same kind of flattery and flirtation they could presumably have found at any other hostess club.

It baffled me that anyone could find Ruth's company soothing, but she spoke fluent Japanese, which gave her a shortcut to establishing a rapport. Many of the customers spoke some English, or tried to. But I'd found that after practising a few sentences on me, they generally got tired of the effort and encouraged me to practise my Japanese on them instead. I'd already learned several new expressions that I'd never have gleaned from any academic journal. For instance, *vamu fechi* was slang for "vampire fetish." I couldn't grasp the precise definition, but it either referred to sharers, or described everyone here.

A new group arrived, led by a florid man who requested Beth. Even she had her regulars. Ruth and I were assigned to entertain his underlings: an undemanding task, since they were already drunk. The man on my right promptly went to sleep. The man on my left seemed content to snigger and nod at his boss's every word.

"Beth is too pale!" bellowed the boss. "She needs a drink!"

I looked up, alert. According to the literature, feedings were supposed to be part of the entertainment at *vamukura*, *but* so far, I hadn't observed any bloodletting here. I suspected the private dance cubicles also served as feeding chambers. But far from demanding privacy, Beth's regular rolled back his sleeve to expose a meaty arm.

Beth sighed and drooped her head.

As if from nowhere, Ogino appeared at the customer's shoulder. I mentally added another item to the maître d's list of duties: lancet-bearer. But I'd barely finished the thought when I saw what he was carrying in a folded white napkin. A knife – a knife? With a blade ten inches long? A *dagger*.

Well, it made sense. If you're going to let your own blood in public, where's the fun, where the macho symbolism, in doing it with a medical tool designed to *prevent* you from hurting yourself? The longer the blade, the bigger the man.

Beth's regular brought the dagger to his arm and drew a steady line in exactly the right place. He'd done this before. Blood welled from the cut. The underlings oohed and aahed at his bravery.

Beth jerked forward.

All the men laughed. "You'll have your drink when I give it to you," the boss shouted. Ogino hovered, close enough to intervene if necessary. The boss hulked closer to Beth, waving his bleeding arm to and fro under her nose. "Smells good, doesn't it? Makes you hot!"

After teasing her for another moment, he allowed her to lap at the cut. Her lips fastened convulsively on the flesh in the way I'd seen before, as if the blood woke some real need in them, as if it wasn't just playacting or a morbid perversion. "Drink! Drink! Drink!" chorused the underlings, clapping in slow time. In my head, I heard Colin saying, *More like cannibalism!*

The customer jerked his arm away. Blood painted Beth's mouth like messy lipstick and filmed her dainty little fangs. Her eyes rolled.

Ogino pinned her in place, holding her upright.

Dorothy rustled to her knees in front of the customer. "Let me fix that up for you." Ogino handed her a first-aid kit. She deftly cleaned the man's now-ragged cut and taped a gauze pad over it. "She's a naughty girl." Dorothy's voice flowed like oil on troubled waters. "But it's because she likes you. Hasn't seen you for a while. Been starving herself, waiting for you. I guess she just couldn't hold back…"

"That's bullshit," Ruth muttered in my ear. "She's been keeping her short. Trying to make her earn it. I guess that strategy just backfired."

"She'll be punished," the customer stated. His features were damp and no longer so florid.

"Sure she will be. How bad do you want her punished? I could take her fangs."

"Take her fangs?"

The customer's underlings bayed that they'd do it themselves.

"No, if it's done, I do it." Dorothy smiled and shook her head. "It's tricky. You got to know what you're doing."

"She files them off," Ruth whispered. "It's not that bad. They grow back."

"They grow back?"

The customer decided on magnanimity. "No need to take her fangs. But she must be punished. Allow me to punish her," he said formally, inflating his chest.

Dorothy sighed. "Beth, Beth, you brought this on yourself." She stood up. "Understood. But no more than ten minutes with the lash. And I have to be there, that's the rule, as you know."

The customer rose as if he was ready to implement Beth's punishment here and now. Dorothy gently propelled him back to his seat. "Don't be in such a hurry. Give her some time to get back to herself, so she understands what happened. You want her to understand, don't you? That's right. We got to get the room ready, anyway. In the meantime, you just relax. Give him a drink, Clare, the gentleman's had a shock…"

On the other side of the club, the remaining customers were singing sentimental karaoke tunes. Exiles was too "high-class" to have a karaoke machine. Instead, it had Aleksey. There was no song, it seemed, English or Japanese, that he couldn't play. I rested my chin on my elbow on the back of the sofa, watching his pale face and listening to the melodious tumult that welled up from under his hands.

Neither he nor any of the customers on that side of the club had reacted to the fracas around Beth. Maybe it happened all the time.

By three o'clock, the only customers left were Beth's regular and one of his underlings. I'd been given the job of helping Irina prepare the "correction chamber," which involved securing wrist and ankle restraints to D-loops on the wall of one of the private cubicles. Now Beth sashayed towards the chamber of her own free will. She'd recovered from her fit. In fact, she was as perky as I'd seen her yet. She looked over her shoulder and made coy eyes at the man she'd bitten.

He followed her into the cubicle at a near run.

The whole episode constituted a kind of ritual, I realized – unscheduled and unorchestrated, but not unwelcome to either party.

It was not, however, *part of the entertainment.* As far as I was concerned, entertainment stopped this side of a supervised spree with a whip.

I helped Ruth collect empty glasses. Suddenly, Dorothy emerged from the chamber. Perhaps it was my imagination, but her eyes seemed to shine brighter than ever. "Clare, you wanna hang with us after this? The trains don't start until half past five, so you got a couple of hours to kill. We generally chill at one of the places down the street."

I shook my head. "I think I'll just grab a taxi."

All the way home, I dwelled on the memory of the affronted look on Dorothy's face. The scientist in me castigated me for refusing her invitation. If I'd stuck around, I would have had a chance to talk to the trio of top hostesses (I'd already sketched out a rebuttal to Professor Kamikawa's thesis: *Self-Made Successes: The Evolution Of The* Vamukura). But I wasn't *just* a scientist. There was a limit to what I could take, and right now I no longer felt as if I had the objectivity to conduct observations at Exiles, much less work there.

50

Chapter 4.

The next morning, I reached Turner Hall on time. Puffy-eyed and dizzy from a whole three hours of sleep, I staggered into the sociology office and found Misaki's desk empty.

"She might be in Kamikawa-sensei's office," the other graduate students told me.

I knocked. "Sensei?" When no answer came, I eased the door open.

The airless heat mugged me. The office was empty. From outside the closed windows, the faint voices of students rose like birdsong. I tiptoed over to Professor Kamikawa's desk, eyes roving greedily over the bookshelves. The door had closed behind me. I slipped around the desk and squatted down on my heels. I'd spotted an entire shelf of back issues of specialist journals: *Shakaigaku Journal, Jinruigaku Ronbun,* and one I'd never heard of, *Kousatsushu,* which translated as *Collected Discussions* and sounded promisingly eclectic. No wonder it had folded... two years ago, going by the date on the most recent issue here.

If I casually cited some argument he'd made in an obscure organ like this, Professor Kamikawa would *have* to take me seriously.

Dust came off on my fingers as I eased the whole slippery wodge off the shelf. In the second-to-last number of *Kousatushu's* run, I hit paydirt.

Too nervous to push my luck any further, I stuffed the issue into my satchel, replaced the rest on the shelf, and fled. Out in the hall, I brushed the dust off my trousers before returning to the department office.

Computer keys clattered against the hum of the fans that supplemented the air-conditioning.

"Does Kamikawa-sensei have any classes today?"

Computerized and paper schedules were consulted.

"Vampiric Psychology, in Building Five, Room Eight, at ten past two."

"Do you have Keita Matsudaira or Seiji Inobe's cell phone numbers?" Surely it must be possible to contact them, even if they seldom put in an appearance on campus.

"We can't give out private information. They're Kami-kawa-sensei's students, aren't they? He might be able to help you..."

I bought an iced coffee from the Starbucks franchise in the dining hall and sat on a bench in the shadow of a giant ginkgo, where the path curved around a small lawn. Students basked in the sunlight. Giant dragonflies skimmed over the grass. Crows weighed down the branches overhead: even they were torpid in this heat. I ate a few squares of chocolate, then took the issue of *Kousatsushu* I'd lifted out of my satchel. With my dictionary at hand, I turned to *Fushigi na chikara o meguru: Wilfred Hauptmann to Nihonryu no maho.*

Regarding a Mysterious Power: Wilfred Hauptmann and the Japanese School of Magic, by Tsuyoshi Kamikawa.

In all honesty, it hadn't been Professor Kamikawa's name that impelled me to liberate the journal from his office. It had been Hauptmann's.

The article opened with an overview of the Swiss magician's early career, which I already knew about – although *knew* was pushing it, since Wilfred Hauptmann had glorified in obscurity, and even his dates (1874-1924?) were open to question. His notoriety in the West stemmed chiefly from Crowley, who'd acclaimed him posthumously as his greatest teacher.

Hauptmann's initial researches into magic had been undertaken in partnership with Baron Otto Reichs, "discoverer" of what Reichs had called "the odic force." In 1905, Reichs and Hauptmann had quarrelled. Hauptmann had then moved to Paris, where he'd plunged into hermeticism and developed the rituals that Crowley would later use as the foundation of his own magic. These had mostly been lost – a fact that gave modern practitioners room for a lot of creativity – but were said to have drawn on ancient Egyptian and Mesopotamian rites, presaging the Golden Dawn's adoption of Thoth, the Egyptian god of knowledge and magic. In fact, contemporary rumor had claimed that the "Swiss sorceror" had the power to summon demons. In the *Collected Papers of Wilfred Hauptmann* published in 1931 by Crowley, the "elder gods" came across as mere aspects of the practitioner's own divine potential. But it was now believed that Crowley had edited the manuscripts to emphasize the spiritual over the practical.

Unlike his more famous disciple, Hauptmann seemed to have had little interest in metaphysics. The portrait that emerged from the historical record showed a man coldly focused on results. His experimental drive, characteristic of his age, may have led him beyond the bounds of caution. In 1919, a scandal erupted in war-weary Paris: one of Hauptmann's pupils was found dead, stark naked, on an island in the Seine, the victim of a murder that the gutter press immediately labeled human sacrifice. In 1920, with criminal charges probably on the verge of materializing against him, Hauptmann embarked for the Orient.

After that, his tracks faded. I'd heard that he ingratiated himself first with the Emperor of Siam, then with the poor, half-mad Taisho Emperor of Japan. But that had the ring of a colonial-era fantasy, and no one could say where or when he'd finally perished. Several sources put him in Japan during the twenties. Certainly, two of his most devoted disciples, Fritz and Eva Stauffenberg, had slogged out here around that time, telling their friends and relatives that they were "going to seek the Master."

Professor Kamikawa's article picked up the thread of Hauptmann's career on May 12, 1921 – the day he disembarked in Yokohama.

I plunged in eagerly.

As the sun rose higher, I followed the shrinking shadows of the trees. No matter how much I adored the sun, I couldn't bask in the open. Even my SPF 50 was no defense. I ended up on the lawn, or rather on the scuffed earth beneath the tallest beech tree, where ants tunnelled in the dirt. Around me, students slept. I lay on my stomach and read on to the end of Professor Kamikawa's article, fascination warring with growing confusion.

From *Self-Created Outcasts* to the most trivial op-ed piece, every publication of Professor Kamikawa's that I'd read used a vague and jargon-ridden academic style. But *Regarding a Mysterious Power* was a colorful polemic. It almost failed scientific standards of objectivity, so loudly did it creak under the weight of an agenda that I slowly identified, through the veil of the language barrier, as anti-Stauffenberg.

Fritz and Eva S. *had* reached Japan, it appeared, in 1924, escaping the war-battered Old World for the booming capital of the world's newest big power. By that time Wilfred Hauptmann had set himself up in Tokyo as the operator of a small "atelier." His only connection with the Taisho Emperor was the acquisition of a rescript to practice "Odic Science." No hint of political influence. Hauptmann had simply got up to his old tricks in a new country, drawing to himself a coterie of admiring disciples. He was one more foreign huckster purveying Western glamor to the nascent Japanese bourgeoisie.

Into this idyll sailed the Stauffenbergs. Having sacrificed everything to seek their "Master," they inevitably came into conflict with his Japanese students. According to Professor Kamikawa, they couldn't appreciate the vast strides that Hauptmann had achieved by incorporating Japanese wisdom into his philosophy of magic.

The article was frustratingly silent on the details of this evolution. I'd speculated that the "Japanese School of Magic" in the title referred to *onmyodo,* the Japanese tradition of sorcery based on esoteric Taoism, which also incorporated elements of Buddhism and *jujutsu,* the Shintoist magic that crudely resembled Western voodoo. I knew very little about *onmyodo,* "The Way of Light and Dark," except that it had been outlawed at the time of the Meiji Restoration. I was keen to learn more, but *onmyodo* wasn't mentioned in the article.

By implication, I gathered that Hauptmann had identified the odic force – aka spirit energy, aka pneuma, aka vitalis, aka orgone – with *qi*, the energy that was believed by Eastern thinkers to flow through all things. That was interesting, but it didn't touch on the points that were, as far as I was concerned, central to any investigation of Hauptmann's life: *Had* he practised human sacrifice? If so, what had he been trying to accomplish? And was there any truth to the charges of satanism?

Far from answering these questions, Professor Kamikawa seemed to assume that his readers were already familiar with the content and objectives of Hauptmann's rituals. He hadn't set pen to paper to discuss the nature of magic itself: he seemed to be out to prove that Hauptman's true heir was a certain Kiyomasa Horibe, star pupil of the Atelier de la Science Odique, who'd quarrelled with Eva Stauffenberg after the death of her husband in 1936. By that time, Wilfred Hauptmann was long cold in his grave. Fritz Stauffenberg had taken over the Atelier after the death of its founder (given here as occurring in 1928). Under Fritz's leadership, the school had enjoyed a prosperous decade, but after his demise, it had all fallen apart. Kiyomasa Horibe had quarrelled with Eva and flounced off to establish a rival atelier – the Tsurukai, or Crane Society – taking most of the Atelier's best students with him. The "Japanese School of Magic" turned out to refer to the Tsurukai. Eva took her revenge by laying legal claim to a number of "precious and unique" magical texts, formerly the property of Hauptmann. The stage was set for a grand battle over the Swiss sorceror's legacy, but a real battle intervened in the shape of the Second World War. Both the Atelier and the Tsurukai were mournfully described as having been obliterated during the conflict.

I closed the journal.

A sad tale, and not as edifying as I'd hoped.

James would be enthralled by the historical revelations,

but given the bias that oozed from the pages, I couldn't feel sure that even the facts were 100% reliable.

The most interesting revelation of all, to be honest, was that Professor Kamikawa took this much interest in magic.

In the past, Aoyama Gakuin's *choshizengaku* department had produced a solid body of publications on *jujutsu* and *onmyodo* – none of which, unfortunately, I'd gotten around to reading – but the force behind all that work had been Professor Masamune Shinozaki, a noted *onmyodo* expert, who'd died a couple of years back. Of course, when this article was published, he'd still been alive. Could he have inspired it? Perhaps even have been its uncredited cowriter? Having read none of Professor Shinozaki's work, I couldn't say whether it jibed with his views. But the article indubitably represented dozens of hours of original research. And where would Professor Kamikawa have found the time? He was busy being the national expert on vampires...

And teaching classes.

A nearby chapel bell struck two.

I slipped into Building Five and grabbed a seat in the back of Professor Kamikawa's class. Room Eight was an auditorium, a hundred students scattered on tiered benches that could have seated three times as many. Most of them were asleep. The minority punctiliously copied down the illegible – to me – characters that the professor scrawled on the blackboard. As far as I could follow his lecture, he was addressing the topic of psychic vampirism. I leaned forward eagerly: field research on so-called psychic vampires was practically nonexistent. But to my disappointment, Professor Kamikawa seemed to have dismissed their literal existence *a priori*. He treated the concept as a metaphor, implying that *all* vampires were psychic vampires. He drew parallels with the charismatic leaders of underworld societies and religious cults. This was the familiar, if unarticulated, contention that ran through his published oeuvre: that the sole source of any power wielded by human beings was the human mind.

The fervid credulity of *Regarding a Mysterious Power*

looked even more incongruous.

After the class, a queue of students formed at the front of the auditorium. I let others go ahead of me until I faced Professor Kamikawa alone. "I enjoyed your lecture, sensei," I began. "And I apologize for being late yesterday. I hoped to meet Matsudaira-san and Inobe-san today, so that I could start my fieldwork. But I couldn't find Yokoyama-san..."

"No, you wouldn't have been able to do that." The professor spoke in Japanese with some asperity, if he'd forgotten our previous conversation in English. He'd been limping to and fro in front of the class for eighty minutes, and looked tired. "She's taken a leave of absence from the university."

"She's *what?*"

His eyes sparkled. "What did you do to her? She was perfectly happy two days ago, and now... It's most inconvenient. She was an excellent office assistant. Perhaps you would care to take her place."

"I... I would be honored to assist you in any way I can. But perhaps I should meet with Matsudaira-san and Inobe-san first? To ascertain exactly where we are in the study. So that I can better assist you."

"That seems reasonable. Your written Japanese, how is it?"

"I do better with a computer, but I can write by hand, too," I asserted, and realized an instant later that I shouldn't have admitted it.

Professor Kamikawa collected his notes from the lectern and folded them into his briefcase. I thought about broaching the topic of magic, but thought better of it: he was obviously exhausted. Out in the sunlight, his face looked like a crumpled ball of paper. "I'll expect you at nine tomorrow morning," he said, exactly as he'd said the last time we met.

"Matsudaira-san and Inobe-san?" I said desperately.

"Oh... If you really want to find them, I should try Harajuku. That's where they usually are." For an instant, he broke into the impish smile that I remembered from the photo in James's office. In English, he said, "Good luck!"

I had little hope of locating two researchers in an area the size of SoHo, and after I got off the train at Harajuku, I had none at all. Colorful crowds funneled into the famous Takeshita-dori, giving the street a holiday atmosphere. Tiny shops spilled their wares into the sunlight: fetish wear, idol merchandise, imported sneakers, risqué lingerie… Spotting a jewelry boutique called Dracula's Crypt, I couldn't resist ducking in, but the crush drove me back out after one glance at the predictably gothic offerings.

Teens slurped icecream cones and squatted on the curb. I felt *old*. Dating couples, kids with purple and white hair, why weren't they in school? The only tartan visible was the Campbell plaid of classic punk, not any school's uniform. The most popular fashion statement was head-to-toe black, accessorized by brand-logo tote bags.

If my agenda for the day had consisted of nothing more than observing vampire shopping habits, I'd have been in paradise.

I reached the end of Takeshita-dori and returned to Harajuku station. On the bridge over the Yamanote line tracks, at the entrance to Meiji Jingu Park, I found another spectacular display. Groups of cosplayers had staked out the bridge, lounging on the pavement as if oblivious to the gawkers around them, yet springing readily into action poses when someone asked to take their pictures. Gothic lolitas, French maids, characters from manga and anime… and vampires. I immediately recognized the setting of Yurika Hamaguchi's most striking photographs. I even recognized some of her subjects: the family of Transylvanian aristocrats, the "vampires from the 24th century" who dressed in black bodystockings and painted their faces silver, defying the heat… Here, the distinction between being a vampire and dressing up as a vampire blurred to the point of irrelevance. Life / "undeath" became coextensive with a performance that inverted the power dynamic of feeding. The vampires / "vampires" invited the public to feed off *them*, to satisfy some widely felt need for morbidity and flamboyance.

I'd thought for a long time that I might find the key to the whole vampire phenomenon here on Harajuku bridge.

Instead, I spotted two young men sitting at the end of the bridge, one with a book and the other with a laptop.

I'd only ever seen one group picture in which they appeared, but I recognized them instantly. They were so out of place.

"We meet at last," I said. "I'm Clare Standing. May I join you?"

Lean and tousled, Matsudaira raised his eyebrows at me. Inobe hastily closed his laptop. They forestalled my apologies for yesterday with apologies of their own.

"We're still gathering quantitative data," Inobe said. He clambered slowly upright. He was bespectacled, soft of limb, and very tall. He mopped sweat off his face with a checked handkerchief.

"What methods are you using?" I said, looking down at Matsudaira, who was holding his place in his book with a finger. Maybe he thought I couldn't read the title. He was right, but I could read the name of the author: Stephen King.

Unblinking, he held up a shiny metal gadget. "We're counting them."

"Well, you just missed one." I pointed.

"Oh. Thanks." He pushed the gadget's button.

"Actually, I think we got him already," said Inobe.

"You're good at picking them out. You'd be better at this than I am." Matsudaira held the gadget up to me. "Just push the button."

"And what are you going to do?" I took the counter from Matsudaira, but I looked at Inobe. "Check your email?"

He stammered. Matsudaira exclaimed, "Gotcha, Politik!"

"Politik?" I said.

"His name's Seiji." At last Matsudaira stood up. "Hence Politik. With a *k*. That was his handle, back in the day. You're looking at a reformed hacker. Now he writes apps."

Inobe – Politik – blushed and demurred. I said, "Fascinating. Do you still work under a pseudonym?"

"Hey—" With an expansive gesture, Matsudaira indicated the cosplayers on the bridge. "We're just trying to blend in."

Both of them laughed.

"How old are you?" Politik said suddenly.

He couldn't tell, I thought. All the customers at Exiles last night had asked my age. I'd thought they were being rude until Dorothy explained the social importance of seniority. At the club, I'd said I was twenty-seven, but I saw no reason to lie now. "Thirty-one."

"Same as me," Matsudaira said. "What month?"

"July."

"I'm May." He smirked as if he'd won.

Politik frowned. I'd thought at first that he had a receding hairline, but it was just a widow's peak. Behind his thick square glasses, he looked to be in his mid-twenties. It depressed me to think that he and I were both Ph.D candidates, whereas Matsudaira already had his doctorate. "Day?" he demanded.

"The twentieth."

"You don't happen to know what time you were born?"

"Half past midnight."

He stared at the sky as if making calculations. Matsudaira loudly instructed him not to waste my time.

"No, so tell me," I said. "What's my birth animal? You're figuring out my Chinese astrological sign, aren't you?"

"Yes! Our system is a bit different, but it's the same idea." Politik's eyes gleamed behind his glasses. "You were born in the year of Wood Rabbit. She's an inner Monkey," he added significantly to Matsudaira, "and a secret Sheep."

"Ugh," I said. "Wood Rabbit? *Sheep?* Couldn't I be something less wimpy?"

"Oh, the animals aren't related to your personality. It's the elements that count. The Monkey is ruled by Fire, you see, and so is the Sheep—"

"Don't get him started," Matsudaira told me. "Go online

60

and look it up if you're interested." He dropped down cross-legged again. Politik and I followed suit. The pavement felt pleasantly cool after my walk in the sun.

"Well, it's good to know," Politik argued. "If we're going to be working together."

"Speaking of which," Matsudaira said.

"Indeed," I said.

I tested the button on the counter. It made a satisfying *thock*. Matsudaira opened his book. I gazed at him until he looked up.

"Hey, I'm working hard!" He clutched his temples and furrowed his brow in mock concentration. "Fieldwork is ninety percent brainwork to ten percent legwork," he gasped. "It's all about insight. Putting your observations together. I'm within grasping distance of any number of conceptual breakthroughs." He grinned at me. "Lesson one: how to keep Kamikawa-sensei happy."

I laughed with them. "The other day, I learned the Japanese word for playing hooky," I said. *"Saboru.* From the English word *sabotage.* Isn't that interesting?"

"You speak Japanese so well!" they chorused.

"I wonder if there's a phrase for *going through the motions?"*

"Katachi dake de yaru." Matsudaira grinned wider. "But if you stick with us, you won't ever need to use that one."

We sat with our backs against the stone, in the shadow of the pillar at the corner of the bridge: a little gang of cosplayers of our own. Two saboteurs and one interloper, dressed up as researchers.

"What happens if I count a vampire you've already counted?" I said.

They looked at each other. If they'd been American, I thought, they would have shrugged. "Then we roll the count back a bit, to make it come out right."

I read the numbers in the counter's little window. 24,703.

"Do you know anything about magic?" I asked Politik a

couple of hours later. I'd decided he would be the easier one
to question. "I read an interesting article about it today."

The shadow we sat in had lengthened to swallow half
the bridge. As the flow of tourists thinned, the cosplayers
had begun to pack their trunks and drift away. Battalions of
crows whirled lazily above the trees in Meiji Jingu Park.

"Majiku?" Politik said. "What kind of majiku, specifically?"

I frowned, not understanding the question. But maybe
he hadn't understood *my* question. Although we shared the
same terminology – *majiku* for magic, *vamupu* for vampire –
we had different reference points. It was unsettling to think
that we might be using the same words to talk about different things.

What kind of magic?

"Wicca? Magick with a K? Qabala?" I hazarded. "The
Enochian Rite? Vaudun? Santeria? Heptarchism? Goetia?"
Normally, I wouldn't have thought to list different systems
of magic like this, since they didn't exist in isolation: magic
was a melting-pot. Even the organized "denominations"
drew on a variety of strains within the loosely defined Three
Great Traditions, the hermetic, Celtic, and shamanistic. That
said, the hermetic or ceremonial tradition was far and away
the most popular. "The Children of Gaia? The New Golden
Dawn? The Order of Neo-Druidae?"

"We don't have anything like that in this country,"
Matsudaira said, leaning across Politik. "Why do you want
to know?"

"I'm just curious," I said. "But it's funny you should say
that, because I read that *majiku* has quite a history in Japan."

"Oh, you're talking about *jujutsu*. Why didn't you say?
We only use *magiku* for Western magic."

Actually, I had been talking about *majiku,* but I decided
to go with the flow. "Yeah, *jujutsu*, then. Do you know anything about it?"

"Well, it's got more popular recently," Matsudaira said.
"You probably saw that article in the Japanese edition of

62

Time."

"Yeah, it was an interesting read." I remembered the piece: magic as the latest celebrity fad, seasoned with a dollop of punditry about unsatisfied spiritual cravings. The way it was described, *jujutsu* seemed to have cross-fertilized pretty thoroughly with Western magic: poppets and gemology shared a mention with *ofuda* – paper talismans to ward off curses – and the mystical manipulation of *qi*. Tokyo could have been replaced with any other world capital, and it would have been just as topical.

Politik snorted. "Interesting," he said, his moon face alive with amusement. "What's interesting is that people actually believe in that stuff."

"Yeah," said Matsudaira. "And it's even more interesting that anyone wastes their time doing serious research on it."

Politik let out a hoot of laughter. I scowled. Presumably, they were aware of my academic history.

"The point is that people *do* believe in it. That alone makes it a worthy subject of study," I said.

Matsudaira snorted. "They're losers." He went back to his book.

The laughter now gone from his face, Politik said more reasonably, "Every movement attracts groupies who just want something to believe in. But from the practitioner's point of view, the whole point of magic is that it promises results. And it doesn't deliver. So... well, there isn't really anything to study, is there?"

I stared at the crowd and pushed the button on the counter. That was a pretty sweeping dismissal, even for students of Tsuyoshi Kamikawa, who was known for his pragmatic approach to paranormal problems.

Except, of course in Regarding A Mysterious Power.

Did magic work? Human beings had been answering that question both ways since the dawn of civilization. My own experience left me reluctant to come down too firmly on either side of the debate. The available statistics seemed to prove that the magical power claimed by self-designated wizards, warlocks, and so forth was – well, *something*. A few percentage points better than a placebo effect. But if you looked closely at those studies, they were poorly designed and relied heavily on anecdotal evidence.In Ireland, I'd been trying to correct that situation by carrying out my own ethnographic field study. Alone, I couldn't employ the quantitative methods that were really needed, so I'd gone into the Skibbereen Coven on foot and unarmed, so to speak, to gather data on a small group of witches and warlocks, and observe their spellcastings with my own eyes.

All I'd been left with, after abruptly wearing out my welcome, was: Absence of evidence is not evidence of absence. Or it *is*. Again, depending on who you ask.

But I'd also been left with a few unpleasant memories of magic's darker side. Although most people thought of magic as the lunatic fringe, it had a lunatic fringe of its own. Like any subculture, it attracted the weird, the socially challenged… and a few certifiable sociopaths.

If Matsudaira and Politik refused to take it seriously, they didn't belong in paranormal studies. Or else I still hadn't asked the right question.

"Hey, guys," I said. Both of them turned to look at me, faces blank and patient in the way that only the Japanese could manage. "Why doesn't Aoyama Gakuin have a professor of magical studies anymore?"

"We used to," Matsudaira said. "Old Shinozaki. He died a couple of years ago, and the tightwads haven't hired anyone to replace him." He shrugged. "The undergrad interest's not there. Why?"

"I just wondered… It was kind of tragic, wasn't it?" At the time of the professor's death, Misaki had confided to me in an email that he'd committed suicide.

"Well, he was no spring chicken," Matsudaira said ruthlessly. "The real tragedy is that they farmed his classes out to Sociology. *I* could have done with the work."

"I know what you're thinking," Politik said with a sudden explosive laugh. "You're thinking it was foul play.

Aren't you?"

"Well, I don't have anything to go on," I hedged.

The two of them exchanged a swift glance.

Politik lowered his voice. "Don't let this go any further, but you just might be right. *We think it was black magic,*" he hissed, eyes bulging.

"Or rather, it was black magicians that drove him to it," Matsudaira said. "Same difference."

"Black magicians?" I said breathlessly. "So he... trod on someone's toes?"

"If *you* were a black magician, wouldn't you go to any lengths to protect your secret?" Politik demanded.

"Which is to say, you want to be careful about asking questions like that," Matsudaira said.

"Are there that many black magicians in Japan?" I wondered if I dared get out my laptop to take notes.

"Oh no," Matsudaira said. "Not many at all."

"There aren't that many who have what it takes," Politik said.

"But they're out there. And they're always on the look-out for... *victims.*"

The last word was hissed into my face; I recoiled. The two of them shared a frat-boy snigger.

I flushed. "How will I know if I meet one, then?" I hid my embarrassment by playing along with their joke. "I mean, what if they don't wear a sign that says *Black Magician ISO Victim?*"

"Oh, but they *do*. Well, not as such, but..." Politik fought back giggles.

"Just ask them for their photo ID," Matsudaira said, expressionlessly.

Politik whooped with laughter.

I gritted my teeth. We were supposed to be working together, and they were acting like junior high school boys. So, fine, I'd sink to their level. "So I guess you've never heard of the Atelier de la Science Odique or the Tsurukai. Oh, well!"

In an instant, Matsudaira's face went from supercilious

to blank. "How do you know about the Tsurukai?"

Triumph warmed me. "I told you, it was in an article. The topic was Wilfred Hauptmann and his legacy in Japan..."

Matsudaira looked at Politik. "The *Kousatsushu* piece. I thought we'd —" He turned back to me. "I mean, that rag isn't around anymore. As a matter of fact, it got banned – for violating the Journalistic Standards Act, believe it or not. They even recalled the back numbers. Where'd you get a copy? Did Kamikawa-sensei *give* it to you?"

In the face of his incredulity, I didn't dare lie outright. But neither could I bring myself to confess the truth, which amounted to unauthorized entry and theft. Despising myself, I muttered, "Yokoyama-san lent it to me."

Matsudaira mustered a smile. He said pityingly, "Did you know she's taken a leave of absence? Gone to stay with her parents in Ibaraki prefecture."

"Yeah. It's so sudden. Do you think she was afraid of something?" I said. "Or maybe some*one?*"

"Course not," Politik said. He grinned, not at anyone in particular. His gaze jumped hither and yon across the bridge.

"**W**ell! I think we've just about completed our work for the day." Matsudaira jumped up. "And there's Skriva. *Skriva!*" He waved.

"Now you can observe our qualitative research methods," Politik said to me.

A small group of vampires approached us. They all wore what I'd started to think of as the gothic grunge look: black tatters, spiky hair, and platform boots in metallic colors.

Matsudaira introduced the leader of the group. "Skriva is the *hakushaku* of the Harajuku vampires."

"Fuck off, Matsudaira," Skriva said. He didn't say *fuck off* – Japanese has no four-letter words – but it was there in his contemptuous smile. He had short, thick fangs. "Those old titles, we don't even use them among ourselves anymore, except as handles."

"So may I call you Count Skriva?" I said.

"You *may*. But I'm not the leader around here. Am I?" he checked with his followers.

"No!"

"Definitely not!"

"We'd never dream of obeying you!"

"See?" Skriva concluded. "We're democratic."

I had yet to verify whether Dorothy Foulkes was a *haku-shaku*, as Leon's sidekick had claimed. But if she was, did that mean she held a position equivalent to the one Skriva disavowed? *Dorothy, Countess of Roppongi?* I couldn't see her renouncing a title like that, regardless of whether any privileges went with it.

"So where are we eating?" Skriva said.

Several of his followers clamored for Japanese food.

"Well, *she* might not be up for that," Matsudaira said. He clearly meant me, since there were no females in Skriva's group.

"On the contrary," I said. "I haven't had a chance to try real Japanese food yet. Let's go for it."

We walked down Omotesando-dori. On Meiji-dori we turned towards Shibuya, and then onto a side street hung with lanterns and the carwash curtains that marked old-fashioned Japanese eateries. Matsudaira led us into a large izakaya, where we sat on zabuton cushions and clinked glasses of peaty Yebisu beer. The vampires commenced feasting with zeal, ordering entire pages of the menu.

"Well, this is why we've got funding," Matsudaira said to me with an air of commiserating over a shared misfortune.

"You know, a lot of people in America believe that vampires don't eat solid food. A lot of American vampires encourage that belief, too. They won't touch anything in public except red wine."

Skriva overheard me and laughed loudly. "A lot of fun immortality would be, without solid food and beer!"

He was in his late twenties, I judged, wearing eyeliner and heavy plugs in his earlobes to complement the spiky hair. And he was smart enough, at any rate, to play Matsu-daira for a free meal ticket.

"Skriva was on TV last week," one of the other vampires said. "*Celebrity Talent Explosion!* They put him on opposite Jaize 3000, can you believe that?"

"At least we got free champagne," Skriva said with his mouth full.

"You haven't tried the sashimi, have you, Clare?" Politik leaned over the table to offer me the dish. He was red in the face, as drunk as any of the customers at Exiles last night. "Try this one! It's *ika.*"

Squid. I captured the morsel with my chopsticks, dunked it in the wasabi-flavored soy sauce, and swallowed it. "Yum, yum. Anything else I should try?"

"Yum, yum!" The vampires fell about. "Yum, yum!"

"Yum, yum," murmured Skriva, looking at my neck.

"The title of my dissertation was *Vampire Democracy,*" Matsudaira said. He, too, was drunk, I thought. "I sent a copy to your professor. Did you get a chance to read it?"

"Sorry, I don't think I ever spotted it in his office."

"Huh. Well, maybe it never got there. I had a contract to spice it up and publish it as a book, but they put a stop to that, too."

"That's a shame," I said.

"You're telling me."

"So have you had any job offers?" I asked, rather meanly.

"You're kidding, right? We don't have it as good here as you do in America. The hard sciences get all the funding, and we get left out in the cold. Then within sociology and anthropology, we have too many Ph.Ds competing for too few academic positions. And with a doctorate in *choshiz-engaku?* I'm as unemployable as they come."

"Well, hopefully this study will pay off in terms of posi-tive publicity for the field," I said.

"So I'm on my fourth one-year contract as a researcher. At first I taught at a cram school to make ends meet. Then when old Shinozaki died, I should have got my assistant professorship, but they decided they didn't need another vampire expert." Matsudaira was in full self-pitying flow. "So now I do proofreading, translation, freelance jobs…"

So what would you do for money, Matsudaira-san? I thought. What have you done?

He downed his beer and poured himself some more. "It's about time this country entered the twenty-first century," he announced.

"I agree," I said. "It's the same in America. The public needs to wake up and pay attention to us, instead of lumping us in with UFOs and Elvis sightings. The vampires are here, and they aren't going away." I looked around at the squabbling, feasting vamps, and sighed.

Matsudaira nodded. "So they put Kamikawa-sensei on TV as a talking head, and they think that's the end of the problem. Now, I respect the hell out of Kamikawa-sensei, but he's more of a theoretician. No one can understand what the fuck he's saying most of the time. That's why he's so popular. But we need to play a role that's more – yeah, the research is important, but we also need to be communicators. We need to give a voice to the vampire community. Tell the real story." He belched.

"I haven't read your dissertation," I said, "but what studies did you use to support your thesis? *Vampire Democracy*… I don't think I've seen that data."

Matsudaira bridled. Quite likely, I thought, there *were* no data – only anecdotes and second-hand statistics. My flash of triumph immediately turned bitter. Was it any wonder the field continued to languish in obscurity, when this was the best we could do?

"Why don't you try listening to our research partners?" he challenged me. "Skriva says they're democratic. You heard him."

"They're democratic because he says so? And just look at them, hanging on his every word. How democratic is that? Oh, never mind," I said in frustration. "What's Politik's dissertation about?"

"He hasn't decided yet. He's kicking around a bunch of topics."

"Maybe he could write a computer game instead and make a bundle," I muttered. "Call it *Vampire Democracy*. First one to get on TV wins."

"That's an idea! And I'd get credit for the concept!" Matsudaira laughed and nudged me, clearly thinking he'd won.

"So who's paying you?" I said, losing patience with him.

Matsudaira squinted at me. "I told you, I'm on contract. And Politik's a grad student. Otherwise known as free labor."

"Oh please." I was drunk, too. I thought about stopping, but didn't. "Someone's paying you not to do any science. Or maybe they didn't pay you. Maybe they just intimidated you. But..." My fury overwhelmed self-control. "This study is an unprecedented opportunity! We've got the support, the time, the academic standing to be taken seriously, and I very much hope that all of us have the theoretical and methodological tools to put together some groundbreaking research on these understudied communities. We have big questions to answer. Who are they? What are they? And what does it mean for human society, in Japan and America and across the world, that their populations appear to be increasing *exponentially*, just a few decades after the first cases of clinical vampirism were documented? We have a dangerous rival theory to disprove. I hope that you've heard of Dr Isaac Brent and his flawed studies. We have the opportunity and the responsibility to stop a lie from being foisted on the world. Just as *you* said, we need to tell the real story. And all you're doing is taking your research partners out to eat and listening to their recycled ideological ramblings? I *hope* someone is paying you, and I hope they're paying you enough to make up for all the times when you can't live with yourself!"

Matsudaira had seemed too stunned to interrupt me. When I uttered the word *truth*, his nostrils had flared and he reared back slightly. But now he recovered his supercilious smile. "I *hope*," he mimicked, "that you never find out the truth about vampires. Because if you did, you would learn that you're wrong. Typically American, and utterly wrong." A muscle under his right eye twitched. "The truth doesn't set you free. The truth just kills you."

"If that's what you think, no wonder you haven't even tried to find out what it is," I retorted.

He flinched. I was right about *that*, at least, I thought coldly.

"Thanks, by the way." He rose on his knees. "Let's all thank Clare! She's paying for dinner today. Her university in America is *very* generous."

"Banzai, Clare-san!" shouted the drunken vampires. "Banzai!"

I forced myself through the rest of the week in the sociology office, paralyzed by the memory of my behavior at the izakaya. Lack of sleep, culture shock, too much Yebisu; it didn't matter what had caused my outburst, or whether I chose to call it an argument, a frank exchange of views, or a quarrel. I'd accused Matsudaira of being corrupt, and he'd accused me of being wrong. After that, how could we collaborate effectively?

Perhaps he felt the same way. Or perhaps he was just glad to have an excuse to ignore me. He and Politik had made no attempt to contact me since that night. I'd got their cell phone numbers, as well as their landline – they shared an apartment off-campus – but I couldn't bring myself to call them.

Professor Kamikawa had given me several articles to translate into English. Wading through his obfuscatory jargon, I felt nostalgic for the frothing partisan tone of *Regarding a Mysterious Power*. I'd secretly returned that issue of *Kousatsushu* to the professor's office, and now I was starting to wonder if I'd hallucinated its existence. With Misaki's dictionaries at my elbow, I slogged through the professor's equivocations and non-conclusions. No one in the office spoke to me beyond "Good morning."

My new cell phone hadn't rung once since I bought it.

At night, I brooded over the gun Colin had sneaked into my suitcase. I'd had the whole thing out with him over the phone. Unrepentant, he referred me to various internet sources that carried tales of Japanese urban violence, most of it vampire-related. "I just don't want you to walk into some dangerous situation without the option of defending yourself. OK, sis? It's not a crime, it's not a *sin*. It's just an option."

"It's an option I don't need."

"And it's an option you won't *have* unless you're carrying. Listen, sis, those little Glocks are idiot-proof. You don't have to worry about it blowing up in your face. But you need to get some target practice —"

"Which won't be possible, because handguns are *illegal* here. Crikey, Colin!" *Crikey* had been one of our mother's words. I only used it when I was really upset. "You did know that? There's a year's waiting period for an air rifle license, and then in another five years you can get a real rifle, and after *twenty* years you can get a handgun, if your record is stainless and you can account for every bullet you ever fired." I'd looked this stuff up, anxious to know how much trouble I was potentially in. "You did know that?" I repeated.

"Sure," my brother said after a moment. "Sure, I knew that."

I closed my eyes, listening with my free ear to the hum of the city outside the open windows.

"Well, at least practise dry-firing," Colin said stubbornly. "Get used to handling your weapon..."

I sighed, but I wrote down his instructions.

Because I hadn't wasted the whole week on Professor Kamikawa's translations. I'd done a little research, aka snooping in Misaki's files.

Ryu Abe.

Born in Asahikawa, Hokkaido. B.A. and M.A. in modern history from Kachiyama University in Hyogo Prefecture – never heard of it. Ph.D from Tokyo University, a prestigious institution which had the only other *choshizengaku* department in Japan. Earned his doctorate the same year as Keita Matsudaira. Dissertation: *Decoding Magic: 20th Century East Asian Occult Symbology*.

Dark-complected and hollow-cheeked, Abe smouldered out of the mugshot attached to his Aoyama Gakuin contract of employment. Professor Shinozaki had hired him to do the grunt work on a research project. Given that Ryu had a doctorate from the Japanese equivalent of Harvard, that either confirmed Matsudaira and Politik's complaints about the nonexistence of good jobs, or it said something about Ryu Abe himself. The project sounded interesting: the goal had been to compile a crossreferenced collection of *jumon*, the mystical mantras that underpinned both *jujutsu* and *onmyodo*. Aoyama Gakuin possessed a large collection of texts on esoteric Buddhism, Shintoism, and Taoism, including some original *jumonsho*, the Japanese equivalent of grimoires. Abe must have had an absorbing time of it, clambering around in the stacks on the scent of material that, after all, bore some relevance to his own specialty. I almost envied him.

Except I didn't.

The study had never been completed, never even received an official title. Sixteen months into his two-year contract, Abe had been fired. One tantalizing letter I found deep in Misaki's desk, from Professor Shinozaki to the dean's office, implied that Abe had been arrested by the police. But why and for what, the professor didn't say.

It didn't look as if he'd been charged. He'd simply been erased from the collective memory of the department.

And three months later, Professor Shinozaki had died.

Ryu Abe: current whereabouts unknown.

On Saturday, my fifth full day in Japan, I called James. It was evening in Manhattan, morning in Tokyo, the air already heavy and hot. I half-intended to pour out my difficulties to my mentor. Instead, I found myself assuring him that everyone was very kind and my fieldwork was producing exciting results. I'd already communicated to him by email that the telephone wasn't safe, so I was spared the need to invent any details. But this put me in the position of delivering hints that could all too easily be interpreted as predictions of groundbreaking discoveries. And I knew that was how James *would* interpret them. He'd been frustrated in his research for so many years, caricatured as a wacko and muzzled by the gentle contempt of the establishment. I was his last hope.

I hung up and said to Yurika's pot plants: "And now all I've got to do is deliver."

Although I hadn't mentioned this to James, I had an additional motivation. I'd learned that withdrawals from what I'd thought of as "my" account at the bursar's office had to be signed off on by at least two members of Professor Kamikawa's team. This regulation obviously posed no obstacle to Matsudaira and Politik, and they'd been making free with the balance.

Chapter 5.

"I thought you'd be back," Dorothy said over the music. "I fired Irina on Wednesday. So you're just on time. Go and sit with Eloise at table five."

I'd moved several paces when she called me back. "Girl, didn't I tell you to see about getting some different clothes?"

Tonight, I wore a floral blouse with frilly cap sleeves – one of my "demure and harmless" standbys – and a pair of white jeans that I'd bought this afternoon at the Banana Republic in Shibuya. I'd obeyed the proscription on black, so I'd hoped I would meet Dorothy's standards. "Aren't I symmetrical enough?" I said.

"That ain't the point. Jeans, we don't wear jeans in here... Well, you got no time to change. See those boys on the end of Eloise's table, they're all alone, they don't have no one to talk to. Go on, go on, I'll pick this up with you later."

The night went by in a blur of men's faces and new Japanese phrases. I bounced from table to table, rotated on by Ogino whenever new customers entered. Jessica and Shinobu performed their "Saturday night special" strip routine, which climaxed with simulated lesbian sex. Angela and Aleksey performed two sets. At last I returned from a snatched trip to the bathroom to find my customers on their way out the door. I bowed them into the elevator – "Get home safely! Come back soon!" and returned to the club.

There were no other customers left. It was four thirty in the morning.

"How time flies when you're having fun," I said, falling onto a sofa.

"Ain't that the truth." Dorothy sat down opposite me. Tonight she wore a sort of cheongsam in heavy black sateen with an exaggerated stiff collar that dipped low at the nape of her neck. The diagonal zipper in front was open far enough to reveal the silver spider pendant between her breasts. The zipper curled all the way around her body to the hem of the garment, making it impossible not to visualize what would happen if you were to give it one good tug.

"You got a gift, Clare," Dorothy said. "I knew it the first time you came here. You make them feel good about themselves, make them feel like they're glad they came here. Make them want to come back." She smiled wanly. "I am always right about this shit."

"But it's all fake," I said. "It's just my fieldwork experience. I know how to seem interested in people. Well, I genuinely am interested in people. But even when I'm not, I can fake it."

"You think they care about that? All this is fake. They come here *because* it's fake."

"Taking blood," I said, "that's not fake."

"You sure about that? I mean, really sure?" She leaned forward to take a cigarette from the pack of Larks a customer had left on the table between us. "You just keep doing what you're doing, Clare, and you won't have no problem. How were your tips tonight?"

I dug in the pocket of my jeans and spilled crumpled bills on the table. Dorothy counted with me, chanting the numbers like a double dutch rhyme, until we reached ¥34000.

"Now ain't that something? You just cleared more than three hundred dollars. I won't lie, Saturday is the best night of the week, plus we just passed the fifteenth, and that's payday at a lot of companies, so you're starting high... but add that to your hourly pay, and once you get your own regulars, then you get drinkbacks. And I ain't even mentioned dohans yet." The twinkle returned to her eyes. "But *first*, we got to talk about your clothes."

"I think the customers were happy with how I looked tonight."

"No, no. You got to make more of an effort. And don't take this the wrong way, but I don't trust your taste no more." She looked past me. "Ruth!"

Ruth was on the stage, talking with Aleksey as he leant

on his mop. She jumped to the floor, nimble in her high heels, and came over to us.

"You gonna take Clare shopping tomorrow. Take her to wherever it is you got your stuff. Shoes, too. How much you made tonight?"

"Eleven thousand," Ruth said.

"Well, she made three times that. So don't let her tell you she ain't got it to spend." Dorothy put out her cigarette, rose, and pushed us together with a hand on each of our shoulders, as if we were recalcitrant children. "Now go run that vacuum cleaner. There was a dish of chips spilled at table seven, make sure you vacuum good in that corner."

When I looked up over the vacuum cleaner, Dorothy was back in her place on the sofa, another cigarette negligently caught between her fingers. She seemed to be a thousand miles away.

"Time for her to crawl into her coffin and die," Ruth said. "When do you want to meet tomorrow? It's our day off, so I'd appreciate it if we could get this done with early."

"Does Dorothy really sleep in a coffin?" I asked the next day.

"Sure. And she changes into a bat when she wants to travel at night, and if you ever get close enough to touch her, she doesn't have a heartbeat... *No*, of course she doesn't sleep in a coffin." Ruth gave me a look of disgust. After a moment, she added brusquely, "Don't feel bad. I used to believe that shit, too."

We were threading through the crowded underground passageways that surrounded Shinjuku station. Ruth led me past cubbyhole shops crammed with cheesy evening dresses manufactured on the cheap in Vietnam and the Philippines. Any one of them would have done, I thought. Wafts of air blew from the grilles in the ceiling, tepid and smelling of plastic. I said tentatively, "Weird shit happens in this country, doesn't it? I bet a lot of people believe..."

"No more so than anywhere," Ruth said. "No, it's in America that people really believe the fucked-up shit. They don't have any way to know better. That's why I *used* to think it was all true about coffins, bats, turning into wolves, can't stand the light of the sun, you can back them down with holy water and a cross... Then I came to Japan and found out the truth."

The truth. "And what's that?" I said.

"That you need to mind your own fucking business."

"I was just asking."

"Well, you've been asking too much."

Her hard little profile quivered with the fury I'd detected in her last night while we were cleaning the club, a fury so disproportionate that it only made sense if she interpreted this shopping trip as a personal humiliation – and that in itself didn't make sense. Her pattern of overreacting made her seem almost unhinged. And top on of that, she seemed to have some kind of personal grudge against me.

Nevertheless, a couple of minutes later I tried again. "So where does Dorothy really live?"

Ruth snorted. "I'm surprised she didn't make a point of mentioning that. Roppongi Hills. You can see it from the window in the dressing-room. It's got a mall and an office tower as well as the residential tower. And if you ever go over there, it's got this giant spider statue thing out in front. That's why she likes it, I guess. It matches her trademark!" She shook her head. "No, she likes it because it's *high-class*."

"I didn't realize Exiles was quite that profitable."

"Do the math. And don't forget she has a stake in most of the other vamp clubs in Roppongi, too."

So perhaps the title of *hakushaku* did mean something, I thought.

"If she ever invites you over," Ruth said, "check out the security system. That's another reason... one of the reasons she moved there. This way!"

We climbed into the basement of Isetan, a vast food hall. Dozens of specialty vendors in long aprons were all crying their wares at once. Smells clashed queasily. The crowds clotted as people stopped to try the free samples.

"When I first came to Japan, I didn't have a yen to my name. I would have starved if not for these places," said Ruth, snagging a chunk of sausage on a toothpick. "Keep moving."

"How long have you been in Japan?" I said as we waited to get into an elevator.

"Depends who's asking."

"If it was me?"

"Five years. Same length of time I've been working at Exiles."

That explained why her Japanese was so good. Still, my mind boggled at the thought of pouring drinks, lighting cigarettes, and making flirtatious conversation, six nights a week... for *five years.* "You don't seem to enjoy it that much," I said.

"Fuck off," she said in a low voice. "I tell you something and you throw it back in my face... well, fuck you."

On the fourth floor, she silently led me between designer boutiques, past suave salespeople who smiled and welcomed us flutingly. We arrived in the midst of pastel silk, fluffy net, and blonde mannequins. "Oh no," I said, laughing. "Welcome to Bridesmaid Country."

"This is where I got my dresses. I told her that was years ago. They might not have the same styles anymore. But she told me to bring you to the same place. You heard her!"

If nothing else, Ruth was psychologically immature, I decided. She was letting Dorothy run her life for her, and then blaming Dorothy for not being God. But did that explain Dorothy's treatment of her? Maybe Dorothy enjoyed playing with matches.

"*Sumimasen!*" Ruth hailed a salesgirl and explained what we wanted. The girl led us around the racks, unearthing comparatively simple gowns from amidst the tulle and satin. I ended up with an armload of things to try on. To my relief, Ruth made no attempt to join me in the changing cubicle. Most of the gowns got discarded before I even zipped them up. At last I emerged to twirl in front of the mirror. Ruth inspected me. "Too long. Makes you look like an OL. What about that violet one?"

I put on the violet one and came out again.

Ruth smiled – the first smile I'd ever had from her. "Much better."

The dress was a fitted shift with a contrasting white trim at the boatneck. The hem came four inches below my crotch. I pulled at it ineffectually.

Ruth stood beside me in front of the mirror. "Perfect," she said dryly. "Now you look just like me."

She wore jeans and a plain red t-shirt and carried a large backpack. We'd looked more alike when I was in my street clothes: baggy black skate shorts, Chuck Taylors, and an old denim jacket. But I knew what she meant. The violet dress resembled her Exiles uniform of a pastel shift. In the semi-dark of the club, we could be mistaken for each other.

The salesgirl effused, "Your sister is so slim! And both of you have such beautiful fair hair!"

"We'll take it," Ruth told her. "Does it come in any other colors?" Switching back into English, she said to me, "This is just what Dorothy wanted."

"Why? Is she trying to collect a matched set?" I recalled that Irina had also fit the general specifications, although she'd been too tall to be mistaken for either Ruth or me. I thought: *dehumanizing the "humans," making us interchangeable, while the vamps are encouraged to express their individuality...*

"No," Ruth said. "It's personal between me and her. And if you're as smart as you're supposed to be, with your advanced degrees and everything, you'll stay out of it."

We bought the violet dress in silver-grey, too. With a pair of strappy silver sandals, the bill came to everything I'd made last night, and then some.

"So tell me about dohans," I said, following Ruth out of the store. "And drinkbacks."

"Shit! Do you *never* stop asking questions?"

"Dorothy told me to ask you."

"All right. Fine! Drinkbacks are when a customer requests you; you get back five hundred yen for every drink they buy you. And if you don't want to get drunk every night, you'd better stick to oolong tea or Sunrise Sours. That's what we call our fake drinks. Soda water with a bit of fizzy lemonade. Dohans are when a customer takes you out to dinner before work. If you bring them to the club, that's three thousand yen. And any presents they give you are *omake* – yours for free. Did you see Shinobu's diamond earrings? That Tiffany heart Eloise has? They go on dohans pretty much every day."

"What about you?"

"Fuck that. Do I look like the type that would sleep with a skanky old sugar daddy for some jewelry?" Ruth flushed. "Besides, it's the kinky vamp shit they really want. They aren't interested in me. And they won't be interested in *you*, either, no matter what she says."

"Well, that's a relief," I said with a laugh.

Ruth sneered at me and walked faster. We were on Shinjuku-dori, heading back towards the station. Even here, among the Greco-Victorian stone buildings that housed Japan's landmark department stores – Isetan, Marui, Mitsukoshi – flyer girls and boys touted the clubs of Kabukicho, and vampires in full costume glided through the crowd. No one bumped into them or even brushed their elbows. To hell with CAIN, the catchy name that Dr. Brent had given his hypothetical retrovirus; the real virus was fear.

Ruth was definitely trying to shake me off.

I caught up with her again. "I'm a network theorist," I said. "That means I study the diffusion of ideas and paradigms through social systems."

"Whatever," she snorted.

"Vampirism is a dynamically chaotic system. It's not a disease, and it's not a supernatural phenomenon. It's – it's a creative way to suck energy from the environment." I was trying to speak her language, avoiding words like *dissipative* and *autopoiesis*. "You've been observing them for longer than I have. You've seen through them. Maybe that's why they

81

treat you like – like…" *Like a slave* – the metaphor popped unbidden into my mind. "But you don't have to play their bullshit games, Ruth! It's really sad that they feel as if they have to sell themselves…" It was the fanghandlers of Thompson Square Park all over again, only with a high-class veneer. "But you've rejected that option, and I admire you for it! There are other ways you can empower yourself apart from sex —"

"You are so full of shit." Ruth's chin jutted; she hurled herself along the sidewalk, forcing me to dodge and weave to keep up with her. "What gives you the impression it's all about sex?"

"Uh… everything?"

"It's all about *power*. And money is power. And let me tell you, I'm *earning*. But that doesn't mean shit to the vamps, because they don't see me as competition. They just see me as human. And when you're up against a vamp, as a human? The only power you can have is to give them blood. *Or not.*" She smiled grimly. "Everyone wants what they can't have, don't they? Even a vamp. *Especially* a vamp. Because they're all about power. Even the fuckups like Beth and Natasha —"

"Please don't tell me Beth is not all about sex. She's so far into her little sadomasochistic spiral, she's lost radio contact with the planet. And Natasha's the same way —"

"OK, yeah, but even Beth and Tasha, they're all about power. Vampires want what they want. And if they can't have it for any reason, it drives them totally nuts." Now Ruth was openly grinning. "Needless to say, they hide it. And they fuck with your head, trying to make you think that a), they could care less, because you're just one of a long line, and b), if they ever set fang in you, they'd be doing you a favor, giving you this big special experience… But if you take one piece of advice from me, since I've been *observing* them so long? If you want to survive in *vamukura*, just remember that you have this power you can work with."

"Ruth, have you ever donated blood?"

"I have *not*. So no! I don't know if it really is this big special experience or not. But you know what? I don't plan on ever finding out."

She dived into the station entrance. I followed her through the wickets. On the Yamanote line, she pretended I wasn't there. She got off at Shibuya, with me a step behind. For a moment, I wondered whether she was going to spite me by leading me to Aoyama Gakuin. But intead of heading upstairs to the Ginza line, she whisked out of the Hachiko exit and into the Scramble Crossing, as the Japanese called the fiveways intersection in front of Shibuya station.

We threaded through a crazy jumble of signage, between tripleparked motorbikes, among nut-brown girls and boys with big blond hair. Speakers on utility poles piped J-pop onto the street. Store clerks balanced cn stepladders, yelling through megaphones. I followed Ruth past 109, the landmark mall, down to the intersection where the Don Quixote penguin presided over an avalanche cf made-in-China electronics, stuffed animals, and vinyl cosplay accessories.

But there was more to Shibuya than this. We climbed the hill behind the Tokyu department store, and all the noise dropped away behind us. Trees shaded the sidewalk. The spotless glass doors of small corporate offices slung our reflections back at us. Alleys twisted off the main road, blocked by jet-black Centurys and Crown Lincolns.

Ruth turned around and howled, "Why are you following me?"

"I thought maybe we could get a coffee," I said. "On me; to thank you for taking me shopping."

She breathed out hard. "Don't you have anything better to do? Because I do. So if you'll excuse me — "

"Do you live around here?" I asked, not believing it. This neighborhood was way out of any hostess's budget.

"No. I live in Nakai," she said grudgingly. "You don't know where that is. On the Oedo line. With the other girls from the club."

"With the *vamps?*"

"It's not that bad. We've got our house rules: no one

brings anyone home. And the only blood that gets consumed is when I fix a rare steak." She stretched out a smile. "I don't even like steak, really. It's just to fuck with them." For a moment I glimpsed a different Ruth, forlornly defiant, trapped in her own hostility. Then she hardened her voice. "All right, you can come with me. You want to learn about Japanese culture, don't you? Now's your chance."

"Japanese culture." I skipped to keep pace with her. "Flower arranging? Tea ceremony? Zen meditation? Am I warm?"

"Stone cold. Are you down for it? Yes or no."

"Sure!" I said brightly.

She fought back a smile. "Well, here we are."

We'd reached a two-storey building set back behind a large parking-lot. I counted four BMWs, two Saabs, and one Lamborghini gleaming in the sun.

"Everyone's here," Ruth observed with satisfaction. She took off her Nikes and stepped onto the sweep of carpet at the foot of the stairs. "Shoes in a cubby."

Kicking off my Converse, I heard faint shouting and thudding overhead. "Ruth! Is this a dojo? Do you do martial arts?"

"I'm still a beginner, but yeah. Karate. This is the central dojo of the Shoto school."

"I do aikido! That is, I only started a few months ago. I've been looking for a dojo —"

"Oh yeah?" She greeted this with a dismissively raised eyebrow. But in the women's locker room on the second floor, she selected a dogi from a rail and held it out to me. "This is my spare. It should fit you. Since we're the same size and everything."

"Uh, well, I was just planning on observing," I said. "I mean, karate's very different from aikido, isn't it?"

"Well, you can't go into the dojo in street clothes."

I bit my lip. Then I went around the other side of the lockers to change into the heavy white cotton trousers and jacket. Ruth had given me a white belt. When I reemerged,

84

she'd secured her own jacket with a black belt and fastened her hair into a ponytail.

We went up to the third floor. Ruth bowed on the threshhold of the dojo. I copied her, then nipped over to the free weights area and placed my bags – the two Isetan shopping bags and my trusty old canvas satchel – amid the gym bags at the base of the dumbbell racks.

On the polished wooden practise floor that took up most of the room, about twenty students kicked air in unison. *"Ich'! Ni! San! Shi! Go! Haaai!"* They took turns to yell out the numbers up to five. Each set concluded with a wordless *qi-ai* shout from all the students at once. Ruth dropped into a kneeling pose at the edge of the floor and touched her forehead to the boards. The ranks opened for her. She joined in. As she kicked and punched in unison with the others, the hard set of her face looked entirely appropriate for once. I'd been wrong about her physique: she wasn't scrawny, she was *wiry*, her dogi appearing empty but for the explosive power that drove her fists and feet. Had anyone else at Exiles seen this side of her? Did the other karate-ka know she was a *vamukura* hostess?

The youngest were teenagers, the oldest looked like a tough eighty. Most of them were Japanese men, but there were a handful of white men, one black man, and a couple of Japanese women. The forty-something sensei leading the class wore a black belt so faded it was almost white. Among the students, every color of belt was represented.

I passed the time noting the technical differences between karate and aikido – no throws, no holds, but a far greater variety of punches and blocks; and of course those dazzling kicks. On the half hour, the students spilled off the floor and surrounded me. "Why don't you join in?" the sensei invited me. He spoke fluent English. "It doesn't matter if this is your first time to do karate. Just do same as Ruth and you'll be OK."

"I have this odd feeling of déjà vu," I murmured as I took my place next to Ruth. She didn't smile.

In the second half-hour, the students paired off to prac-tise. Ruth took me through the basic punches and blocks. Our forearms collided with bruising force. "Good! Good!" exclaimed the sensei. "You're using your core muscles nicely."

I knew how to do that from aikido, but I wasn't used to this kind of contact. How did Ruth keep her arms un-marked? Well, she was a black belt. From experience, I knew that the better you got, the less it hurt. Over the months I'd been doing aikido, I'd got used to the shock of being thrown and controlled. But the philosophy of aikido was based on cooperation. You worked with your partner in a sort of gymnastic ballet. This was pure violence filtered through rules. No wonder it suited Ruth so well.

The dojo was air-conditioned, but the furious pace of the exercises had everyone sweating. Bare fists and feet cracked loudly against soaked dogi. Comparatively out-of-shape, I was breathing hard and streaming wet.

"All right! Free bouts!" the sensei shouted. "Same oppo-nents. Begin!"

Ruth's stance changed. She was no longer braced on her forward leg, but lightly balanced, fists up. I copied her, bob-bing on the balls of my feet, and she came at me with one of the punches we'd just been practising. I bounced it off with the block we'd just been practising. "Good," she said mock-ingly. "But we're not taking turns anymore. That's why it's called a free bout. Look for an opening and — " She interrupt-ed herself with another punch. I blocked and threw a punch of my own. She turned it with a flick of her wrist and retali-ated with a slow and easy kick. I didn't know how to block a kick, so I just dodged. She came after me with a flurry of punches. I batted at them with my wrists, but one landed hard on my shoulder. The jolt of pain drove everything else out of my mind.

Too impatient to wait for an opening, not even knowing what one would look like, I rushed at her with the lunge we'd practised. She danced sideways. Her foot lashed out, catching me on the hip. I spun, but she was already on my other side, powering a punch at my head. Without thinking, I whirled again, letting her chase me into the spin. I grabbed her wrist and threw my weight forward, flinging her away. She staggered and came back at me, smiling fiercely. This time, her punch was almost too fast to see, but by now I'd worked out one of her favorite combinations, and could predict what came next. I soaked up the punch with an inept block and was in position to seize her wrist when she delivered the gyakuzuki. I pulled her into her own momentum, shifted my grip to her elbow, and threw her. She went down hard, sprawling. I laughed out loud.

"Mixed disciplines!" someone hooted in English. I became aware of vertical patches of white in my peripheral vision.

"Have I won?" I shouted.

Ruth leapt back to her feet. *She* wasn't laughing. "Say your fucking prayers, bitch," she spat. "Cause I am gonna kill your ass."

She whirled at me with a roundhouse kick. I dodged that one, but I couldn't dodge the piston kick that she followed up with. The side of her foot slammed into the back of my shoulder. I went down in a forward roll. The wooden floor was a lot harder than the matting at Colin's dojo. Ruth waited for me to get up. Then she drove me back across the room. She'd figured out that I could work with her punches, but I had no answer to her kicks. She hailed them at me, aiming at a different part of my body every time. Some of them connected, albeit lightly, since I was moving backwards. I stumbled off the raised edge of the practice floor and reflexively threw my weight forwards to catch my balance. Her foot glanced off my temple, snapping my head sideways on my neck.

The impact eliminated any sense of restraint I had left. I turned and darted across the room to where I'd left my bags. She came after me, a flickering streak of white like grounded lightning.

I dived my hand into my satchel. My fingers closed on

the butt of the Glock, which I'd been carrying fully loaded but without a round in the chamber, as per instructions. This could hardly have been the self-defense scenario Colin imagined. But the whole point of carrying a concealed gun was to be ready for the unexpected, wasn't it?

I am gonna kill your ass, Ruth had said, her voice momentarily taking on a rhythm that reminded me of Dorothy.

If that last kick had hit me squarely, it could have broken my neck. And it would have looked like an accident.

With milliseconds to spare, I brought the Glock up in both hands, whirling on one knee to aim at the center of Ruth's dogi as she plunged towards me.. "Back off," I panted. "Come on, Ruth, you may not enjoy life very much, but you don't want to get shot."

"Bitch. You wouldn't fucking dare."

"You were trying to kill me." I forced my voice back to something like its normal tones. "I'm perfectly capable of returning the favor. Want to try again?" I sighted on the center of her body and let out my breath. The trigger felt alive under my finger. It wasn't me versus Ruth, after all; it was me versus the gun.

I registered movement in the background, just a blur behind Ruth, who herself was just a blur beyond the white dot of my front sight.

She slapped her thighs and forced a smile. "All right. 'Nuff respect." A tiny frown creased her face. "So drop the fucking gun," she howled, and took a convulsive step towards me, as if fighting some invisible force that held her back.

Jesus, I might really have to shoot her. I lowered my aim to her knee. The ring of students tightened. They all had their arms extended stiffly, the heels of their hands together, fingers starring out.

"Give it up, Ruth," a man's voice called from behind me in accented English, familiar but temporarily unplaceable. "She's right: you don't want to get shot. And anyone crazy enough to bring a gun in here is crazy enough to use it. Better not to provoke her. I like you the way you are – alive."

The words, or the voice that spoke them, had an extraordinary effect on Ruth. She seemed to shrink, all her fury dissipating. She approached me at a shambling walk, and I tensed again, but she went past me as if I wasn't there. I uncurled my finger from the trigger, realizing that I hadn't racked a round into the chamber: I couldn't have shot her even if I tried.

The moment I relaxed even slightly, I started to tremble. At the same time, my head started to hurt. I touched my hair where she'd kicked me. My fingers came away red. Ruth needed to cut her toenails. And I needed some antiseptic cream. If not stitches. Not to mention a shower.

"I could file assault charges," I said to the gathered students in English, not knowing whether I *could*, under Japanese law – or whether any of these weekend ninjas would support my story. They probably considered a gash on the scalp a love tap.

"I don't recommend lawsuit." The sensei stood over me. "You're American, yes? Well, you violate every rule of this dojo, and Firearm and Sword Control Law, too."

Through my dizziness, I said, "I'd like to know what the rules of this fucking dojo *are*. She was trying to kill me, and none of you stopped her! I'm sorry, sensei, but if that's the ethos of your school of karate, I'll keep my gun."

"The Shoto school is very spiritual. It can be difficult to understand," the sensei admitted. "Especially for foreigners."

An American man said, "But we did stop her." The others laughed again.

"Scott-san," the sensei warned.

"She's a coworker of Ruth's, sensei. She can't be *that* naïve."

I turned to see where Ruth had gone. She stood in the far corner of the dojo, with Aleksey.

"What's *he* doing here?" I said to the man named Scott, who was tall and smiling, with a dark mustache to match his black belt. A beaten copper medallion glinted amidst the

89

curls in the gap of his dogi.

"Aleks? Oh, he just comes to watch the practise. Doesn't join in; too worried about his hands."

"He just comes to watch Ruth," said one of the Japanese women.

A ripple of laughter followed. Tension broken, the students drifted apart, picking up their gym bags, toweling their faces, swigging sports drinks.

Scott and the sensei lingered, casting glances at me.

"That could have been very unpleasant," the sensei observed. I pricked my ears, realizing they thought I couldn't understand Japanese. "Thank you, Scott-san."

"All in a day's work," Scott said. "But we shouldn't be too judgemental. I take that as a cry for help." He paused. "You know, it just might be that she's come to exactly where she needs to be."

The sensei raised his eyebrows. "She won't last long in Tokyo with that attitude."

"Not without protection." Scott half-shut his eyes and grinned under his moustache.

The sensei pooched his lips dubiously. "Do you think the boss...?"

"Only thing I think about the boss is, you can't second-guess him."

The sensei laughed and moved off.

Scott turned to me and dropped into English again. "You need something for that cut. I live near here. Go shower, then you can come home with me and get patched up. That's the least I can do." His eyes crinkled ruefully. His tan helped me to place the accent: California. "These boys are pretty big on the spiritual aspect. They tend to forget that what we're doing here is fighting, and when you lose, it *hurts.*"

I didn't think I'd lost. Ruth and I were both still alive, and as far as I was concerned, that meant I'd won. But after overhearing Scott's exchange with the sensei, I'd started to wonder if I hadn't stumbled into yet another situation I couldn't control. If it would forestall any serious consequences, I'd gladly apologize first.

90

Chapter 6.

"I've been misjudging people and situations ever since I arrived in Japan," I said. "Things haven't been going the way I expected. And I suppose I'd begun to think the rules were different here, or that the normal rules didn't apply. But I shouldn't have pointed a gun at Ruth. I do know better than that. I'm sorry."

"Aw, now there you go, Ruth," Scott said. "That's manners. Where's yours?"

Ruth scowled. "Sorry about your head," she muttered.

"It's OK." I touched the cut. It had bled rivulets in the shower at the dojo, but had now stopped. "I'm as right as rain already."

Scott didn't take my hint. He drove on, smiling, around a small park. We were all squeezed into his BMW, me in the deep leather passenger seat, Aleksey and Ruth in the back. Behind the park, a woodsy hill raked up to meet the sky. It was incredible that we were just ten minutes from Shibuya. The homes up here nestled amidst lush, walled gardens. In front of one of these, a silver van was parked – the only vehicle on the street. Scott pulled in behind it and we got out while he parked the Beemer in the adjacent garage, domed with a rose perspex roof, which held the BMW and a Jeep stacked on top of each other by means of an elevator system. Strolling back to us, he used a second remote control to unlock the metal concertina-style front gate. A black Ferrari lay sideways across the skirt of concrete in front of the house.

"Looks like the boss is home," Scott grinned, squeezing around the Ferrari. He held tree branches aside for me to follow, but let them snap back in Aleksey's face when I'd passed.

Majestic pawlonias and ginkgos shaded the house. Scalloped tiers of roofs evoked traditional Japanese architecture, but once inside the front door with its electronic keypad lock, we were back in the 21st century. Techno thumped faintly overhead. Scott led us down the hall to a black-marble-and-chrome kitchen. "Hu-whoa! What have we here?" Lacquered caterer's trays flanked an icebucketed bottle of champagne on the central island. "You guys had lunch?" Scott ripped the cellophane wrap off the tray of sandwiches and stuffed one into his mouth. "Come on, have some, you'll be doing us a favor," he said indistinctly. "Too much food. Just gets thrown away."

"Well, in that case," I smiled, and took a sandwich. It was shrimp and avocado, and tasted heavenly.

Scott seemed to have forgotten about his promise to "patch me up." In no hurry to remind him, I let myself enjoy the sandwiches and the casual conversation, and even enjoy the weirdness of the whole situation. In Japan, you just had to roll with the bizarre and the inexplicable, didn't you?

In response to Scott's questions, I explained that I was working at Exiles but I was primarily a researcher. "I'm affiliated with Aoyama Gakuin."

"Yeah? Great, great."

"I'm in *choshizengaku*. Paranormal studies?"

"Isn't that a coincidence!" Scott took another sandwich.

"She's studying vampires," Ruth said. "She wants to find out what makes them tick. I already told her, but she thinks there's more to it. Like there's some *big secret*."

Scott swallowed his mouthful and leaned forward, holding my gaze. "Well, Clare, there's a few things I guess you may not have learned at school, and maybe Dorothy Foulkes didn't tell you, either. She's a good lady, in fact she's a personal friend of mine..."

"Ha!" said Ruth, and Aleksey smiled.

" —but she's first and foremost a businesswoman. What I'm saying is, you may not be aware that vampires are *dangerous*. You go around asking questions, even if you call it research, you're asking for a world of trouble. Unless you've got protection."

My heart beat slightly faster as I recalled the snatch of

conversation I'd overheard at the dojo. But I didn't want to seem too nosy. I gestured at Scott's hands. Karate might explain his callouses, but not the myriad tiny scars and burn marks where the dark hair didn't grow. "So what do *you* do?"

"Little ol' me? I'm a designer."

"Oh, how fascinating. What do you design?"

Before Scott could answer, Aleksey spoke up for the first time. "Jewelry," he said, with the exquisitely bored look he often used at work. "Have you seen the shops called Dracula's Crypt? Yes."

"I'm the lead designer for the chain," Scott said. "Show you my workshop if you like, it's out back. I do custom, one-of-a-kind pieces as well."

"That would be lovely," I started to say, but a voice from the doorway cut me off.

"Shit, Scotty, how unsubtle can you get?" A masculine chuckle followed, a little cough of infectious glee that took any sting out of the words.

In the doorway stood the most beautiful man I'd ever seen in real life. Soft peaks of red hair tipped with black, like the petals of some exotic flower, flopped over a smooth ivory forehead and curled into warm brown eyes full of laughter. A diaphanous, ruffled black shirt hung open to reveal sculpted and hairless pecs, framing a medallion similar to Scott's, but gold. Black leather jeans encased snaky hips and long legs so graceful I could hardly take my eyes off them as their owner ambled into the kitchen. In fact, it was hard to decide which part of him I most wanted to feast my eyes upon, but when he spoke again, his lips won out. Long, curling, and slightly too thin, they elevated mere perfection into heartpounding sexiness.

"So you're Ruth's co-worker. Enjoying your lunch?"

"Yes, very much. I'm afraid we seem to have..." I gestured at the depleted tray of sandwiches. "Nice to meet you, too," I said, raising my eyebrows.

Scott roared with laughter. "Boss, she doesn't recognize you. Don't feel bad," he added to me. "It's good for his ego."

"Scotty, with you around, my ego is in no danger." His faint lisp was no accent: it resulted from the elegant little fangs that peeked through his smile. "I'm Jaize."

"Nice to meet you," I repeated. "Jaize 3000? The – the TV tarento?"

"There you go, Scotty, she does know who I am." Jaize's English was flawless. He couldn't be Japanese, I thought. Japanese-American, maybe.

"Jaize 3000," I repeated. "Wow."

"Wow," Jaize mocked me, kindly. He swung a lanky leg over the stool beside me and popped a leftover sandwich into his mouth. "Pretty good."

"Jaize is like the vampire Paris Hilton," Ruth said loudly. "Or the vampire Donald Trump. A celebrity entrepreneur. But mostly he's just famous for being famous."

A girl with an organizer entered the kitchen. "What time shall I order the limo for, Jaize?" She was a jaundiced little thing with a grating voice.

"Oh, sevenish. And tell Makiko I need her upstairs now." Jaize turned back to me. "So you're working for Dorothy Foulkes. Do you sing? Strip?"

"No talent in either direction, I'm afraid."

"Still, every *vamukura* girl knows a little something about showbiz." His eyes held mine, and I felt as if he was looking into my soul, descrying the none-too-noble motives behind the act I put on at Exiles, the act I was putting on now. Those warm eyes seemed to tell me there was an alternative to faking it. There was *honesty*… "Can I get you to do me a favor?"

"Sure," I managed. He was already rising.

We climbed a switchback staircase, Ruth and Aleksey trailing behind. The second-floor hall retained its original wooden pillars, and calligraphic scrolls hung on the paneled walls. Jaize stopped at a solid Western-style door, clearly more recent than the sliding *fusuma* doors on the other side of the hall. I noted that it had an electronic lock, and recalled Ruth's comments about the security system at Dorothy's apartment. The vampires of Tokyo, it seemed, were paranoid.

Did they have any good reason to be?

We followed Jaize and Scott into a bedroom so big it was more like a luxury hotel suite. One wall was entirely mirrored. Only the bed in the center of the floor spoke of everyday use, and even that wasn't particularly mundane, being circular and... what was the next size up from king?

Aleksey flopped down on the chaise longue and ate strawberries from the bowl on the coffee table. Ruth slipped into position in front of the mirrored wall and began to run through her karate *katas*, sneakers soundless on the white pile carpet.

Jaize shook his head at her, then announced to me with a straight face, "Welcome to my parlor, said the spider to the fly."

"I'm duly impressed," I said, thinking: Leon Foulkes, eat your heart out.

"Jaize?" A door opened in one of the un-mirrored walls, and a Japanese girl popped her pink-dyed head out of a brightly lit walk-in closet.

"Right there, Makiko." Still looking at me, Jaize lifted his gold medallion over his head, placed it in my hand, and closed my fingers over it. "Hang onto this for me." He vanished into the closet.

Scott was talking to me again. Preoccupied with the warmth of the medallion in my fist – Jaize's body warmth – I had to force myself to listen. "You heard of Takahisa Ise? No, not many people outside of Japan have. He started off making pornos, pink films as they call them here, now he's one of the hottest J-horror directors. His next project is going to be the sequel to *The Turning*. Tentative title, *The ReTurn*. The original starred Jekyll, the visual-kei idol, and some kid from a Taiwanese boy band..."

"Oh yeah, they're remaking it in the States," I recalled.

"Right. Typical Hollywood overkill. How are you going to improve on a little gem of B-movie perfection? Actually, Ise *will* improve on it: the sequel's going to be box-office gold, you betcha. But the problem is, he killed off Jekyll's character,

95

so he needs a new star to play the vampire. And who do you think's on the shortlist? But it's not a sure thing yet. So it's important for Jaize to be seen with Ise in public, take every opportunity to schmooze… hence this premiere tonight."

"Of course." I opened my fingers to show the medallion. On its disc, a gold relief formed a pattern that looked like a stylized kanji, but not one I'd ever seen before – maybe a Chinese character. "Is this one of your designs?"

"It's an old motif. But I designed it, yeah, hell, I made it. This one, too." Scott touched his own medallion, which bore another complicated kanji. "How about I make one for you? Just like Jaize's."

I started to say that would be lovely, even though I wasn't into this kind of heavy ethnic jewelry. Ruth called over, "Fuck off, Scott, she doesn't need any of your shit. She wouldn't be able to wear it at work, anyway."

"I could do you an anklet," Scott said. "Real discreet. Classy."

"That would be —"

"Scott." Ruth turned from the mirror. "Have you ever seen Dorothy mad, I mean *really* mad? Do you want to?"

Scott held up both hands in jesting defense. "Dorothy likes art, she's interested."

"Ta-da!" Jaize emerged from the closet and stalked towards us in a gold lamé tank top, a black velvet sombrero on his head. An enormous medallion swung on his chest, gold studded with rhinestones, an oversized version of the one I held. His tight black pants laced up the sides, leaving glimpses of skin visible to his hips. His boots folded over at the knee. Snapping his fingers and tipping his hat down low, he looked like a toreador crossed with *Pirates of the Carribbean*, with accessories by Flavor Flav. "What do you think?"

"Noooo," I said, trying not to smile. "Just… no. Maybe at a club. Not on the red carpet." If the favor Jaize wanted from me was fashion advice, he'd come to the wrong person. But as my father's daughter, I'd appeared in front of the TV cameras often enough to know what would get you laughed at.

"Unless this kind of thing is, uh, fashionable in Japan?"

"It depends," Jaize admitted. "This might be pushing it."

"In that case... You know what? You should go with what you were wearing earlier. That was just right. Maybe add a studded belt if you want to funk it up."

Jaize sighed ruefully. "I'm the second most powerful vampire in Tokyo. My mission is to expand the boundaries of what a vampire can be... what a vampire *is*. But I can't get away with expressing my goddamn originality. If I had a dime for every time I've had to wear an opera cloak!"

"Honestly? I think you'll expand a lot of people's boundaries just by showing up. In terms of the outfit, less is more, trust me." A thought struck me. "What's your date wearing? She'll have to coordinate..."

"I don't have a date." Jaize headed back to the closet, chewing one perfect fingernail. Then he turned, his face alight with mischief. "You've got the right look. What do you say? Come on, it'll be a blast. Good publicity for Exiles, too. We've got all the girl-vamp stuff here, don't we, Makiko?"

"Sure," the pink-haired stylist said, running a professional eye over me. "Definitely we can find something to fit her."

Feeling giddy, I said, "Wouldn't that be false advertising? Since I'm not, you know, a vampire." *Expanding the boundaries of what a vampire can be,* indeed. I clutched the medallion for strength.

"How can she think under such pressure?" Aleksey barked, crossing the room. In one hand he carried the bottle of Burgundy from the table, and in the other a wineglass. "Everyone needs a drink, then we can talk about it. Drink, drink!" His cold, unfamiliar smile seemed to underline his abrupt mood swing. "In Russia we do nothing without a drink." He came straight up to me and held out the bottle and glass. To take them, I had to give him Jaize's medallion. Aleksey seized my wrist and tipped the bottle up. *"Ya vas!"*

Wine splattered my arm and glugged in a stream to the floor. I twisted away, and wine arced onto the front of Jaize's lamé top. The vampire seized the bottle. Aleksey gave it a final jog, spilling the last of the wine. "Sorry!" he grinned. He was very pale.

The palms of my hands felt cold, and I had the mental clarity that often accompanies a catastrophe. Stiffly, I apologized to Jaize. He shook his head, took off his sombrero, and sent it spinning onto the bed. "So we get the carpet cleaned. No big deal. And I was going to change, anyway, wasn't I?" He stripped off his top to reveal a devastating sixpack and a smile to match. "You, too. I can't wait to see what Makiko finds for you."

I shook my head. "I'm sorry, but I don't think I can make it." My voice was small, but clear and determined. I sounded like *me* again. "I have work to do."

A giant hand seemed to push us out of the room, the wry regret of Jaize and the disapproval of Scott buffeting our backs, making me cringe. I caught sight of myself in the mirrored wall: my face red, my hair a staticky halo, the cut in my hairline angrily visible. I even had a zit coming on my chin. I looked like no one's idea of arm candy, far less the ethereal vampire maiden I'd momentarily imagined myself as.

Still playing his brusque role, Aleksey threw Jaize's medallion down by the door. "Your trinket. Take it back."

I followed Aleksey and Ruth – not downstairs, but up. The staircase turned into a ladder, and I protested in vain as we climbed into an attic, little more than a crawlspace with cardboard boxes and packing cases jammed beneath the rafters. The air-conditioning didn't reach up here. The floor-level windows in the gables were open, but the air felt like hot liquid. We picked our way through the boxes to an open space in front of the far window where a futon lay unrolled. On it was a tuxedo in a dry-cleaning bag. I'd last seen that red cummerbund at Exiles.

"Aleksey," I said. "Don't tell me *you* live here, too?"

He kicked the tuxedo aside and dropped full-length on

his back. "Alas."

Ruth collapsed on the futon beside him. "I didn't plan on bringing you here! I didn't think Scott would be at the dojo today! And even if he was, I didn't know you were going to go and draw attention to yourself!"

"Hush," Aleksey said.

"She just had to follow me!" Ruth glared up at me. "Well, don't blame me now Jaize has leeched onto you!"

"He has not leeched onto her," Aleksey said. "He just wanted to take her to the movie thing to – to tease Dorothy. To annoy her. But Clare said no. So his pride is hurt, and he makes himself forget it. He's already forgetting it." His voice was empty.

"I didn't deliberately try to get you into trouble," Ruth insisted. "I wouldn't do something like that. I'm not that type of person."

I leaned against the wall, arms folded over the lump of the Glock under my denim jacket. I'd put my holster back on when I changed out of my dogi. My paranoia was starting to seem more and more rational. "Is Jaize a *psychic* vampire?" I said.

They both stared at me. Aleksey said, "No one is meant to know that."

"It's not that hard to work out." I pinched the bridge of my nose. The mental fuzziness had receded, but the fatigue was as overwhelming as my attraction to Jaize had been. It gave me a peculiarly bitter feeling to know that attraction had been false. But it had been, of course. Pretty boys weren't even my type. "He used his – his psychic energy on me." The karate-ka group had done the same thing to Ruth at the dojo, I thought. "Are your karate friends all psychic vampires, too?"

"The Shoto gang? No! Jaize is the only one. He's like some kind of freak mutation. But he's taught them all how to do that forcefield thing. They call it '*qi* craft.'" Ruth hesitated. "Uh, I'm studying it too, but only as much as I need to improve my karate... *But* none of the Shoto gang can fuck with your mind. Only Jaize can do that. Luckily for the rest of us."

"What about Scott?" Giving in to my fatigue, I sat down by Aleksey's feet.

"Him? He's just a plain vanilla human. Oh, he's good at *qi* craft. But basically, he's Jaize's boyfriend." She made a disgusted face.

"All the best ones are gay," I sighed in a feeble attempt at humor.

"Jaize is bisexual," said Aleksey. "For a vampire, boy-friend, girlfriend, it means something different. It's mostly about blood, not sex. So he feeds from Scott, but he fucks everything he can seduce. And he's very good at seducing." I winced. Aleksey grinned humorlessly. "You can understand why all the other vampires are jealous of him!"

"Jealous," I muttered. "Is it true that he's the second most powerful vamp in Tokyo?"

"Not even close," Ruth said.

"Well," Aleksey countered, "I'd say he's in the top ten. He did take this territory by force."

"And they're still arguing over whether it was legit," Ruth said.

Aleksey shook his head. "Possession is nine-tenths of the law, don't you say?" He turned to me, half sitting up. "A decade ago, Shibuya and Harajuku were one territory. Jaize killed the old *hakushaku* and took Shibuya. But he couldn't take Harajuku; the vampires there refused to accept him!"

He meant Count Skriva and his gang, I realized. Maybe there was more to that crew of feckless punks than I'd seen last week.

"So the territory – the *clave,* as they call it – was split. They're still at war, unofficially. But Jaize is making gains all the time. Also unofficially. He has more human followers than any other vampire, and *that's* why I put him in the top ten." Aleksey flopped onto his back again.

"I see," I said. "Do the other vampires know what he is?"

"Duh, how do you think we found out?" Ruth said. "We didn't all go to college to study this shit. Dorothy told us about him. But she wasn't supposed to. Only the high-ranking vamps know, and they have a kind of a pact to keep quiet about it. *Officially,* there's no such thing as a psychic vamp. So most people just think Jaize is one sneaky mother-fucker, and they call him *hakushaku,* even though he doesn't have any official title... which suits him fine!"

"Yes." The vampires' pact of silence was easy to under-stand. If it got out that even one vamp could, in Ruth's choice phrase, "fuck with your mind," the limited tolerance they enjoyed as the performing freaks of Japanese society would vanish. There'd be a fucking *pogrom.*

I flapped the collar of my jacket, trying to whoosh air down my front. This secret was too large for me. Apart from the potential danger that a Jaize 3000 presented to the public – if, say, his ambitions had lain in the direction of politics, instead of the movies – how could I possibly keep from writ-ing it up? How could I deny Professor Kamikawa the revela-tion that his psychic vampires were more than metaphors, they were real? I'd been mesmerized, half-seduced, and it had left me as weak as a kitten.

"If you're too hot, you can take off your jacket," Aleksey said.

Oh well, they already knew I was armed.

"The last time I saw one of those," Aleksey said, his eyes opening wider as I stripped off my jacket, "it was on the FSB bastard who had come to arrest me. I escaped on the way to jail and crossed the continent with a herd of pigs on the Trans-Siberian Railway. They keep the carriage heated for the livestock. That saved my life. I then worked on a fishing boat from Vladivostok to Hokkaido; it almost destroyed my hands. Let me tell you, I started to question what am I doing. But in Sapporo there is an industry of fake ID papers for Russian defectors. And so I came to Tokyo."

"Out of the frying-pan and into the fire?" I said.

"I have a great feeling for this English expression."

Below the window, the treetops burned in the deep or-ange light of late afternoon. I could see the wall that separated Jaize's garden from the neighboring houses. It looked high.

"I know it's a lot to take in," Aleksey said. "The world is mad, but at least we can have a cold drink. There's lemonade in the fridge."

Ruth crawled to the minifridge in the corner of Aleksey's space and took out a bottle of CC Lemon. With irritated movements, she chucked ice into three glasses that looked to me as if they'd already been reused without washing.

I cradled my cold glass, the condensation wetting my hands. "Why did Scott try to sell me a medallion? Is there any significance to those symbols?"

"The one Jaize wears is the Dracula's Crypt logo." Aleksey rolled onto his elbow to sip his lemonade through the straw Ruth had provided him. "If you wore it at Exiles, Dorothy would think Jaize had claimed you."

"She'd fire your ass. Boy, would she ever," Ruth said, looking not displeased with the notion. She might not have brought me here on purpose, but she hadn't tried very hard to alert me to the danger I was in, I remembered. It was Aleksey who'd saved me with his magnificent bit of playacting.

"I met him on the set of a television drama," Aleksey said suddenly. I nodded to encourage him, but his eyes were closed. "I had the job of a pianist in a bar, one day of shooting and the pay is shit, but they don't ask to see my visa. Jaize played the part of the evil vampire, the hero defeats him to impress the girl. He often gets little parts like this, it's for comedy. But when the hero hit him – he *really* hit him. Maybe it was an accident, maybe not. Jaize went over cold, and I was close by, so I helped him up. I took his hand." As if reenacting the memory, his hand stole out, seeking Ruth's. She squeezed it. "I took his hand," Aleksey repeated. His eyes opened wide and locked on mine. "Don't touch him. Whatever you do, *don't touch him!*"

The urgent warning gave me pause. I swallowed. "I'll – I'll bear that in mind. Some sources say that psychic vampires operate by touch. So I believe you." However, Jaize had already touched me once, and I'd felt nothing unusual.

Ruth coughed. "So, Clare. How come you were able to break away from him? Usually when he leeches onto someone, that's all she wrote."

"I might as well ask you why he hasn't leeched onto *you*," I said.

"Easy. He isn't interested in *this* scrawny white coochie. So he never tried." She gave me the cold assessing stare that I'd come to know from Exiles.

"I can't explain what I don't understand," I said tightly.

"Obviously! Well, just so you know: I did *not* plan to introduce you to Jaize. But that's just because I knew he wouldn't be interested in you! He might have thought for a minute that it would be fun to steal you away from Dorothy, but he's not interested in you for *you*. He's looking for someone special. Someone like Aleks." Her voice was hoarse with anguish. "And that isn't you, no matter how special you think you are!"

"Please," Aleksey said. His eyes were closed again. "This special person has a headache."

Ruth flinched. She said, "I'm sorry, Clare. I'm just venting my stress on you. Sorry. Same as at the dojo. It's what I always do. Sorry." On the first *sorry*, Aleksey's hand crept into hers; by the last *sorry*, they were holding each other's wrists, a quaint gesture that made me think of some sort of secret-society handshake.

"That's quite all right," I said. "I apologize. I mean, I understand."

If only I did. But now I understood one thing about Ruth and Aleksey, at least. My heart briefly twisted with envy. What does it matter if your life is a car wreck, as long as you've got someone to hang onto?

"I'm going now," I whispered, slipping my jacket on. "Thanks for the lemonade. I'll see you both at work."

Aleksey withdrew his hand from Ruth's and said in the same empty voice as before, "Go with her. Make sure she doesn't run into Jaize or Scott on the way out. We don't want any gunfire; that would *really* give me a headache."

I paused, looking down at him. "Thank you. Aleksey, I forgot to say – thank you."

He moved his head minutely. "My pleasure."

Ruth and I met no one on our way out except Jaize's anorexic PA, who whisked past us with a glare, her arms full of files. I noted a inflammation on her neck. I knew that vampires tended to feed from the same place over and over. Frequent "sharers" carried puncture wounds or cuts that never had a chance to heal and sometimes developed into abscesses. Someone was obviously feeding from the PA regularly. I guess Jaize wasn't even faithful to Scott in the vampiric sense.

Outside, the sun had slipped behind the rooftops, and cicadas shrilled in the trees. I smelled gardenias. As I slipped through the gate behind Ruth, a sudden blast of wind buffetted my back. I lost my balance and almost fell out to the street.

Ruth picked hair out of her mouth. "That's Jaize telling us to fuck off. Well, fuck you, too!" she yelled at the house.

The wind did seem to be pushing us away from the house, spitefully slapping at our backs. "Is this his – his *qi* craft? It just feels like – wind." The gusts susurrated in the trees, jerked petals off the white roses spraying over the garden wall. But the boughs on the other side of the street hung immobile.

"Oh, it's him, all right."

Torn leaves and bits of twig stung my neck. We stumbled down the street, blasts of air shoving at our backs. At the bottom of the hill, the wind died in an instant. I looked back at the trail of fallen leaves marking our path. "*God*, that was spooky."

"You noticed," Ruth said.

In the quiet of Sunday evening, the residential streets lay empty beneath a sky gradated from lemon to dark blue. Not a sound emerged from behind the high walls and gates that surrounded every property.

"Ruth. What are all these people so scared of?" *Jaize*, I

thought.

"Crime. Especially vampire crime We aren't that far from Harajuku, and you must have seen the news stories – rape, murder, corpse drained of blood, yadda yadda. Personally, I think Jaize is behind it. The bad publicity, I mean. At least he doesn't go around draining the blood out of his victims!"

"There are so many ways to manipulate people," I said hopelessly.

Ruth sighed. "If you take my advice? Because I've been there, where you are now. Angry and scared and wishing it would all go away. It's easier if you just give up trying to understand how they do what they do We're not vampires, we *can't* understand. But you only need to know enough of the rules to fight back."

I scuffed my sneakers along the street. "I wish… I wish I could do something for Aleksey."

"Like what? Eventually, I'm going to save enough money… Jaize and I have a deal. Five million yen. That's how much Aleks is worth to him. I'm halfway there."

I did a quick mental conversion. "Fifty thousand dollars? Ruth, surely…"

"All right, I wish I had a Humvee, a sawed-off Remmy, and enough backup to go in there like a fucking SWAT team. Oh, and after I've punched Jaize's ticket and grabbed Aleks? Open up with a fucking rocket launcher and put the hurt on this whole goddam neighborhood. Monkey see, monkey do, monkey watch za funnee vampire on TV and say, '*Omoshi-rowwwi!*' Assholes."

"Ah," I said, casting about for a suitable response. "Uh… sounds like a plan?"

"Want to lend me your gat? And if you've got any extra clips to go with it. 'Just me and my nines…'" She sang a snatch of an R&B tune that had been a hit about five years ago. Recognizing it, I smiled. She tossed her head. "That shit doesn't play here. But I'm getting desperate enough that I just might try."

"There's got to be a better way," I said.

"I'm working on it."

Chapter 7.

There was a new vampire at Exiles.

He was a customer.

Or maybe not, I thought, watching Dorothy swish across the club to greet him. All smiles, she ushered him to a table in the far corner.

I'd never seen Dorothy give her undivided attention to a single man before. Especially not when the club was three-quarters full and Angela was onstage, performing her week-night enka set for her fan club of regulars.

In Dorothy's place, Shinobu got up and managed the room, visiting with each group to keep them civilized. That left me to hostess the table of salarymen she and I had been sharing. But as I talked, I couldn't stop my gaze from returning to that corner. The new vampire was six feet six if he was an inch -- when he came in, he'd had to duck under the lintel of the door -- with wild black hair in an Edward Scissorhands mop, and the pale complexion to go with it. Definitely Japanese, though. He wore an odd complicated black outfit, a tailcoat and wideleg trousers with overall straps hanging loose around the thighs. It looked like the male equivalent of one of Dorothy's costumes. Tonight, she was resplendent in a Cinderella gown that would have made her look like a debutante if it hadn't been black, with the inevitable zippers in place of bodice seams.

"Know who that is?" said the salaryman facing me. I jumped guiltily. "That's the *kami* of Tokyo."

"*Kami* as in god?" I said, opening my eyes wide.

They all laughed. "No, no, he's just a *koshaku*."

"Don't they still call it Edo?" interjected someone else.

"Edo was the feudal name of Tokyo," a third man informed me, and began to expound the history of the Tokugawa era.

"I guess when you live for centuries, you get stuck in

your ways!" the first man interrupted him. They all laughed.

"Do you," I said, "do you write *koshaku* with this *ko*? Or this one?" I drew the kanji, as near as I could remember them, on a napkin. When the group got through correcting my calligraphy, the bloviator informed me that the first *ko* indicated a superior rank to the second *ko:* Duke or Prince versus Marquis.

"And which one is this guy?" I said, concealing my impatience.

None of them knew. One ventured that the new vampire might be a marquis. *A* marquis? *The* marquis? Japanese lacked articles, so I couldn't tell. In either case, that would put him one level above Dorothy. But what did these ranks mean, anyway? And what was a *kami?* Japanese had so many homonyms, differentiated only by the written kanji. *Kami* could mean paper, wife, hair, god, above...

I'd been working at Exiles for almost a week now, sacrificing sleep to combine it with my job in the sociology office at Aoyama Gakuin, and this was the first real chance I'd had to learn anything about vampire society. As soon as Shinobu returned to our table, I made an excuse and stood up, ignoring her glare. I crossed the club in my new four-inch heels, pulled a hassock up to Dorothy's table, and sat down. The trick in this dress was to sit down sideways, as if you were getting into a car. *"Konbanwa,"* I trilled, deploying the cutesy act I'd copied from the top hostesses. I extended my hand, fingers dangling. "Clare-*chan dehhhsu!"*

The *koshaku* took my hand and lowered his face to it. Almost no customers had the nous to do this; the gesture was just a way of embarrassing and pleasing them. I nearly jerked back in surprise. But I didn't. Cold fingers closed around mine. His lips barely brushed the back of my hand, but he must have kept his mouth slightly open, because I felt twin spots of pressure that could only have been the curves of his fangs. Hot breath flared between the cool lips, momentarily scorching my skin.

"This is my new girl," Dorothy said in Japanese. "She's

VAMPIRE DEMOCRACY

American. And she's educated, so don't you try to impress her, cause it won't work."

"Have you had her?" The *koshaku's* voice was a low rumble, felt as much as heard.

"Now I know you've got your old-fashioned ideas, but where we come from, we like to keep work and play strictly separated," Dorothy said.

"Play," the *koshaku* said. "A matter of life and death. *Play.* I suppose it is, to you." He grunted and looked around the club. "Have you disposed of the other one?"

"Irina? Sure. I fired her ass."

"Not the Russian. *That* one."

I didn't have to look to know he was talking about Ruth.

"Why would I do that?" Dorothy's laugh sounded forced. "She's my lucky mascot."

"It *is* a game to you," the *koshaku* rumbled.

Now Dorothy's fangs showed like pointed daisy petals in her smile. "Haven't you ever heard the saying: 'Keep your friends close and your enemies even closer'? Those are words to live by, Gore. You should note them down. Could have been invented for you." She squeezed my knee. "Clare, this is my boss. *You* might wanna take notes right about now: his name is Gorozaemon Edonokami. Try saying that three times fast. But he don't mind if you just call him Gore."

"Gore," I said.

He cocked his huge head and smiled at me. Beneath the messy bangs, black eyes sparkled with impish humor, and the wide lips peeled back to expose bone-white fangs that looked as thin and worn as needles. "As always, Dorothy has good taste." The rumbling voice had dropped to a murmur that I could still, somehow, hear through the music. "You are an amazingly beautiful woman."

"I told you, Gore, don't start that shit with her."

Was Gore another psychic vampire? No; I could tell his charm was all natural – because it wasn't working.

"We had none like you in the days of my birth. None so delicate and fair."

"She's fair because she is *Caucasian*. You didn't have any Caucasians around back then. And she's delicate because she overworks herself." Dorothy turned to me. "He has trouble with the whole concept of race," she said without lowering her voice. "To him, ain't but two races: vampire and mortal, as they call it. And ain't but *one* language: Japanese. He don't think English is a language at all. To him, it's just like birds tweeting in the sky!"

I said, "Gore-san, may I ask when you were born?"

"In the third year of the Kyowa emperor's reign," he said, still smiling at me.

I summoned up my history. The Japanese used to calculate dates from imperial successions. Going backwards from the Meiji Restoration in 1865, there'd been the Keio, Genji, Bunkyu...

Gore had just told me that he'd been born in 1803.

However, since that would make him more than two centuries old, a likelier explanation was that the fake birthdate went with the antiquated name and courtly speech. It was all part of his shtick. I reminded myself of my objective. "I thought Dorothy owned this club," I said ingenuously. "If you're her boss, does that mean Exiles is part of a larger corporation?"

"There is no reason for you to know such things. A beautiful woman does not need knowledge. However, because you are beautiful, I will indulge you this far: I do not represent a *corporation*, but what we call a *kuni*. In today's legal terminology, it is a non-profit organization." But his smile was fading. "That does not excuse *you*," he suddenly snarled at Dorothy, "from accountability!"

Dorothy held herself straight. "I am the Countess of Roppongi," she said. "I got the right to spend my own money how I like. Are you going to gainsay me on that?"

"Ten million yen! That was not yours, it was the Emperor's!"

"And I told you I am going to make up the shortfall next month. I'm not cheating you. If I was cheating you, I wouldn't tell you *openly* what I had done." She rolled her eyes.

"You have no responsibilities outside your *kuni*," Gore fumed. "Certainly not to your mortal family!"

Dorothy almost looked at me. It didn't get beyond a twitch. "My brother is not mortal," she said calmly. "He is the first of our kind on the east coast of the United States of America. That is a country, Gore. It is a *large, powerful* country. And while I would never ever presume to criticize the Emperor, it does seem to me that some people around him could stand to brush up on their long-term planning skills. Because if you had the ghost of a clue about the modern world, you would understand that ten million yen to secure our foothold in the only superpower is a fucking *bargain*."

Gore's huge body lurched forward. I stiffened. Dorothy sat absolutely still. But the *kami* of Edo only picked up his wineglass and drank off its contents. When he lowered the glass, he was frowning, the needle-like fangs barely visible between his lips. "You speak boldly on your own territory. I would like to hear you say the same words in front of the court."

"Any time," Dorothy said. "I'll even give them a crash course in geopolitics if they want. Or maybe Clare here could do it. She knows all about that shit, and her father is a politician, too."

Gore studied me. "No one may come to court – and live – unless he or she swears allegiance to the Emperor. Would you do that, fair one?"

What Emperor? The Emperor of where? *Kuni* meant *country*. But when Gore said *kuni*, he obviously wasn't using the word in the same way that Dorothy used it for the USA. So we weren't talking about the Emperor of Japan.

By virtue of my bi-national background, I sometimes thought of myself as a citizen of some invisible country yet to be defined… but this wasn't what I'd had in mind.

"Gorozaemon-san, I come from a democratic tradition," I said, while I noted with a jolt: *this puts "Vampire Democracy"*

111

in a whole new light. "I believe that in the political sphere, allegiance should be contingent. When allegiance becomes absolute, we tend to see every threat as existential, and to lose sight of genuine existential dangers. So…"

Dorothy laughed. "I think she just told you to go fuck yourself, Gore."

Gore didn't seem to hear her. His dark eyes travelled down my face and stopped at my neck. "Existential danger is not to be ignored," he murmured, "but you should try to develop a keener sense of *personal* danger, if you intend to work here." He smiled and rose with a sweep of his tailcoat. Dorothy and I were just in time to close the door of the club behind him.

She leaned on the handle for a moment. "I sent that money to Leon so he'd get himself some treatment," she muttered. "Since I can't be there for him right now. At least if he's got money, the doctors won't turn him away. But Gore don't need to know that, Ruth, you hear?"

I wished I was anywhere else. But there was no help for it; I had to say, "I'm not Ruth."

"Oh." She straightened up and gave me a tiny wince of a smile. "My mind slipped for a minute there. But I hope you don't take this wrong, but you're just *like* her in some ways." Her voice sharpened. "I hate to agree with old Gore on anything, but he spoke the truth that you don't know the meaning of fear. What was you *thinking*, to ask him about the organization? You could have just asked me!"

"I didn't even know there was an organization," I said. "Is it strictly hierarchical?" The word in my mind was *feudal.*

"It is strictly bullshit. But we all got to live with what we can't change." She looked past me. "And you got to get back to your table. Ask your questions on your own time in future, because we have a job to do here."

For the rest of the night, I couldn't manage to catch her eye, but I was constantly aware of her voice behind me, rising in loud sallies and peals of laughter. After the last customers trickled out, she whirled around the club, issuing orders. "Over there, Tasha! You ain't vaccumed around table two, Clare!" I said that I had. "Well, it don't look clean to me. Go over it again!"

I went over that corner again, then switched off the vacuum cleaner, put it away behind the bar, and headed for the dressing-room. Dorothy stopped in her tracks and pointed dramatically at me. "Clare-*chaan!* You ain't trying to creep off home?"

I'd been taking a taxi back to Jingumae every night after the club closed. If I didn't get at least a few hours of sleep, I would doze off over my translations in the sociology office. I started to explain, but Dorothy cut me off.

"Tonight, you are coming out with us."

"I can't go to work tomorrow with a hangover," I complained.

"Oh, you won't have a hangover. You're gonna feel better tomorrow than you ever felt in your life... Ruth! You're coming with us, too."

Ruth scowled. "What about Aleks?"

I'd learned that Ruth and Aleksey normally went off by themselves after the club closed. For the two of them, these hours were a precious slice of time stolen from the vampires.

"He can go to McDonalds and hang out until the first train." Dismissing Aleksey with a few words, Dorothy stared at me again. "You want to know the reality behind the hype." Her smile was feline. "Well, now you're going to find out."

We left Exiles in a chattering mob. Beth and Natasha weren't invited, and Angela had a date, but all the other girls came: Shinobu, Eloise, Jessica, and Ruth. We'd changed back into our street clothes. It was strange to see Dorothy in jeans, even if they were black, paired with black Ferragamo sandals and a black camisole printed with a silver spiderweb. The other vampires and Ruth wore variations on the same theme. In my Plastikman t-shirt and sloppy denim skirt, I lowered the tone.

We turned right at Motown and clattered down a steep

hill lined with bar entrances. Ruth fell back to walk beside me. She hissed in my ear, "I hope you know what you let yourself in for. Just remember, they can't do anything if you say no. That's the rule. Hell, it's the law."

"*Where* are we going?"

Before she could answer, we'd arrived. The small blue neon sign over the door said *Twilight*.

"*Irrashaimase!*" It was like walking into Exiles. That was our chorus of welcome. But the voices were all male, and the figures hastening to greet us were men. *Young* men.

OK, maybe some of them weren't so young. The light was very forgiving. But they were all Japanese. They wore black suits with white shirts open to mid-chest, and their hairstyles ran to blond crests and surfer shags.

Scanning past them, I saw that almost every table was occupied by women in tight denim, false eyelashes, and high-piled curls that wouldn't have looked out of place in 18th-century Versailles. By now, I was familiar enough with Roppongi dress codes to identify them as off-duty *mizu shobai* workers: snack bar girls, strippers, and *vamukura* hostesses. And among them sat more pretty boys in black suits, pouring drinks, lighting cigarettes, and making flirtatious conversation.

We were in a host club.

I'd heard about these places: they were supposedly the male equivalent of hostess clubs. An advance for gender equality in Japan, so the standard sociological interpretation ran. Clearly, however, the management of Twilight didn't believe that Japanese womanhood was ready for throbbing reggae and male strippers. The place resembled a West Village café that was trying too hard to be funky. Syrupy muzak washed over the deep sofas and minute tables. Copies of Renaissance statuary stood in niches around the walls. The light came from electric chandeliers set on dim.

Attended by a retinue of hosts, we paraded through the club to a cluster of tables that had magically opened up. Two hosts sat on either side of me and gave me their cards. The adolescent with silver hair was Yuta; the older one with the lazy smile was Makoto. Dorothy ordered champagne. We clinked our glasses and shrilled, *"O-tsukare sama!"* As soon as I'd drained my glass, another drink appeared in front of me. Relishing the tang of Jose Cuervo, I sipped and watched Dorothy flirt with her own pair of hosts – a slender blond, the only gaijin in the place, and a stocky Japanese with a comically animated face. Her fangs had extruded to their full length, giving her laughter a tigerish aspect. Yet there was something febrile about her display of lightheartedness. It had the opposite effect to what was probably intended, reminding me of her moment of vulnerability after Gore left the club.

The three top hostesses were table-hopping. Ruth ate mixed nuts with an expression of boredom.

Inattentively talking with Yuta and Makoto, I'd finished my drink, and now another one was in my hand. I could feel my mind losing traction, but what did it matter? Dorothy had promised to show me the reality behind the hype... and so she had. Even vampires got tired and stressed out. So they went out for a drink after work. They gossiped with their friends and soaked up synthetic affection at places like Twilight. I, of all people, shouldn't have needed Dorothy to remind me that vampires were human, too.

When I leant back, there was an arm around my shoulders. I was too tired to make a fuss about it. I stared at the nearest of the plaster statues ensconced in the walls, a plump cherub two feet high. There was something odd about it, although I couldn't have said exactly what. I needed another drink.

I must have said it aloud, because no sooner had the thought occurred to me than someone as blurry as the cherub placed another drink in my hand. "Thank you," I murmured, and realized that there was a hand on my thigh. Before I could do anything about its presence, it moved under my dress and slipped inside my panties.

Paralyzed with shock, I gradually worked out that it was

115

Yuta whose arm was around my shoulders and Makoto who was touching me. Meanwhile, I was drunk enough that my body responded automatically. "This is completely unacceptable," I said loudly.

"Relax," came the whisper in my ear. "Dorothy's taken care of it."

Dorothy. I could see three of her. They were all blurry, but I could tell that they were all smiling at me while they toyed with the blond hair of the boys whose heads lay on their cleavage. As I stared fixedly at her, I became convinced that it was *she* who was playing with me. Then her first two fingers slipped inside me, and I gasped, "I'm going to come."

"May I?"

"I suppose so..."

"May I have you?"

There was something about that phrasing that chimed in my sodden brain. Dorothy pushed her fingers all the way inside me. "Oh God," I muttered. That was her hot breath on my neck: those were her lips on my skin —

I heard a distant crash. Her mouth pulled back from my neck. I sat up and squinted hard. Dorothy wasn't anywhere near me. At my side cowered one of the Twilight hosts, Makoto. Ruth bobbed in a fighting stance in front of him.

"That was *so* wrong," she hissed. "If she wants to get bit, that's her problem, but you don't get her drunk and then start messing with her and make her think she's saying yes to something else! That is just *wrong!* Now are you gonna apologize or do I have to make you?"

"Dorothy said it was OK," Makoto protested.

I swayed upright. My heels crunched on broken glass, and I skidded in the remains of the drink I'd dropped. Makoto seized the opportunity to retreat. I watched him grab a wet towel off another table and wipe his hand. I said, "I didn't want to get bit. Bitten. Thanks, Ruth. God. Thank you. Thank you..."

She snorted in disgust. "You are totally hammered. I guess I should have warned you, but I didn't know..."

116

We both turned to look at Dorothy.

Incredibly, she didn't seem to have noticed Ruth's intervention. She and the stocky Japanese host were bent over, their heads together, concentrating on something on Dorothy's lap. Ruth kicked away the table in front of them to reveal the body of the young blond host. He knelt on the floor with his head in Dorothy's lap. Despite the fracas, he hadn't moved. Dorothy lifted her head. A single drop of blood ran down her chin, bright red on her bronze skin. In the instant before the other man lowered his head, I saw the blond host's face. His eyes were closed in an expression of tranquil bliss. The wound in his neck was a straight welling line to his jaw, obviously the work of a lancet.

Dorothy turned her head, hawked, and spat red onto the floor. "What you two gaping at? Didn't your mommas teach you no manners?"

"You cut him," Ruth said, "but you were going to let them bite her."

"That sound like sour grapes to me, Ruth. You want her to not get bit, that's *your* issues talking."

While Ruth protested that she didn't have any issues, I focused on the cherub statue behind Dorothy. I now saw what was odd about it: not only did it have a wee erection, it had fangs protruding over its plump lower lip. Why hadn't I guessed? Dorothy had a stake in most of the vamp clubs in Roppongi (ha, ha). And Twilight was one of them.

Wherever I looked, I now glimpsed fangs in the hosts' smiles. Their tans came from salons, not the beach, and open shirts exposed Gothic tattoos on pectorals. The boy with his head on Dorothy's lap, I supposed, was the Twilight equivalent of me and Ruth: the house human. In fact, with his blond hair and slender physique, multiple parallels seemed to converge in a very uncomfortable way.

At the sound of my own name, I dragged my gaze up to Dorothy's face.

"*She* said she wanted to know the reality, Ruth. So I set that up for her all nice. Makoto is real good, she would have enjoyed it, but you just had to…" Dorothy shook her head. She glanced down at the vampire feeding from the boy on her lap. She stroked his black head and cupped the shoulder of the blond in her long-fingered, bloodstained hand. "Get," she said without raising her voice. "Out that door, Ruth. Clare, you stay here."

"I had no idea you meant for me to get bitten," I slurred.

She smiled, showing bloody fangs. "What the hell you think I did mean?"

"I thought I'd made it clear that my comment -- commitment to science does *not* extend to blood donation."

Ruth laughed mirthlessly. "Come on, Clare, let's go before you say something *really* stupid." She took my elbow. I looked back to see Dorothy gently shifting the head of the blond host onto the lap of the vamp host beside her. She rose and came after us at a graceful saunter. Ruth and I left the club. The street was still dark, the air cool. A couple of those enormous Tokyo crows took off from the gutter, their wings flapping audibly.

"Excuse me, Ruth," I said. "I'm going to throw up."

While I retched, I heard Dorothy emerge from the club. Ruth stopped holding my hair, and their voices moved off, arguing. My stomach empty, I straightened up. Ruth and Dorothy were standing at the bottom of the hill beneath a streetlight that yellowed the foliage of the trees around it. I wobbled down the hill to join them.

"Never again will I touch anything stronger than a Sunrise Sour," I joked weakly.

Their faces turned to me, identically blank with fury. "All right," said Dorothy. She shot a ferocious yet triumphant glance at Ruth, then modulated her voice for me. "Clare, I can see you ain't feeling too good, so I'm gonna take you home with me. Put you to bed and let you sleep it off." She moved towards me. I moved back.

Ruth's fists clenched; her face screwed up childishly. "Can't you see she doesn't want to?"

"Quit fighting her battles! If she don't want to, she can

say so herself. It's up to you, Clare." Dorothy smiled at me confidently.

"Actually, she's right, Ruth," I said. "I appreciate it, but I can fight my own battles."

"You cute little thing," Dorothy said. "I'd like to see how scientists fight." She giggled, probably picturing a fistfight between hapless nerds. Her lips were still stained with blood. "Uh huh, I surely would like to see that."

Suddenly, I realized that I was no longer capable of speaking a civil word to Dorothy or anyone. I turned and started up the hill.

"Clare!"

Without slowing down, I shouted, "Yes, what is it?"

Dorothy drew level with me. She matched my pace and said breathlessly, "Now you're all in a huff. Don't just walk out on me like that!"

I shook my head. "Dorothy, I... I... I just can't be around you right now. I'm sorry."

"You been listening to Ruth. Don't get me wrong, I'm glad that you and her are tight, but I... I guess I trusted her too far. The trouble with her is, she's jealous," Dorothy said bitterly. "She's got her little boyfriend, but she wants to be the dog in the manger, too. And now she's trying to turn you against me. I done *everything* for that girl, and this is how she repays me!"

"You ordered them to... to bite me," I said, immersed in the frightening and humiliating memory.

"And what you think would have happened if they did? You think that would Turn you?" We'd just passed Twilight. She nodded across the street. "If you didn't know, none of them little punks can Turn anyone. You got to be a *danshaku* at the minimum before you can breed."

Danshaku, baron: two ranks below Dorothy in the aristocratic system that they seemed to use in parallel with the feudal system that had historically preceded it. At some point tonight, I'd remembered that *kami* had been a bureaucratic rank under the shogunate, roughly equivalent to district tax collector. Gorozaemon Edonokami was the *kami* of Edo as well as the, or a, marquis. But this was the first I'd heard about any of these ranks having to do with variants of the vampiric condition, or…

…the holy grail of vampire research.

The "transmission mechanism."

Forgetting that I was angry, I said, "Dorothy, can *you* create new vampires?"

"Me? I'm the one that Turned most of the girls at Exiles, ain't I? Except for Shinobu, she came to me all strung out and I fixed her up."

"Uh… and Beth and Natasha?"

She grimaced. "Yeah, well, they ain't *Turned* out so good, did they?" The pun caught me off guard. We both laughed. "Strictly in confidence, I never tried Turning anyone before I got to be a *shishaku*. I'm a *hakushaku* now. But it ain't easy: I mean, in the first place it takes time, and then once you Turn them, you got to support them until they find their feet. That's just common decency. And that means you got to have the financial wherewithal, too. So what I'm saying to you is, let's say you been misinformed by someone, and you think one bite would give you fangs of your own, then you can stop worrying about that, because it just ain't true. Hell, if it was, we would be running the world already!"

Exultation bubbled inside me. Maybe in twenty years, I would look back on this night as the start of my career proper-er, and the date when James's legacy was assured. Yet while I tried to imprint Dorothy's every word in my memory, unease niggled at me. "So what went wrong with Beth and Natasha?"

Dorothy sighed. "It's like baking a cake from a tricky recipe, you know? First couple of times, it don't rise or whatever, and you got to throw it away. Happens to everyone. But I got too soft a heart. Since it was my fault, in a kind of a way; although you won't find many vamps that care about that… So I kept them around. And it ain't worked out too badly. As you know, they got their own fans!" She smiled ruefully.

We were nearing the top of the hill. Neon blinked on the rooftops, reflected in the blank dark windows of the buildings. I shivered and drew imperceptibly closer to Dorothy. With deceptive ease, my exhilaration had given way to a sense of peril. Each additional spark of understanding only revealed the depths of the shadows around me. And those shadows had already touched me. *And how.*

I said quickly, "Dorothy, when they – they didn't *only* try to bite me —"

She watched me as I spoke. When I finished, we were almost at the top of the hill, but we'd stopped walking. She said without taking her eyes from mine, "Yeah. I told them to do that. Your first time, it should be in bed. That's ideally. But even if there's no one you would want to do that with, it still amplifies the experience."

"In bed," I echoed.

"Yeah. Just picture your naked body wrapped around that person, and they're inside you." She spoke deliberately. "And right at that same moment as you climax, they sink their fangs into you. Ain't no drug in the world that feels that good. And I'm not exaggerating."

I swallowed. "You sound like you're speaking from experience."

"How you think I got started on this path? But oh, that was way back in the day." Her lips curved. She'd licked the blood off them; they gleamed dark in the streetlight.

I said, "But why do you – why do vampires cut their sharers instead of biting them? I mean, that's all I see at the club!"

"Oh, that's simple. It's an intimacy thing. As a vampire, you got to feed, but you only want to share your bite with someone that you love. Or at least you got to *like* them. Or else you got to be a pervert like Beth!"

"Or... or like Makoto?"

"Makoto? Well, it's different for guys, ain't it? He likes anything that has two legs and a rack. But me; no. I really got to like that person."

I took an involuntary step towards her. I could smell her rich patchouli-tinged perfume.

The voice that rumbled, "Stop!" seemed to come from my own brain. But it had spoken in Japanese. We both whirled . A few meters off at the top of the hill, Gore stood with his arms folded high on the breast of his tailcoat. "Dorothy, have you no shame? No sense of decency?"

"Fuck that, yo," Dorothy gasped, then switched into Japanese. "Gore, have *you* no decency? Why are you all up in my private life?"

"There is no private life on a public street. So this *is* your new mortal toy." Gore strode down the street towards us. I started to retreat. My internal danger alarms were going off for the first time tonight. I wished I hadn't let the Shoto sensei's lecture dissuade me from packing the Glock. Not that I had anywhere to conceal it in these clothes... and at work, I'd have had to leave it in the dressing-room, which would be no different from leaving it on a low shelf in a house full of children. But I missed it badly in the instants that it took Gore to close with me, catch me by the right wrist, and twist my arm behind my back when I tried to break his grip. I squeaked in pain and rose on tiptoe. He jerked me closer so that I stood with my back against his chest. My head just reached the top button of his tailcoat. His enormous hand closed over my left breast and squeezed. His voice vibrated through my bones. "Have you truly not had her yet, Dorothy?" *Dolosi?*

"I told you, I keep that separate. Let her go, Gore, won't you? She's new to all this! Doesn't know hardly anything."

"Ah," sighed Gore, as if he understood at last. "These days, it *is* difficult to find a mortal who is truly innocent of our ways. But how sweet it was, I recall, to take them with not only their bodies, but their minds, pure and empty."

"This one isn't pure," said Dorothy hurriedly. "She's just ignorant, is all. She's American. They don't know anything —"

"Perhaps I will have her, first." Gore's hand moved to my other breast. I threw my free elbow into his iron-hard stomach and tried to stamp on his feet. They were so large I couldn't miss, and I didn't. He betrayed no sign of having felt it through his heavy leather shoes, but his fingers fastened on my nipple through my t-shirt and bra. Pulling it between thumb and forefinger, he said reflectively, "We would learn then how true you are, Countess. Are you faithful to your own? Or do you betray them as soon as they cease to meet your needs?"

"If this is all about that ten million yen... Gore, let her *go!*"

"That was merely the last of the abuses that have led me – and those greater than I – to question your loyalty." On the last word, he brought his other hand around and pinched my other nipple. I now had my arms free, but held in this excruciating way, I couldn't do anything with them. "It is necessary for you to reflect seriously on the duty you owe the Emperor, and the value you place on your own life. To that end, I will take this one with me."

"You're hurting me," I gasped. "I never did you any harm!"

"Oh Clare," Dorothy sighed, and she came off the ground in a flying kick.

I ducked my head instinctively. The stiletto heel of her sandal punched into Gore's upper arm. He let go of me and staggered backwards. She stumbled to one knee on landing, but in a split second she was up again, driving another kick at Gore's stomach. Her style was different from Ruth's: the airborne kicks made me think of tae kwon do. But she had the same explosive power, and a grace that made her seem almost to float.

Gore dropped into a wrestler's crouch, arms hanging wide. He growled, "Countess, is *this* how you mean to convince me of your loyalty?"

I didn't wait to find out how Dorothy replied.

I was free.

I ran.

Two blocks on, I spotted a taxi and dashed into the street to hail it. I'd left my satchel at Twilight. Fortunately, I kept my wallet in the pocket of my skirt. It contained my tips for the night and my key in its fold-out holder.

As soon as I got in the door of the apartment and locked it behind me, I started to shake uncontrollably.

I fetched the Glock from under my bed and hugged it for a while. The tooled metal was a poem of life and safety under my fingertips, a strange inversion.

With a lustreless grey dawn breaking in the sky, I showered, hoping to wash off the sense of damage that clung to me. I put on my black skate shorts and a sleeveless khaki sweatshirt. I fumbled my shoulder holster on and snapped the Glock into it. I put my denim jacket on over that. Then I stood at the window with my cell phone in hand, listening to the silence outside. I couldn't hear so much as a crow cawing.

Yurika Hamaguchi had claimed that this was a good area. That was patently not true in one important sense: Jingumae lay within Jaize 3000's territory. Ergo, Yurika didn't know what she was talking about... or else Jaize had "leeched onto" her, which would explain a lot of things, including his approach to me. Maybe I was being overly suspicious. But when I emailed her to ask for clarification of her cryptic note, her reply had been a bright, funny email about her experiences in New York. She hadn't even mentioned my questions.

And anyway, even if this was a "good area," even if it lay under Jaize's "protection," what did that mean in practical terms? Nothing that would stop Gorozaemon Edonokami, if he were determined to kidnap me as a hostage to Dorothy's good behavior.

I'd abandoned Dorothy when she was in danger. She'd seemed perfectly capable of looking after herself. But that was merely a justification for my own cowardice. I'd abandoned her, and I didn't have her cell phone number, so I couldn't even call and make sure she was all right.

I scrolled through the brief list of numbers in my phone and dialed, half hoping there would be no answer. But when a voicemail service clicked on, I felt a surge of despair.

"Hi," I said. "Uh, Matsudaira-san? This is Clare. Uh. Your colleague on the vampire study." My Japanese was deserting me. "Listen, I'm really sorry about last week. I said some things I shouldn't have. Uh... I need to talk to you and Politik-san. I met someone who... well, I found out a few things that raise some interesting new issues with regards to the study. I'd like to bounce my observations off you. But... but... Anyway. That's not why I'm calling. Uh..."

The machine cut me off with a beep.

I hadn't even got around to asking for advice —

—no. For *help*.

I needed help. But I couldn't bring myself to call back and leave another message.

I snapped my phone shut and sat on the floor, wondering if I had any other options, or if my only realistic course of action was to catch the next flight back to New York... just when I'd finally started to get somewhere.

125

Chapter 8.

I was lying on the floor, staring up at the ceiling. The land-line phone on the table was ringing. Groggy, I grabbed the receiver. *"Moshi moshi."*

"Clare? It was good to hear from you. Sorry I couldn't get back to you earlier."

"That's OK." I scarcely recognized Matsudaira's friendly tone. "This phone isn't safe," I blurted.

"I know. I just called to make sure you were home. I'll be there in five minutes."

I went outside. It was late afternoon – I'd slept away most of the day. A haze of cloud covered the sun. There were no shadows in the sultry air.

It occurred to me that I should have been at work in Turner Hall, surrounded by dusty reference books. Slowly, a smile spread across my face. I crossed the street, lifted an overhanging red rose to my face, and inhaled its fragrance. Then I defiantly picked it and tucked it behind my ear.

I heard an engine approaching. A motorbike coasted around the corner, engine spluttering out. The rider halted and pulled off his helmet. I smiled broadly, at the bike as much as the rider: it was one of those heavy skeletal jobs with the wheel shoved way out in front, fireball decals on the engine case, contrasting comically with Matsudaira's frayed jeans, pink t-shirt, and hiking boots.

My smile faded, however, when he didn't return it. "Sorry it took me so long to get here. Traffic." He climbed off the bike, swung its seat up, and produced a spare helmet. "Let's get out of here."

"I thought we could go for a walk and talk," I said.

Raising his eyebrows, Matsudaira looked around at the placid houses and trees sweltering in the grey afternoon. He started to say something, then nodded at my building. "You're staying at Yurika's place. I didn't know you knew her that well."

"I've never even met her. She just..." *She warned me to keep away from you.* Even though I'd decided to disregard Yurika's warnings, that part of her message still niggled.

"So she never warned you to keep away from me and Politik?" Matsudaira grinned.

I laughed in relief. "I gather it wasn't a terribly successful working relationship?"

"Yeah, well, sometimes you just can't hit the right note with a person, you know? They take everything the wrong way. I'm not saying I wasn't at fault, too, but..."

"OK. OK. Let's go to a café or something and..." I sighed. "I don't know, Matsudaira-san, can we just start again?"

He shook his head. "Our place. Politik wants to talk to you, too."

"Fine," I sighed. Pushing away my misgivings, I put on the shiny black helmet and climbed onto the pillion.

Swinging this way and that through the alleys was rather fun, but out on 246, the traffic was as bad as Matsudaira had said. As we overtook bus after car after truck, my anxiety flared. I held on for dear life to the grab bar behind me. Matsudaira turned his head and yelled something from behind his tinted visor.

"What?"

"I said, scoot forward! You're too far back!"

I didn't want him to feel the Glock under my jacket. I scooted forward and lightly placed my arms around his waist. He turned his head. I yelled in English, "Keep your bloody eyes on the road!"

"Hold on!"

Down the broad, dusty slope of 246 and through a maze of construction cones behind Shibuya station, around bulldozers squatting in pits. North on Meiji-dori. Matsudaira didn't slow down for traffic jams... or amber lights... or even red ones, when there was nothing coming the other way. Through Harajuku and the long bleak canyon of the Yoyogi business district. The needle never dropped below 80 km/h.

How had he ever qualified for a bike license, let alone managed to hold onto one? I told myself that he didn't usually
attack the streets like this; he was just trying to impress me.
Which meant I'd better fail to be impressed. Still, when he
gunned the bike through infinitesimal gaps between cars and
trucks, I clung panickily to his waist.

Circling Shinjuku station, we idled in a traffic jam that
even the bike couldn't penetrate. To the west towered the
skyscrapers that housed the city administration, which I'd
seen from the Narita Express on my arrival in Tokyo. Had
that really been only eleven days ago? Matsudaira pointed
across the street to a dead neon arch. "Kabukicho!" he shouted from behind his visor. "Stronghold of the Shinjuku
household. The conducator of Shinjuku is a friend of Skriva's."

I'd heard of Kabukicho, of course. It had a reputation as
Tokyo's premiere red-light district. Pedestrians filtered beneath the arch, pallid and furtive beneath black parasols.
Nothing moved in the maze of streets beyond. There's nothing deader than a nightlife district before dark, I reflected...
except maybe the vampires who inhabit it.

We cruised away from the center of Shinjuku, still heading north, into a congested district of small factories and grey
apartment buildings. Little old houses filled in the chinks,
but these weren't impeccably maintained like the houses in
Jingumae and Omotesando. Their second storeys sagged,
their roofs had been mended with corrugated iron, and their
wooden siding was falling off. We swung off the main street,
whipped around a couple of tight corners, and came to a halt
at the mouth of an alley flanked by tall apartment buildings.

I jumped off the bike, removed my helmet, and flapped
the hem of my jacket, wishing I could find a cooler way to
conceal my gun. Without the roar of wind in my ears, it was
very quiet. "So where are we?"

"Meiji-dori is over there. This is Nishi-Okubo. Lot of Ko-
reans here, which makes it affordable."

I followed him as he wheeled his bike down the alley.

128

"Whoa, whoa," I said. "*Affordable* is great and all, but how's your earthquake-proofing?" Damp-streaked concrete walls the color of ash, studded with blank windows, leaned over us to a height of four storeys. The alley dead-ended in a garbage collection site. Pigeons strutted, pecking at scraps of trash. Matsudaira paused, squatted down, and cooed in his throat. A pigeon cocked its head and walked up to him. He cooed again. The pigeon came closer. Matsudaira waited, hand extended. The pigeon thought about it, then took off in its bouncing flight.

"Damn," Matsudaira said. Smiling, he wheeled his bike on, scattering the rest of the pigeons. A gate with a funny little tiled roof blocked the much narrower alley that continued through to the next block – a mere chink between the buildings, half-choked with the kudzu that festooned the entire side of the building on the left. As Matsudaira wheeled his bike into the alley, a familiar voice hailed him from above.

Politik clattered down the concrete stairs to the street entrance of the building on the left. "Hiromi's here," he panted.

"Clare's here, too," Matsudaira said, grinning, swinging the bike helmets in his hand.

"Hi, Clare." Politik was sweating visibly. "Uh, Kay, I thought you might want her to —"

"Hiromi's welcome any time. And I'm just as glad to get her input on whatever Clare has to say."

Politik wore wooden *zori* on his big bare feet, which set up exotic thocking echoes in the stairwell. I wrinkled my nose at the rank air. Garbage littered the dim halls leading off the first- and second-floor landings. A horrible suspicion dawned on me: the building was uninhabited. What was I walking into here?

"Slated for demolition," Matsudaira said in response to my unspoken fears. "But with any luck, it'll be a while yet. The Japanese court system moves at approximately the speed of continental drift. All the other tenants moved out years ago. That's when we moved in." He looked mischievously over his shoulder at me.

"I guess that's one way to save on rent," I murmured.

Kicking an empty beer can off the stairs, Politik nodded. "We've got the whole building to ourselves. It's great! Apart from the vamps in the basement."

"Some of Zuleiko's people," Matsudaira said. "I mentioned her, didn't I? The conducator of Shinjuku."

"I'm not familiar with that term," I said. "Is it Japanese?"

"Not originally. I'm still trying to track it down, but I think it might be Transylvanian."

I groaned silently. Why were guys like this? Get them alone and they were relatively manageable, but put them together and you might as well talk to a pair of llamas. "So is *conducator* a rank? Or..."

"More like a job description. Technically, Skriva's a conducator, too. It just means the top vamp in a clave."

Clave. I'd heard that term before. Was it the same as *household*? I didn't ask; I was tired of displaying my ignorance. I could only hope that the "vampires in the basement" weren't allies of Gorozaemon Edonokami... or that if they were, they didn't find out I was here.

The fourth-floor hall was comparatively garbage-free. As we approached a door wedged ajar, I detected the savory aroma of tomato sauce. Despite my nerves, my stomach twinged, reminding me that I hadn't eaten for almost twenty-four hours.

"Well, here we are," said Matsudaira, bending to unlace his boots.

The living-room presented a scene of clutter that immediately felt familiar. Books and papers overflowed a low round table, covered the tatami floor, and lapped towards the walls, which were lined with bookcases. Matsudaira and Politik were clearly hard at work on something, even if it wasn't *Macrotrends in Vampire Culture.* While they vanished through an inner door, I lingered to glance at the volumes on the table. These were mostly in Japanese as old as the books themselves, but I could make out a couple of kanji compounds: *Mikkyo, Reiki, Jajutsu...* Well, well. Maybe my questions the other day had spurred them into brushing up their Japanese magical history. On the floor underneath the table, I caught sight of a stack of leatherbound tomes titled in roman script. *De Heptarchia Mystica – Alf Layla wa Layla...* Good Lord, *De Praestigiis Daemonum.* What did *those* have to do with vampirism?

A possible explanation popped into my mind. Matsudaira had said that he did editing and research jobs for spare cash. Maybe that was what I was looking at. And maybe that was all Yurika had been talking about. *They join a bad agency to get money for their work...*

If true, those words could have two meanings. Either Matsudaira and Politik were selling their academic integrity to the highest bidder – *or* they were just taking on some odd jobs to make ends meet, so they could continue their academic work. Right now, I favored the latter interpretation.

I *needed* them to be trustworthy. Which was exactly the problem.

My thoughts stalled as I caught sight of another journal on the table. This one I knew: *Kousatsushu.* It poked out from the overlapping tomes far enough for me to see that it was the same number as the one I'd "borrowed" from Professor Kamikawa's office. From its pages protruded several sheets of Japanese manuscript paper, the vertical lines of squares filled with handwritten characters. I squatted down to read them. *Hauptmann instantly recognized the natural ability that distinguished Kiyomasa Horibe from his other students. Of their first meeting, he later wrote, "Never have I experienced such an overwhelming sense of a stranger's qi..."*

"Clare!" Matsudaira looked back into the room. Seeing where I was, he said evenly, "Find something interesting?"

"Yes," I said, my heart beating fast. "Quite interesting."

He didn't take the bait. "Well, come on through and be introduced."

Open windows barely alleviated the steamy but enticingly scented atmosphere of the kitchen, where a girl in camo pants and a black tank top stood over the stove. She put down her wooden spoon and turned to smile at me. Olive-skinned, black hair scraped back in a ponytail, she was about ten years my junior. "Hi! I'm Hiromi. Doing my best to see these two nerds don't starve to death in their ivory tower here." She extended her hand. I accepted it, amused to realize that I'd already got out of the habit of expecting to shake hands when introduced to someone. Hiromi squeezed my hand. I squeezed back. She withdrew. "Keita," she said, turning to Matsudaira. "Kay?"

"Smells like it's time to eat," Politik broke in with a laugh.

"It's always time to eat, according to you." Matsudaira sent a playful slap at Politik's stomach. He opened the fridge, took out two cans of Sapporo, and tossed one to Politik. "Something to drink, Clare?"

"Nothing alcoholic, thank you," I said quickly.

"I'll have my usual poison, Kay," Hiromi said. "Diet Coke."

"That works for me, too." Hopefully it would suppress my hunger pangs, since it didn't look as if we were about to eat, after all.

We all sat around the kitchen table, which was crowded with houseplants and potted herbs that matched the profusion of plants on the windowsill. Outside the open windows, a lumpy carpet of rooftops unrolled to the spires of Shinjuku. The neon had started to come on, hastening the twilight. I could feel, rather than hear, a rhythmic bass vibration from somewhere far down in the building. Probably the vampires in the basement, starting their night with a dose of rock 'n' roll.

Take the initiative, Clare. Where to start? Exiles. Everything had started there.

But before I formulated my first sentence, Matsudaira said, "So." He took a gulp of beer and wiped his mouth with his sleeve. "You did well to get into Exiles. It was Dorothy Foulkes's first club, and it's legendary among the *vamu fechi* crowd. In general, Roppongi is a great venue for fieldwork… with one significant drawback: Dorothy. She's politically toxic. Gorozaemon, the *kami* of Edo, styled Marquis, has had a grudge against her ever since she reached *hakushaku* rank, and now he's closing in on her. But I don't need to tell you that, do I? You've met him yourself." Matsudaira's supercilious smile emerged. "Not a very pleasant experience, was it? So you see why our work would be jeopardized if he got wind of it." He nodded, letting that sink in. Then he leaned forward. "What did you tell him about our project? How bad is the damage? That's what we're here to determine."

I lowered my can of Diet Coke from my lips without tasting it. I said, "How on earth? Have you been *following* me?"

"Oh, I've got ways of finding things out, if I know what I'm looking for," Matsudaira said.

I rallied. "And right now you're looking for proof that I've screwed up." Considering that Matsudaira had a network of vampire contacts, the question of *how* he'd known that I was working in Roppongi seemed less important than the fact that he was blaming me for doing my job to the best of my abilities, while he and Politik were sitting around and spending my grant money on beer. The thought of my dwindling bursar's account fanned my indignation. "Maybe it wasn't advisable for me to be in Roppongi. But if you knew I was working at Exiles, why didn't you warn me? You have my cell phone number, don't you? Even if you lost it, I've been in Turner Hall all week."

Matsudaira reached for a pack of Marlboro Reds that lay on the table. He lit one and exhaled hard.

"Well?" I pressed, seeing that I had him. "All it would have taken was one phone call. How was I supposed to know any of this stuff?"

Matsudaira turned to Politik. "*This* is why. It would take the rest of the year just to get her up to speed. She doesn't know about the *kami* regime, she doesn't know about the taxation system… Tell the truth, Clare. If we'd warned you off, would it really have stopped you? Or would it just have encouraged you?"

"Naturally, I wouldn't want to jeopardize the viability of our study," I said.

Matsudaira's lips stretched humorlessly. "So give me at least one reason to be optimistic. You didn't mention me or Politik to Gore. *Did* you?"

"No. As a matter of fact, we discussed the Emperor and the morality of unconditional allegiance. I think he took a fancy to me." I bent the truth with an inner wince. "But he didn't display the slightest interest in my academic background. Does that reassure you?"

"I knew it!" Politik exclaimed. "They'll trust a gaijin where they'd never trust a Japanese. She might even be able to get into the Court! This could be our big break, Kay!"

"Cool your jets," Matsudaira snapped. "It's still risky, and it gets riskier the more you shoot your mouth off. There's no reason we should give her anything to repeat to them."

"We need her," Politik argued. Like Matsudaira, he seemed to assume I couldn't understand him if he spoke fast enough. "You're making the same mistake they do. You're underestimating her—"

"I am not, and we don't. Get that straight in your mind. The only question is whether we can use her or not."

My breath caught with anger. Then I heard the resentment in his tone, and saw the truth. Matsudaira simply couldn't bear to acknowledge that I'd got further in a week than he and Politik had in months. Even when he found out that I'd tangled with Gore, he'd waited for me to call *him*. It was incredibly unprofessional.

Unfortunately, I was all too familiar with the corrosive power of pride.

I wasn't going to grovel to Matsudaira. And I wasn't going to apologize for doing my job. I could get their attention by revealing Jaize 3000's secret... but would they even believe me? No, that revelation could wait until I'd regained their trust. *Somehow.*

"Gore invited me to visit the Court," I said. "He said I'd have to swear allegiance to the Emperor, but..."

Hiromi burst into laughter. I scowled. If Matsudaira and Politik were so big on discretion, why were they letting some random friend of theirs sit in on this discussion? Who was Hiromi, anyway? I'd never seen her on campus...

Matsudaira sat forward, an unpleasant smile animating his lean face. "I guess he didn't say what *swearing allegiance* is. There *are* humans at court. They're blood slaves. Oh, and sometimes they even come out again... when they're so used up that even the hungriest *danshaku* doesn't want their veins anymore. You've probably seen them wandering around the train stations. Sleeping on cardboard. Talking to themselves in Martian."

I scowled, afraid to seem gullible. "Well, if we want to understand the sociology of this community, we've obviously *got* to learn more about the top levels of their hierarchy. Can't Gore be circumvented? Aren't there any other officials who could be bargained with? Bribed? *Distracted?*"

Matsudaira shook his head. "Blood, or brute force. That's all they respond to. Money? They've got plenty of *that*. Blood! That's all they need; and all they *want* is to take over the world."

I stifled an incredulous giggle. "Then they need better PR," I said. "For a monarch, the Emperor doesn't have much of a media presence."

"And that's exactly how they like it," Hiromi said. "It's so much easier to expand your sphere of influence when no one believes in you."

I reflected with something like panic that I certainly had come a long way since I sat on the floor beneath Leon Foulkes's throne, interviewing him about his media strategy and listening to him complain that no one believed he was a *real* vampire.

"If that's so, I must say they're succeeding remarkably well," I said. "There's nothing about any Emperor in the literature. No suggestion of a formal hierarchy — "

"Oh – I thought – but I guess your department in America never subscribed to *Kousatsushu?*" Politik said.

"No; was there something in there?" I cringed.

"Was there ever! *The Emperor Underground: The Unifying Mythos of the Vampire Race.* That was the word, *race,*" Politik added glumly. "We wanted to use *nation,* because that's the word *they* use, isn't it? But we thought that would be *more* likely to push the wrong buttons. So we went with *race.* And it blew up into a major controversy."

I gazed at my hands for a moment, adding this information to the manuscript of *Regarding a Mysterious Power* that I'd seen in the other room. There was only one conclusion to be drawn, but I feigned ignorance to elicit it. "Did *you* get in trouble?"

"Oh, not me; I only helped with the research. He was the one who wrote the article!" Politik sketched a bow in Matsudaira's direction. "And of course, it was published under Kamikawa-sensei's name. That's how it works in Japan. The lowly postgrads do the work and the tenured professors collect the kudos. Or the smacks on the wrist, as the case may be. But in *this* case… well, Kamikawa-sensei is a celebrity! They couldn't touch him."

"You see, Politik is an eternal optimist," Matsudaira said. "The truth is, that article almost destroyed Kamikawa-sensei's career."

Could one brush with the censors have scared the professor into virtually abandoning his life's work – farming it out to a pair of incompetent postgrads? I was sceptical. "Well, that certainly explains why *you're* still just a researcher," I said, smiling to show that I was teasing. "If you want a job in Japanese academia, you're going about it in an interesting way."

"As opposed to your approach?" Matsudaira gave me a derisory stare.

"There are no jobs in Japanese academia, anyway," Politik muttered.

136

"Oh, come on," I said. "I'm the one trying to make this study happen. Although I get a feeling I'm the only one." I swallowed down an all-too-familiar pang of panic. "My future is on the line here. And hell, what about you guys?"

Unexpectedly, Matsudaira smiled. "If I had tits, I might flash them at Gore, too. But do you understand what we're trying to tell you?" He stubbbed out his cigarette in a plant pot. "If the Marquis decides we're a threat, we're finished. There won't be a vamp left in Tokyo who'll be willing to talk to us."

"I get your point," I muttered, thinking that we could learn more from talking to Gore himself in the first place. Or at least, *I* could...

Hiromi broke her silence. "Oh Keita, why don't you just tell her? She'll think you only care about your publications and your job prospects. She won't understand how serious it all is! And maybe she can help. I just know she's got potential." She hunched her shoulders and looked down at her lap as if embarrassed.

At first, my irritation flared in response to her outburst, but as it sank in, I felt humbled. I'd needed an outsider to remind me of what was really at stake here: not just our professional rivalries, but the fate of vampire communities across the world. "Listen, I *know* how serious it all is. But that's just one more reason why we can't afford to mess up..." Their blank faces told me to try again. "At the risk of repeating myself, if we're going to produce valid science, we *have* to collaborate effectively..."

It was like trying to sculpt the Parthenon out of dry sand, I thought wearily. Did they even know what valid science *was?*

"So, tell me more about what you've been doing in Harajuku," I said eventually. This time, I didn't make it into a challenge or imply by my tone that I was poised to sneer at them. "I'm open to ideas as to how I could work more effectively within your methodological format."

Politik and Hiromi traded significant glances. In the end,

both of them turned to Matsudaira.

"It's a long-term project," Matsudaira said at last. "But as you saw for yourself last week, there are progressive elements in the vampire organization. You might even call them revolutionary elements. And baby revolutionaries need all the support they can get. Just someone with academic credentials who'll tell them they're *right* – it's hugely important to them." He snorted, drained his beer, and started to push dents into the can with his thumbs.

Politik had a nerdy glow in his eyes. "You're American, you'll get it. We're supporting the democratic movement. Actually, it's more like the anti-Gore movement. But we're giving them the ideological foundation they need to believe in themselves."

"*Vampire Democracy*," I said. "Skriva and his crew. I get it."

And I did. Finally, I understood why Yurika had warned me to stay as far away from these two as possible.

Matsudaira nodded. "Sooner or later, there's going to be a revolution. We may not be able to give them any *material help* – " he twisted the words bitterly — "but we can prepare them to succeed in other ways."

I sifted my memories of that night at Gin No Tsuki. Nothing I'd just learned gave me a reason to alter my impression of Count Skriva and his boys. Probably they did resent Gore, for economic rather than ideological reasons – given their scrounging lifestyle, it must be hard for them to pay their "taxes" to him. And doubtless, they did harbor fantasies of abolishing a "regime" that seemed to be nothing more than a gigantic protection racket. I knew nothing of their actual capacity for rebellion, beyond Aleksey's vague allegation that they'd resisted Jaize 3000's takeover of their territory. But based on experience, I had a cynical view of revolutionaries: ten times out of ten, their zeal faded when they sobered up.

"It sounds like it might take a while before the revolution bears fruit," I said delicately.

"Like Keita said, it's a long-term project," Politik emphasized.

"A long-term *gamble,*" Matsudaira said.

"And I expect they have to be very careful not to betray themselves to the regime?"

All three of them laughed. Matsudaira said, "They call it *Radio Transylvania.* Instead of batteries, it runs on fear. The Court knows all about Skriva's ideas, but they consider him an asset. The Harajuku vamps are the best advertisement for the lifestyle: the mainstream media loves them. So Skriva can say whatever he likes. And we're tolerated: from their point of view, we look like Skriva's mortal toys. The only time we've run into trouble was when Zuleiko, the Princess of Shinjuku, started to wonder what Skriva was getting out of our relationship. *She* knew it wasn't blood or sex. So she incited some of his rivals in Harajuku to threaten us... but Hiromi took care of them." What? I blinked. Had I misunderstood? I glanced at the younger woman. Preening at Matsudaira's praise, she spared me a smug look. "Well, we ended up winning Zuleiko's support," Matsudaira finished. "Not that it's made a whole lot of difference."

"In the long term, we just have to hope that Gore is wrong about Skriva, and we're right," Hiromi sighed.

Politik said intensely, "When your goal is the survival of the human race, you can't afford to ignore a single option. But the fact is, we were a little short on options. Until *you* came along!" He giggled as if he'd said something clever.

"Don't get too excited," Matsudaira snapped. "We haven't decided to bring her on board, and she hasn't agreed, come to that."

"But you *will,*" Politik stated. "I mean, you're American! You can't like the idea of the vamps taking over the world."

I took a deep breath. "Let me get this straight. You're suggesting that I redirect my efforts towards the destruction of the *kami* regime?"

"That's the objective," Matsudaira said.

"In Roppongi? Or—"

"What?" Matsudaira reared back, genuinely surprised. "No, stay away from Dorothy, whatever you do."

"We could find some people for you to talk to in Shinju-ku." Politik reached for a pen, as if to give me the names right now. "Zuleiko's household is full of revolutionaries in the making. They just need inspiration."

"I see." So my role would be to provide "inspiration," aka "ideological guidance." With the ultimate goal of defanging the vampire nation... pun intended.

If I agreed, my colleagues would presumably help me to evade Gore's clutches. And that was all I really needed from them.

Unfortunately, it was out of the question. Matsudaira and Politik might use the arguments of critical theory to legitimize their meddling. *I* believed my role was to seek the truth... *not* to dabble in social engineering. "Vampire Democracy" might be a reasonably good bet as a long-term prospect for destabilizing the *kami* regime. As science, it... well, it wasn't.

I'd spent years in paranormal studies, one of the most politically sensitive fields in existence. Most recently, the public hysteria that had coalesced around Dr. Isaac Brent's CAIN theory and the Citizenship Act had reinforced my conviction that there was nothing more reprehensible and dangerous than an academic who succumbed to an ulterior agenda.

From the fate of *Kousatsushu,* it would seem Matsudaira and Politik had also learned the hard way that when science clashed with politics, we lost. *They should have known better.* Yet here they were, suggesting that our fieldwork ought to take the shape of ideological formation!

Their apparent failure to comprehend just how far out of line they were triggered every sensitivity I possessed.

But I was one against two – or three. So I didn't argue with them in those terms.

"If the vampires really were planning to take over the world," I said slowly, "that would be all the more reason why the world needs to know the truth about them. As I said, I believe we'll be much more effective if we share our data. But I'm not prepared to –" *to subordinate my academic integrity to your political objectives.* My stomach churned, and I took a trembling sip of Diet Coke. "If the revolution takes off, would you expect me to *participate?* To take sides?"

"To help us destroy them!" Politik said. "That's the whole point."

"I see." I spoke calmly. Inside I was shaking with anger. "Unfortunately, if I were to commit to an agenda like that, it would completely invalidate any data I gather. So if that's the price of your cooperation, I'm afraid we'll just have to work separately. Maybe we can recommend that the study be stopped and devise our own alternate proposals."

The three of them shared another moment of silence. Matsudaira said, "You know what'll happen if you go back to Roppongi? They'll kill you. They do that, you know."

This morning, I would have said that nothing could induce me to go back to Roppongi, but now I found myself determined to do exactly that. I forced a shrug. "I have a pretty high tolerance for risk. And some ability to defend myself."

"The Countess won't protect you," Politik said.

His casual reference to Dorothy reawakened all my fears for her safety and my shame at having abandoned her last night. Out of this tangle of emotions emerged a resolution: I wouldn't betray her any more than I already had. "She saved my life last night," I said.

Politik put down his pen and nudged it with a finger, aligning it with the edge of the table. "But if she knew you'd been talking to us, she'd kill you."

The tension in the room was escalating faster than I could handle it. My years of studying Japanese journals and academic publications had gone for naught: I was competent in the language, but clueless about the people. I couldn't read their cultural cues to save my life.

"We're not saying she's a monster like Gore," Matsudaira said. "But her position is very delicate."

I shook my head. They could try to sow doubts in my mind, but actions spoke louder than words. "I'll take my chances," I said.

"With what?" Matsudaira said, anger boiling suddenly in his voice. "That?"

He nodded at my left side. Shocked, I touched the outside of my denim jacket.

"Oh, I saw it straight off. What is it, a nine-millimetre?" He smirked. "Illegal in this country. As I'm sure you're aware. But the vamps don't let that trouble them. Handguns, shotguns, tactical assault rifles, AK-47s, you name it, they've got it."

"Yeah, and at the Court?" Politik's face twitched. "They've got *maaajor* firepower. Black-market military stuff. We're talking anti-tank guns, rocket launchers. *Chemical weapons.* That's the whole problem in a nutshell!" He backhanded sweat from his temples.

"Shut up, Politik," Hiromi said. "Clare," she said, contorting her face into what I now understood was merely a mask of friendliness, "would you like to think about it? Just reflect on what we've told you."

"I'll give it serious thought," I said sincerely. I knew now that I wanted nothing more to do with any of them, yet as I started to stand up, I felt a sort of wrench, like a tooth coming out under novocaine.

Hiromi jumped out of her seat and pushed me back down. Holding my shoulders, she said, "Just stay here for a few minutes, OK? We'll leave you to think about it." For an instant, her grip tightened to the point of pain.

"No," I said. The physical contact snapped my last thread of control. I twisted my shoulders to break her grip, and when she tried to take hold of me again, I knocked her arms away and sprang to my feet.

Matsudaira jumped up. "Calm down, everyone. Just calm down. You two, don't you have stuff to do? Let *me* talk to Clare... I'm sorry. It's our fault. We've never had to explain all this stuff to anyone before—"

"Well," I said, heart pounding. "I think you did a fairly good job, actually. I don't see what more you can... But, OK." Thank God someone was being rational around here. It should have been me. "OK."

Hiromi shot me an oddly triumphant glare, then left the kitchen by the far door. Politik followed her. I sank down at the table again and glanced around, seeking reassurance. On top of the fridge stood a lucky cat figurine and several stacks of manga tied with string. Judging from their titles, it was a fair bet at least some of them contained tentacle sex. *Not* very reassuring.

"One thing," Matsudaira said. "Would you mind taking off your gun?"

"Why?"

"Because it's making me jumpy."

I laughed ruefully. "Fair enough." I placed the Glock on the table amid the houseplants – nearer to me than him. "Better?"

"Some." He rose and took another can of beer out of the fridge. "Sure you won't have one?"

"No, really..."

"Well then, how about some... what's this... spaghetti bolognese?"

Anger and fear had stolen my appetite, but I nodded. "Please."

He heated the spaghetti up, and as the savory odor filled the kitchen, my hunger returned.

We ate in silence, with forks. I had to hand it to Hiromi, her pasta was a thing of beauty. But after what had just happened, Matsudaira's silence felt as if he was judging me. As I searched for something to say, I heard the faint sound of music from deep in the apartment. It sounded like some kind of tribal chant, and from the way it stopped and started, I understood that it wasn't a cassette or record. *They* were chanting: Politik and Hiromi. The sounds were those of Japanese, but as far as I could make out, they didn't add up to words.

Unease skipped down my spine.

Matsudaira seemed oblivious, but I could stand it no longer. Brightly, I nodded at the top of the fridge. "Are you into manga? I feel like this country is weird enough that manga artists probably don't even have to make anything up."

"What?" My comment seemed to startle Matsudaira out of a reverie. He twisted around to see what I was pointing at. "Oh, those! No, I don't read manga. Those were, uh—" He caught himself.

"Those were?"

He grunted. "Ryu's. Reality was never weird enough for that guy."

"Ryu Abe?"

Matsudaira nodded.

I put my fork down. Ryu Abe, the graduate student who'd been arrested for assault.

Funny how the dots were starting to join up.

"Yurika warned me to remember what happened to Ryu," I said. "I had to do a bit of digging to find out what *did* happen to him. But he got fired, didn't he?"

"Yeah." Matsudaira's gaze didn't flinch. "He took the rap for something... a total accident. Smartest guy I ever met, and he'll never work in academia again. Left Tokyo, isn't answering his emails anymore, and I can't say I blame him. But it's a pain in the ass. I mean, what am I supposed to do with all his junk?"

"So what exactly happened?" I said, not sure I wanted to know.

He shook his head. "You've got spaghetti sauce on your face."

"What? Where?"

"Here." He touched his own temple. "How'd you manage to get it up there?"

I reached up and felt stickiness at my temple. In my scuffle with Hiromi, the cut on my scalp had opened up again. Now that I knew it was bleeding, it stung to the touch. "Ugh, how annoying. But it's just a graze. I've had it for a week."

"Oh. Well…" Matsudaira grabbed a paper towel from the roll near the gave stove. Crumpling it up, he reached for me.

I flinched back. "It's really all right."

"Fine."

Now I'd offended him again. I sighed. "Sorry. Go ahead, Matsudaira-san." I bent my head.

"Oh, call me Keita, or Kay. It seems kind of dumb to be on formal terms at this point, doesn't it?" He moved forward and clumsily dabbed at my head with the paper towel. I could smell his body odor. Deodorant was obviously not a priority item for him. "So have you had time to wander around the city? Done any sightseeing?"

I struggled to wrap my mind around the fact that he was making small talk, and decided it was a good sign. "I've been to Shibuya… that was kind of fun. But I haven't really had time to do the sights per se."

"You should check out some of the older neighborhoods. Asakusa, Ueno. Get away from the glitz and you can see what Tokyo used to be like."

"Are you originally from Tokyo yourself?"

"Sure. I grew up fifteen minutes from here. It's changed a lot." He gave one more dab to my head. "There, that's a bit better."

"Thanks," I said.

"No problem." He stuffed the bloodstained paper towel in the pocket of his jeans.

"Actually, there was something else I wanted to discuss with you guys," I said, deciding to gamble. "I think I mentioned on your answering machine—"

"Oh, yeah. So what was all that about?"

"Well, a friend introduced me to a vamp named Jaize 3000. Have you heard of him?"

Keita – as I would now have to think of him – sat down hard. I'd managed to surprise him at last. "Who hasn't heard of him? You've got some well-connected friends." He waited a moment. "So what's he like in person?"

"Charming," I said. "Ridiculously charming. Of course, he's a very powerful vampire…"

"Yeah, the conducator of Shibuya." Keita nodded. "There was almost a war when he murdered the old conducator, Arima *hakushaku*. Hang around with Skriva, and I guarantee you'll hear the story before long. Originally, you see, Shibuya and Harajuku were a single clave —"

"Which split in half when Harajuku resisted Jaize's takeover," I finished. "Yeah, I heard the backstory. And I also found out something else."

Keita smiled. "Let me guess. The secret of Jaize's success? The reason he's the only unranked vampire to hold even half a clave? *Without* a household of vamps that owe their allegiance to him? The reason he's also a filthy rich celebrity in what we quaintly call the real world? Yes?"

"I suppose so," I said grumpily. I knew before I made it that my "revelation" was going to be an anticlimax. "He's a psychic vampire."

"Everyone knows that," Keita said, not sparing me.

"I was told it was a deep, dark secret."

Keita pushed away his plate and lit a cigarette. Exhaling, he said loftily, "I guess your friends aren't as well-informed as they make out. Everyone knows about Jaize… everyone who *matters.* He didn't make a secret of it himself, at first. He actually bragged about it, until Gore cornered him one night and told him that if he wanted to keep his ill-gotten gains, he'd better wise up. So now the official story is that he's powerful enough for *hakushaku* rank, but the Court has blacklisted him on account of the way he killed old Arima – he used that *qi* craft of his - so they've refused to ennoble him." Keita gazed at the tip of his cigarette. "Of course, it's possible he *is* that powerful by now. He didn't have a corporate empire ten years ago, either."

"But he still doesn't have his own… household… of vamps?" Curiosity overrode my humiliation at being forced back into the role of questioner.

146

"Who knows? Maybe you can tell *me.*"

I had to shake my head, although I did add, "I didn't see any other vamps there. Only human flunkies."

"Figures. He doesn't interact much with the organization. Keeps to the real world. Pays his taxes."

"Cultivates his army of fans," I said half under my breath.

Keita leaned forward. "Did he try anything on you?"

The eagerness of his expression was oddly heartening. No matter what his faults, I realized, he had the insatiable curiosity that made a scientist. If I opened up to him and shared information, maybe we'd be colleagues again.

"He tried to stake a claim to me," I said softly. "And he almost got me."

I related my experience *chez* Jaize in the detached language of a field report, trying not to omit anything that might be significant. I also mentioned my speculation that Jaize had seduced Yurika Hamaguchi in the past. My queasy sense of disloyalty abated when Keita nodded.

"Yeah. She was a total Jaize groupie. She didn't admit it when we confronted her about it, but she wore one of those amulets – it's like a fan club. The mark of the well and truly flipped."

"The sources are so contradictory. Most of them say psychic vampires don't even exist. But…"

"Fuck the sources," Keita said. "Hearsay and myths." He put his cigarette out on his plate, then looked straight at me. Maybe it was just the fluorescent overhead light, which seemed to have grown brighter as darkness fell outside, but I didn't like the gleam in his eye. "Listen, I know I was kind of harsh about your work in Roppongi. But I was just being realistic. No one can get into the Court. But psychic vampirism is a topic of – of equal importance. And the only way to do the research is to go in there. Politik and I can't do that… but you can."

I bit my lip. The prospect of a repeat encounter with Jaize appealed about as much as taking a swan dive off the

Rainbow Bridge. Yet I was also aware of a deeper resistance to Keita's proposal. Everything he'd done since we met had been one attempt after another to bully and manipulate me. This was just more of the same.

"Are you thinking of publishing a paper on psychic vampires?" I said.

"Maybe in the long run."

"Maybe under Professor Kamikawa's name?"

Keita scowled. "Kamikawa-sensei doesn't believe in psychic vamps. Better keep him blissfully ignorant of this particular wrinkle."

One finger to my lower lip, I pretended to think. "I would have to tell James," I said. "If Jaize is the real thing... this would be *big*. And if we did get some concrete data, we'd have to publish."

"In Japan? The Ministry of Internal Affairs keeps a close watch on everything coming out of our field. We've tangled with them before -- Politik mentioned that ridiculous fuss over the word *race*. And there was an even nastier episode over – ah – another paper I wrote for Kamikawa-sensei."

"Regarding a Mysterious Power," I said.

Keita didn't even blink. "Yeah. It went through five revisions before they let us publish it, and then, after it was out, they changed their minds and shut the fucking journal down. All because of a little harmless magical history. And you want to publish an expose on psychic vamps? Good luck."

"So we'll publish in the States," I said. "Look, I hear you on the censorship. In America, it's informal censorshop, but still – whenever we get a few inches in the mainstream media, it's pure fluff, and they crop the requisite 'expert opinion' all to hell. But what happened to your articles – that's a total scandal. *That* doesn't happen in America."

"That you know of," Keita pointed out.

"Well, yeah. But still, I think we have to try." I grinned, my excitement growing as the prospect became more concrete. I hadn't forgotten my qualms about breaching the vamps' pact of silence, but the public's right to know did come first. "It would make quite the splash! We could be co-authors, if you like."

"You'd really do that?"

"Sure. I mean, we're in this together —"

"Don't you get it, Clare?" Keita raked his messy bangs back. "Jaize is the most dangerous vampire in Tokyo. If I ever get to him, I'll only need one research instrument, and it won't be a questionnaire... Listen! When I started in paranormal studies, I was like you – I wanted to tell the truth. But then I realized they don't want to hear the truth. They won't even let you publish it. That's what happened with my dissertation, too. After that, I realized... oh, never mind." He shook his head. "Just, never mind. That's not the world you live in."

"I've spent six years of my life —"

"Just forget it." He glanced over his shoulder at the far door. "Things can get pretty wacky around here." He sounded tired.

"Strangely enough, I believe you." I said.

"Well, believe this: I'm the most reasonable person you've met today. You don't want to get involved with our project, and I don't see any reason to needlessly ruin your life. So, come on. Let's get you out of here. If you were really smart, you'd go back to America. But that's up to you. All I ask is that you keep quiet about everything... everything we talked about today. Jaize 3000 included."

In the nearby room, I could clearly distinguish Hiromi and Politik's voices rising and falling. One of them was also tapping a drum in a skittering seasick rhythm. I said, "What *is* that?"

"Just don't say anything," Keita repeated, louder. "Not to Kamikawa-sensei, or Merriwick-sensei, or anyone. Can you do that?"

"Sure," I said.

The chant was increasing in volume. Keita shifted his weight anxiously. He didn't seem to doubt my easy assent. "Here, let me show you." He gestured me towards the windows. Standing in front of the sink, I looked out at the patchy field of lights and the technicolor blaze of Shinjuku on the horizon. "This isn't the best neighborhood, but you'll be OK if you don't get lost. When you get out on the street, just head for Meiji-dori. Can you see it over there?"

I leaned over the sink. This part of Tokyo was more of a snarl than a grid, and the lights made no obvious pattern. "I can't see," I started, and then I saw the reflection in the windowpane before me.

Keita was gone. There was someone else in the kitchen with me.

Where my colleague had stood behind me, I saw the chiaroscuro reflection of a thin man whose face sagged off his skull, the cheeks pocked and discolored. His mouth hung open in a gape beneath a scraggly pencil moustache. His nose had been smashed and badly mended. Deep lines rutted his forehead. His eyelids drooped wearily as he gazed past me out of the window. He wore a faded t-shirt like Keita's, and he resembled Keita in a nightmarish way: twenty years older, beaten and broken on the wheel of life. I saw all of this in a split second, and then I involuntarily closed my eyes.

Pulse hammering, I stood immobile. It had been an optical illusion. My own anxiety and the uncertain light had combined to produce a hellish vision. I'd imagined what I saw...

...and I dared not let Keita suspect that I'd seen it.

When I opened my eyes, he'd moved aside from the window. "Is that better?"

"Yeah. I think I can see which way to go." I turned back to the room. My whole body was shaking. I darted a glance at him, making sure his face was normal. It was, but still I couldn't look him in the eye.

"Quietly now," he whispered, herding me towards the living-room.

The chant grew suddenly louder when we left the kitchen. The smell of incense drifted from the dark little hall to the back of the apartment, which opened off the living-room without an intervening door. I picked my way through the clutter. The pieces of information I'd gathered were like magnets in my head: I was holding them apart by force of will, but they were trying to come together. The smell of incense. The mantra. The grimoires, with paper scraps stuck in them for bookmarks. And —

"You remember the way out," Keita urged me. "What are you waiting for?" He touched his pocket, and the last piece of information clicked into place.

"Give me that paper towel," I said. "It's got my blood on it."

His face altered. All at once, now that I'd seen through him, he allowed the hostility and contempt I'd seen at Gin No Tsuki to resurface. "Off you go," he said, standing out of my reach.

"I want that." I stepped around him and made a vain swipe at his pocket. What a clever little deception it had been. The kind of thing magicians excelled at.

"It won't make any difference even if I give it to you," he taunted me. "We've got the Diet Coke can you drank from. And Hiromi picked a hair off your jacket."

I backed off, sickened as much by his gloating as by the revelation.

"That's right! Go!" His expression was unfriendly, but his voice held an edge of urgency that convinced me he was telling the truth. He really did want me gone. But not for my own good. More likely, it was an automatic reflex to exclude me, a judgemental outsider, from whatever was going on in the back of the apartment.

Unfortunately for him, I didn't have to see the circle and the pentacle to guess what was happening. They intended to use my blood and hair in some disgusting ritual that was probably designed to ensure I never interfered with their precious project again. A "benign" spell of dissuasion… or one of deadly harm?

"Fine. I don't believe in that shit, anyway," I said, trembling. "I've seen poppets made and invoked. They only work if the intended victim believes in their power."

"They work on fear. And you're not scared, oh no!" Keita's expression hardened into a mocking smile. "But don't worry. We don't believe in that shit, either."

"What's that paper towel for, then?"

"A souvenir?" he simpered.

I swivelled. Then I stopped. "My gun. I left it in the kitchen."

"I'll give it back to you another time, OK?"

Through the chant, I suddenly heard what sounded like the frightened screech of a cat. *They had a live animal in there! They were going to make a sacrifice!*

Blind fury took over. I launched myself past Keita. He grabbed me from behind. The chant dissolved into confused exclamations that mingled with a muffled howl like wind sweeping through a narrow aperture. I could hear too many voices.

"How fucking stupid can you be?" Keita snarled, shoving at me. "Get *out!*"

My nerve broke. I turned and fled, skidding on the scattered books. It seemed to take an eternity to force my feet into my sneakers. As I opened the front door, Hiromi burst into the living-room in a storm of black robes. I threw myself into the hall. Which way were the stairs? Shit! I blindly swung left. I turned a corner and stumbled to a halt. The next leg of the hall led to a dead end. I'd gone the wrong way.

And behind me I could now hear more than one pair of footsteps. I hit the end of the hall: a blank wall with a large window that offered a view of the city lights, partially obscured by tendrils of kudzu. Behind me, Hiromi shouted breathlessly, "Clare-san! Stop! No one's trying to hurt you!" and then, *How'd she get out?*

The window opened with a crackle of rotten rubber. I straddled the sill and tested the strength of the kudzu. Huge spade-shaped leaves rustled in the dark. The biggest vines were woody like the branches of a tree, thicker than my wrist.

What was I worried about? "The weed that ate the South" was practically invincible. It would bear my weight.

As Hiromi and Politik pounded down the hall towards me, I dropped out of the window. The vine I'd looped around both arms peeled loose from the old concrete, and for a terrifying moment I was falling. Then I jerked to a halt in mid-air. My shoulders protested, but the vine held. I dangled within reach of the leafy face of the building. I grabbed the nearest vine. The stuff grew deep: my elbow had vanished into it before I touched the rough concrete of the the wall. I dug my sneakers into the rustling mass, finding footholds. Above me, the window squealed wider. "Shit!" Politik exclaimed. "She jumped! Gotta get down there – if she's dead –" His terrified voice receded.

But Hiromi's voice was so clear that I knew she was leaning out of the window, two or three meters above my head. "If she's dead, it'll be your fault. But I don't think she jumped."

Trying not to make a sound, I clung to my footholds and handholds in the leaves. Acrid dust rose from them, as if I'd disturbed crevices of the plant that were never cleansed by rain.

"Clare?" Hiromi called softly. "Are you there? I bet Keita scared you off. That's him being selfish. Because you have potential, and he's afraid you might have more potential than he does. See? Totally selfish. But it *is* tough for him." I held my breath. She sighed loudly. "Are you there? I *wish* you wouldn't run away."

Silence fell. Hoping she'd left the window, I started to ease myself down through the kudzu, probing with my toes, dropping my weight from one handhold to the next. It was as easy as climbing down a rope ladder. When I passed the second window, I glanced over my shoulder. This side of the building faced a narrow parking-lot. A little further and I'd be low enough to jump to the weeds that bordered the asphalt.

"Well, just to let you know." Hiromi said overhead. "If

you're trying to climb down, you'd better sing out right now. You thought that kudzu was pretty convenient, didn't you? Wrong. It's my security system."

I'd frozen in the act of switching handholds when she spoke. Awkwardly suspended, I tried to shift my grip to another vine. It broke in my hand and I slipped down several feet, the kudzu crackling like a fire.

Shit!

Something whippy and tough curled around my left wrist. I jerked, caught.

Eyes popping, I struggled, shoving my feet deeper into the kudzu to get some leverage against the wall – and another vine fastened around my ankle. Woody splinters driving into my bare skin, it hauled my foot up to the level of my groin. I fought madly. It was just a plant, just a *plant* –

My struggles twisted me around, giving me a view of the parking-lot. A gutted van up on blocks. A couple of fancy sedans gleaming in the lemony streetlight. Beyond them, an empty street. . If I could just get *down* –

I swung my full weight from my wrist, and managed to jerk it free of the kudzu. That didn't improve my position. I tumbled upside-down to swing from one ankle. Blood rushed to my head, blurring my vision. I tried to catch hold of the vines in front of me, but they darted away, lashing my face as they went.

With a rustle that sounded like a laugh, the vine released my ankle.

I plummetted.

My hours at Colin's dojo paid off. I hit the ground in a perfect ukemi fall, throwing my momentum sideways, head over heels, and bounced to my feet.

I'd fallen more than two meters, head-first. If not for my training, I would probably have been an unconscious heap of broken bones. As it was, I was jarred and shaken, but otherwise unhurt. "Screw you!" I shouted, giving the building the finger as I retreated across the parking-lot. The kudzu rustled innocently in the dark.

154

A small object arced down from the fourth-floor window. Yipping, I dodged. Then I heard the ching and skid of metal on asphalt. I darted over to pick it up.

My Glock.

Feverishly, I popped the clip out, then reloaded it. An instant later I felt like an idiot, realizing that the thing could have been rigged to explode in my hands. But it hadn't. So why had it been thrown down to me? Was this Keita's way of "giving it back to me later"? Never mind. It appeared to be in working order. Three cheers for German manufacturing excellence. "Thanks!" I shouted, watching for any movement in the window I'd climbed out of. "Sorry, let me rephrase: Thanks for *nothing!*"

"Clare! Clare!" A breathless shout; Politik. He squeezed out of the chink between the buildings, pushing through the kudzu that almost choked it at this end. "You're alive! I thought... you jumped. It's a long way down. I would never have forgiven Kay... any of us. Let me explain," he gasped.

Staring at him across the parking-lot, I shook my head. Then I deliberately aimed the Glock at him. "Back off. You had a chance to explain. Instead, you figured you'd cast a spell on me. And now, funnily enough, I don't feel like listening to you anymore."

He stumbled backwards, hands rising into the air.

God, it had been this easy all along, hadn't it? I sighted on Politik's chest, hoping I wasn't being targeted from the fourth storey with a rifle or something. I wasn't going to shoot him, of course. But I'd seldom been so angry in my life, and I meant him to know it.

His glasses had slipped to hang from one ear. Not attempting to right them, he stood with his hands limply raised. "It didn't work, anyway," he said hopelessly. "We've tried everything, *everything* – and it never works."

Steadily retreating, I hit the smoother asphalt of the street. I spared a last glance for Politik's sad-sack form, and then I clicked on the Glock's safety. Holding it loosely at my side, I started to walk without looking back.

Chapter 9.

Not soon enough for my twitching nerves, I reached Meiji-dori, and followed the crowds to the south side of Shinjuku station. The simple actions of buying a ticket and getting on the Yamanote line were comforting. But as the train carried me south, confusion tainted my relief. I *hadn't* made a clean getaway. It had been dirty – and painful. When I fell from the kudzu, I'd landed on my left shoulder, and now it hurt to move my arm. The furtive stares of other passengers worried me, too. I got off the train at Shibuya and ducked into the restroom.

Horrified, I saw a tint of spaghetti sauce mingling with the crust of blood in the roots of my hair. God! Keita could at least have left me looking as if I hadn't been in the wars! Stains marked my jacket, and my bare wrists and ankles were scored with scratches from the kudzu. Dust clung to my hair, making it a lank cobwebby sheet. I splashed my face with water, but only succeeded in moving the dirt around.

I couldn't show up at Exiles like this. To top it all off, another worry nagged at me: to walk into a gathering of vampires looking like a bloodstained victim might be a very bad move.

Reluctantly, I turned for home.

Padding dolefully up the stairs of Yurika's building, I held the Glock naked in my hand. It was a bad sign that I was starting to rely on it like this. But in the circumstances, I thought, even my father would understand.

"Ruth," I said in shock.

"So you *are* as dumb as you look." She rose from where she'd been sitting in front of the door of my apartment and brushed herself off. "If it was me, I'd have been on the first plane out of this burg."

She wore a black hoodie, much too big, over her pale

green dress. She was made up for work. But instead of high heels, she wore Nikes without socks.

"Did Gore come after you, too?" I asked excitedly.

"Fuck, no! He doesn't even know I exist." I doubted that, remembering how the Marquis had asked Dorothy, *Have you disposed of the other one?* But it might be true that Gore didn't see Ruth as a potential hostage – and he'd probably be right: I guessed that she would go down fighting before she let herself be dragged off to the vampire court. "It's you he wants," she said. "And it's a good thing you didn't come to work tonight, because he's posted one of his *kenin* at the club."

"What's a – *kenin*?"

"A household warrior. Nowadays they just call them soldiers, but most of Gore's soldiers are as old as he is... like, from the days of the samurai. With *chonmage.*" She pulled her hair off her forehead to illustrate the traditional samurai hairstyle. "The old ones pick and choose their modern technology. Most of them don't use the telephone. Can't understand television. Some of them won't even ride the trains. But they don't turn up their nose at modern weaponry. This guy's packing a Colt semiauto. Also a .22, and I think I saw a stun gun in his jacket." Her gaze travelled to the Glock in my hand. "How good is your aim?"

Embarrassed to admit that I'd only fired live rounds once in my life, and that was on a range with an instructor at my elbow, I holstered the gun inside my jacket. "Sounds scary," I said lightly. "I can't imagine that's doing much for the atmosphere at the club."

Ruth laughed. "Oh, Dorothy's got him serving drinks. But it's not good, you're right about that. So as soon as I got into work, it was, 'Go and find Clare. Keep her out of Gore's way until I get a chance to settle his ass, you hear?'" Dropping her mimicry, she gestured at the door of my apartment. "Anything you need out of there?"

"Wait," I said. "Fill me in on the plan, Ruth, for God's sake. Are you saying I have to go into hiding?"

She nodded, lips tightening. "For a day or so, maybe.

Gore thought you were living with us in Nakai. Showed up right before dawn, foam all dripping off his fangs… Shinobu told him where to stick it. She's one mean vamp when you wake her up half an hour after she's gone to bed. But fucking Eloise… whenever some statusy motherfucker from the Court shows up, she just melts. So she had to go and tell him that you live in Jingumae. Which narrows it down for him. Which means we should really get going."

She seemed completely uninterested in where I'd spent the day, or where I'd picked up my cuts and scratches. Watching her eyes flick towards the stairs, I realized that she was more nervous than she let on.

"I was looking forward to a shower," I said, and then as she opened her mouth, "But under the circumstances, I guess I can skip it."

She rolled her eyes. "Mind if we skip the pore-cleansing mask, too? And I don't think we've got time for you to fix your manicure."

"The hell with it," I said, and unlocked the door of the apartment. I grabbed the knapsack I'd been taking to work at Turner Hall and threw some toiletries, a clean t-shirt, and underwear into it. While Ruth fretted in the genkan, I added a couple of books I'd borrowed – legitimately – from the university library. As soon as I got a minute, there were a couple of things I wanted to look up.

As we scurried through the alleys, Ruth's gaze ticked back and forth in an intent way that reminded me of her manner at the karate dojo. She enforced a pause at every crossroads to make sure the coast was clear. When I tried to speak to her, she shushed me. But when we emerged onto 246, where a trickle of pedestrians seemed to temporarily ensure our safety, I overrode her hisses to say, "Where are we going? At least tell me that!"

"I thought I did." She swung right, towards Shibuya. "We're going to Jaize's place."

"You're kidding," I said in shock.

"I wish. But that's the only place in Tokyo where Gore

won't dare look for you. Dorothy called ahead and set it up."

"Ah. I didn't get the impression that she and Jaize were such… good friends?"

"They aren't. But they're neighbors. Shibuya borders Roppongi in the south. And they've got a kind of a mutual benefit agreement. That's how come Aleksey gets to work at Exiles. Just like in nature, right? The wolf eats the meat and the coyote gets the bones."

"But which is which?"

"OK, so that was a bad example. The point is, they cooperate on their mutual goals. Such as keeping Gore off of their backs. Dorothy is all like, 'Look how well we work together. All you gotta do is have some faith in people.'" Ruth wrinkled her nose. "But the way I see it? No one else has any faith in Jaize. The royals and the old nobility won't give him the time of day. And just *mayyybe* those old bloodsuckers are right."

I pursed my lips noncommittally. We were passing the long, ivied wall of Aoyama Gakuin on the other side of the street. Earlier in the day, the campus might have been a haven for me. Now Turner Hall would be locked, everyone gone home but for security guards and a few library rats. At night, the whole city belonged to the vampires, I thought.

Ruth's jaw set harder. "What I'm saying is, I think Dorothy could have made a bad call on this one. I mean, by the fact that she's calling in a favor to get Jaize to protect you, she's basically told Jaize that you're worth protecting. Do you follow my logic? So we're going there because we don't have any choice, but we might have to end up protecting *ourselves*."

"So what if we were to just take off somewhere and lie low until the fun is over? I've got some money –"

"If you want to try it, fine. But then I'd have to try and stop you. And then we'd find out if you have the balls to shoot me for real." Her lips stretched in a mirthless smile. "Don't forget I have to live in this city. At least as long as Aleks is still in his power."

She walked on ahead of me.

Depressed, I reflected that she would allow herself to be relatively friendly as long as I was meekly accepting her leadership, but the minute I expressed any initiative, she reverted to hostility. Did she even realize that her every action was governed by fear, or did her simmering anger give her the illusion that she was in control?

Then again, in her world, it probably made sense to trust no one. I was rapidly coming to that conclusion myself.

And yet… Dorothy was looking out for me. Dorothy had taken steps to ensure my safety. If I rejected her plan because I thought I knew better, I'd be even more stupid and ungrateful than Ruth.

I bumped into Ruth before I knew she'd stopped. She backed up, pressing me into the shelter of the wall that bordered a deep, paved plaza. The gigantic modern sculpture behind us marked the University of the United Nations. The fiery nimbus of Shibuya's neon silhouetted the buildings ahead. "Other side of the street," Ruth muttered. "No, down there."She pointed. "That's a *kenin*."

A skinny little guy in a baggy t-shirt and jeans. His gait gave him away, once I'd spotted him. He seemed to wander along, zigzagging across the straight vectors of the other pedestrians, head swivelling as if he were sniffing the air. "He moves more like a cat than a person," I whispered.

"And he'd kill you like a cat, too. How'd you like to have that play with you for a few days before you die?"

The *kenin* was less than two blocks away on the other side of the street, his aimless-looking progress deceptively fast.

"He won't spot us over here," I said. "And even if he does, look at all these people. He can't do anything to us in a public place —"

"Wanna bet?"

"Oh my God, look," I gasped. "There's another of them. On our side of the street."

Ruth cursed. "So that's their plan. Going to go through

the whole area like a finetooth comb."

"What do we do?"

"Cover your hair." She pulled up her hood. I had no way to cover my own head. Ruth shoved me to her other side, away from the *kenin*. We waited for the walklight to turn green, then moved into the crosswalk. The *kenin* was less than a block off. I felt horribly exposed. "Don't look," Ruth muttered. "Hasn't seen us. Don't hurry! We're gonna go straight down this cross street. Just keep walking."

In my peripheral vision, as we crossed thirty meters in front of the *kenin*, I saw him break stride, the sharp-planed face turning towards us, and I even retained an impression of strangely pale eyes – but then we were past. We walked briskly down the hill towards Shibuya, losing ourselves in the foot traffic.

"Still want to go off on your own?" Ruth said. When I didn't answer, she pressed her point home. "The only reason he didn't spot you? He was looking for *one* white girl. Not *two*. If you'd have been on your own, you'd be dead. They can smell fear, you know. Like sharks…"

"Ruth," I said, my voice admirably steady, "my idea was for *both* of us to hide out somewhere. But I see now that was a dumb suggestion. You enjoy this way too much."

Having circled out of our way, we reached Shibuya via the stretch of Meiji-dori that led to Ebisu. Ruth threaded us through the maze of pedestrian flyovers outside the station, all jigsawed by construction barriers. We cut through the station itself, crossed the Scramble, and climbed Dogenzaka hill amidst the chaos of cycling neon and touts' cries. Between one block and the next, the sensory assault faded, and we plodded into Jaize's quiet neighborhood.

The streetlights glowed misty white, but the trees limited their reach, allowing the residents to slumber in peace – if they could sleep through the cicadas that droned in their gardens. The noise drowned out even the sound of Ruth's and my footsteps. Humidity thickened the night air. I wiped sweat off my face.

Jaize's bubble-roofed garage was empty, and the concertina gate was shut, a red light glowing on its lock. Within, the house loomed blank, dark.

"I don't fucking believe this," Ruth said.

She shook the gate, yelling in Japanese for someone to come and let us in. It seemed impossible that her voice should penetrate the racket of the cicadas, let alone the house itself. But a lamp went on over the front door, and it swung open to reveal Aleksey's slight figure.

"Ruth?"

"God! Aleks! Come and let us in before I have to fight off the entire Court by myself out here." As he approached, Ruth whirled, feinting at the darkness. I jumped in fright. Both of them laughed at me. But when Aleksey had opened the gate and relocked it behind us with a remote, Ruth made an little sound of distress and dropped her head against his shoulder. "What are you doing here?" she muttered, lightly beating her fists on his back. "You're supposed to be at work!"

"I am to stay home tonight, Jaize said, without a word of explanation." Aleksey stroked the folds of sweatshirt that draped Ruth's thin back. "I suppose you can tell me what's going on."

She shook her head back and forth against his neck. "If the shit is gonna hit the fan, I don't want you in the way. I thought you'd be at work. You'd have been safe, as long as Clare was *here*. Oh, that doublecrossing psychic faggot, I could fucking kill him."

"Maybe we should get indoors before the aforementioned shit becomes airborne," I said uncomfortably.

Pulling away from Aleksey, Ruth shot me a look of hatred. "What's it to you? This just proves that Jaize is already turning squirrelly on us. He kept Aleks home tonight as insurance that Dorothy wouldn't try to doublecross *him* by siccing Gore onto him. He knows Gore would be happy for any excuse to call him out, so he's using Aleks as extra leverage to make sure that Dorothy keeps her end of the bargain—"

"Whoa," I interrupted. "How about running that by me again, slowly?"

Ruth stomped towards the house. "Whatever," she threw over her shoulder. *"You* don't care!"

I grimaced at Aleksey, meeting the pale eyes in the sensitive, gaunt face. "I *do* care," I mumbled. More than I'd known, I cared about Aleksey, who seemed to have got the sharp end of life since the day he was born, but endured it with stoic grace. I cared about Ruth, who made herself so vulnerable by wearing her heart on her sleeve. I cared about the fragile tenderness of their feelings for each other.

But in all honesty, I thought that neither Jaize nor Dorothy cared about Aleksey very much. Ruth was letting her emotions blind her on that one. Talented pianists weren't *that* rare.

In response to the question in Aleksey's eyes, I said awkwardly, "It would seem that Gorozaemon Edonokami is trying to kidnap me. That's why I'm here. I'm very sorry that you appear to have been dragged into it."

"Gore? Ah, that explains it," Aleksey said. We followed Ruth towards the house. "For a long time he's been trying to provoke Dorothy into a fight. He's lacked only a, what is the word—"

"A pretext?"

"No. Ah, a *bait*, that's it. He intends to trap her into destroying herself. I've been predicting this for months. He can't—" Aleksey interrupted himself as the light fell on my face. *"Mat!"* He stared at me. "Have they attacked you already? Are those stains of blood?"

"Sort of and yes. But what actually happened was..."

"Yes? You're hurt?" He led me towards the stairs.

"Where *is* he? Where is everyone?" All I could hear was the cicadas, so loud that they might have been in the house with us.

"Jaize? Some party." Aleksey shrugged.

"So we're all alone. How reassuring."

Aleksey's upper lip quirked. "Disappointed?"

"Not at all," I said. "Just wondering if we really are safe from Gore here."

"Nowhere is completely safe from Gore. He's a monster."

"Ye-es. But actually, Gore didn't do this to me," I said as we went up the stairs. Aleksey looked back at me, but was too short of breath to respond. We climbed the third, narrow flight into the attic, where a small lamp glimmered between the stacks of boxes. Ruth sat crosslegged on Aleksey's futon.

"Alley alley, home free," she said with a twisted smile.

"Now all we have to do is pray," Aleksey agreed.

Their laughter gave me an insight: in a sense, they *enjoyed* their dread of the vampire court. They thought they knew what evil looked like and where it lived. They were complacent in their "knowledge"… and by God, I was going to disturb them.

"Let me tell you what I did today," I said. "I went to meet with my colleagues from the university. I thought – well, never mind what I thought—"

"I can guess," Ruth said. "You thought they'd stand by you. But they turned out to be wimps. What were you expecting? When you went to work in *vamukura,* you left behind everything they know. This shit isn't in any books."

"Maybe not," I said tartly. "But plenty of other stuff is. They're experimenting with black magic."

Ruth let out a cry. Aleksey backed up until his head hit the steeply pitched roof. "Hush! I don't want to hear any more about this."

I looked slowly from one of them to the other, not entirely displeased. "Yeah, I was freaked out, too. Of course, I don't think they're getting anywhere with it, and they probably never will. How much can you hope to understand, when you're getting it all out of books? But—"

"Plenty," Aleksey said. Gabbling under his breath in Russian, he crossed himself. *Superstitious,* I thought, conscious of the irony: I used to wear a cross myself, but too many of my vampire interview subjects had complained. "There are books that, that have evil words, I mean spells."

His English was more broken than usual. "I see. Have seen."

"That's enough," Ruth exclaimed. She floundered to her feet, hooked his arm over her shoulders, and lowered him onto the futon. She rummaged in the minifridge. "Sure, there's books of spells," she said over her shoulder. "Just like there's books that tell you how to get rich in ten easy steps. It's all a bunch of hoodoo. Basically, what we have here is a couple of college students talking out of their asses, and this dumb bitch believed them."

I flushed. "Shall I tell you what happened to me?" The kudzu had come alive in my hands and tried to kill me. "I – I – it – "

"Her Japanese is crap. She probably didn't understand what they were talking about."

"Excuse *me*," I said. "I may not have your skill at flirtatious banter, but I do have a certain competency. I also have some background in this stuff. Black magic is fairly accessible, as it happens. Grimoires – your 'books of spells,' Aleksey – aren't that hard to get hold of. You can even find them on the internet. The rituals tend to be unpleasant; they often involve sacrifices, which is the main reason most practioners of magic refuse to admit that black magic even exists. But it does, and there is a certain amount of evidence that it works." I was breathing hard, fighting memories of my ill-fated months in Ireland.

"Back in Russia," Aleksey said loudly. "There were stories. Even in the Kremlin! The system is rotten and so they prop it up with these filthy practices. That's what some people say." Ruth handed him a glass into which she'd poured two inches from an Evian bottle. He glugged it back. "How else to explain why we are still not free?"

I said, "You left Russia because you were in trouble…"

"Yes. But sometimes I think it was a waste of time to run. Because it's easier there. In Russia, yes, it's very easy to die." He hunched over his glass, nursing it like an old man.

"You're not dying," I said stupidly, as if it were a protest against the deep lines on his young face, the greyish cast of his skin, the horrible boniness of his wrists and elbows. Even as I spoke, I understood at last that Aleksey was very sick.

He leaned back against the wall beneath the window, balancing his glass on his belt buckle. "I'm not dying. Yet."

"Jaize won't let him die," Ruth said harshly. "Not as long as he needs him. Or until he finds a replacement."

Aleksey gave a tired smile, as if he wasn't so sure of that.

"What are you to him?" I said bluntly, dreading the answer.

"Oh, nothing. I'm nothing to him. Just a shadow, a noise in the dark... nothing!"

Ruth said, "Have you heard the expression *mortal toy?*" Watching my face, she nodded. "Well, for a psychic vampire, that means something a bit different. It's all to do with *qi*... Yeah, now you're getting the picture."

I rubbed the bridge of my nose. "I thought vampires were supposed to cherish their mortal toys. Protect them. Not..."

"That's the etiquette. Which Jaize doesn't give a shit for."

Aleksey said, "I'm nothing. I'm just the pianist at Exiles." He hummed a snatch of melody.

I said, "Couldn't Dorothy help you? To... to get away from him?"

"She does help me. She gives me a job where I can play the piano. And when I am too sick to show up, she telephones Jaize and tells him to go easy on me. Oh yes, she is very helpful."

"It's just a little power game between them," Ruth said bitterly.

"I'm serious. Oh, maybe this is part of his strategy, to keep me happy. But Exiles is my – my haven; it's a place of normal life. Here, everything is evil. I'm surrounded by Jaize's evil. It's inside me. This," Aleksey gestured around the attic, "this is what it is to be the mortal toy of Jaize 3000. Perhaps it looks glamorous from the outside. But do you know what's in these boxes? His old clothes and things. I'm hidden up here with his *junk*, waiting for him to need me

166

again!"

Disgust and pity rolled over me in slow waves. I grabbed the Evian bottle that Ruth had set down, drank from it, and choked. It wasn't water. It was neat vodka. My splutters should have amused Ruth, but neither she nor Aleksey so much as smiled. I took another drink, pacing myself this time.

"I don't boast," Aleksey said. "But I used to be talented. I could have been great, if I didn't lose my place at the conservatoire in Moscow. And now – look at this body. Look at these hands." He held them out. "They shake," he said with fury. "He's killing me, one day at a time. And I can't say no to him."

I'd seldom heard a more depressing claim. I would have liked to argue with Aleksey, but I hadn't meant to start an argument in the first place. OK, so maybe I *had,* but that was before I understood what I was up against.

Aleksey and Ruth leaned shoulder to shoulder, swapping the Evian bottle back and forth. I spiked my bottle of green tea and tasted the mixture. Not bad, although it could have been sweeter. I was starting to get a feeling of unreality. The house was too quiet. Were Gore's vampires massing outside right now, preparing to storm the gate? Would the Marquis risk Jaize's ire to get hold of me? I almost wished he *would.*

But with his psychic abilities, Jaize would be a formidable foe. So why would Gore want to pick a fight with *Dorothy?* Surely Jaize posed a greater threat to the Court?

With that thought, a new hypothesis presented itself: I'd been deliberately situated here to provide Gore with a pretext for attacking Jaize. And since it was Dorothy who'd sent me here, she must have colluded in the plan. In fact, she might have *originated* it, reckoning that she could thus achieve the elimination of her dangerous neighbor at no cost to herself – or at the relatively low cost of my, Ruth's, and Aleksey's lives. *Had she sacrificed us like pawns?*

I rolled my shoulders, glad of the pressure of my holster.

167

But the Glock was cold comfort when I had no one to aim it at. And were we to sit here on our asses, stupidly waiting to die?

"Guys," I said. They both looked at me, faces pale and bleak. "Guys, I don't like this. It's too quiet. Let's get the hell out of here while we still can."

"We have to stay here until Dorothy calls," Ruth began. But with no further prompting, Aleksey jumped to his feet.

"An excellent idea!" Stumbling slightly, he gathered loose pages of sheet music off the floor, jammed them into a binder, and put that in the softshell briefcase I'd seen him carry to work. He snapped his fingers and added the Evian bottle of vodka. "She's right, Ruth! *He's* not here; you are. I'll never again have another opportunity like this. And even if I do, I may not have the strength to take it." He sent a last look around the room, then stooped to the tiny mirror that stood on top of the minifridge. He spat on a finger and slicked his fringe sideways. Turning to me, he said in a creditable cowboy accent, "Let's blow this two-bit whorehouse, pardner."

I giggled. Ruth didn't. "You can't," she said, getting to her feet. "You mustn't."

"Ruth—" Suddenly serious, Aleksey put out his hand to her. "I'd rather die than go on living like this. I know I've said this before, but this time I mean it. If you love me…"

"I don't want to lose you," she muttered, clutching his hand to her cheek. Her eyes glittered with tears.

"We'd better hurry," I said.

"The security system," Ruth protested.

Aleksey grinned and held up the remote to the front gate.

Footsteps pounded sharply on the stairs. Ruth and Aleksey backed up. A black leather glove slapped onto the floor at the edge of the hatch, and a tiger-lily head shot up into the attic.

And all I could do was stare, not so much attracted as simply intimidated by Jaize 3000's sheer beauty.

Biker leathers hugged his graceful limbs, black with scarlet flashes. In the open collar of his jacket, his logo medallion winked over a tight black t-shirt. His face glowed, and his wide mouth curled in a delighted grin. "Clare! Great to see you again. I gotta head back out; it's my night to volunteer. Can't let the guys down. But you hang out. Make yourself at home. When I get back, we're going to talk, just the two of us, OK?"

I ducked my head, my heart in my throat.

The house was no longer quiet. Downstairs, sharp male exclamations collided with the noise of opening and closing doors. Jaize turned to Aleksey. "You're on," he said quietly. "Sorry, Aleks. It's showtime."

"What's happened?" Ruth said.

"No one's sure," Jaize said, still gazing at Aleksey. "But we're under attack. Patrol ambushed down south. We've got people hurt, Aleks. People bleeding. Dying. I had to leave an important shindig: drop everything and go. Whoever they are, they won't get away with this."

"No." It cost Aleksey an obvious effort to force the words out. "Take care of it without me. I'm not going."

Jaize's face hardened. His voice took on an aggrieved whine. "Oh, get over yourself, man! Do you think I *like* having to defend everything I built up like this, every fucking night? But that's the vampire way. If we let them get away with this, they'll be back for more. So we slap them the fuck *down*, right? You and me. Come on."

Aleksey wilted visibly. "No," he said again, but it was barely audible. Mechanically, he moved towards Jaize.

"There you are," Jaize said softly. He took Aleksey's hand and led him towards the stairs.

"Hey, boss!" Scott shouted from downstairs. "Aleks! Down south! We have another report of hostile activity! C'mon, gentlemen, let's hustle!"

Aleksey twisted against Jaize's grip for a moment. He looked from me to Jaize. Then they vanished through the hatch in the floor.

Ruth dropped onto the futon. "Goddammit," she said emptily.

Downstairs, Scott shouted at Aleksey, and there were more voices I didn't know. The front door slammed. Out in the street, motorbike engines revved and then faded away. The drone of the cicadas flooded back into the silence.

"Guess it's bad," Ruth said flatly. "He always has Aleks by his side when he's gonna work some heavy mojo with his *qi* craft. He uses him like a *battery*, is what it is. And if need be, he'll drain him flat."

"Well, come on," I said. "Let's go after them."

She looked at her hands for a minute, flexing her battered knuckles. Then she stood up. "All right."

I grabbed Aleksey's briefcase on our way out of the room. It was awkward to carry, and I was still trying to stuff it into my own knapsack when we reached the first floor.

A female voice called out, "Hey, Ruth. You're supposed to wait here with me."

"Jaize didn't say anything about that," Ruth answered, walking into the nearest doorway.

I followed her. A dark living-room with a piano; a girl sprawling immobile in an armchair. It took my eyes a minute to make sense of the fluttering glimpses of paleness down her torso; then I saw a bare breast. Her strappy silk camisole had been ripped down the middle and hung from one shoulder. Blood crusted the pulpy puncture area on the side of her throat. I belatedly recognized Jaize's PA.

"So the boss had time for a quickie, huh?" Ruth said. "Jeez, Naomi. Put some clothes on."

"I remember you," Naomi greeted me. "Yurika's replacement."

I swallowed. "Naomi, do you… Uh, sexual harassment is against the law, you know. You don't have to put up with it."

Ruth laughed. "It's in her job description. She *likes* it. Oh, she'd do aaaanything for Jaize. But he'll kick her to the curb when he's through with her, too. How long have you been working for him, Naomi-chan? Three, four years? Shit, she's so spacey right now she doesn't even remember."

Naomi clutched the arms of her chair. "I'm the best personal assistant he's ever had. He promised me he'd never — "

"And you believe him?" Ruth guffawed. "All right, if you're such a good assistant, you can assist us. Go and fix us a bite to eat. A burger. A sandwich. Shit, whatever you've got in the fridge." She flopped onto the sofa and stared expectantly at Naomi.

Naomi shook her head. "No. You'd just sneak off while I was busy. You're supposed to *wait* here."

"Well, shit," Ruth said, rising. "I guess you saw right through me." She pounced on Naomi and swept her off the sofa into a bear hug. While Naomi's arms flailed uselessly, Ruth jammed her right thumb and forefinger under the Japanese girl's jaw. Naomi bucked, making a strangled noise through her teeth. Ruth staggered backwards. They collided with one of the floor lamps. I rushed to catch it. Ruth counted under her breath. "Ten and one and two…"

Naomi went limp, her eyes fluttering closed. Ruth laid her none too gently on the floor. Then she shook her head. "Help me move her."

I took Naomi's shoulders, satisfying myself that she wasn't dead. We laid her on the sofa. Naked to the waist, with the toes of her fashionable sandals pointing at angles, she looked like some appalling piece of performance art.

"I should just kill her," Ruth said. "Put her out of her misery."

I touched her arm. "Come on."

But when we pushed the front door open, the air split into arcs of piercing noise.

Ruth threw her weight on the gate.

We ran.

The alarm chased us through the hot night, reinforced by the whoop of a police siren. The noise had barely faded behind us when I developed a stitch in my side. I stumbled to a walk and sucked in huge gulps of air. Ahead of me, Ruth halted. When I could speak, I said, "I think you just saved my life. Again."

"I don't give a damn about your motherfucking life. I

just want to save Aleks. God! He can be so *stupid...* He gets drunk and thinks he can just walk away, when he can't even say no to him..."

"I guess that means we have to say no *for* him," I said. "But first we have to find him."

Ruth pulled herself together. "That won't be hard. He said *down south.* There's only one place they're likely to be."

According to Ruth, Jaize 3000's "clave" encompassed about two-thirds of what had once been the Shibuya-Harajuku clave. It sprawled across the municipal ward of Shibuya and thrust a leg into Minato ward, the district that contained Roppongi. Ruth told me that a group called *Ningen-no-Heiwakai,* or the Human League for Peace, patrolled its boundaries nightly. These were Jaize's "volunteers." They sounded like the groups of "concerned citizens" who patrolled many towns in America to keep the "bloodsuckers" off their streets – with a twist: the group had largely been taken over by Jaize's followers from the Shoto karate school.

They usually concentrated their efforts in the north: "Those Harajuku vamps are always picking fights," Ruth said softly in English, with one eye on the back of our taxi driver's head. But tonight's attack had come from an unexpected direction... from Roppongi. So that was the way we went.

Neither of us mentioned that it was also the most dangerous direction we could go.

We'd almost reached Nishi-Azabu, the western terminus of Dorothy's turf, when Ruth exclaimed, "Here we are." She gestured for me to pay.

To the south, the neon of Roppongi lit the packed skyline. We stood on the curb, looking across the street at a dank, mature forest.

"Aoyama Reien," Ruth said.

"A graveyard."

"Sure. Where else would you come looking for vampires?" She laughed. I scurried after her across the street.

"Naw, but a lot of *zako* stay in here, so Jaize's people patrol it... looking for trouble. And tonight, I guess they found it.." She pointed down the street. I saw a row of brawny motor-bikes parked single file along the curb. "The League is so full of shit," Ruth said, smiling.

I felt less sanguine, but I followed her between a pair of stone bollards that blocked an opening in the wall. Trees leaned over a narrow asphalt path, untamed and limby. The only light was the dim luminosity that filtered out of the city sky. I said, "*Zako?*"

"Homeless vamps that don't belong to any household. Stay on your guard. Anyone that comes in here at night is liable to get chomped."

Headstones towered amidst the trees, receding in more or less straight rows, their raised plinths surrounded by knee-height railings. Devoid of whimsical decorations, the stones were flanked by shelves for offerings and niches that held clusters of wooden laths incised with Buddhist death names. Our footsteps rustled on leaves and broken twigs. I smelled the untouched accumulation of humus.

Ruth stopped dead. She put a finger to her lips, then stepped off the path. I followed her, keeping to the shadows beneath the trees.

All in a split second, I heard something charging straight at me, and then a human figure barreled past, running flat out. I swallowed a scream. In other parts of the graveyard, people were running in different directions. A blast of wind roared through the trees, its trailing edge tossing the leaves above my head. But all I could do was huddle against the trunk, shaking. The man who'd passed me, close enough to touch, had had a long white face, prominent fangs in a leering mouth, blood trickling down his chin...

Another noise drew my attention to Ruth. She was moaning – no, giggling helplessly. "A Dracula mask! Moth-erfucker was wearing a *Dracula mask!* Damn smart for a *zako*," she gasped, then drew a deep breath. "Help! Heeelllp!" she shrieked in Japanese. "It's a vampire! Eeeek! It went that

173

way!"

Getting the idea, I added my screams to hers. Then, silently, we zigzagged between the rows of graves, circling around in the direction the guy in the Halloween mask had come from.

"Get back!" a man yelled in Japanese. "Bloodsucking scum!"

I flinched into the shadow of the last headstone. On the far side of the next path, a grave with a particularly grand obelisk stood on its own plot beneath a spreading tree. Within the railing of the plinth, a bulky man in black leather straddled another man who sprawled face-down – a casualty. Soon, they would both be casualties. A dozen scruffy, skinny people clustered around the grave, and as I watched, they rushed the man. He sent two of them spinning back with impossibly fast punches, but several others pounced on his back. He collapsed to his hands and knees, still sheltering his fallen comrade. "Vamp scum!" he bawled.

"I guess those are the *zako*," I whispered to Ruth.

"That's Aleksey," Ruth said.

Between the flickering bodies of the *zako*, I got a second look at the man who lay face down, in his black leather jacket – borrowed, too big – and yelped in horror.

Ruth exploded across the path. Empty-handed, she sailed into the *zako* with a *qi-ai* yell that momentarily turned every head. Her first kick crunched into a *zako* face. The Human League vigilante surged to his knees, hands forming a V at his chest, as if he was about to throw a ball. He pushed his hands sharply outward, and the heads of two *zako* cracked together.

I moved.

Most of the *zako* had crowded around Ruth on one side of the grave's stepped plinth. I leapt onto the other side of the plinth. As I scrambled over the railing, hands snatched at me. I caught them blindly in my own and dropped flat, pulling my assailant face down onto the railing. Something crunched, and the hands spasmed violently, releasing me.

Afraid to look around, I crawled across the grave, behind the vigilante, and yanked Aleksey upright. He was able to stand with my help, although when I asked him, "Where's Jaize?" he only jerked his chin. Broken branches scattered the grass to that side of the grave, and I could actually see the trail of destruction continuing on the other side of the path.

So, we'd go the other way. I manhandled Aleksey over the railings and dragged him to the path, fumbling the Glock out of my pocket en route. I hit out at the *zako* with its barrel. But there were too many of them. They were abandoning Ruth now, streaming towards me and Aleksey. They knew easy prey when they smelled it. They knew all about the scruples that kept me from shooting them. God damn their young faces, their angry, deprived, heartbreakingly *young* faces, damn it all—

Back on the grave, the vigilante stretched out a hand and helped Ruth up onto the plinth. They swayed face to face for a moment. I didn't see what happened, but I saw the vigilante crash down like a black leather punching bag. Ruth jumped up. "Hey, kids!" she hooted. "Chow's up! Lotta blood in this one!"

The *zako* turned. They fell on the vigilante like starving cats.

Overhead, crows circled, waiting for them to be done.

Ruth and I ran, half-steadying and half-supporting Aleksey. Once, we almost ran straight into a pair of *zako* feeding on another fallen vigilante. One of them sprang after us and chased us a few paces before returning to his meal. The Human League for Peace was a lost cause, I thought. They obviously had some martial arts-inspired ethos of unarmed combat, and that was just suicidal. Even with the help of Jaize's *qi* craft, humans couldn't compete against this primal compulsion… this *hunger*. Our only hope would be to escalate the conflict and kill them all.

Ahead, lights glowed through the trees. We burst onto the street and kept running straight into the momentarily stalled traffic, zigzagging between the red-hot flanks of trucks. Shocked faces blinked from car windows. My lungs burned, my legs ached, Aleksey was getting heavier and heavier, and Ruth and I kept getting out of step. The traffic started to move again. We stumbled up onto the sidewalk. Like robots, we limped on for a while, and then Aleksey sagged between us, his knees giving way.

The passersby streamed around us. Ruth cajoled Aleksey to keep going just a little further.

The passersby?

And the flyer girls, the touts and the scouts, the posses of American servicemen and the prowling gangs of vampires.

We'd got away. By dashing straight into Roppongi.

Chapter 10.

T he vampire pinned Ruth against the wall of the alley. "Looking good enough to eat," he lisped, and jerked the zipper of her hoodie down, exposing her throat.

"Hey, did you hear the one about the vampire who took a cab to New Jersey?" Ruth said. I hoped I was the only one who could hear the tremor in her voice. "He said, 'Great Neck.' Get it? Shit, humor never translates."

"Actually, I prefer a softer bite." The vampire barked a command, and one of the other vampires knelt to raise the hem of Ruth's dress. She tried to kick him. He pinned her dress up with one hand and pulled her panties down with the other. Now I knew for sure that she wasn't a natural blonde. The leader of the gang pinched her upper thigh. "Tender." He made a sucking sound. A drop of saliva fell from his mouth to stain the front of Ruth's dress. "If the *kami* hadn't already claimed you, I'd sink my fangs into this."

He had short hair gelled into spikes, and he wore a sort of B-boy uniform of baggy jeans and an oversized Bathing Ape t-shirt. His face contrived to look cruel and yet wounded, as if he'd had some huge horrible surprise in the past that he'd never recovered from. His companions, male and female, sported more designer gear than an outlet mall, but their eyes were as empty as the *zakos'*. They'd surrounded us and hustled us off the street into a dark alley where only a couple of crows, pecking at a puddle of vomit, would witness our fate.

"Do we have to give her to the *kami*?" The smallest vampire spoke up. "Does he want her for himself? Or does he just want her dead?"

God! I went rigid as the truth dawned on me. They thought it was *Ruth* that Gore was looking for!

I could understand their mistake. A fragile-looking blonde in a short dress with her hair pinned up, Ruth fit my description, based on the way I'd looked last night. By contrast, at this point I looked like something the cat dragged in. But I couldn't let their mistake stand. "It's me," I piped up from my position on the ground. "It's me you want. Let her go."

The vampires ignored me. Muttering incomprehensible slang at each other, they closed in around Ruth – all except the one who'd taken my gun, who stood over me and Aleksey. He held the Glock at his side, looking comfortable with it.

Aleksey stirred in my lap, but didn't open his eyes. I laid the back of my hand against his cheek. Clammy, colder than the air.

The knot of vampires around Ruth exploded outwards. "Clare!" she screamed. I bumped Aleksey off my lap and scrambled to my feet. "Get Aleks out of here!"

The thug who'd pinned her reeled backwards, clutching his face. Blood gushed from between his fingers. My guard turned, distracted for a moment. That was all I needed, and I pounced on him. He was fast, but I was desperate. I twisted his wrist, yanked the Glock out of his hands, and fired into the air. The shot echoed like an explosion in the narrow alley. Ruth delivered a kick to a vampire gut. Her hair flew loose and blood sprinkled from her nose. "Shoot the motherfuckers," she croaked. "Blow them away!"

Dry sobs tore from my throat as I found the vampire furthest from Ruth, aimed, and fired. My target jerked and slumped. His associates caught him. Spitting threats, they retreated down the alley. I stared after them in a daze.

"I could use some fucking help here!" Ruth was trying to pick Aleksey up.

As I stuffed the Glock into its holster, my hands were shaking badly. *I'd shot him.* Self-defense. *He was only a vampire.*

We lugged Aleksey back to the street. The sound of gunshots had raised no panic among the titivated women and pimped-out guys passing by. I didn't want to think about what that said about Roppongi.

Twenty meters from the mouth of the alley, we settled Aleksey against a wall, half-sitting on a lightbox sign that glowed with pictures of naked girls.

"I thought he bit you," I gasped. "Did you catch him off guard?"

"Took his fucking eye out." Ruth showed me a long silver pin lodged in the breast of her hoodie. Rhinestones dangled off the blunt end; blood darkened the sharp end. It was the pin she'd had in her hair, and now I knew how she'd felled the vigilante back in the cemetery. "But if it was me with the gun, not one single one of those fuckers would have walked away from there."

"Sorry," I said, adjusting Aleksey's weight. His breathing was slow and stertorous.

"We need to move him. They're going to be back. We can't stay here. So—"

"Ruth, I don't know what's wrong with him, but he needs to be in hospital."

"Hospital won't help him. He's... he's *out*. I've seen this before. Jaize has drained him flat. He'll come back eventually, but he's going to be like this for a while, like a day or so. We need somewhere..." She wiped her still-bleeding nose with the sleeve of her hoodie, then drew in a breath. "Call your friends."

"My friends?"

"Your friends from the university that you were bragging about."

"My..." I gaped at her.

"Yeah. The black magicians."

"Are you kidding? They tried to kill me." But as I spoke, I remembered my gun flying out of that window. Keita, or someone, had given it back to me, and that gesture had ended up saving our lives. "Ruth, they're dabbling in some seriously messed-up shit. They're scared of anyone finding out."

"Just like Jaize. He doesn't like to leave witnesses, either. But I guess he'll have to take a number, because the *kenin* are going to get here any minute."

"I thought those were *kenin*!"

"Them? *Zako*. The difference between them and those kids in the cemetery is about two paychecks."

I stared distractedly at the crows that had followed us out of the alley and were now stalking around in the gutter, unafraid of the cars whose wind ruffled their feathers.

"Listen, I know you don't trust them. I wouldn't either, if I had my choice. But I don't know if you ever heard this saying," Ruth went on. "The enemy of my enemy is my friend."

Looking at her, I knew she was thinking of Dorothy, too. We were only a few blocks from Exiles, but it might as well have been a hundred miles. And for us to be safe, it would have to be a thousand.

"You can get in touch with them, can't you? Call them," Ruth persisted, and now I could hear the edge of panic in her voice. "Or do you want to just sit here until the *kenin* come?"

Slumped between us, Aleksey moaned. His deathly pale face decided me. I transferred his weight to Ruth's shoulder, stood up, and moved towards the gutter. The crows cocked their heads and stared at me.

A rusty blue Subaru crunched to a halt, wafting the crows into the air. The passenger door flew open. "Get in the car!" Keita brushed past me.

"Not without my friends," I said blankly. Keita didn't seem to need me to identify them for him. He charged straight towards them and helped Ruth lug Aleksey back to the car.

"I told you to stay away from Jaize," he said furiously when we'd all piled in. Politik yanked back on the gearshift, and we hurtled through Roppongi Crossing at roughly the speed of sound. My two colleagues might drive very different vehicles, but they had a similar style: suicidal. Keita twisted around in the passenger seat. "So what's the story? Did Yurika pass you along to him? Did you run straight to him to report on us?" He grinned, his eyes wide and glinting. "That's what Politik thinks." He banged Politik on the shoulder. "He was like, what the fuck were you thinking? She'll run straight to Jaize and give us away."

"Please," I said, my voice steady. "Give me some credit. I just *escaped* from Jaize's, uh, decidedly *ambiguous* protection. "

"See? I told you so," Keita exclaimed, reversing himself without a blink. Why was he acting so strangely? "I'm the one that talked to her, dude. And if she was lying, she's the best liar I have ever encountered in my life. That's what I said, isn't it?"

"That's right," Politik answered. "That's what you said."

"Besides, when you wasted one of Jaize's precious *qi* warriors in Aoyama Reien – yeah, that indicated pretty conclusively that you're not on his side." Keita laughed loudly. "Politik, get off this street. They're checking the traffic at the next light."

"Gotcha." Politik swung the Subaru into a tiny lane.

"How did you know where we were, anyway?" Ruth said.

"Magic," Keita said, and uttered another loud laugh.

Ruth looked impressed. She steadied Aleksey's upper body on our laps. "Jaize is scared of magicians," she said. "According to Scott. Because he can't leech onto them. That's why I thought Clare might be —"

Politik said, "Oh. Kay."

"Pure speculation!" Keita shouted, hanging onto the frame of the window as we zipped past the entrances of bars, through blasts of heavy music. "We don't know anything about Jaize, really. But he doesn't know anything about us, either! And we want to keep it that way."

"I hear that." One of Ruth's rare grins spread across her face, her bloody nose making it look especially fierce. "Black magic? I could get used to this shit. Have you ever tried beating the stock market? What about currency trading?"

The Subaru popped out onto Roppongi-dori and turned right, careening down the long dark slope towards Akasaka. I thought the silence of Keita and Politik boded no good, and

I was right.

"You don't know what you're talking about," Keita said without turning around. His strange jitteriness had gone, and he spoke in the cold, grumpy tone I knew. "You don't even belong in this country. I've saved your life twice today, and that's enough." OK, so he was talking to me. "We're taking you to the American embassy. They'll repatriate all three of you... We'll cover your ass with Kamikawa-sensei," he added. "Don't worry, we'll think of something good."

"Oh no, you don't," Ruth said. She reached over the seatback and grabbed Keita's chin. He wrenched violently away. "See this guy here? He's Russian. He's a defector. And you know what American policy on Russian defectors is? No more political asylum, because they might be terrorists. They'd sling him out on the street —"

I interrupted her sharply. "Guys, just take a look at him. He's dying."

In the brief silence that followed, Aleksey drew a single ragged breath.

"I'll do whatever you want me to," I said. "I'll go back to America. I won't tell anyone that you're the second coming of Wilfred Hauptmann. I'll keep my mouth shut about everything. But don't let him die. His name is Aleksey. Aleksey —"

He was dying in my lap, and I didn't even know his last name.

Politik carried Aleksey up the stairs of their building and laid him gently on the living-room floor. Ruth knelt and stroked his hair. Keita just watched. Politik vanished into the depths of the apartment.

I clenched my fists, staring at Aleksey's pale face. "I think what we have here is massive *qi* loss," I said in a monotone. "Aleksey is Jaize 3000's mortal toy. Jaize has been using him like a sort of... a sort of *portable battery* for years, and now he's drained him flat."

"He'll get over it soon," Ruth insisted. "He just needs to

lie quiet—" but she no longer sounded as if she believed it.

Keita, leaning against the jamb of the kitchen door, shifted to let Politik back into the room. The younger man carried an armful of flowered velour blankets. I helped him tuck them around Aleksey. The room was hot, even with a breeze blowing through from the kitchen. I'd personally have been more comfortable with fewer clothes on. But Aleksey's skin was clammy, his lips bluish. All the way back here, he'd seemed to grow colder to the touch. Whatever else was wrong with him, he was presenting the symptoms of shock, and the extent of our collective knowledge about shock was that you should wrap the victim up warmly. Years studying the paranormal, and I'd never studied elementary first aid. What an asinine oversight.

Politik tucked a pillow under Aleksey's head. His big soft hands cradled Aleksey's shoulders gently. He really did mean well, I thought. It was Keita I'd have to watch out for.

He *had* come to pluck us out of danger, and for that – as well as for giving me my gun back earlier – I owed him the benefit of the doubt. He surely had good intentions on some level. But I couldn't forget that he also had other priorities, and Aleksey's life might mean nothing to him.

"Stop that," he said. "I need to examine him."

Dropping to his knees on Aleksey's other side, he tossed the blankets back. When he began to lift Aleksey's t-shirt, Ruth snapped, "Leave him alone!"

"Do you want to find out what's wrong with him or not?"

"We *told* you what's wrong—"

"You have a hypothesis. Which I don't necessarily endorse."

I clenched my teeth at the sight of Aleksey's torso, the skin so tightly stretched that the overhead light cast shadows between his ribs. Keita raised the t-shirt to his armpits, then rolled him onto his front with Politik's help. After one glance, they rolled him back again, raised his sleeves to peer at his shoulders, and then started to unbutton his jeans.

"No," Ruth cried, arching her body protectively over

him. "I know what you're looking for. It's – it's down *there,* OK? Now quit messing with him."

"You could have told us that to begin with," Keita said. "Sorry, but we've got to see it."

Ignoring Ruth's protests, they pulled down Aleksey's jeans and then the back of his boxer shorts. High on Aleksey's bony flank, I saw... there was only one word for it... a *brand.* The size of my palm, it formed an intricate but familiar tangle of scars that had faded to pale pink, lumpy in places.

Keita said, "Photograph it. Politik, get the camera."

I said, "What the hell are you doing? Research?"

"As it happens, yes," Keita said. "We have to find out what this is."

"Don't bother. I can tell you. It's the Dracula's Crypt logo."

"I know," Keita snapped. "But that doesn't tell us what it *is.*"

I said, "Jaize wears it as a medallion. Clearly, he uses it as a mark of... ownership. I shouldn't be surprised if it were a common vampiric practise to mark their mortal toys in some way. Are you aware of any such custom?" My mind forged speculative links between Aleksey's brand and the Japanese tradition of *irezumi* – dragons on yakuza backs – the tattoo as the mark of the social outcast... But this was no aesthetic statement. It was just the Lazy Y Ranch gone upscale, and I was just trying to distance myself.

"It would generally be considered vulgar," Keita said. "Oh, you might find them getting a tattoo with the vampire's name. That's more what I was expecting here, to be honest. But this makes sense, of course. He can't remove it."

Ruth surprised me. "If it has to be removed," she said, looking levelly at Keita, "you have my permission."

Keita reared back, scrunching his face up. "That's a bit premature."

"You'd have to cut it out," Politik said. He ran one finger over the brand, then covered Aleksey up again. "Scalpel, graft... but he hasn't got enough spare skin anywhere. Maybe you could just cauterize the whole area. Blank it out."

Ruth gritted her teeth, but she said, "If it's necessary, I know he'd agree."

"We don't know if it's necessary," Keita said. "It might do him more harm than good, and I don't just mean in the medical sense."

"You're stalling," I said. "Tell us the truth."

"I don't *know* the truth!" Keita exclaimed. "I'm guessing, that's all!" Incredibly, he started to laugh. His face turned dark red, and finally he was able to share the joke. "Hey, for all I know, he might just be going through drug withdrawal."

Ruth said quietly, "Aleks isn't a junkie. I know junkies, and if he was on anything, I'd know that, too."

"I was just kidding," Keita said. He shrugged and stood up. "Politik, take his temperature and his pulse. We should have done that straight away. And see if you can get any more useful information out of *her*. Clare, can I talk to you for a minute?"

Full of forebodings, I followed him into the kitchen. He took a bottle of whiskey from the cupboard under the sink and poured a finger into each of two mugs, tossing in a few ice cubes for luck. I thought about telling him that none of the last few hours might have happened if Ruth, Aleksey, and I hadn't been stuck into Aleksey's stash of vodka. But as it so happened, a stiff drink was exactly what I needed right now.

A minute later, I needed it even more.

Leaning against the sink with his back to the windows, Keita said, "Well, you can forget about publishing anything on psychic vampires."

"If you think it crossed my mind to treat Aleksey as a case study, you're even more insensitive than you act," I said furiously.

"Oh, it did. Don't bother lying to me. But that's not the point. I've suspected for a while... but I didn't have any proof... and I still can't say categorically that there are no such things as psychic vampires. But I can say with ninety-nine percent certainty that Jaize 3000 isn't one."

I blinked. "I assume you have an alternate theory?"

"Doesn't amount to a theory. Just a hypothesis. But yeah, I'm fairly sure that mark is a sigil. And if that's what it is, Jaize isn't any kind of über-vampire. He's just a regular, low-level bloodsucker who's got hold of some magic."

"Magic?"

"That's what I said."

"*Black* magic."

"Sure."

I sipped my whiskey. It slid down my throat, soothing fire. "In that case," I said, "my theory about Jaize feeding on Aleksey's *qi* would be wrong."

"Completely. It's impossible to *feed* on *qi*. It's better to think of it as a frequency: it can be manipulated, but not consumed. That's where the Western concept of spirit energy is misleading—"

I interrupted, "So what's wrong with him?"

"I'm not a doctor." Keita sighed. "You're thinking of him as a victim. But victims make choices, too. He chose to stay with Jaize. And then he chose to leave him – according to you." I nodded, uncomfortably aware that on his own, Aleksey might not have followed through on his impulse. Ruth and I had done it for him. "Well, the mind-body connection would have done the rest."

"The mind-body connection?"

"Surely you know that's how magic works. Mind over matter."

"Yes, but..." I bit my lip. "So what did you say, the Dracula's Crypt logo is a *sigil?* Are sigils like runes? When I was working in Ireland, I saw..."

"No, those would have been Celtic runes. Sigils are something different. You could say they're words – but words that can't be spoken. Or at least, we don't know how to pronounce them."

"I actually thought they might be Chinese characters, some of the complicated old ones that no one uses anymore.

They – Jaize and Scott – seem to have a bunch of different ones. They sell them – "

"As pendants, bracelets, etcetera. Yeah. We've always thought they looked like sigils – but we couldn't be sure…"

"But now you are?"

Keita raised his mug, momentarily hiding his lower face. "No. I told you, all this is just guesswork."

I spread my arms. "Then how do you – "

"I've done a lot of research in this area, OK?"

"I'm aware of that," I said tightly. In the other room, Politik was patiently interrogating Ruth. I heard him asking her what time of day Aleksey had been born, and Ruth replying that she didn't have a fucking clue. I knew how she felt.

But now that I was thinking in terms of magic, I did begin to see parallels with Aleksey's plight. The leaders of the most unsavory covens and sects often employed rituals involving theatrics, sex, and drugs to "initiate" their followers. I'd never heard of a case involving branding, but in satanist cults, these hazing rituals could get quite sadistic. They forged group identity and inspired unconditional loyalty to the cult leader – always an attractive, charismatic individual. In the long run, the effect on the members could be terrible: they lost their moral integrity, their autonomy, sometimes even their will to live. And then there were the cases of unsuccessful deprogramming leading to suicide – a cause-and-effect relationship that abruptly seemed questionable to me…

I'd rather die than go on living like this.

I said, "Do you mean to say Aleksey's doing this to *himself?*"

Keita took a sip of whiskey before answering. "Frankly, I think if he wasn't in shock, he'd be on his way back to Jaize right now. But that's karma for you. He made the choice to endure and, yes, and *facilitate* Jaize's evil. And now he's dying of it. What goes around comes around!"

I shook my head. "Sorry, but now you *are* blaming the

victim. I don't know Aleksey very well, but as far as I do know, the only reason he's stayed with Jaize this long is because – well, I suppose a degree of inertia – but mainly because he's scared of being deported. And to begin with, he literally just stumbled into Jaize's orbit. It was pure bad luck."

"Exactly. Bad luck and ignorance. It's a scandal," Keita said, suddenly animated. "People just don't *know*. So magicians prey on them in all shapes and forms – "

"Let's try to stay focused, shall we? Is there any way, short of cutting that brand out of Aleksey's skin, to – to liberate him from Jaize?" Keita had used the phrase *Jaize's evil*. So had Aleksey himself, come to think of it.

Keita huffed out an impatient breath. "Probably not. And even removing the brand might not do it, now that he's had it for a while."

"That's not much help," I said wryly.

"What do you want from me?" Keita lowered his mug, flushing dark. "You wanted to know what was wrong with him. I made an informed guess to the best of my abilities, based on my research. And I've told you a lot more than you needed to know. Congratulations, you are now in the possession of information that could get you killed! What *else* do you want?"

"How about some straight answers, since you know so much about magic?" I shot back, losing my temper. "How about some *help*?"

Keita showed his teeth. "Try a hospital. I'm sure they'd be able to diagnose him. You'd end up with a bunch of medical jargon, and he'd still be lying there like a fucking corpse. Would that *help*?"

"Are you trying to tell me he can't be cured?"

"Can you unshoot a bullet? Can you unbreak a heart?"

"That's why they call it magic, I believe," I snarled.

"Only in the movies. In real life, entropy is irreversible. Done is done. And your friend is screwed." Keita set his mug down on the draining board with a clink. "If you give him back to Jaize, he might live a while longer, I guess." He moved towards the door that led into the hall. "You tell Ruth-san. I'm not going to be the messenger who gets shot. And also—" he turned on the threshhold, his expression ugly— "this can wait until tomorrow, but if you *don't* give him back, Jaize is going to come looking for him. In fact, if I'm right, he'll move heaven and earth to get him, and I for one am not going to stand in his way. So if you're not planning to give him back, you need to take him somewhere else. Otherwise, I'll do it."

He started down the hall. I went after him and caught his bare elbow. "Tell me how to cure him."

"Don't touch me." He wrenched away.

My head was spinning from the whiskey. "What's the use of knowing what's wrong with him if we can't fix it?"

"There speaks an American," Keita declared to the walls. "Sure, you can cure him."

"Just tell me what to do." I kept following him down the hall.

"Kill Jaize 3000. Ha!"

"Then that's what we've got to do," I said, mouth dry.

"Talk to Skriva. He's been trying to kill him for years." Keita wrenched open the door at the end of the hall. The light was on; I saw a typical student's lair, a laptop and an overflowing ashtray on the desk, sheets rucked up on a single bed. The obligatory framed reproduction looked like an Italian Old Master, although I didn't know the artist. Keita started to close the door in my face.

"Wait," I said. "What if we just turn Jaize over to the authorities?"

Keita laughed. "You blow me away, you really do. Just go home. For the last time, go home, forget you ever met us, and take your friends with you."

He slammed the door so hard that it shook.

I sat bolt upright. Where was I? Heart pounding, I strained to orient myself in the darkness.

On the far side of the tatami room, Politik stirred and

said, "Huh?"

"Nothing. Sorry. Go back to sleep." My throat was dry. Sweaty strands of hair stuck to my neck. After a moment, I silently stood up and made for the kitchen. I didn't need to dress, since I hadn't undressed before dropping onto the sheet that Politik spread for me on the floor of his room.

Moving around the kitchen by the ghostlight from the windows, I swallowed some water from the tap and then reconnoitered the fridge. An enormous Tupperware box, half filled with offal. I *hoped* it was offal. They did eat that in Japan. Beer. Condiments. And a half-empty carton of chocolate milk. I could do something with that…

"Clare?"

Politik's hair bristled on end, and his face looked naked without his glasses.

"Oh God, sorry. I didn't mean to wake you up." I spoke in a whisper, since Ruth and Aleksey were asleep in the living-room. I fanned my face with a hand. "It's so hot."

"It's all right."

Helplessly, I held up the carton of chocolate milk. "Care for a cold toddy? It'll be an experimental recipe, but it ought to help us get back to sleep."

"Experimental is good." Politik's head bobbed. "At least, that's all we ever do around here. We're on the cutting edge of human history, experimenting with forces that no one has ever harnessed successfully… except for a few old Taoist monks, and they're all dead!"

I found Keita's whiskey and mixed some of it into two mugs of the chocolate milk, completing the concoction with a dash of corn syrup and a sprinkling of cocoa powder. Politik took a slurp and made a comically surprised face. "This is good." He stood with his big, flat, bare feet splayed on the lino. After an awkward pause, he said, "You were talking in your sleep."

I cringed in embarrassment. "I had a nightmare," I confessed. I couldn't actually remember much of it. "My little brother was in danger, and I couldn't help him." It had been

190

one of my water nightmares – I'd woken up when I thought Colin and I were both drowning. "A fairly standard anxiety dream. My brother would stand in for all the people—" I gestured in the direction of the living-room— "who I'd like to protect, but can't."

"That's a bit too Jungian for me," Politik said. "So you have a brother?"

I nodded. I didn't really want to talk about my family. It would have felt like dragging them into it. "What about you, have you any sisters and brothers?"

"Yeah, an older sister. She's married; I've got a little niece, too."

"How lovely. And what about Keita?"

"Oh, he's an only child. His family is those books in there!"

"I knew it," I said darkly.

"Really? How come?"

"Oh, just something about him." I sipped my toddy. The syrup had sunk to the bottom. "He doesn't seem to play well with others." I was actually leaning towards a diagnosis of narcissistic personality disorder, a condition so common in academia that to weed it out, you'd have to decimate entire departments. But Keita was an extreme case.

"That's an unfair judgment on him," Politik said with a hint of hostility that made me grimace. I'd forgotten how quickly he would leap to the defense of the friend he worshipped. "He's got a lot to cope with, and I can't help him as much as I'd like to."

"I imagine you're busy with your own thesis."

"No, it's not that," Politik dismissed his academic obligations with a wave of his hand. "But there's a lot of stuff that only Kay can do. The Harajuku vamps don't listen to me; they listen to him. And there's our research. Kay's the one who pulled it all together, so he feels responsible…"

"What about Hiromi?" I said, although I would have preferred to forget the girl's existence.

"Her! She's – she's a natural. She has a lot of skill, but

she's… well." Politik's face wrinkled; his gaze searched my face in the near-dark. "She's saved our lives a couple of times, so I feel like an asshole for saying this, but she's not actually very much *help.*"

I cut my eyes away, depressed by the thought that Politik was indirectly asking me to involve myself with their "research," much as he'd earlier asked me to join their Vampire Democracy project. He probably thought I owed him and Keita some repayment for coming to my aid tonight: some *help.* But as far as I was concerned, they'd owed *me* that much for the way they'd treated me earlier.

"It seems to me that Keita's life would be a lot simpler if he quit experimenting with black magic," I said bluntly.

"I really wish people wouldn't call it that," Politik said softly. "It's not what most people think of as magic. And I don't think it means anything to call it a black art."

I shuddered. Now that I had the confession I'd been seeking, I felt slightly ill. I said, "Yes, well, I'm actually having trouble with the fine distinction there."

A look of pain clouded Politik's big face. Turning away to rinse out his mug, he said, "Jaize 3000 is a typical black magician. They use and abuse people. We respect free will. Do you think that's a fine distinction?"

They hadn't exactly respected *my* free will when they tried to use my blood in a spell earlier, but I didn't point that out. "Ah," I said. "I see. Them bad, us good."

"It's not that simple. Our research is based on a theoretical foundation that most magicians wouldn't even recognize. And our goals are different. Have you read *Faust?* He was a typical magician: gimme the girls, gold, and guns. We're different. We're doing this to – to…" Politik's mumble was lost beneath the sound of the running water.

"Sorry, what?"

Politik turned off the tap. It dripped. He turned it off harder. "To save the world," he said defiantly.

"Ah. I see," I repeated.

"You think that's unrealistic?"

I murmured a demurral.

"Well, Keita's grandfather could have won the war for Japan, if he and the rest of the Tsurukai hadn't been arrested for practising magic."

"Keita's *grandfather?*" I said.

Politik wet a dishrag, wrung it out, and started to wipe up the drops of chocolate milk I'd spilled on the draining board.

"Go on," I said. "Too late now."

"It's not a secret. But…"

"Oh, go on."

"All right! You read that article on Wilfred Hauptmann, didn't you? Well, Kay's grandfather was in it. His name was Kiyomasa Horibe."

"Oh, wow," I said. "So *that's* how Keita knew all that stuff." I laughed, half-admiringly. "He didn't do any bloody research at all!"

"Yes, he did. We've done *mountains* of research. For the last two years, we've been working every day to… to…."

I sighed. "Politik, I'm not here to judge you. Just tell me."

He hesitated another moment, then faced me squarely. "You know that sigil on – on your friend's body? Well, that's just one of a set that originally numbered in the hundreds. And if you knew them all, you'd be able to do magic scientifically. No more rituals and *jumon*. No more sacrifices and potions, no more grubbing around in people's garbage. No more *mess*."

"Well. That certainly would be a breakthrough."

"It *was* a breakthrough. It was the discovery of the millennium! The result of fusing Eastern and Western methods." Politik stammered with urgency. I realized with amusement tinged by sorrow that he wanted my approval. "Hauptmann, Horibe, and… and another guy. From 1921 through 1923, they were in contact with an angelic entity named Horobiel, and it taught them the whole set of sigils. The continuation of John Dee's work with the hieroglyphic monad. The Angelic Runes, as Hauptmann called them. The algebra of reality itself."

"Incredible," I said.

"It could have led to universal magical literacy. It could have changed the world!" Politik drooped. "But then Hauptmann died, and the war came, and everything was lost."

"Oh, dear."

"Yeah. Which is why," Politik wound up with an air of having hopelessly committed himself, "we've been trying to duplicate the Atelier's work from scratch. We do have some notebooks that document the procedure." His hands clenched on the edge of the sink. "But it doesn't work. We've tried everything we can think of. And *nothing works*."

"Oh no," I said insincerely.

"We were doing well at first. We *were* making progress. But then… then Ryu left town. And ever since… zilch." Politik's voice shook with a depth of frustration I hadn't thought he would be capable of. For a moment, he sounded more like Keita. "And meanwhile, Jaize 3000 is using *our* sigils to build himself an empire!"

"But if they were lost during the war, how did Jaize learn them?"

Politik shook his head. "One of those cosmic coincidence things; it happens in science all the time. And this time it happened to a vampire. A cosmic *joke.*"

I spread my hands. "So why don't you just buy a set of his medallions and use them yourselves?"

"We've tried. Of course. But we can't – we don't – they aren't made for any of us."

Of course not, I thought. The world was full of magicians touting revolutionary discoveries, and they always managed to dodge any real test of their claims.

But whatever ailed Aleksey was no illusion. And there was that other little issue…

"So if I can ask," I said, half-dreading the answer. "How did Keita know where to find me and Ruth tonight? Luck?"

Politik snickered, sounding more like himself. "I'm not at

liberty to divulge the details. But no, it wasn't just luck. "

"So your – your procedure *does* work."

Politik made a face. "OK, so I was exaggerating. It's worked a couple of times." His frustration bubbled up again. "Out of *hundreds* of times! Can you imagine what it's like to get a result, and not know how you got it, and not be able to duplicate it? And we weren't even trying for f— for Kay's, uh, magical ability. That was an accident. And after that, we, uh, decided that wasn't a direction we wanted to pursue."

Far from reassured, I said, "So what are you working on now?"

Politik sighed. "We're at the point now where we're just trying to solidify our grasp of the basic grimoiric procedures. Enchantments, hexes, you know the kind of thing."

I said, "That's what you were going to do with my blood. You were going to hex me. So I'd have an accident or... or anyhow, stay away." I stared at him, daring him to deny it.

"No, no," he protested. "We would never do that. It was a spell of *protection*. It was obvious that you were going to go your own way and get yourself killed – and that's what almost happened, isn't it? So we —"

"Are you trying to take credit for my survival? Good God."

"No." Politik's lower lip jutted sullenly. "You interrupted us. It never goes well if you break off in the middle. But it probably wouldn't have worked, anyway."

"I heard a dog barking. Who performed the sacrifice? Was it him or you?"

"It was Hiromi, actually. You know, I really think girls are better at some things —"

"You *sacrificed* someone's *pet*."

"Not a pet," Politik corrected me crossly. "A stray. You have to show two forms of ID at pet shops."

My gorge rose. I wanted to storm out of the apartment all over again. "You guys make me sick."

"Some scientist you are," Politik retorted.

Once again, I cringed from my own awareness of the cultural gulf between us. But it wasn't fair to conclude that my colleagues thought nothing of cruelty to animals because they were Japanese. They thought nothing of cruelty to animals because they'd internalized the principles – or *lack* of principles – of black magic.

To hell with *fine distinctions*. My colleagues could give Hauptmann himself a run for his money. All in the name of science.

Yet as I worked up to another outburst of righteous indignation, I recalled that I'd told Politik I wasn't here to judge him. And what's more, I didn't have the right to judge him, did I? Earlier tonight, I'd shot someone (but he was just a vampire – no, a *human being*) with the intent to wound if not kill. Sure, it had been self-defense. But the point was that I'd pulled the trigger. My moral high horse had thrown me and galloped off, maybe forever.

But… maybe it was the English animal-lover in me, but I couldn't forgive them for that dog.

As I turned my mug around in my hands, Politik coughed to get my attention.

"You've got to help him," he whispered.

I looked up at him, and then at the windows, which were angled so that I couldn't see his reflection in the glass. "You know, something I've noticed," I said. "There aren't any mirrors in this apartment. Not even in the bathroom." I sniggered. "How do you guys shave?"

Politik winced. "You've got to help him," he repeated. "You're the only person who's ever come along that knows anything about this stuff. You're not scared, are you?"

On his last words, I suddenly realized that I'd left the Glock in his bedroom. It hadn't even occurred to me to take it when I went to get a drink of water in the middle of the night. Because I *hadn't* been scared. After everything I'd been through, this apartment seemed like a haven of safety. In comparison to the rest of what was out there, my colleagues had looked like heroes. And something in me had let go. Some dormant instinct had kicked in and shut down my paranoia. I'd gone to *sleep,* lulled by a subconscious trust in the chivalry of men. God, the social conditioning ran deep! Politik hadn't threatened me, but if he *had*…

My own assumptions could get me killed.

Holding my ground, I shook my head sadly. "Politik, I'm not going to help you… *research* black magic. Or whatever you're calling it. That's a non-negotiable no."

"Please."

"Sorry."

He wheeled. As he left the kitchen – a dramatic exit rather spoiled by the fact that I would have to follow him back to my bivouac on the floor of his room – he muttered, "I'm just telling you what he's going to say."

Chapter 11.

"**S**omeone at the door." Ruth shook me.

I followed her into the living-room, rubbing sleep out of my eyes. Keita was already at the front door. I glanced down at Aleksey's pale, still form. We were going to kill him like this: he should have been in hospital, where they had IV machines, feeding tubes, catheters.

"Yeah, she called me, and I told her I can't make it," Keita was saying. "We've got a sick friend here. Can't leave him."

Encouraged that Keita referred to Aleksey as a friend, I sidled into the genkan behind him. Morning sunlight filled the hall. The heavy-set man at the door wore baggy black shorts, flip-flops, and a faded black Danzig t-shirt. He saw me, and beneath a mop of black hair as tousled as Keita's, a shit-eating grin split his broad pale face. He had fangs. "Well, it looks like you've got friends over. So leave the nursing duties to them and lug your ass down to Shinjuku. But if I was you, I'd take some backup, because it sounds like she's plenty pissed." He grinned at me in a way that suggested I was better suited to nursing than backup duties. "Howdy," he said, using the English word. "Name's Juroku. I live downstairs."

"Just a friend from the university," Keita said.

"Oooh, I get it. Hands off the nice white meat." Juroku chuckled. "Don't worry, I like them with a bit more blood in their veins." He leveled a stare at Keita. "And believe it or not, I don't appreciate being woken up at an hour like this, halfway up the crack of dawn's rosy pink ass, to give you a message you already got."

"Told her I'm busy. Not my fault if she can't take no for an answer."

"You're crazy, man! You don't say no to the Princess of Shinjuku." Abruptly, Juroku seemed to tire of the exchange.

He turned and plodded away down the hall, saying over his shoulder, "If I get in trouble over this, you'll know it."

Keita closed the door. "I'll know the wrath of the terrible Juroku," he jeered. "I'm so *scared.*"

Politik raised his face questioningly. He was holding Aleksey's head up while Ruth tried to tip hot milk from a mug down Aleksey's throat.

"Maybe we should take him downstairs," Keita said. "Ni-chan's good at this kind of thing. She nursed Sanjusan and Sanjunana through their Turns when no one else thought they would make it, remember?"

"I'm not handing him over to some vampire," Ruth said. Last night's mascara had smeared, giving her raccoon eyes. Welcome to life without mirrors, I thought.

"That's just as likely to go down his windpipe and choke him," Keita said. "Which is why you might want to ask the advice of someone who knows what she's doing." He rubbed his face with both hands. "Crap. I need coffee."

I lingered in the door of the kitchen while he shook grounds into the coffee-maker. Unlike the other appliances, it was a top-of-the-line machine, bringing a wistful smile to my lips. "Caffeine sounds great. But I think we could all use some solid food."

"No time for that. Got to get down to Shinjuku." Keita measured water into the coffee-maker.

"I thought you weren't going?"

"In Juroku's words, it's not smart to ignore princesses. But don't get any ideas about coming with me," he said as I opened my mouth. "There's a fair chance that whatever she wants, it's something to do with you."

The rich scent of coffee began to fill the kitchen. From the living-room, I heard Ruth and Politik coaxing Aleksey to swallow just a few drops of milk. I recalled my conversation with Politik last night: *Nothing works!* A sense of futility overwhelmed me.

"There's bread in the freezer," Keita said, his back to me. "Margarine and natto in the fridge. You won't like the natto, but I'll have some, and so will Politik."

I bristled at being ordered around, but I was the one who'd suggested breakfast in the first place. The natto – a glop of fermented beans – smelled like week-old socks. Customers at Exiles invariably asked me if I liked the stuff: it seemed to be some kind of litmus test for gaijin. I'd never actually tried it, and the smell was revolting. But if I refused it, Keita would have another reason to sneer at me. Breathing through my mouth, I mixed in the tare and mustard. As I buttered the toast, Keita silently placed a cup of coffee at my elbow.

"I'm going with you," I said, turning. "Don't say no. I've got to."

"This is no time to indulge your professional curiosity."

"It's not that," I said, knowing that on some level, it was. "If this is anything to do with me, I've got to be there."

"Zuleiko might decide to take you captive herself."

I shook my head, suddenly excited. "She's never seen my face. If anyone asks, I'll be Ruth. The *zako* in Roppongi last night thought she was me!"

"What's that?" Ruth yelled from the living-room.

"If you don't mind," I yelled back, "I'm going to go see the Princess of Shinjuku as you."

A moment later she was in the kitchen. "Fuck that. I'm going, too."

And then it would be obvious that *one* of us was me. And if this Zuleiko character tried to take Ruth captive in the mistaken belief that she was acquiring me, I knew I wouldn't be able to stand by and watch. "Ruth, I've got to," I gabbled in English. "These guys aren't telling us everything they know. It may be a slim chance, but I've got to find out what's really going on. Right now, we don't even know if it's safe to show our faces on the street. But if we split up, you can stay here and phone Dorothy. That way, even if I can't find out why –"

Keita made a sudden movement. When I fell silent, he went to the table and retrieved his packet of Marlboro Reds.

He lit one, took a deep drag, and blew the smoke in my direction.

"Jeez, Clare," Ruth said. "Just because they're Japanese doesn't mean they can't understand English."

Shrugging, I leaned against the sink and drank my coffee. I didn't care if Keita had understood everything I said. In fact, I hoped he *had*. He should know that our loyalty to Dorothy went deeper than a bad encounter with a bunch of thugs who infested her territory without her permission.

He spoke. In English. I hid a smile. "You two don't look anything alike, anyway."

"Damn straight," Ruth said. "I'm Irish on my mother's side and Swedish on my father's side. Not that he ever gave me anything besides the genes. *She's* just a cookie-cutter WASP."

"Hey, I'm Catholic," I said, smiling.

Keita grunted.

Ruth said, "Well, I'm not calling Dorothy, anyway. She'd be home by now, and I bet you dollars to donuts it would be someone else that picked up. Besides, she couldn't even save our asses in Roppongi, so what could she do for us up here? I'll tell you: squat. I guess you still haven't figured this out, but she's a gaijin trying to make it in *vamukura*. That means she's the lowest of the fucking low." Her eye fell on the plate of breakfast I'd just fixed. "Hey, natto." She grabbed a styrofoam packet and spooned it into her mouth. "I love this stuff." Her words were indistinct, but her eyes glittered too brightly.

"Ruth," I pleaded, and bit my lip.

"Save it." She wiped her lips and managed to wipe her eyes with the same motion. "You can go. I'd like to... but I can't leave him."

Politik stayed behind, too, ostensibly to search Keita's collection of inherited grimoires for some way to deactivate Aleksey's brand. In reality, I suspected, Keita had told him to make sure that Ruth neither placed any phone calls nor snooped around the apartment.

Ruth had agreed to trade clothes with me, so climbing onto the pillion of Keita's bike was an interesting exercise in modesty under duress. The skirt of her pale green dress (now stained and dusty) rode up to the tops of my thighs. I held onto Keita at arm's length, trying not to slide against him as we rocketed through the narrow streets. I'd expected him to be sullen that I'd insisted on coming, but far from resenting my company, he seemed to appreciate it. At every stoplight he turned to shout at me from behind his visor. Straining to distinguish his Japanese from the roar of motors around us, I built up a sketchy profile of the vampire we were going to see.

Princess Zuleiko of Shinjuku, it appeared, was the closest thing in Tokyo to a power independent of the *kuni* that Gore served. While she derived her legitimacy from her "family connection" to the mysterious Emperor, her high rank allowed her to go her own way – and keep her own money. Gore could only dream of taxing her as he did Dorothy and the other conducators. She maintained formal links with the Court, refusing to set herself up as a rival to the Emperor. But at the same time, she supported misfits and dissidents such as the would-be revolutionaries of Harajuku. It was a given, Keita said, that the Court knew of Zuleiko's tenuous alliance with Skriva. Thus, no one could say for sure whether the alliance reflected her true aspirations, or if it was just a way for her to remind the Court that she could do as she liked.

I said that it sounded like a delicate balancing act.

"There's nothing delicate about Zuleiko, *or* her methods," Keita snorted.

We coasted in under the dead neon arch that surmounted the main entrance to Kabukicho. I hopped off, and Keita parked his bike in a row of equally flashy machines at the center of the pedestrian concourse. He spoke briefly to a vampire youth who lounged in the shade of a spindly ginkgo, then came to join me. It was not quite ten in the morning.

The sun baked down on our heads. In the narrow strips of shadow in front of the pachinko parlors, queues of sad-faced men waited for the doors to open. "Gambling," Keita said. "That's Zuleiko's main source of revenue. Ready?"

I nodded. "I have to get out of this sun or I'll burn."

He chuckled. "No wonder they're all attracted to you. You're half a vampire already."

"Is it true? That they can't go out in the sun? Your friends in Harajuku don't seem to have any problem with the light. Nor does Juroku," I fished, squinting. The concourse was so empty that our footfalls echoed off the facades of the multiuse buildings, with their queasy mix of pornographic and cute signage.

"Only the old ones have trouble with the sun," Keita said. "At about a hundred, they start to burn easily. They say the really old ones would burn right up if they ever went out in the daylight." He laughed. "I'm going to test that theory someday."

"How old is old?"

"Zuleiko might tell you she's twenty-one, or she might tell you she's twelve hundred. But whatever she says, just be polite. Don't ask any questions. In fact, don't say anything at all if you can help it. If she doesn't hear that barbaric accent, she probably won't even notice that you're not Japanese."

"You're telling me to shut up and trust you."

"I've been here before. And here we are."

Keita thrust open a plain metal door beneath a sign that featured two red kanji on a yellow background, which I couldn't read. Darkness blinded me. Brisk steps approached. "Welcome, honorable guests, welcome. May I see some ID?"

"Come on, it's me," Keita said. "I've had a summons from Her Highness."

"I still need to see your ID, Matsudaira-san. And your companion?"

I produced Ruth's alien registration card from the pocket of her black hoodie. A small flashlight came on, and I saw the impassive face of an elderly man, spiffy in a waistcoat and bowtie. He returned the card along with Keita's driver's license. "This way please, Matsudaira-san, O'Meara-san."

We followed his flashlight up a steep carpeted staircase. At my side, Keita breathed into my ear, in English, "I never have to show ID. This isn't good. Want to make a run for it?"

"Quit messing with me," I whispered.

On the first landing, the concierge led us into a curtained-off security area with a cash register and a metal detector. Now I knew why Keita had refused to let me bring my gun. Not that it would have stayed concealed for long, anyway, if I had to take Ruth's black hoodie off... Right now, I was glad of the hoodie. The air-conditioning was cranked down to arctic.

Walking through the curtains after Keita and the concierge, I saw men hunched over mahjong tables, playing with grim concentration, or sagging half-asleep over melted drinks. Some of them looked as if they'd been here for days on end. A girl wheeled a dim sum cart between the tables, carving a wake through the heavy veils of cigarette smoke that hung in the air.

"See?" Keita said, not bothering to lower his voice. "I told you. Highly illegal, but—" He pretended to give a start of surprise. "Look over there, I do believe that's the chief of police."

"You are mistaken, Matsudaira-san," the concierge said without turning. "The honorable chief of police plays at the Lotus Room, our sister establishment."

"The corruption, the corruption," Keita said, shaking his head.

At the far side of the room, the concierge led us through a door marked STAFF ONLY. It was hot, and we were going downstairs again.

The stairs led to an industrial-grey corridor that seemed to be a service passage connected with the underground shopping complex around Shinjuku station. People hurried past, pushing dollies that held pallets of fresh produce, crates of booze, frozen sides of meat, cardboard boxes of senbei and potato chips. Others jogged, bearing velvet pouches or little trays that held change and receipts, giving a new meaning to speedy customer service. Everyone in sight wore some sort of uniform. Restaurants, I thought, mahjong parlors, baccarat clubs, probably snack bars and hostess clubs, too. Up on the surface, the night's last customers were toddling off into the sun; down here, an army of staff was prepping for the next rush. Did all of this belong to Princess Zuleiko?

Cooking smells wafted from swinging doors, reminding me that a slice of toast and a mouthful of natto did not a meal make.

I had little sense of how far we'd come, or in what direction, when the concierge led us into a service elevator. Ears popping, I whispered to Keita, "Where *are* we?"

"The Princessa Royale," intoned the concierge, in the manner of the elevator operators at Japanese department stores. "Highly exclusive, with membership granted by peer review, upon the approval of the Princess Zuleiko. Her Highness will see you in the VIP lounge." The elevator clanked to a stop. "Please enjoy your Princessa Royale experience. I hope to see you again, Matsudaira-san."

"I hope so, too," Keita told him without a smile..

We stepped out of the elevator into pitch darkness. I stumbled after Keita through a door into the stepped bowl of a casino. The blackjack and poker tables were fuller than I would have expected at ten in the morning: I guessed that many of the "gamblers" were actually holding discreet business meetings. At the roulette tables, by contrast, the croupiers outnumbered the bettors. We slunk between the tables, descended the split floor levels, and passed a sunken central pool where koi swam beneath overhanging ferns in the glow of a black light. High on the far side of the casino floor, we reached a bulge of tinted glass where a bouncer rechecked our ID. His fangs showed when he spoke into his two-way radio to confirm our invitation.

"Thanks, Hyaku-hachijuni," Keita said as the bouncer ushered us into the VIP lounge.

Without thinking, I hissed, "Am I hearing this right? Do *all* of her vampires go by *numbers?* And is that guy number *one hundred and eighty-two?*"

"He is," said an amused female voice. "And they do. Your education in our ways continues, O'Meara... *san.*"

Half lost in the gloom, several people sat on the floor around a low smoked-glass table that bore square white coffee cups and a minimalist flower arrangement in a black crystal dish. Very mod, but not more so than their stark black Mao-collared suits, or the fitted jumpsuit in a clownish pattern of multicolored circles and squares that clung to the fragile frame of the woman who'd spoken. I knew it had been her because she was the only female in the group. She was also the only one with a chair, or rather a black leather couch on which she reclined like a *Vogue* fashion spread. Her needle-straight platinum shag contrasted with her small, perfect Asian features, completing her aura of artificial beauty. I didn't need the diamond tiara on her head to tell me this was Princess Zuleiko.

"Your Highness." Keita approached the couch and bowed. Belatedly, I did the same, watching him out of the corner of my eye to get the angle right.

"Sit, sit." As we arranged ourselves on the lush black carpet, the Princess's companions melted away. "Not you, Ichi." Zuleiko fastened her gaze on Keita. "Have you anything to tell me, Kay?" she asked softly.

"I – I – Highness, no. I mean, I don't know." Keita had turned dull red, his flush visible even in the low light. My heart sank further. He tried to recover. "I mean, I don't know why you summoned me this morning, Highness. I haven't seen anything that would – would interest you. If I had, you know I'd have contacted you myself."

"But surely you saw *something*," she said in the same gently chiding tone. "It would have been in Aoyama Cemetery. A party of mortals belonging to Jaize 3000, the Conducator of Shibuya, mounted an unprovoked attack on the rank outsiders who call the cemetery their home. It's hardly

206

the first time they have done so. This time, however, the *zako* seem to have fought back with unusual vigor and coordination." Zuleiko stretched out a hand for the toasted galette on the saucer of her coffee cup. Nibbling it, she went on, "At this show of resilience, Jaize's mortal rabble broke, and he himself made a sortie to put heart into them."

All in all, Jaize's version was more plausible, I thought. It probably *had* been the *zako* of Aoyama Cemetery who attacked the Human League first, and they probably had had provocation – from Gore.

"But the conducator was ambushed, and his party allegedly suffered three fatalities. Scattered fighting in the cemetery continued until the arrival of the police, who promptly arrested every vampire they could find." Without warning, Zuleiko's voice rose to a raw growl that tightened my skin. "And you say you saw *nothing?*"

Keita stammered, "Your Highness, don't I always tell you the truth?"

"Yes. You do. You have." Zuleiko shifted on her couch, her small face tensing with irritation. "Ichi, our guests should have something to eat and drink! What are you thinking?"

A rock-faced vampire with a gray ponytail that trailed down his back, seated in martially correct seiza on the floor, turned and barked an order into the darkness of the lounge. *One.* Did Zuleiko's naming convention reflect seniority, in which case Ichi would be the first vampire Zuleiko had ever Turned? How old would that make him? How old was *she?* My curiosity had a practical function: it insulated me from the fear that grated on the edges of my mind like a distant scream.

"Kay, your crows have made a significant contribution to my security arrangements." Zuleiko leant forward over her knees, her voice almost a coo.

A shiver passed over my skin. The crows. Gutter birds, vermin, Spenser's "hateful messengers of heavy things."

Keita's crows.

Well, I'd guessed as much, hadn't I? It was always nice

to be right.

And that was why we were here, wasn't it? Because Keita's crows played a part in Zuleiko's "security arrangements." *Damn.* This was no "alliance." This was Keita dancing to the tune of a woman who might – might – support vampire democracy, but showed every sign of believing in only one cause: her own.

All the same, it was a relief to know we weren't here because of me. Zuleiko was just fishing for information, like the good little paranoid business mogul she was.

A waitress in a miniskirt placed a coffee cup and a blueberry Danish in front of me. I ate the Danish and swallowed the excellent brew, with cream out of the thimble-sized jug that had accompanied it.

Keita turned his own cup around in his hands, listening and nodding as Zuleiko reminded him how she relied on him. She wasn't even aiming her flattery at me, and it still took my breath away, it was so pseudo. "You may smoke," she added. Fumbling, Keita shook out a cigarette and lit it with a Princessa Royale matchbook from the saucer on the table. Zuleiko rested her chin in the V of her hands. "There's only one thing I *really* want to know, Kay. *Who ambushed Jaize 3000?* You know what the rank outsiders are: pathetic, unclaimed younglings. They've never stood up to Jaize's mortals before, and I don't believe for a minute that they did so last night. No, they had help."

I remembered the man in the Halloween mask.

"The feeling is that they were probably led on by some hotheads from Roppongi. Our dear cousin Dorothy doesn't have quite the grip on her household that one might wish. But no one witnessed the attack except Jaize's followers themselves; that's the trouble. They might name anyone. And since *someone* is likely to be punished – well, one would like it to be the right man. Or woman."

I held very still, feeling as if the slightest motion might give me away.

"I don't know who it was," Keita said. "I wasn't looking."

Zuleiko huffed and flung herself back against the couch. "I hope you understand this could be serious. Apparently, one of Jaize's mortal toys was taken captive. Jaize has communicated with the Court, indicating that he'll send an envoy to present his terms for compensation. Read between the diplomatic lines, Kay. He means to press for official recognition of his rank, and I don't doubt expansion of his clave to boot. That would be the end of our little friends in Harajuku, I hardly need to tell you. Oh, it won't happen, of course: with that unwholesome trick of mesmerism, he must be kept at arm's length. The Court will never allow him into their counsels. But if he were to take offense at a refusal... it might lead to even worse trouble."

"I saw nothing," Keita lied again. Then he raised his head and said, "What if it was Gore?"

"What? Keita, you surprise me. Edonokami would never commit a pointless blunder like that." Suddenly, Zuleiko sat upright again. "But since you mention our Gorozaemon – I heard an interesting bit of gossip yesterday. He has apparently laid claim to one of Dorothy's mortals, but she's refusing to hand the creature over. What do you think of that? I wonder if there is any connection with the incidents we have been discussing."

"Shockingly bad judgment," Keita said expressionlessly. "'All that is mine is the Emperor's, and when called upon to yield it up, that will I do joyfully.' Isn't that how it goes, Highness?"

She tittered. "Touché. But I never took that imbecilic oath in the first place. Why should I? I am the Emperor's own daughter." Her voice hardened. "And a good thing for you, too."

Keita inclined his head. "I am in your debt, Princess."

Ichi said something guttural in a language that sounded like Japanese but wasn't. At least, I couldn't understand it.

"That's so," Zuleiko conceded. "I value your counsel as well as your crows, Kay. So tell me, have you any idea why this mortal should have interested our Gorozaemon? I suppose she's pretty."

The bated laughter in her voice felt like a razor tickling my eardrums. I could hold still no longer. "I know who it was," I said. "It was a girl named Clare Standing. She's not that pretty, unless you're into the anorexic WASP type. But anyway, it wasn't me. Ruth O'Meara. That's me. And he doesn't even know I exist. He was after *her!*" I kept my chin up as Keita turned furious eyes on me.

"No," Ichi said in his gravelly voice, this time in Japanese that I could understand. "It was not you, Ruth O'Meara. One wonders what you are doing with our Master of Crows, but you are both of the same social class. I daresay you enjoy scuffling with him in the gutter. This Standing-san is another matter. She is descended from British nobility and is the daughter of an American lord, a senior member of Parliament."

Keita let out a soft grunt.

"No wonder Gorozaemon wishes to lay claim to her," Ichi concluded. "Think what the Court could do with *that!*"

I had to close my eyes for a minute. *Christ.* How could I have failed to realize that this wasn't about who I was, but who I was related to?

I'd thought Gore lacked any sense of the world outside his *kuni.* Maybe so… but there was clearly *someone* in the vampire hierarchy who recognized leverage, no matter what shape it came in.

Silently vowing to Nilson that I would never let these criminal deviants use me against him, I opened my eyes. "Incidentally, it's not called Parliament in America," I said. "It's Congress, and the members are known as representatives or senators."

Keita's hand shook as he stubbed out his cigarette in the black crystal ashtray. I winced, realizing I'd slipped out of character.

"Congress, of course," Ichi said. "Thank you, Ruth O'Meara. Your country was not yet an independent nation when I was born."

I lowered my head to avoid his dark gray eyes. My gaze fell on Zuleiko's torso. Under the heavy fabric of her jumpsuit, her abdomen appeared oddly lumpy. Botched liposuction? Surely she could afford the best? And why was she covered up to the neck and wrists, anyway? I reeled my thoughts back in before they could flee any further.

Keita said, "Excuse me, Highness. I wish you wouldn't play with me like this. If you and Ichi-*sama* already knew who Gore was seeking to claim, why ask me?"

Zuleiko made a moue. "I just wanted to be sure that you're still telling me the truth." She tossed her blonde hair. "At least your little friend is honest. That's one of you." She looked at Ichi. "I think it's time, don't you?"

Keita rose on his knees. I pushed back from the table, adrenaline surging at the thought that we were going to make a run for it.

"*Sit,*" Zuleiko ordered.

Again, Ichi shouted over his shoulder in that language that sounded like Japanese. Or maybe it *was* Japanese, circa 1100.

Tension crackled through my body, depositing cold sweat on my back. Keita tore off matches and lined them up on the table, acting bored. Zuleiko glared impatiently into the darkness.

Dorothy walked up to the table. She wore skinny jeans tucked into combat boots and a black chemise with ruffles at the neckline. "Clare!" she exclaimed. "Damn, girl, I had the whole city out looking for you last night." She beamed at Zuleiko. "You are a dark horse, cuz. I owe you one. I won't ask how you found her. I know you got your *eyes.*" On the last word, she directed a narrow stare at Keita. Her expression subtly altered as she understood that Keita and I were together in some way.

Keita was already dragging me to my feet. I barely dared to look at Zuleiko and Ichi. When I did, I saw the last thing I anticipated: naked shock. They hadn't expected this.

They'd expected Dorothy to recognize *Keita.* That's who

they intended to spring on her. After all, they hadn't even known I was coming.

And on the word of their own security, they'd accepted that I was Ruth.

Until now.

Keita and I jostled each other as we backed away from the table. Ichi was growling into a handheld radio. The only question was whether casino security would reach us before Zuleiko did.

She stalked across the low table in one impossible stride, knocking over the flower arrangement. "You traitorous little shit. You have the ethics of your own carrion birds. Give her to me."

"Come on, Your Highness, it was just a gag," Keita said. "I brought her here, didn't I? Obviously, I was going to turn her over as soon as the joke wore thin."

"Oh my God," I said, and reeled away from him.

Dorothy was quietly backing up in the other direction. The moment our eyes met, she crooked her finger. *This way.*

I sidestepped between the tables.. Ichi moved to intercept me. He was barely my height, and his legs were short and bowed. "We're on the eighteenth floor, Standing-san." I almost laughed at the new respect in his tone, now that he knew I was descended from someone with a title. But it obviously had limits. "You can't get out, and I wouldn't want you to get hurt trying."

"Lay off, Itch," Dorothy said. Her hand locked around my wrist, dry and cool. "You located her for me, and for that I thank you. But she's mine, and now I'm taking her. You got a problem with that? Let me say again, you got a problem with Court law?"

"You, Countess, may leave. Without her." But for all his implacable tone, Ichi didn't close with us. Perhaps he knew that Dorothy was far from helpless. He might be equally proficient at martial arts, but if it came to unarmed combat, Dorothy's reach would put him at a disadvantage.

Screams ruptured the air. I whipped around, pulling on

Dorothy's grip, and saw Keita recoiling from Zuleiko as she shrieked hysterically into his face. Three security guards piled into the lounge, only to halt and give their mistress space for her tantrum. The gist seemed to be that Keita had betrayed her, he was unworthy of the blood in his veins, he deserved to die in excruciating pain, etc, etc. Oddly enough, I agreed with most of her points, but not that last one.

"Hey!" I screamed. If Keita made a dash for it, the three of us together might have a chance. "Princess! You use him like toilet paper and then you're surprised when he turns on you?" Across the room, her face swivelled briefly in my direction, a pale blank heart. "Haven't you learnt any better than *that* after twelve hundred years?"

"Oh, Clare," Dorothy said. "I only had you back for two minutes, and I've already got to be schooling you again." Her laughter tickled my ear. "You do *not* trash-talk royalty."

The flicker of movement in my peripheral vision was all the warning I had before Dorothy thrust me away. I hit the carpet with my forearms a split second before a glass table sailed through the space where we'd been, to land on another table with a deafening crash.

"Then again," Dorothy said breathlessly, "I forgot that you don't have no respect for Court law in this part of town. None at all." She drifted forward, bearing down on Ichi as he stalled his hammer-thrower's spin. "So I guess I'm just gonna play it your way." She swayed into one of those blurring kicks. Her boot heel crunched into the back of Ichi's neck.

On the far side of the room, something exploded.

I screamed, "Keita!" and started to run towards the pillar of flame that had sprung up where he'd been. Beyond it, the lounge was filling up with people, and they were all shouting. Someone switched on the lights, flooding the lounge with white brilliance that dulled the wall of glass to black.

Keita broke out of the mêlée around the explosion. Smoke was already hazing the air. "Burn!" he shouted at the vampires who were trying with a ridiculous mixture of haste and delicacy to put out the fire with blankets. "Burn, baby,

213

burn!"

Ichi pounded past us, short legs pistoning. He ploughed through the mêlée and straight into the fire.

"Did *you* do that?" I screamed at Keita. "What was it?"

"Her Royal fucking Highness the Princess Zuleiko! Now let's get out of here, before they remember about us."

"Dorothy," I coughed.

"Let the vampire bitch find her own way out."

"I heard that," Dorothy said, shimmering out of the smoke in front of us. "Keep a civil tongue in your head, Crow Boy, unless you want to find your own way out, past *them*, because that's the only other way. No? That's what I thought."

I stumbled after her, tripping over fallen furniture, eyes burning. At the back of the lounge, we broke through a door into a narrow golden corridor, and suddenly the air was breathable again. "Back here is where they had me wait," Dorothy said. "Told me they got someone they want me to meet, and in the meantime, how's about a glass of Cristal and some caviar? When you operate at Zuleiko's level, even the VIP lounge got its *own* VIP lounge." We passed a door that stood open on a private room, tastelessly done in black and gold with some kind of animal head on the wall, and then rounded a corner. LADIES, said one door, and GENTLEMEN, said two others. "Reverse of how the natural order should be. Well, they don't get too many *ladies* up here." Dorothy faced Keita. "OK, I guess this is where we part ways... no, I'm just messing with you."

Keita stumbled sideways, hitting the wall.

"Vampire bitch. You're all the same," he said thickly. "Think it's all so funny, until the joke's on you. *She* was like that, too. Wasn't expecting... wasn't expecting..."

"Clare, get on the other side of him, quick — "

Keita sagged between us.

"He's gonna pass out," Dorothy finished. She pulled open the second door marked GENTLEMEN. It wasn't a bathroom. It was an elevator, the old-fashioned type with a manual door. We jostled inside. "Now this," she said, "is the Royal Flush." She hit the ground floor button.

My laugh turned into a cough. Keita's weight hung heavily on my shoulder, and my knees were buckling. "These skinny guys," I said. "What do they have, bones made of solid iron?"

"I'll fix his shit."

While the elevator hummed down so smoothly that it seemed to be standing still, Dorothy braced Keita against the wall and slapped him in the face.

"We're just gonna walk on out of here, nice and smooth. So you got to be able *to* walk."

The elevator ejected us into the corner of a marble-floored foyer, behind a rubber plant. Dorothy strutted past the security guards with her nose in the air, followed by Keita, shaky but moving under his own power. I brought up the rear, glancing around at the salarymen spilling noisily from the main bank of elevators. It was an ordinary day, and these were ordinary office workers heading out for lunch, their shirtsleeves rolled back in anticipation of the heat outside. But hadn't we been in the middle of Kabukicho?

Outside, the sunlight fell on my head, a solid weight. On planters full of dusty azalea, OLs perched with their lunches on their knees. Keita craned up at the kanji over the doors of the building we'd just emerged from. "Well, that's one thing settled."

"You mean you never knew where the Princessa Royale was?" I questioned distractedly, following his gaze up – and up. I shaded my eyes with my hand. Was I going mad? "I'm only counting nine storeys. We were definitely higher up than—"

"Up," Keita said. "You mean *down*. We were eighteen storeys underground. You just assumed the elevator was going up. I made the same mistake the first time. Too nervous to think properly." A smirk danced on his lips. "So much for scientific observation," he said, and the words twisted in my mind like the jet of flame that had gouted up in the middle of the VIP lounge.

A crow swooped over the forecourt, jinked in the air, and landed on one of the young maples in the planters. I said, "So what's the deal with you and the crows? It's magic, isn't it?"

Keita's smirk vanished. He was a mess, his hair wild, his face and t-shirt smeared with soot. "I can see through their eyes. But it's not as cool as it might sound. Everything's divided in half and black and white. You have to know what you're looking for. And if the government found out, they'd lock me up until the next ice age, so keep your mouth shut about it, OK?"

Dorothy strode back to us. "You want to stay here until they raise the alarm? Well, that's your choice, Crow Boy. It ain't no concern of mine if they catch *you!*"

"Like fuck." Keita coughed. "I'm going to get my bike. Who wants a ride? The other one will have to walk." He looked at Dorothy.

"I'll walk," I said, nerves jangling. I started off between the planters, glad when Dorothy matched my steps.

"No way. You're coming with me," Keita said, shouldering between us.

"Wait up, wait up." Dorothy's combat boots clunked hard on the sidewalk. "Clare, you been hanging out with this guy? Where's Ruth? I sent her to look for you last night. Didn't she find you? Yeah, then where's she at?"

"My place," Keita said. "With her boyfriend. He's in bad shape. Jaize 3000 has really done a number on him."

Dorothy hissed between her teeth. "So," she said after a moment, and I was mildly surprised when she asked the right question. "You got another identity, Crow Boy? You ain't *just* the bird whisperer that Zuleiko hired to spy on old Gore, and Jaize 3000, and the White Duke, and whoever else she thought was trying to edge up on her?"

"And you," Keita said. "I did a good bit of spying on you, Countess." He grinned, but his eyes were taking on that wide and distant look they'd had in the car last night.

"That's taken for granted. I'm saying, what other tricks you got up your sleeve?"

Burn, baby, burn! Flames seemed to flicker again at the edges of my vision, as if the intense sunlight was igniting the asphalt.

While Dorothy waited for Keita's answer, we emerged on the broad sweep of Ome-kaido. We were in southwest Shinjuku. To retrieve his bike, Keita would have to cross to the east side of the station and double back into Kabukicho. "I work at Aoyama Gakuin," he said. "I'm a *choshizengaku* researcher. That's how I know Clare."

Dorothy exhaled. "Fucking college kids," she said. "Always stick together, don't you?" Tapping one boot heel, she waited for the walk light.

"Don't go," I pleaded with her. "Aleksey needs help." What did I think Dorothy could do for him? But as I spoke, the true urgency of the situation came home to me. "Keita *killed Zuleiko —* "

"Wanna tell the whole city about it? Just because they're Japanese, it don't mean — "

I lowered my voice. "He *killed* the Princess of Shinjuku. Her people are going to be all over his place. They might be there already!" I hopped in agony at the thought of Juroku and his vampires receiving an order from Ichi (or whoever had taken over Ichi's command after the grey-eyed vampire flung himself into the fire), swarming up from the basement; Politik and Ruth barricading the front door and preparing to die. "We've got to get Aleksey and Ruth out of there, if it's not too late already!"

"What do you think I was up here for? Zuleiko told me she had someone for me – I thought it was Aleksey. Why, because I already had Jaize on the phone this morning, wanting to know where I got him hid away. Lord, I never heard that man lose his cool like that." Dorothy chuckled. "I told him, go hire another pianist and tell them to play something nice and classical, soothe you down. But I know why he's so worked up. Aleksey *is* special. He's got a gift. And it's a pity

217

what Jaize done to him." The light changed and people surged across Ome-kaido. Dorothy stayed where she was. I nervously looked around for Keita, but he must have given up on us and gone off to get his bike. "Anyway," Dorothy said. "I can't leave Ruth in the lurch, after she did what I asked her to last night. And more. That was my bad: I didn't know that anyone knew about Hachioji. Well, but Ruth got you out of there before they rolled up on the place, didn't she? I owe her for that."

Disoriented, I said, "Hachioji? I don't even know where that is. We went from my place straight to Jaize's."

Dorothy blinked. "Say that again, because I don't think I heard you right."

"We went from my place straight to Jaize's," I repeated, apprehensively.

"Is that so." The silver spider pendant in Dorothy's cleavage rose and fell as her breath quickened. "I do not *believe* that girl. Still betraying me after all these years." Her freckles stood out starkly against her skin, as black as crumbs of glass from the table that Ichi had smashed. "I *told* her to take you to my other house. I got a little hideyhole out in Hachioji, that's forty minutes out of the city. At least, I *thought* it was a hideyhole. Come to find out someone broke in there and tore up the place —"

"Good thing we weren't there, then," I offered.

"That is not the fucking point. She —"

"She probably thought we'd be safer with Jaize," I said, numb but still trying to find a justification for Ruth's actions. "And she was right, wasn't she? At least..."

"Nuh uh." Understanding dragged Dorothy's face into unfamiliar lines, bitter and yet complacent. "She must have thought, after Gore set up to catch you – she must have thought you were special. Something special that she could trade away to Jaize for her boy's life. But she don't understand – what Gore thinks is special, and what Jaize thinks is special, it's two fundamentally different things. I told her... I *told* her. But she don't ever learn. And now she goes behind my back—"

"But she said you called Jaize to arrange it!"

"And I picked up a little bit of that in what Jaize said. I thought he was just ranting. Now I understand: Ruth must have made that call from the club herself. All right, we're going." She stepped off the curb and waved at the nearest taxi. A moment later she retreated. "You try. I tend to forget sometimes. Chicago, New York, Tokyo, it don't make no difference – I'm still black."

A taxi swerved to the curb the moment I stepped forward.We swooped under the JR tracks and glided along Shinjuku-dori. The noon crowds masked any pursuit of us that might have been afoot. I asked rhetorically, in an effort to calm my pounding heart, "What am I worried about? Keita's on his bike. Look at this traffic. He'll get there before anyone else could."

"Crow Boy? I'd say they caught him already. As you did point out, he put the hurt on..." Dorothy giggled quietly, her brown eyes sparkling. "*Barbecued* her ass. Hoo!"

"I think he'll be all right," I said. "After all, he can see them coming."

"Yeah. There is that."

We got out of the taxi on Keita and Politik's corner, after driving in circles for ten minutes while I tried to remember the way through the maze of streets. The sunlight filled the canyon between the aged tenements. Keita's bike stood in front of the door to their building. That was reassuring. On the other hand, it was less than reassuring that he'd been in such a hurry he hadn't even bothered to put it away. Tension cramped my chest as we ran up the stairs.

"Nice building they got here," Dorothy panted. "Reminds me of the old Cabrini-Green."

I was swinging up two stairs at a time to keep up with her, my thighs protesting. "Are you from Chicago originally?"

"Nope, that's just where my moms lived for a while." Dorothy held up a hand. Three vampires swung around the landing above us. Dorothy swept me back against the wall.

The vampires pulled up short, and I saw that one of them was Juroku. "After you," Dorothy said in Japanese. "Look like y'all are in a hurry."

The youngest vampire, short and husky with a shaved head, spat a pink loogie on the stairs above us. "Trouble up there. Stay away, if you know what's good for you."

"What kind of trouble?" I jerked away from Dorothy. The vampires shuffled out of our way as we reached the landing.

"Wait," Juroku said. "You're – you're... Sanjusan! Yonju! This is the Countess of Roppongi! *Hakushaku*," he choked, and fell to his knees. Sanjusan and Yonju copied him, touching their foreheads to the dirty concrete.

"Quit that kowtowing shit! I don't hold with it, even if you were mine, which you aren't. Save it for your Princess. She oughta be pleased with you, as long as she don't object to minions who run away from trouble." As Juroku scrambled to his feet, Dorothy gave him an open-handed push on the shoulder. "Anyone hurt up there? Fighting?"

"No, but—"

"They don't want our help," the third vampire broke in. He was small, with a pinched face. "Fine! We'd like to do what we can, in our own small way, to piss in the Princess's colostomy bag. But if Matsudaira-san doesn't want us—"

"Do *not* tell me what you think I want to hear," Dorothy said.

"It's true! Why d'you think we came away to live in this shithole, instead of staying in Kabukicho with the rest of her numbers?"

"Packed four to a six-mat room," said the shaven-headed vampire. "And it's a good day when you get something to drink that isn't dead. No, thank you! Only reason they all stay is because they're cowards."

"Well, forgive me if I don't see a lot of difference between you and them on that count." Dorothy pushed the shaven-headed vampire and Juroku again, one with either hand. "Go on! Get on with your business, and the next time I have royal tea with the Princess, I'll be sure and give her your love."

I was dancing with impatience, but as we started up the stairs again, I slowed down enough to whisper, "I understand why you didn't tell them about Zuleiko, but they're not going to shed many tears for her, are they?"

"I guess not." Dorothy smiled tiredly. "Ain't loyalty a wonderful thing?"

Voices echoed down the fourth-floor hall. I distinguished Ruth's, Keita's – and Hiromi's. When we burst into the apartment, however, my was gaze drawn to a stocky woman in her fifties who knelt on the floor, facing Ruth at a distance from Aleksey's supine body. Her round, calm face betrayed no reaction to the abuse that Ruth was hurling at her in Japanese.

Keita shouted at Ruth, "She's only trying to help! Either you let her take him, or you leave him here for the Princess's thugs. Which is it going to be?"

"I'm staying with him!"

"Fine! You can stay with him, and they can kill you, too! Sorry, Ni-chan," Keita addressed the older woman. "I'm not wasting another second –" He saw me and Dorothy. So did Ruth.

The horror on Ruth's face gave me all the proof I needed. Jerkily, she rose and stumbled backwards to the kitchen door, where she bumped into Hiromi.

In the sudden silence, Dorothy laughed. Perhaps only I could tell that it was as fake as Zuleiko's laughter back at the Princessa Royale. "Ruth, Ruth. You act like I'm gonna strike you down with a thunderbolt. Relax. Yeah, I got a bone to pick with you, but that can wait." Her tone chilled. "Or was you planning on going somewhere?"

"Not me," Ruth said. She indicated Keita and Ni-chan. "They want to take Aleksey, but they won't let me go with him. So it looks like I'm all yours again, doesn't it?" Ugly emotion clotted her voice.

"We shall take sanctuary in Harajuku," Ni-chan said,

standing up. Short and dumpy, she wore a flowered blouse and brown slacks, and her salt-and-pepper hair was in a crown of braids. When she spoke, fangs showed. "Count Skriva has offered us shelter: a mere hole in the ground, but at least the Princess did not know of it." Ni-chan faced Dorothy. "She was not like you, Countess. She barely tolerated our independent existence here. We have long thought that we may have to drop out of her sight altogether, some day... and it seems that day has now come."

"Sorry," Keita said.

"What are you sorry for? You have slain the cruellest vampire in Tokyo. Many will thank you, as do I. It is not your fault her numbers remain alive to take vengeance." Ni-chan moved closer to Dorothy, tipping her head back to meet Dorothy's eyes. "With your leave, Countess. We have no quarrel, so let me gather my men and go."

Dorothy pulled herself up. "Let you go, hell. I got a proposal, Ni-chan. As it do so happen, I would like to offer you sanctuary myself. If you'll accept, and if you don't mind company. See, our friend over there is not in the best of shape, and as long as we got options, there's no need for him – for any of you – to be shut up in some nasty old basement." Dorothy was trying to sound decisive, but I'd never heard her sound so unsure of herself. Something about Ni-chan had her rattled. "No, Ruth, I'm not talking about Hachioji," she added more sharply, making Ruth flinch. "You think we could fit this crowd in there? I'm talking about Nero's. Yeah, I still got the keys. See, not even *you* knew that." She looked down at Ni-chan again. "Will you accept... Mevrouw van der Zeeuw?"

I gaped. Ni-chan half-smiled at the words, then brushed the back of one hand across her lined cheek. Just like that, I saw that she wasn't Japanese. Where her hair wasn't gray, it was oak-brown, not black. And yet I still couldn't see her as white: she was so solidly herself that no racial category applied, but for that very reason, she seemed more *other* than if she'd been an Inuit or a Pygmy.

"No one has called me that in decades," she said.

"Well, I guess it was a low trick. But I just want you to know you can trust me."

"Very well. I accept your offer. And I thank you." With that, Ni-chan looked at Keita. "May I use your telephone? We have no time to waste. I will instruct Juroku to bring our truck to the front of the building. Do you need the help of my men to carry this poor boy downstairs?"

"Not necessary, but they could do with the exercise." Keita was kneeling on the tatami, sorting through the bookshelves. With methodical speed, he pulled volumes out and stacked them in a large cardboard box that was going to break, if my experience was any guide.

"That's too many," Hiromi said, expressing my thoughts. "You're not going to be able to carry that."

"I'm going to send them with Aleksey and the vamps. There should be room in the truck. If not, they'll just have to kick Sanjusan's fat ass out to walk. I'm not leaving *everything* here for the Kabukicho mob to tear apart."

"We don't have *time —* "

"So go and help Politik pack!"

"Hell," Dorothy said. "You might as well come too, Crow Boy. Bring your birds. Bring your friends."

"What about you, Clare?" Keita said without looking up. "You've been pretty quiet. I guess your delicate sensibilities took a beating back there. More than you bargained for, huh? So are you going with them, or coming with us?"

"I think we should all go to Dorothy's place," I said. "I trust her. After all, she got us out of the Princessa Royale, didn't she?" I tried to appeal to Keita's pragmatism.

"Only because we could have put her at the scene if they caught us," he sneered.

"No, because I liked what you did with that Molotov cocktail," Dorothy said. "Or whatever it was. I'd like to pick your brains about that."

"So maybe we can do lunch sometime." Keita stood. "They're coming up Meiji-dori. They'll be here in about five

223

minutes. I can see two SUVs and a Beemer that I recognize from Kabukicho, but there could be more of them."

Politik staggered into the room, lugging two gigantic suitcases. "I packed all your stuff, Keita," he gasped. "And I think I can carry a bit more. Are you going to take the big duffel?" Hiromi came behind him with a cardboard box full of kitchenware and plants.

Keita blinked. Then he threw down the book he'd just picked up. "We're out of time. Forget all of this, it's no use. Let's go."

Chapter 12.

Having made the choice to go with Dorothy, I thought I really had seen the last of Keita and Politik. They would drop out of sight just as Misaki had, jumping off this runaway train before it was too late.

But once again, I was wrong. Towards night, they showed up at Dorothy's hideout to collect their suitcases. The vampire on sentry duty looked shaken as he escorted them in. "Don't know how they found us. Swear to you, Countess, no one knows about this place. No one!"

"Ha! I saw you arrive," Keita said to Dorothy. "I was watching you the whole way."

"All I can say is, it's a good thing there's only one of you in this city," Dorothy said. "Take a seat."

Dorothy's hideout was the premises of Nero's, a former dance club in the fashionable district of Nishi-Azabu, east of Roppongi. She'd sold the club last year to a shell company of her own with the intention of repurposing the building as a theme restaurant. (She was slightly coy about this transaction. I began to see that Gore's dissatisfaction with her might run quite deep.) Thus the place had vanished off her business records, but she hadn't yet got around to renovating it. You entered via an overgrown courtyard with its own gate. The first floor underground still held the bar (which was still partially stocked, to the delight of Juroku and friends), swing seats suspended from the ceiling, and pool tables – Ni-chan had turned one of them into a bed for Aleksey. Below that was the dancefloor and another bar with its own seating area. Here some of Dorothy's vampire "household" – employees from her Roppongi businesses – were squatting: they'd strewn their possessions over the dance floor and pushed together all the tables in the seating area to create a communal board, with a purple velvet curtain for a tablecloth. This stab at domesticity touched me painfully, the more so because most of them were boys so young that they probably missed their homes and families. They dressed hip-hop and spoke in a streetwise mumble. Only Dorothy, I thought, stood between these kids and the *zako*.

They padded silently down the stairs, gathering at a distance from the communal table as Keita and Politik were ushered to seats.

"I just want my stuff," Keita grumbled.

"You too, Clare," Dorothy said, ignoring him. "Have a seat."

I cautiously took the place on her left.

I'd spent the afternoon, while she was out "taking care of business," looking through Keita's box of books. Most of them were in ancient Japanese or German: treasure troves of information on hermetic magic, esoteric Buddhism, Taoism, and Egyptian spirituality... all locked away from me by the language barrier. When I tired of trying to decipher them, I'd turned to my own library books. There, I'd found more questions than answers. When I re-emerged from the pages, it had been to an atmosphere of suppressed excitement. Ni-chan's vamps and Dorothy's kids were sharing rumors in street slang. I couldn't understand much of what they said, but the tension in the air spoke for itself. The murder of Zuleiko had ignited the whole vampire community.

One of the youngest vamps now placed cups of green tea in front of us, as if this were a business meeting. Keita curled his lip and pushed his cup a few centimeters away.

"Go ask Madame Ni to join us," Dorothy said to the server. "I want her to hear what Crow Boy got to say for himself." She smiled at Keita. Her eyeteeth were ever so slightly pointed. "You inconvenienced a lot of people today."

"Yeah, well, sorry about that," Keita said. "But she had it coming."

"Oh, I ain't disputing that. Trouble is, though..." Dorothy inclined her head as Ni-chan waddled across the dance-floor and took the chair at her right. "Thanks for joining us, Ni-chan. How's Aleksey doing?"

226

"There is nothing I can do for him," the older vampire said sadly. "If we could persuade him to take some food and water, we might slow his decline... but his soul is swamped in the mesmerist's evil."

Dorothy nodded, her lips pursed. "Well, Ni-chan, Crow Boy here was just explaining why we shouldn't hand him over to the Court for incinerating the Emperor's very own daughter."

Keita stiffened. Politik made a stifled sound, and my heart beat faster.

Ni-chan took a noisy slurp of tea. "As to that, I think there are mitigating circumstances. She used him hardly, Countess: she made his service to her the price of her lenience to her neighbors in the south. As you know, unrest is brewing in Harajuku, change is afoot: they desire to throw off the chains of oppression..." Catching Politik's eye at exactly the wrong moment, I had to smother a laugh. A vampire Marxist! Oblivious, Ni-chan continued, "It is they who will lead the revolution, and this young man, Keita Matsudaira, has done much to encourage and support them. For their sake, he served Zuleiko for more than two years. Yet this put him in the position of spying on the agents of the Court – a death sentence for any mortal."

"I would have spied on them anyway," Keita said mildly.

"Precisely." Ni-chan's face remained calm. "Knowing Zuleiko, I can say without a doubt that she would have summarily executed him if he ever showed a sign of less than total loyalty to her. His skill with the crows is unique, and it makes him dangerous."

"It's not a skill," Keita sighed, but I could see that the edge of his wariness had been dulled. "I just... get along with them. Anyone could do it, if... well. And I'm not as dangerous as I'd like to be. The Court doesn't meet in the open air, unfortunately."

"I don't know about that," Dorothy said. "Maybe anyone could do it, but I never met anyone else that *can*." She stared at Keita restlessly. "What possessed you to hook up with

Skriva and his boys? All they do is twiddle their guitars and flaunt on TV, and they're *still* broke."

"They are the future of our race," Ni-chan said.

"I've met Skriva and some of his friends," I offered. "They were a lot of fun to hang out with, but I'm not sure I'd trust them with my life."

"They're good guys," Keita said hotly, turning on me. "None of this absolute loyalty, drain you dry, *Homo sapiens draculus* crap. They just want to live and let live."

"Yeah," Politik said. "And they don't think money is the only thing worth living for."

"I'm sure of that," Dorothy said. "And I expect you know there's nothing to them worth dying for, either. According to Ni-chan, you been pimping out your skills for them. You been risking your life for them. And now you're in trouble, but you haven't gone near them for help. *Have* you?"

Keita and Politik's silence spoke volumes.

"You haven't. And I'm gonna assume that's because you have good instincts." Dorothy's attempt to flatter Keita would have come off better if she hadn't had to raise her voice. "You know where they stand with the regime. You know they couldn't —"

" — refuse to put them in danger!" That was Politik.

" — look after myself!" That, of course, was Keita.

"Don't give me that shit!" Dorothy's fangs had extruded and she lisped slightly. On instinct, I pushed my chair away from hers. "You need me, Crow Boy," she said, spacing the words evenly. "And I ain't gonna beat around the bush: I need you, too." She nodded at Politik. "And your friend, what does he do?"

"I'm working on a theory of problem-specific intervention, targeting at-risk communities —" Politik broke off suddenly, as if Keita had kicked him under the table. "Nothing." He swallowed. "I don't do anything."

"Can you use a gun if you need to?"

"I – I've never...."

"Well, you'll pick it up. Anyhow, Crow Boy's got enough juice for the both of you." Dorothy sat back in her chair and took a sip of tea. Her fangs had retracted to feline points. My pulse steadied... and then lurched back into high gear when I saw that the vampires had closed in behind us, Ni-chan's men from Shinjuku mingling with Dorothy's squatters. Haunches planted on their bare heels, they watched the argument with bright-eyed interest. With their fangs and their flat Japanese faces, they barely even looked human to me right now. *Human...* I'd always hated the way that the vamps spoke of "humans," as if they thought they themselves were a new species. *Homo sapiens draculus.* But right now I was in their territory. And to adopt their terminology for the sake of politeness, Keita, Politik, and I were the only humans in the room.

Keita spoke boldly, but a muscle under his eye twitched. "All I want is my stuff."

Amusement rippled through the vampires.

"And I guess you also want to stay alive," Dorothy said, playing to the gallery.

Keita's eye twitched again. He pressed his fingers on his cheek to still it. "Sorry, Countess, but I've had enough of being at the beck and call of your kind. And even if I was looking to trade for protection again..."

"I'm not suggesting that," Dorothy said, too quickly. "I'm suggesting a working partnership of equals. A win-win situation."

"An alliance," I supplied. My voice was horrifyingly reedy. Keita gave me a disgusted look.

"A fine alliance that would be." He spoke in deliberately clear and formal Japanese. "What would I gain, Countess? The honor of dying at Gorozaemon Edonokami's own hands, after he finishes with you?"

Ni-chan hissed on an indrawn breath.

Dorothy reached into a zippered pocket of her skirt. My heart skipped a beat. But all she took out was her silver cigarette case and her Zippo with the spider embossed on it.

229

Without offering the case to anyone else, she lit one and blew the smoke at the ceiling. It was exactly what I'd seen her do on several occasions at Exiles when a customer had annoyed her and she wanted him to know it. "I'll give you this, Crow Boy. Your little stunt back there? You really made Gore's day."

"Why were *you* there, anyway?" Keita said.

Dorothy shrugged impatiently. Remembering that Zuleiko had tricked her into coming to Shinjuku, I broke in, "Zuleiko suspected you of organizing those attacks on Jaize's patrol last night, Dorothy. I don't know what your motive was supposed to be. But she said the *zako* fought back with unusual coordination, and that must have made her think Keita was involved. And since the attacks originated in your territory, she thought the two of you had formed a secret alliance." *So why not take a hint?* I tried to inject some persuasive humor into my words. "She would have seen red at Keita's betrayal. So she invited you there to confront you with her brilliant deductions. You were supposed to break down and confess…"

Dorothy let out a laugh. "Zuleiko fucking Poirot. If that ain't just like her. Sniffing around on her freelance, playing detective… Liked to think she saw through everything that goes on." Her voice was oddly soft. "Can't you just see her in a pair of them little round eyeglasses, with a walking cane and a bowler hat on the top of her head? Oh my, what a picture."

"You would never have hurt her," I said.

"Oh, hell no." The mirth drained from her tone. "But that ain't going to stop Gore from saying I did."

"Ah."

"*Ah* yourself. That's what the street is saying, Radio Transylvania as they call it, and it's never been wrong yet. He's gonna pin it on me, and he's gonna finger me for that *zako* attack, too. Two birds with one stone. A stone that got my name on it." She gazed at me, her face unreadable. "And when I'm dead, everything of mine goes to the Court, for

230

them to do with at their own discretion. Everything... and everyone."

"That's vampire law," Keita said. "But Japan is a democratic country. We've got our own laws, thank you very much, and we're also a signatory to the International Convention Against Human Trafficking." He stood up and held out his hand to me. "Don't worry. Even by vampire law, she hasn't claimed you, so you don't belong to her."

I left my chair and walked around the table to him.

"Only thing is," Dorothy said without moving, "I don't plan to give old Gore one single drop of my blood. He thinks he's gonna kill me as easy as a... a baby." I knew she'd been going to say *a human*. "He's wrong. He's going to find out what it feels like to go up against someone that can fight back." Her face was as bright as a bronze mirror, cracked by her smile, and the reflection of myself that I saw in it was ugly and weak. "I'm gonna paint the town red with his blood and throw the party of the decade. And believe me, you want to be invited."

"I'll be rooting for you." Keita turned away. Politik hurried after him.

The vampires shuffled on their heels, drifting together to block their path.

Pretending that he'd just stopped to make sure I was following him, Keita grabbed my hand. He lifted it and made me wave at Dorothy. "Good luck, *hakushaku*."

"That's right," Dorothy mocked him. "Turn down the opportunity of a lifetime, and see how far you get."

The nearest vampires hunched forward over their knees. Still squatting, they tensed to spring up off the floor.

"Get your skates on! I ain't gonna turn you over to the Court. I might be too tender-hearted, but I wouldn't wish that on my worst enemy. But when they find you, because they *will* find you, don't expect me to lift one little finger to help you." Turning her face away, Dorothy crossed her legs and dragged on her cigarette.

The vampire at my feet snapped his teeth, making me

jump back. Hair matted, sharpened fingernails braced on the floor, he might have been fifteen. "Hungry," he hissed.

The murmur went up from a dozen throats. "Hungry."

"We want the female."

"Tender. Sweet."

"Give her to us," growled Sanjusan, the shaven-headed vampire from Shinjuku.

"Hungry."

Keita walked me across the dancefloor. At the foot of the stairs, I twisted free. "I still don't understand," I said desperately. "What does Gore have against you, Dorothy? What's it all *about?*" Tax fiddles, I thought, unreported income, a thousand dollars here and five thousand there wired back to the United States. I wanted her to admit how petty it all was.

"Still asking questions. You want to stop using your brain and start using your eyes." Dorothy's chair scraped back. "I am a black woman running the most profitable nightlife district in Tokyo. I beat the Japanese competition to get where I'm at, and I beat vampires ten times my own age. And if that wasn't enough reason for Gore to want me dead? I got it in me to be more powerful than all of them." The vampires growled restively. She silenced them with a gesture and stared across the dancefloor at me. "Do that answer your question, Clare-*chan?*"

Not really. But it did tell me one thing: I couldn't stay in this room any longer.

My thoughts in a maelstrom, I slunk through the upper basement after Keita and Politik, past the pool table where Aleksey lay comatose and Ruth lay asleep beside him.

"Don't forget your books." I pointed at the box in the corner. "After all, that's what you came for."

"Oh yeah. Politik, you've got the duffel." They scooped the books into a khaki sack. Downstairs, all was horribly quiet. Keita said, "But actually, that's not what I came for."

"What, then?" I hissed. "Professional curiosity? If so, you should have taken her up on her offer. You're going to miss all the fun when Gore kills her for what *you* did."

"Do I look like I care?"

"Asshole. You're lucky she has too much integrity to hand you over to the Court."

"Had to risk it. I came for you."

The night breeze blew cool on my bare legs. Little frou-frou restaurants and bars glowed in between blocks of condominiums. People strolled past, chattering, unaware or indifferent to the war brewing under their feet. If it had been up to me, I'd have run. I just wasn't sure if I'd have run forward, or back.

The heavy swish of wings pulled my gaze up. Several crows circled over the roofs, their black pinions briefly silhouetted against the blazing columns of Roppongi Hills.

If we needed to run, Keita would know, I supposed. Even so, his overconfidence made me want to scream.

Out on Roppongi-dori, Politik unlocked the Subaru and heaved the duffel into its back seat.

Pull yourself together, Clare.

"I had time to do some reading this afternoon," I said, looking at Keita. "I came across a few… interesting facts."

"Didn't know your Japanese was that good. Or your German."

"Not your books. A couple of library books I've been meaning to get to."

"Oh yeah?" Keita opened the passenger door for me and climbed into the back. Politik craned his head around and angled the Subaru into the steady flow of traffic. For a pair of guys who'd just escaped a den of hungry vampires, they were strangely subdued, I thought.

"Where are we going?" I said.

Keita laughed. "We've got a hideyhole, too. Everyone has one in this city."

As Politik slowed for a light, I gazed at the faces in other cars, the faces of men and women who didn't have hideyholes and didn't need them. I could board a plane and be back in my own safe, sheltered life tomorrow. I just wouldn't be able to live with myself afterwards.

"Wilfred Hauptmann spent his Paris years trying to summon... spirits," I said. "It became his obsession. But he never succeeded. Until he came to Japan."

"*Spirits,*" Keita said. "I like that."

"It was an angel who taught him the sigils," Politik said. "Horobiel. That's in the notebooks."

"So I was wondering," I said. "How did he suddenly gain the ability he'd been seeking for so long? And I think I know. He discovered the Japanese art of *onmyodo,* didn't he? The Way of Light and Dark. The art of the magicians who advised the Imperial Court in the medieval era, who specialized in divination... and invocation. This library book has a transliteration of the *jumon* that the legendary *onmyoji,* Abe no Seimei, supposedly used to summon the spirits." I filled my lungs with a slightly shaky breath. "How did it go?"

Politik's wordless cry overlapped with Keita's snarl. "Mad," he panted, "Mad." His arm came around the back of my seat, his hand slapping over my mouth.

I indicated by my struggles that I would shut up.

Keita breathed heavily in my ear for a moment, then let go and slid back. "His name was Kamigari. At least, that's what he called himself, my grandfather said. He was descended from one of the old *onmyoji* clans. Of course, even back then, *onmyodo* was already illegal. Nowadays, all that's left is the books... as a matter of fact, I think I know the book you're talking about." He slapped Politik's shoulder. "I told you we shouldn't have returned it to the library – we should have destroyed it!"

"You didn't want to pay the fine," Politik answered him.

Keita shook his head. "All those books should be burned, and the law against *onmyodo* enforced. Because it's easy to say the words and get – *something.* Trouble. Disease. A demotion. A war. But it's next to fucking impossible to get what you want. Unless you're an *onmyoji.*" He grunted a laugh. "Even if you are an *onmyoji.*"

"Like your friend Ryu," I said, feeling my mouth for

damage. Ryu *Abe;* his very name hinted that he was descended from one of the ancient *onmyodo* clans. I should have
put the pieces together earlier. Too shaken to move, I sought
Keita's gaze in the rearview mirror.

And stared in terror at his ruined face, the drooping eyelids and depraved leer that I'd half forgotten, but which now
etched themselves into my brain, and surely his cheeks
hadn't sagged like that, nor had the skin of his forehead been
marred by those blotches? I saw all this in a millisecond, and
then his arm shot over my shoulder again. He knocked the
mirror up to face the roof.

Politik readjusted it. "I need that to drive." Drops of
sweat glistened on his face. "Deal with it, Keita. She'd have
seen it sooner or later, if she's going to hang around with us."

"All right for you," Keita responded.

"I don't have any marks yet," Politik explained tautly,
his eyes on the traffic. "Keita usually leads our experiments.
He's the only non-*onmyoji* who's ever successfully travelled
into the qliphotic realm."

"Once," Keita said. "When I was high on weed and PCP."

"Better magic through chemistry?" I said.

"Yeah, but sacrifices are more efficient," Keita said.

"What a *splendid* procedure," I said. "No one could ever
mistake it for a black art."

My sarcasm didn't translate. Politik nodded. "For real. It
just has this one weird side-effect, the way you change in the
mirror... Keita, can I take Gaien-higashi-dori?"

"All clear," Keita said from the back seat.

"I won't look," I said. "All right?"

When I looked anyway, Keita had shifted to the far side
of the car so that I could no longer see him in the mirror.

I hitched around. In the moving shadows of the car, I
hooked one elbow over the back of the seat and stared at the
taut, strong features that looked unreal to me now, so trau-
matic had that momentary glimpse of his... marks... been.

"I'm usually careful around mirrors," he said, shifting
under my gaze.

235

"Is there anything else I should know? Because these little surprises are getting tedious."

"Don't play dumb. You'd already figured it out. And you've probably also figured out what I did at the Princessa Royale this morning." His voice held an odd note of anticipation... of *hope?*

I flopped back into the front seat. "All right. You invoked... *something.*"

Keita made a buzzer noise: wrong answer.

"That would be impossible," Politik said. "You can't control spirits without a ritual binding, and then they're stuck in the circle. Besides, they aren't *weapons.* They're greater than we are."

Vinyl creaked. Keita leaned forward between the seats. "This morning? That was the first iteration of the mastery of fire, or —" I shook my head at the incomprehensible string of syllables. "No, well, that's what they called it in the old days. It means something like *affinity of the qi for the essence of fire.* Sounds like some hoity-toity Buddhist metaphor, doesn't it? But it's not. The theory comes from *onmyodo,* and the technique I used was one that should be familiar to you from our little talk a couple of nights back." He watched for my reaction. "Did you see those matches? I made the First Sigil of Fire, using the matches to represent fire itself, which links the cognitive plane with the material plane. That's called focusing your *qi.* And then I *felt* the power... the *fire...*" His voice hushed in awe. "It was... *incredibly... cool.*"

I rubbed my temples, as if I could erase the memory of flames gouting towards the ceiling, the shock wave that had rolled through the room. "The First Sigil of Fire? Is that one of Jaize's?" Surely, if Jaize had *that* power, he would have unleashed it on the *zako* in Aoyama Cemetery.

"Hell, no, it's not one of Jaize's," Keita said. "It's mine."

"So all the sigils *weren't* lost in the war," I said resignedly.

"What gave you that idea? They weren't lost until my grandfather died." A note of pride entered Keita's voice. "He was one of the original members of the Atelier, the founder of the Tsurukai – and he died twenty years ago with all the sigils locked away in his head. Except that one. He gave it to me on my tenth birthday."

"Quite the present for a ten-year-old," I said. "It was like a bomb going off."

"I know!" Keita grinned. Then he looked slightly uncomfortable. "Actually, I didn't know it was going to work that well. It must have been because she was a vampire. The old ones are supposed to be very flammable…"

"Admit it," Politik said.

"All right! I actually didn't think it was going to work at all. It's never worked before." He gazed at me, eyes bright. "It was like my conscious mind had been blocking my *qi*. And then… it suddenly stopped getting in the way."

"Well, when was the last time a vampire princess threatened you with death by torture?" Politik said.

"Last week?" Keita said. They both sniggered.

"Yeah, but this time she meant it. You could tell she meant it, couldn't you? And lo and behold, suddenly your conscious mind and your *qi* were on the same page."

"Alternatively," I said, "practice makes perfect."

"Possibly," Keita said. His gaze lost focus. He sat upright. "Politik, don't take Omotesando-dori. Some of Skriva's guys are hanging out in front of the station."

We passed the turning for Omotesando-dori and continued towards Shibuya, then swung off 246 and crossed over the JR Yamanote tracks. It seemed as if we were doubling back, and then the road stretched out wide and almost empty, bounded on the right by a complex of public facilities, and on the left by a dark and apparently natural forest.

"You don't want to run into Skriva's friends, do you?" I said.

Politik slowed down as he spotted a parking space. "Can't be too careful."

"I thought they were supposed to be the good guys?"

"Everyone's got their limits," Keita said.

"Don't you trust *anyone*?" I needled.

"Well, obviously," Keita said, "we trust you."

There was an unexpectedly awkward silence. Politik rescued the moment: "Us humans have to stick together." He parallel parked.

We climbed the low railing and tramped through the forest. Underfoot, twigs crunched on dry ground. The smell of earth mingled with the scent of dusty summer foliage. I said, "If this place is infested by feral *zako*, please warn me now."

"Oh no," Politik said. "Skriva wouldn't allow that. The only homeless who live in here are human." He pointed, and I saw a row of tarpaulin lean-tos against a fence, half-hidden by the undergrowth. Most likely, I surmised, we were heading for one of those tents ourselves. Keita and Politik were doing exactly what anyone would do when abruptly evicted by vengeful vampires: they were camping out in the park.

"Here we are," Politik said presently. He tipped his head back and whistled.

I looked for a tent or other bivouac. There was nothing to see except trees – Japanese cedars in this part of the park, massive trunks shooting up to bristly crowns.

"No need for that. I heard you a mile off." The soft voice seemed to come from overhead.

"Hiromi?" I whispered.

"Yeah. This is her place," Keita said. "She's lived here for years. Ever since – well, *almost* ever since she ran away from home."

"Got any more of your stuff?" Her voice was barely distinguishable from the rustling of the leaves.

"One bag," Politik said. "We had to leave the suitcases again."

"Oh. Well, come on up."

A rope tumbled from the top of the closest tree, and I jumped as its end hit the ground with a smack. Disbelievingly, I waited for the men to shin up it. Rope-climbing wasn't one of my talents. And even if it had been, I'd already vowed never again to climb anything that Hiromi had had to do

238

with.

But instead, Politik tied the duffel to the rope. Then he began to climb the tree. Dwarf branches stuck out of the trunk at regular intervals, parallel to the ground: stepping and reaching, Politik heaved his big body around the trunk in a spiral. "It's a *staircase*," I said. "How did she make it?"

"Ask her yourself," Keita said. "But don't hold your breath. She can do all kinds of things with plants. Once, she even faked an earthquake... ever seen weeds growing through concrete? Now imagine that happening in less than half a second. *Very* impressive! But she can't explain how she does it."

He gestured for me to start climbing the tree.

"You first," I said, residually aware that I was in a short skirt. "So, do you think you could do your trick with the matches again?"

"That? I expect so, now I've got the hang of it."

"Go on, then." I pointed at some dead twigs on the ground. "Those should burn nicely."

"Mad," he said.

"Scared?"

"Of starting a fire in the middle of Yoyogi Park when it hasn't rained for a month? Yeah." He started to climb.

"Bullshit," I whispered. "You're just scared that you won't be able to do it again." I didn't believe he would be able to, either. As Politik had suggested, people could perform extraordinary feats when it was a matter of life and death. So why not *paranormal* ones? And those stimuli couldn't be produced under experimental conditions, or duplicated, period. The example of the Human League for Peace suggested that this stuff could be taught, and learnt, to an extent... but their *qi* craft was only gray-zone paranormal, lying pretty much within the scope of ninjutsu and kung fu. It was orders of magnitude away from setting a vampire on fire with a handful of unstruck matches.

I started up the "staircase" of branches. If it held Politik, it would hold me. As for Hiromi, I'd just have to trust that she no longer wanted to kill me. Still, the floor of the forest seemed to recede into the darkness with terrifying speed.

Sticky sap gluing my fingers together, the smell of cedar sharp in my nose, I hauled myself between two broad branches, into a treehouse. A plywood floor rested on a cradle of boughs that would mask it from the ground, just as the foliage masked half of the sky overhead. Living branches and sprigs formed the walls and a partial ceiling, their weave painfully tight and un-treelike, making me think of bonsai on a massive scale. I saw all this by the light that the city threw into the sky, plus streetlights along a park path visible from this height.

Hiromi sat crosslegged amidst tortuously fashioned branches that served as a table and shelves. In her lap she had something that looked like raffia work. "Shoes off." She grinned at me. "What do you think? Not bad for a high-school dropout, huh?"

"This place is amazing," I said, sitting down. Then I thought of something. "But where's the toilet?"

"*Sei-no, yoshhha!*" Keita and Politik hauled the duffel bag up through the hole in the floor.

Hiromi nodded at the hole. "I just shit on the tourists' heads... I'm *kidding*. There are public restrooms over there. And I shower at Keita and Politik's place... or I used to."

"Yes, well, as to that," Keita said. "I'm going over there now to see what's what. They may not have trashed the place too badly. At any rate, I've got to see if I can salvage the rest of my books." He gestured for Politik to empty the duffel. "I'll take the car. And I'll take Clare with me."

"You haven't even sat down!" Hiromi said.

"Wise," I said. "Sit down, and you won't want to get up again." But with the words, I sat up straight. I'd noticed that the whole treehouse swayed slightly. It was like being on a boat, and I was prone to seasickness. "What are you working on?" I asked Hiromi, nodding at the handicrafty mess in her lap.

"My sigils," she said, after a glance at Keita. "This one's

grass, this one's cherry, this one's – uh..."

"Kudzu," I said.

"It's really hard to weave them together in the right shapes."

Keita cuffed her gently on the head. "You don't need those stupid weeds. All *you* have to do is *visualize* your sigils."

"They help me to focus," she protested.

"Hiromi knows the Angelic Language," Politik said. "She's —"

"A natural," I finished with him. A woman with *innate* paranormal abilities? There was no such thing, regardless of wild claims from the fringes of the field. "That's pretty amazing, Hiromi," I said. "So you were born bilingual, so to speak? Ha ha."

Hiromi scowled down at her work. "No."

"She learnt the hard way," Keita said. "And Politik, *don't* call it the Angelic Language."

"The Language of the Gods, then," Politik said in an uncharacteristic, yet familiar, sing-song. I realized that he was imitating Keita's own jeering tone.

"Better not to call it anything at all," Keita said flatly. "All right, Clare, let's get going."

"Whenever you're ready," I said, standing up with alacrity. I was starting to feel distinctly seasick.

"I've just got to change." He stripped off the grey t-shirt he'd been wearing, wadded it up and sniffed it, then slung it into a corner. "Stinks of vampires. All that fucking perfume they use, and you can still smell the decay."

"You haven't even told me how it went," Hiromi said. "Politik just said you didn't get the suitcases —"

"In a nutshell," Keita said. "The Countess of Roppongi offered me a position as her spy. Now that I'm conveniently unemployed in that capacity. I said no." He had a pectoral tattoo, or maybe a scar, shaped something like a crow with spread wings. He pulled his fresh t-shirt over his head, and the fabric slid down to cover the tattoo. "Acrimonious words were exchanged. We left. Oh, and that other gaijin, Ruth?

241

Left her, too, but she should be OK. She seems to be immune to the vamps. What's the name of that little fish that swims with the sharks and cleans their fangs for them?" He chuckled.

"But *you're* not immune to the vamps," Hiromi said. "They could have killed you!"

"You forget, Dorothy saw my demonstration this morning. She knew I could have roasted the lot of them."

There was a silence. Neither Politik nor Hiromi believed him, I realized. They thought that if he could do it again, he *would* have.

On a sudden impulse to back him up, I said, "We were down in the second basement. If anything… happened, we would have been trapped like rats. Keita got us out of there without resorting to violence. *I* was pretty impressed." *Now can we get down out of this tree?*

"But the Countess," Hiromi said. Obviously, she couldn't comprehend why Dorothy hadn't resorted to violence. In her mind, that was what vampires did.

Keita sighed. "I knew she wouldn't touch us, Hiromi. I also knew she wouldn't hand us over to Gore. He wants her blood. The only thing that's held him back in the past is the fact that he'd have to explain himself to the Court. And now he's got a perfect excuse to take her down. He probably knows she didn't kill Zuleiko, but *he doesn't care.* So she knows it wouldn't do her any good to produce the real culprit." Keita moved past me to the hole in the floor. "On the other hand, if she let me go, I might feel indebted to her and change my mind about joining her utterly hopeless campaign to survive." He laughed and swung his legs through the hole. "If I was a different person."

"Psychology," Politik said to us. "You see, Keita's greatest strength is psychology."

"Coming, Clare?" Keita's voice drifted up through the hole.

By now, I could hardly think about anything except not throwing up. But as I neared the ground, it did occur to me that Politik had been speaking ironically.

Chapter 13.

Rounding the corner of Keita and Politik's building. I saw no evidence that Zuleiko's vamps had been here. The windows were vacant, and the scarred threshhold told no tales. Upstairs in the apartment, I thought again of that blank façade, reflecting how odd it was that a place could look untouched from the outside, when *inside...*

"Do you think someone's trying to send me a message?" Keita stared at the pile of trash in the middle of the living-room. Books, futons, clothes, computers, TV and DVD player, cups and plates, posters, notebooks... Revoltingly, the whole heap had been drenched in blood. It had soaked into the tatami, and had already started to dry. The odor turned my stomach. "They hate me," Keita said. "They really hate me, don't they?"

"Mm." Kneeling, I put down my candle – every lightbulb in the apartment had been smashed – and picked at the bottom of the pile. "If they hated you, I think they'd have done a more thorough job. This was just someone following orders. It's not as bad as it looks. See? It hasn't soaked all the way through."

"These were my grandfather's." Keita dropped to his knees and snatched a book up. He shook bits of broken glass out of its spine. Tacky blood desecrated the open pages. "I can't believe I let this happen." He blotted the pages on his t-shirt.

"Well, I bet Tokyo wasn't overrun with vampires in your grandfather's time," I said.

"True. All *they* had to worry about was the censors, the informers, the military police... the shortages, the air raids..."

"My grandparents lived through the Blitz," I offered.

Keita shot me a sideways look. "What, they didn't hole up in the ancestral castle?"

"Everyone mucked in together during the war," I said,

embarrassed. "Anyway, my grandfather was just a viscount. That doesn't qualify you for a castle."

"*Just* a viscount," Keita echoed. Rather dreadfully, the word translated into Japanese as *shishaku,* a vampire rank. "And were you planning to mention that at any point?"

"I didn't think it mattered," I said bitterly.

"OK. Now try thinking about it from the point of view of a vampire who was born in the feudal era." Keita shook his head.

"Yeah, well, that's not even the worst of it." Misery clutched me. "My father's a United States senator." I had to force the words out, barely able to admit how stupid I'd been. *"That's* why they're after me. And the really ironic thing? He's in the middle of fighting a bill that would take away the civil rights of vampires in America. Goddamn it, he's on their side." Now the words tumbled out. "He believes in democracy. There's something for you. He believes in the Bible and the Constitution; it's the same thing to him. One nation under God. And sure, he's media-savvy, but he practises what he preaches. He's never taken a penny from lobbyists, never run a smear campaign, never even *responded* to a smear. When he was the Massachusetts state prosecutor, he got on the wrong side of the liberal media, and they've never let up on him since. They accuse him of all kinds of things. But he doesn't have any secrets. He just cares about the poor and the marginalized." I rubbed my eyes with the backs of my hands, since I had blood on my fingers. "Goddamn it. Why don't they try to kidnap the daughter of some fire-breathing Republican who's calling for anything with fangs to be shot on sight?"

"Because someone like that wouldn't be here in the first place?"

I acknowledged the point with a lopsided smile. We went to work in silence, sorting out the books that weren't irreparably ruined, but my thoughts were in turmoil. After a few minutes, I stood up and went into the kitchen. I stared at the smashed windows and the scattered contents of the cupboards, seeing the wreckage of my hopes. When the light from Keita's candle wobbled around me, I said tightly, "I thought I'd be helping the cause of liberty. I mean, this study could have been an incredibly powerful tool for the human-rights lobby. When the opposition starts hyping the crime statistics and playing on the public fear of disease, you have to be able to hit back at them with something solid. I never thought—"

"You thought the truth was on your side," Keita said, gently, for him. "And now you're starting to find out that maybe it's not."

"Truth doesn't take sides." I kicked an empty bottle. It bounced off the wall. "I'm prepared to learn things that I may not like. Vampires are human, so it stands to reason that some of them are criminals. But I'm *not* prepared to be a pawn in some sordid kidnapping drama orchestrated by thugs who couldn't even find America on the map!" My hands itched to throw something, but I wasn't far enough gone to miss the irony of adding to the ruin that Zuleiko's thugs had made of the kitchen.

Keita leaned against the fridge, smiling. I sensed that he relished my loss of control. "If only they were all uneducated bozos. But unfortunately, some of them read the papers. A few of them even watch TV."

"So it would seem, wouldn't it?"

"And I'm afraid it's probably occurred to them that an American senator's daughter would make a great advertisement for the culture."

"You think they'd *Turn* me?"

"I think they'd try."

"I was under the impression that it's a voluntary process."

"After a few days of the Emperor's hospitality, even you might volunteer. So best to just stay away from them altogether, huh?" Keita opened the fridge. Its door scraped back debris. "Here's something to be cheerful about, anyway. They didn't take the beer." He handed me a can of Asahi. "A reward for your exertions."

"Fuck it." I peeled back the tab and drank. But despite the smooth chill of bubbles percolating down my throat, helpless rage filled me. I was well and truly in over my head, playing chicken with forces I didn't understand. One false step and I would not only endanger myself, I'd expose Nilson to a disaster that could overshadow his whole career. But was that any excuse for cowardice? Was that any excuse for letting myself be pushed around like a pawn?

What would Nilson himself tell me to do?

All at once, my indecision cancelled out. The answer lay in the way he'd raised me after my mother's death.

I knew right from wrong. And it was high time I acted like it.

Keita popped the tab of his own beer. Before I could form my thoughts into Japanese, he said, "You've got incredibly strong *qi*. Especially when you're mad. I can practically feel it from here."

"Bullshit," I said, instantly forgetting that I'd just resolved to be more Christian to him. "Even if there is such a thing as *qi* – "

"You can train yourself to be able to sense it." Keita reached for my hand. "Ow!" He grinned. "See what I mean? It's almost like a static charge. You're *dangerous*."

I pulled away, having felt nothing. "Is that why you were going to turn me over to Zuleiko?" It popped out.

"I what?"

"Sorry to disappoint you, but I hadn't forgotten about that."

"Fuck. That was just the first thing that came into my head."

"It would be."

"I was just trying to stop her from killing us both!" He fished for a cigarette. "Don't believe everything I say."

I studied his face in the flare of the lighter. At last I sighed. "Sorry, Keita. But at this point, I don't believe *anything* you say."

The odor of smoke was almost welcome, masking the

246

stench of blood and spilled food that had already started to turn in the heat.

"Well, whether you believe in me or not, it's always interesting to talk to you," Keita said, in such a churlish tone it took me a minute to understand that he was saying something nice. "And things seem to go better with you around."

At that I had to laugh, looking at the wrecked kitchen.

"Thanks for coming here with me."

My laughter faded as I remembered again that his priorities were different from mine. In my time, I'd worked with some pretty odd and obsessive people. It was an occupational hazard in paranormal studies. But Keita was off the charts.

Every time he'd been nice to me before, it had been the prelude to some bruising reversal of my expectations.

Still, his conciliatory attitude gave me the opening I needed. "Keita, I think you ought to reconsider Dorothy's offer. She's not like the rest of them. She has standards, ethics—"

"And enemies that I don't want, even second-hand."

"She'd probably pay you. That would make a nice change, wouldn't it?"

"She couldn't pay me enough."

"What would it take? Listen, I don't understand why you turned her down in the first place. She's standing up to the Court. That's exactly what you want to accomplish. You have the same goals—"

"All she wants is to hang onto her territory. That's not revolution. That's business as usual, and I can already tell you how it'll end: Gore will kill her and the Court will appoint some up-and-coming vamp to take her place. They'll change the names of a few clubs, fire a few people..." Keita shook his head. "I'm not getting involved."

"You're already involved." Paranoia was one thing, but denial was another.

"It's a different level of risk." Puffing on his cigarette, he said bad-humoredly, "As you rightly point out, too many of them know about me already. But I'm just a mortal, and they don't take us seriously as individuals. That's their blind spot. On the other hand, their arrogance is justified. Do you *know* what kind of an organization Gore runs? It's a killing machine. You haven't seen a fraction of what they can do. I guarantee you that everyone who sides with the Countess, mortal or vampire, will end up dead. And I like my life." He made a slashing gesture. "This conversation is over."

"This is what you call a life?" I did a theatrical glance around the kitchen.

Keita simmered and smoked. "They've trashed my apartment. Big deal. Politik and I will stay at Hiromi's place until Gore finishes with the Countess. Things should quiet down after that. Of course, it partly depends on who'll be running Shinjuku. It'll probably be some duke or marquis... the Court won't make the mistake of giving a royal their own clave again. But fortunately for us, the created nobles tend to be more practical than they are vengeful. I may be labeled a magician and a murderer, but they'll see how useful that could be."

I understood his bitterness, I thought: it came back to the agonizing fear that he wouldn't be able to do his "Molotov cocktail" trick again. "So you don't want to get involved in a fight. OK. But you won't deny that you're already involved in a revolution. And even revolutionaries have to train." I moved to the draining board and blew out the candle. "Wait until I've moved back – OK. You can try from the other room, if you think you might cause an explosion. Or else we could go out in the parking lot. It would be fun," I coaxed, with hazy memories of playing in the garden in London when I was very small: Colin's new chemistry set, a kite...

It was a moment before Keita spoke. "Come here."

I retreated, half-expecting the whole sink to explode. The darkness thinned as my eyes adjusted, but nothing happened.

"This is pointless," Keita said, his exasperation creeping back.

I let my arms slap to my sides. "Well, why do you have

248

to make everything into a trial of your magic, or your art, or whatever you want to call it?" I was aware that *I* was the one who'd suggested a trial of his magic – but the responsibility still rested with him. "Why not just help Dorothy because *it's the right thing to do?*"

There was a pause. "Come again?"

"It's the right thing to do. But I guess that doesn't mean much to you. What do I have to do to change your mind?"

There was another pause; longer. "You really want to know?"

I frowned, suspicious of the smile I could hear in his voice. "Enlighten me."

He stood in front of me, arms folded. "Sleep with me."

Embarrassment ignited somewhere under my breastbone and raged up to set my cheeks on fire. I was glad of the dark, at the same time as I would have liked to see his face, to be absolutely sure he was joking. "Excuse me?"

"Have sex with me. Let's fuck. I know there are a hundred other ways to say it in English, but you get the idea."

"This is absurd." I made for the door.

He stepped in front of me again. "You're a virgin, aren't you?"

If before my face had been on fire, my whole body now felt like the epicenter of a conflagration – no sigils, rituals, or even matches required. "That's not any of your business, and I would appreciate it if we could keep this relationship on a professional level."

"I knew it!"

I remembered his reaction to the news that I was a Catholic. It figured: even in Japan, the only thing people knew about the Church was *that.*

"Not that that has anything to do with it," he added quickly. "Clare." Broken glass crunched under his feet. "It doesn't have to be a big deal. It's just a little thing, really. And if you do it, I'll accept Dorothy's offer."

"You'd just try to get out of it another way."

"I promise I won't. You believe that, don't you? I may be

a total asshole, but I keep my promises."

"Why? Why do you want to… sleep with me?" I winced. It sounded as if I was open to the idea.

"Because you're pretty, and I haven't gotten laid in ages. You *are* pretty. I thought you'd be some hairy feminist, and you turn out to be a blonde with a great figure. Couldn't believe my luck."

"I've had colleagues hit on me before," I said, shaking my head. "But you get first prize for utter shamelessness."

"What's the problem? Is it because I'm Japanese?"

I shook my head again. "Are we talking about *once?*"

"Once would be enough… for me to persuade you to repeat the experience."

"Very funny."

"So do we have a deal?"

"We do not." I spun on my heel. Escaping from the kitchen by the other door, I shuffled blindly down the hall, my one idea to terminate this disastrous conversation. I pushed open the first door I came to. The room before me was pitch black; windowless. I realized immediately where I was. "Bluebeard's chamber," I said.

Keita crowded up behind me. "Never mind about in here," he wheedled, trying to close the door in my face.

"How bad can it be?" I reached around the door and found a lightswitch. Flipping it up and down, I remembered the bulb must be smashed. "I'm going to get the candle."

I was back in the kitchen when he called after me, "OK, OK, don't freak out. I'm going to try —" Light billowed down the hall.

Heart thudding, I eased back the way I'd come. Keita stood in the doorway, his lighter flaring as if forgotten in one hand. He was gaping at the flames that had sprung up at a dozen points on the floor inside the room: the wicks of fat ceremonial candles lying amidst a welter of destruction. As we watched, the splintered remains of furniture started to catch. Varnish bubbled, puffing out oily smoke.

"Go get some water!" Keita shouted, stamping on the eerie flames.

"In what? Everything's broken!" I grabbed the nearest large object, a taiko drum two feet wide. Even this had been spoiled, its skin rent. I crunched it down on the flames and rolled it. Sparks hit my bare legs, points of pain so hot they felt cold.

"Shit," Keita howled. He seized what looked at first like a heavy black curtain – it was a robe, torn down the center – and threw it over fire, taiko, and all. We trod on it, our shadows dancing with us in the bluish-yellow light that failed, not slowly enough. My Converse would never be the same.

"OK, I guess you were right about not trying this at home," I gasped. My legs stung, my eyes watered, and I felt exhilarated. Maybe it wasn't much of a triumph to have put out a fire that Keita had started himself, but damn, I'd had a long day. "At least your control is improving—"

In the darkness, something exploded with a pop and a flash.

"Damn it all to hell! My fucking stereo!"

Another small flame leapt up on the floor: one of the candles we'd just put out. It reminded me of those joke birthday cake candles that won't stay blown out. Before I could stamp on it, Keita picked it up. It tilted in his hand, burning too fast, molten wax falling in a continuous stream, and its light was oddly blue, like a gas flame. Keita kicked disconsolately at the stereo, or what was left of it. I saw the remains of furniture, pieces of a barbecue grill or maybe a cage, and the one thing the vampires hadn't been able to smash: a stone slab, slightly thicker at one end than the other, with a runnel at its thin end for the blood to drain off. A universal design. I scraped at the floor with my sneaker, looking for the other thing I'd expected to find. Debris shifted over floorboards that were singed but otherwise unmarked. Then I spotted a half-melted wad of red duct tape as big as my head. *Ah.* Keita and Politik had used duct tape to outline a circle and pentacle on the floor, and the vampires had taken the trouble to rip it up. They seemed to have a special animosity towards magic. I empathized.

The flame reached Keita's hand. He cursed and dropped the candle. No sooner had he stamped it out than a different candle flamed up. He seized it off the floor and held it high, seeming not to notice the wax dripping down his arm.

"Stop that! You *are* doing it, aren't you?"

"I'm trying—"

I sidled closer to him, my exhilaration giving way to misery. There was something odd about the flame of the candle. There'd been something odd about the fire we put out. I hadn't noticed it consciously at the time, but now it was gnawing at my perceptions: something very, very wrong.

The realization escaped me in a soft wail. "It's not hot."

"Same… this morning. You weren't… close enough."

I stared wretchedly at the candle, which was blazing when it should have been guttering. I raised my hand. Six inches from the flame, I felt a stinging sensation in my palm, like the instant when you accidentally touch a hot pan, before it registers in your brain as *hot*. But I had no reflexive urge to pull my hand back. This "fire" was tricking my nervous system. Clutching my hand to my chest, I wanted to weep. "Can't you put it out?"

"Sure," Keita said. He stooped and ground the candle into the floor.

"It's not normal fire."

"No."

"What is it?"

"'The essence of fire.' I never thought about what that actually means."

Afterimages floated on my retinas. I thought about the fire that burned in old pictures along the blades of angels' swords.

"What does fire do, essentially?" Keita mused.

"The Promethean revelation," I said. "The source of civilization. It's *supposed* to be warm."

"It destroys." His voice was bleak. "It destroys."

252

Outside the smashed kitchen windows, rooftops emerged like Cubist clouds in a drizzly grey dawn. It was the first rain I'd seen in Japan. The coffee-maker was broken, of course. I stood beside the gas stove, waiting for water to boil in a dented but usable kettle. Keita was asleep. I wished I could have slept, too, but my emotions had given me no rest, twisting into a tight and ugly knot as my thoughts went round and round.

After all these years, my first confirmed experience of a paranormal phenomenon should have made me feel thrilled, vindicated. It should have been the greatest triumph of my life. Instead, I felt miserable… and miserably scared.

Of course, with hindsight, I'd seen paranormal phenomena before. A ball of blue light bouncing from standing stone to standing stone, singeing the grass, burning a ring around the menhirs, and the static electricity in the air had seemed to pull my hair on end. *Wyrdfire.* Another night, crowding with the Coven into a damp underground barrow: the tip of Ceannaire O'Callaghan's staff had begun to glow, a point of light that swelled gradually into a white globe of radiance. *Werelight.* Then there'd been that second night in the barrow, when the shadows of things that weren't there moved on the stone… Back then, I'd taken refuge in scientific skepticism. Now I no longer had that option.

It was like being six years old all over again. No Santa Claus, no Easter Bunny… and no first law of thermodynamics.

Goddamn it. I shook Nescafe from a mercifully unbroken jar into the sole unbroken mug. Then I yelped and jumped back across the kitchen as three enormous crows dropped out of the sky and landed on the windowsill. They beat their wings for balance, blowing loose rubbish around the room.

Keita stumbled groggily into the kitchen and crashed against the sink. One of the crows stepped onto each of his wrists and walked up to his shoulders. The third one hopped onto his head.

"Ow!" Keita shook his head from side to side until the bird swooped to the floor. "Dammit, Flash! What's the problem? Feeling a little insecure?"

"*Flash?*" I said.

"Got to call them something." Keita stepped around Flash to open the refridgerator. The crows on his shoulders clumsily groomed his hair with their beaks. "Ow, guys, that hurts... Someone's coming," he added to me. Taking care not to tip the crows off his shoulders, he stooped and took out the tupperware container of mystery meat that I'd noted the last time I was here. As I watched the birds snap fatty scraps out of his fingers, some part of me decoupled from the weirdness in front of me and registered the last thing he'd said.

"Someone's coming! Zuleiko's vamps? Shit!"

"It's your friend Ruth. There you go, Killer. Eat up, Ranger... Here you are, Flash."

The bird called Flash hopped up onto the edge of the sink, momentarily displaying an awesome wingspan. It turned its sideways gaze on Keita. For a second, man and bird seemed to commune in silence. My scalp tightened.

Keita laughed out loud. "Sure. Good idea. Go for it!"

All three of the great creatures bounced back to the windowsill and soared heavily into the rain.

Keita gazed affectionately after them. "That's loyalty! Coming out in the rain to wake me up... I can't hear them when I'm asleep." He picked up the kettle I'd dropped. "Were you making coffee?"

"Keita, this is just−" I shook my head. ""It's far out. You can't act like it's no big deal."

"It doesn't seem like a big deal to me anymore. But yeah, I know." He sighed. "A couple of years ago, I astral-travelled to the qliphotic realm. I don't remember much of it, but it wasn't an experience I'd want to repeat. I woke up on the bathroom floor with Politik dumping cold water on me, and my chest ... I had this burn. It was pretty serious. My amulet that I used to wear... the sigil my grandfather gave me. It had *melted*. Left me with a scar..." He touched the left side of his chest. "Funny. Anyway, I had a fever for a few days after that, and while I was out of it, I had these strange images running through my head. Black and white and changing every few seconds. Rooftops. And I could hear voices. I got better, but the voices didn't go away. I thought I'd permanently damaged my brain. But finally I figured out how to talk back to them, and they told me what they were." He grinned. "And the moral of the story is kids, just say no to drugs."

I laughed. In fact, I felt a new sense of respect for him, and I knew why. The warmth in his voice when he talked to the crows had been the first uncomplicated, positive emotion I'd ever seen him display. "Your bond with the crows is pretty cool. *I* wouldn't mind having familiars," I confided.

"Familiars, yeah, I guess that's what you'd call them." He grimaced. "But they're not crows, you know."

"What? What are they, then?"

"I don't know... crow spirits. Minor demons. Yes, I mean they are crows, but they're also more than that."

Minor *demons?* That was a claim too far for me to untangle right now. I sipped from the mug of Nescafe I'd made – lukewarm, bitter – and changed the subject. "What are the Sigilaries?"

"Is that the only cup left?"

I held it out to him. "The Sigilaries. You mentioned them last night. Just before you passed out."

"The Sigilaries... Is this professional or personal curiosity?"

"Both."

"Well, as you might guess, they were the books that held the sigils. Dictated to Wilfred Hauptmann by the so-called angelic entity Horobiel. My grandfather collated them into five, maybe six volumes."

"And now they're gone," I said. "I suppose the vamps took them."

"Did I say that?" Keita looked slightly worried, perhaps

wondering what else he'd said. He needn't have; very little of it had been comprehensible. "No, they've been gone for longer than that. My grandfather was the only member of the Atelier to survive the war, and the way he did that was to, well... after they were all arrested for practising magic, he testified against his friends. They were executed. Grandpops was allowed to go and serve in China with the Kwantung Army. At the age of forty. What a reprieve, huh? By a miracle, he survived, but... In 1945, your air force carpeted Tokyo with fire-bombs. So he got home to find that everything he owned had been destroyed. Including the Sigilaries." Keita tapped one foot restlessly on the floor. "If I could go back in time and change one thing—"

"And he never taught you any of the sigils from memory," I said. "Except..."

"Yeah. He told me he'd kill me if he ever found me messing around with magic, and then he gave me an amulet in the shape of the First Sigil of Fire. Typical of his contradictory ways. My mother always said he'd gone crazy during the war." Keita touched his chest. "I wish I still had it. Well, it doesn't matter, I know it by heart. But if only I had *more* of them! I wouldn't have to put up with this... this *shit.*" That muscle under his eye twitched.

I remembered the flames that had sprung up from the floor of the lab, bright and cold and voracious. "Haven't you had enough already?" I said. "You could have burned the whole building down last night—"

"It was you that suggested it!" he exploded. "You just had to see it for yourself. And now you won't be satisfied until you've *tried* it for yourself. Oh, I know how it goes." He left the kitchen. From the living-room, I heard, "I *told* you to go back to America!"

As I darted after him in a fury, he flung the front door open. "Yes? What is it now?"

"Control your fucking birds," Ruth cried. "They practically chased me here."

"You shouldn't have started running. Does the Countess

know where you are?"

"I sneaked away." Ruth pushed wet hair out of her face. Rain spattered her clothes – *my* clothes. "Damn, what hit this place?"

"How'd you know where to find us?" Keita demanded. "Or did you just come to see if they'd missed anything valuable?"

"Fuck you. I didn't really think you'd be dumb enough to have come back here, but I had to… I had to try…"

"Ruth, what's happened?" My anxiety surged. "You look like —"

"Like shit. I know." She plucked at her – my – jacket, undoing the buttons with clumsy fingers. There was another dark smear on the chest of the sweatshirt. It wasn't rain, or not *all* rain. I guided her to the undefiled patch of tatami where Keita had been sleeping. We knelt face to face, but she looked at Keita. "First of all, they attacked Nero's, OK? We weren't expecting it. I mean, people were getting ready to go to work. That's the etiquette. You show how not scared you are, then you fight when everyone's good and ready. But they – Gore sent the *kenin*. They took out the sentries and came down the stairs —"

"I thought Nero's was supposed to be safe!" I said.

"Someone must've squealed. Like rats off of a sinking ship. My money's on fucking Eloise… Anyway, we lost three or four guys right there. Then we retreated to the lower basement, and that was a standoff for a while. It's the middle of fucking Nishi-Azabu, so they're using knives and throwing stars, right? Anything louder's gonna draw the cops. But Dorothy has her .38 Special, and we don't give a fuck about the cops, we just want to survive. So she's picking them off as they come down the stairs. *Bam, bam!* I think she dropped six or seven of them before they figured out what was happening." Ruth shivered and giggled, caught up in her own story. I reached out and rubbed her shoulder, feeling helpless.

"We don't need the play-by-play." Keita said. "Who's

dead?"

Ruth's face clouded. "I don't know, maybe fifteen of their guys... There's another way out of the lower basement. The delivery entrance. It was padlocked on the outside, so we had to cut through the hinges. But before we got through, they used tear gas. The motherfuckers threw tear-gas canisters down the stairs. Well, the funny thing was, that's what covered our retreat. I guess they thought they could come on down and roll us up at their leisure. I would've liked to see their faces when there was no one there! Well... no one alive. We lost... I guess five, no, eight or ten guys, including the sentries. But Dorothy's OK. So is Ni-chan. Her guys gave their lives to defend her in the first attack."

"Juroku?" Keita said. "Sanjusan?"

"That was the skinhead, right? And Juroku was Ni-chan's lieutenant?"

Keita nodded.

"Sorry. I guess they were your friends."

"Not really," Keita said, and dragged on his cigarette. "Fuck it."

"So we got out of there," Ruth said. "But it was just luck. Gore was trying to take Dorothy out before she could damage him. He broke their own fucking rules. That's because he knows she *could* damage him. So look at it one way, he's scared. But look at it another way, Dorothy only has about fifty in her household at the best of times, and only about half of them can fight worth a damn. And now half of *those* are dead. And when they hear about the attack, everyone in Roppongi is going to run for cover. So now she's all alone, except for the four or five guys who survived."

"Did you get Aleksey out all right?" I asked.

"Yeah. Luckily, I'd just brought him downstairs so I could try to feed him."

I bit my lip. "How is he?"

"He's recovered some. His eyes are open, he's sitting up. He drank some water."

"Well, that's great!"

"No, it's not." Ruth drew a shuddering breath. She blurted, "Jaize says he'll take him back. That's his price: Aleksey, plus all of Nishi-Azabu. And Dorothy just says, 'Beggars can't be choosers.'"

Keita barked a laugh. "Holy hell! The Countess of Roppongi and Jaize 3000! No wonder Gore's afraid of her. Jaize is supposed to be *mura-hachibu*, you know – one simply doesn't talk to him, much less ally with him. She *must* be desperate."

"So after you escaped from Nero's, you went to Jaize's place?" I tried to put myself in Dorothy's position, caught between Gore and Jaize 3000. Which way would I have run? Then I remembered that was more or less my own position.

"We spent the rest of the night at the hospital. We had a couple of guys badly wounded, so we had to stay and yell at the doctors so they wouldn't get left in a corner to die. Then there's the blood transfusion issue—"

The blood transfusion issue? I thought with the small part of my mind that still cared about the scientific debate over "vampiric syndrome."

"And the paramedics took Aleksey in, too. They thought he was vampire bit, so they gave *him* a transfusion. And they put a drip in his arm and shit. But they wouldn't let me stay with him. So I was just like, fuck you anyway. I made them disconnect the IV and I took him away. But when I finally get back to the waiting area, Dorothy's getting off the phone with Jaize, and they've set up a meeting at L'Aqua. You know, near Tokyo Dome." At this, Keita started laughing again. "Well, where would *you* go? It's the same place they've used before."

"No, no," Keita said, straightening his face. "L'Aqua. The day spa. It makes perfect sense. That's in Prince Chigusa's clave, isn't it? The old guy's a stickler for etiquette. Ought to be safe."

"But Ruth," I said, "is Dorothy really going to trade Aleksey back to Jaize? Surely..." No matter how much trouble she was in, Dorothy would find some way around Jaize's demands. Unless— "Does she think Jaize has some kind of rightful claim to him?"

"Just out of curiosity, what's Jaize got to trade?" Keita's voice overlapped mine.

Ruth clutched her head as if she couldn't answer all these questions at once. "He says he can teach Dorothy and all her people this super *qi* technique that will make them invulnerable. And I'm like, yeah, that really stopped the *zako* from tearing your people up on Friday night, didn't it? No offense, but you got any Kevlar? Then he was like, no this is a different technique that you haven't seen, it works with amulets. And Dorothy was all, get out of here, you're ruining my concentration. So I sneaked away. But she's going to go for it. I could see that. And I even understand. I mean, she's desperate. And she doesn't have much to lose anymore. *But I do!*"

Keita raised his eyebrows. "Amulets, did you say?"

I gave him an impatient glare. "I agree. We have to save Aleksey —"

"He's already dead," Keita said.

"I told you, he's starting to recover —"

" — but Ruth, I don't see exactly what we can do —" I trailed off. *We could kill Jaize 3000. And all our problems would be solved.* Except for the little problem known as Gorozaemon Edonokami...

"Sorry, Ruth," said Keita. "I really think you're just making it worse for yourself. How about a cup of coffee?"

Ruth shook her head. She rose to her feet. "I know what went down when you came to get your stuff."

Keita folded his arms.

"If she had you on her side, she wouldn't need Jaize. She *said* that."

"No," Keita said, and went into the kitchen.

Ruth followed him, her face contorted with emotion working loose. She slid to her knees in front of Keita and banged her forehead on the floor. "Please," she said in time to the thumps. "Please. Please. Please."

I grabbed her under the arms and hauled her to her feet.

Tears rolled down her face.

"I'm begging you. I'm not even sure what your name is, but I'm begging you."

This is what love does to you, I thought. "Don't cry! We don't need him. We'll find some other way."

"Quit talking out of your ass. And get away from me," Ruth sobbed. "It's all your fault in the first place."

"Careful how you talk to Clare." Keita looked slightly shaken. "She's actually the only one who can help you; and the Countess. Maybe even that pathetic vamp-toy you're so attached to."

Ruth wiped her nose, eyes swimming.

"That deal's still on the table," Keita said, suddenly smiling at me.

My head reeled. "Have mercy." I said.

"If you'd excuse us for a moment," Keita said.

Standing in his room amidst the wreckage of his over-turned desk, I said, "You can't do this to us."

"I think I'm being generous."

"You're being sadistic. There are lives at stake."

"And your virtue is more important?"

"Damn you," I said, staring at the Italian reproduction that lay smashed on the floor. It depicted a red, horned devil whispering in the ear of a robed figure who looked like Christ, only the face was wrong in some way. "Just... damn you."

"So do we have a deal?"

All I could do was nod.

"Say it," he wheedled.

"We've got a deal," I said in a low monotone, vowing to myself that I'd find some way out of it. "When this is over. One way or another."

"The chances are that one or both of us will end up dead. You do know that."

I scowled. "Do you want this, or don't you?"

"Oh, I want it." He stepped towards me. "Sealed with a kiss, Clare. That's traditional. Sealed with a kiss."

261

His arms snaked around me. I turned my head away and jabbed with my elbows, and then I thought, what the hell. I'd already agreed to have sex with a man I hated. What was one kiss?

I opened my lips, aggressively sliding my tongue into his mouth. He kissed me back, deeper. Caught in my own trap, I felt a tiny pulse of desire. I instinctively wound my arms around his neck. He made a little sound and slid his hands lower. His groin crushed against me.

I prised his hands off and stepped away, breathing shallowly.

"Tease," he said, his voice low.

"When I tease you, you'll know it."

"Oh hell, Clare…"

"I was just testing your honor." After all, my life would soon depend on it, I thought.

"So did I pass?"

I shrugged and left the room to tell Ruth that we had a new ally. Keita wasn't the only one who could do ambiguous.

The truth was, my body had responded to him… and it was a monumental relief. But I didn't want him to see that, in case he got the wrong idea.

Chapter 14.

On the way to L'Aqua, Keita drove with one hand and juggled his cell phone with the other, talking to Politik. To my disappointment – perhaps because Ruth could overhear him, too – he didn't go into detail about the wyrdfire incident. Most of the time, in fact, it sounded as if they were discussing astrology. What did that have to do with anything? I thought back to Keita's comments a couple of days ago about the nature of *qi*. He'd said it was like a frequency... The tall buildings flashing past in the rain carried my mind on a free-associative glide. When I was preparing to come to Japan, I'd read up on seismology and the science of earthquake-proofing. Along the way, I'd learned a bit about vibrations, the way they travelled through air and solids, causing each medium to resonate at its own particular frequency... Was *qi* craft just a matter of broadcasting your personal "frequency" to make your target "resonate"? Could that theory be extended to explain wyrdfire? Well, it was as good as any other theory I had, and it would also explain Keita and Politik's insistence that their art wasn't magic – although in my opinion, that would still be splitting hairs. But where did the sigils come in? *Don't call it the Angelic Language...*

Deep in thought, I failed to ask Keita or Ruth what this place called L'Aqua might be. A *day spa* – as we rode up in the elevator, I pictured Dorothy and Jaize 3000 negotiating their alliance in the café of some upscale gym.

I was wrong again.

"O'Meara-san? Your party is in the mixed bathing area." The clerk led us around the reception desk and down a hushed, carpeted corridor. "This is the gentlemen's changing room, and here is the ladies'."

"Mixed bathing?" I said faintly.

The clerk gave me a look of pity. "We also offer rental

swimsuits."

Well, there was some logic to it, I thought. Hadn't the Mafia once held meetings in the public baths? Not to mention the ancient Romans. You can't conceal a weapon when you're next to naked. You can't conceal much of anything.

Ruth and I stripped between rows of tall wooden lockers. The air hummed with the noise of hair-dryers and smelt of chlorine. "My gramma would be embarrassed to be seen in this," Ruth huffed, wriggling into her blue-and-white polka-dotted rental suit. "Shit, when did I get fat?"

"It's not you, it's the swimsuit," I said grimly. Mine was even worse: a brown-and-orange plaid bikini with yellow plastic flowers on the straps, which did nothing to hide my growing collection of scrapes and bruises. The burns on my legs had come up in blisters. Wyrdfire might not *feel* hot, but it had the same effect on skin. That was oddly reassuring.

"Clare?"

Bundling my hair into a complimentary terrycloth band, I looked over at Ruth.

"I'm… oh, damn. I'm sorry about Friday night. Taking you to Jaize's."

Oh, *that.* "It's OK," I said, heading for the entrance to the baths. "I'm not looking forward to meeting him again. But…"

"Well, if Dorothy doesn't agree to an alliance, he'll just have to back the fuck off. He can't join up with Gore, anyway. Gore wouldn't have him." We squeezed between women doing their faces at individual mirrored cubicles. "But about Friday night…"

"Honestly, it's OK. I mean, I understand why you did it." God, I sounded sanctimonious.

"Oh," Ruth said rather blankly. After an instant she pursued, "But do you… do you forgive me? I mean, if I was you, I wouldn't get over that in a hurry."

We walked into a cloud of steam. *To understand everything is to forgive everything,* they say, and I'd once thought that was a restatement of the importance of knowledge, until I heard James's interpretation: *It's a warning. Understanding has its dangers, and one of them is moral laxity. Theoretically, everything may be understood – but not everything should be forgiven.*

"It's forgotten," I said. We'd escaped from Jaize's house two nights ago. It felt like a lifetime.

"You rock!" Ruth beamed at me in relief. I smiled back at her, but an uncharitable thought crossed my mind: she was like a child who'd got her way by crying, and was now all smiles again.

And why had I agreed to Keita's bargain? A large part of the reason had been that I couldn't stand the way Ruth was falling apart in front of my eyes. Yet she was the same person who'd planned to sell me to a vampire black magician for his metaphysical lunch. She might think I'd turned the other cheek, but that wasn't true. My heart had simply taken over from my head.

I felt as if I could trust her now – but I was really just trusting my own instincts.

We picked our way around sulphur-scented pools where men and women lolled up to their chins in the bubbling hot water.

"There's Ni-chan and everyone," Ruth said. "What are they staring... oh."

"Oh God," I said, staring, too.

The mixed bathing area ended in a wall of clear glass. Outside, a thatched roof sheltered a rocky grotto where hot water gushed into yet another pool, sending up clouds of steam. Ferns and vines trailed down the rocks. It would have been a postcard-perfect recreation of a traditional Japanese *rotenburo*, except that we were nine storeys up. The view beyond the pool held distant skyscrapers shrouded in rain. The only two bathers in the grotto were Dorothy and Jaize 3000... and it looked as if they were engaging in foreplay.

For an instant. Then the steam swirled, giving me a clearer view.

Half-submerged in the water, Dorothy had her arms wrapped around Jaize's waist. Lounging on a crag with one foot drawn up, he wore baggy black trunks with a white

265

skull-and-crossbones print, and around his neck hung not one medallion but two. He sat calmly, while Dorothy appeared to be trying to pull him down into the water … and now Dorothy lost her grip. She flew backwards, splashed into the pool, and came up spluttering. Jaize languidly turned aside and drew a pattern with his forefinger on the rock.

"That's got to be a sigil," I whispered.

Dorothy rose a few inches out of the water, panting. Then she plunged her face back into the pool. She came up, gasped for air, and plunged down again.

Ruth plopped into the long narrow bath that banded this side of the plate glass wall. Belatedly, I saw that the people crouching in the water were Scott and several of the vampires from Nero's. The only person not intent on the action was Ni-chan, who floated at one end of the pool with a towel folded on top of her head. "It is as it must be," she said to Ruth.

"It's not *fair*," Ruth exclaimed passionately. "The whole reason for meeting here was to keep everything on the level!"

"Shut up," Scott said without taking his eyes off the fight. "Your Countess started it."

I slid into the pool up to my chin, then sat up, dizzy with the shock of the hot water. I tapped Scott on the shoulder. "Hey, remember me?"

Face puce with the heat, he raised his eyebrows. "Old Kamikawa's American protégé. Proper little trouble magnet, aren't you?"

Outside, Dorothy kept on plunging beneath the water, surfacing for barely long enough to breathe. She looked as if she'd gone mad. Jaize was smiling. "Is this your idea of a civilized negotiating process?" I demanded, echoing Ruth's outrage.

"These are two very powerful vampires," Scott said shortly. "Stands to reason there'll be some arm wrestling initially."

"Was there a challenge?" Ruth demanded. "Who started

it?"

Scott started to speak, but Dorothy's vampires were louder. With a shrug, he let them tell it.

"Three G brought a sample of those amulets he was talking about."

"Looked like the same cheap crud he sells in his stores."

"So Dorothy asked him for a demonstration."

"And he started inventing excuses."

"So Dorothy handed the shit back to him – and *wham!*" The vampire who'd spoken mimed a pounce, and laughed gleefully. I recognized him as the youngster who'd whined for my blood last night. A ragged cut now disfigured his neck, long enough to need stitches. I wondered why they'd let him in here. Then again, like the fabled 600lb gorilla, a posse of battle-weary vampires could probably go wherever they wanted.

On the other side of the glass, Dorothy smashed her head on the rocks and slid back into the water as if stunned. The vampires around me sat up in alarm.

"Is that enough of a demonstration for ya?" Scott sounded bored.

I was on the point of dashing out to save Dorothy myself when she broke the surface, coughing and wiping her eyes. Jaize still hadn't moved more than his index finger.

"This needs to end before someone gets hurt." I looked around, hoping to see some staffer hurrying to intervene... or even better, Keita. Where was he? Had he decided to wait for Politik out in the lobby? Or was he already having second thoughts?

"Justice will be done," Ni-chan said behind us.

"Where's the justice here?" Ruth cried. "It's all about power. It always is."

"Dorothy is lucky." Pinkened from the heat, Ni-chan looked almost young, and her square little face suddenly gave me déjà vu, as if I'd seen one like it before... but not at Nero's or the apartment in Shinjuku. "Luck is a gift like any other. But sooner or later, all gifts run dry."

She sounded oddly satisfied about that. My mind tingled with suspicion. But my thoughts had no time to take form before Jaize's finger moved, tracing that figure in the water again. It *had* to be a sigil. The water smacked at the backs of Dorothy's thighs, swirling around her knees. She collapsed back into the pool, and I'd had enough.

I stood up, the rush of blood to my head dizzying me. "Jaize is cheating," I said, and the vampires leapt after me. I got to the door first, a nubby rubber floor mat catching my slide. The humid air outside was scarcely cooler. "Quit it!" I felt ridiculous. "I declare a violation!"

Jaize lifted his head and looked at me.

"Clare! *Down!*" Ruth tackled me, driving me to hands and knees as a blast of wind thundered over us. It actually jolted me back, my knees skidding on the cobbled border of the pool. I heard shouts from the vampires behind me, then Ni-chan ordering them to stay where they were.

"Justice," I shouted into the wind. "It's only justice when it's happening to someone else."

It felt like I was fighting a gale-force wind. The skin of my face pulled back, and yet the water stirred only slightly, and the steam curled in lazy clouds around me. Exhausted from the effort of trying to move, I dropped flat. A shape floated in my disoriented brain: the sigil that Jaize had drawn in the water. I saw it behind my eyes, the way I could visualize print when I wanted to recall a passage from memory – black on white, perfectly clear.

I hauled myself forward to the edge of the pool, reached down, and started to draw the sigil in the water with one finger. Suddenly I realized that I might just be reinforcing Jaize's spell. But it was too late: I'd completed the sigil. I fell flat on the stones, just managing to roll and keep my arm out of the water.

The water jumped after me.

It crashed down on me in a hot wave, rolling me across the cobbles. Suddenly, I was five years old again and drowning within sight of the beach at Brighton; twenty years old again, out in a yacht on Nantucket Sound, puking my guts up as a freak squall shot the boat across the waves like a paper boat in a gutter. It was no good. I would never get over my fear of water.

At least I didn't throw up this time.

I raised myself on one elbow. The flash flood was leaking off the tiles through hidden drains. Dorothy stood up in the pool, which was now all of six inches deep. Miniature torrents gushed noisily from the feed grilles in the side walls. Water streaming off curves emphasized by her black bikini, she stared at me. "Who gave you permission to butt in?" She coughed and spat. "And since when did you learn how to do that?"

"You told Gore my father was a senator," I croaked. "You just couldn't stop yourself from bragging about it, could you? I didn't ask to be involved in your petty little feud. But now I'm involved in your war." I picked up a plastic flower that had come off my bikini and tossed it into the pool. "So may I suggest you deal with it."

The answer to her second question was that I didn't actually think I *had* done it. But since Jaize, now standing on the edge of the pool beside Scott, was staring at me as if he thought I'd done it, too, I decided that to set them straight would be counter-productive.

I stood up. My hair hung dripping around my face. I was the center of attention. And I was still wearing the world's ugliest bikini. Guess I'd have to distract them.

"You cheated," I said bluntly to Jaize. "You weren't using that amulet at all. You were using the *pool* to hold her back!"

"Hey, good-looking girl," Jaize said. He took off one of his gold medallions, the one I hadn't seen before, and swung it from its chain. "You kind of walked into the middle of the movie. Guess you don't know what this is."

I shrugged. "I don't know what it is. But I know what it's not. There's no such thing as an amulet of invulnerability." I was going entirely on Keita's hint, and it was a satisfaction when Jaize's face went thoughtful. He murmured in Scott's ear, keeping his gaze on me.

Dorothy stepped out of the pool. One of the Nero's vampires rushed forward with a towel. Wrapping herself in it, Dorothy sighed, "So you *were* trying to doublecross me, Three G. And here I thought we had a good business relationship." She patted her hair dry. Muffled by the towel, she added, "I would have had you in another couple of minutes. Amulet or no amulet, blood."

"Pretty to think so," Scott burst out. "That amulet is *Loath Stringless*. Every time you moved, it turned your own *qi* against you. You'd never have overcome it."

"Oh, I believe I would." Dorothy lowered the towel from her face. "I was hungry. Matter of fact, I still am." She looked Jaize up and down, eyes sparkling. "All that exercise, I done worked up an appetite."

"*Hakushaku*," one of the Nero's vampires exclaimed. "He still has the amulet. Don't piss him off."

"Ain't nothing but a piece of costume jewelry. That's what Clare says, and I believe her."

"Treachery." Ruth heaved herself to her feet. "*Sabotage.*"

The vampires growled. They might have trouble with complex sentences, but they understood treachery. They'd all lost friends last night.

Jaize shook off Scott's protective arm and moved to face Dorothy. I'd never seen anyone look so supremely confident in bare feet and swimwear – unless it was Dorothy herself. "I admit it," he said softly. "The amulets? They don't work very well. It's a new design, I'm still refining it. But it's better than nothing, huh, Dorothy? It's better than facing Gore's entire household with a handgun."

He was going to bluff straight through my revelation that he'd cheated. He no longer even cared if Dorothy saw through his masquerade. He was willing to sacrifice his reputation as a psychic vampire to seal this alliance with her... and get Aleksey back.

"You gotta be flexible, Dorothy. You can't go on sticking

to your tried and true tactics when the *kenin* are out for your blood. I learned that lesson a long time ago. And you know what? You're good people. One of the few in this whole medieval clusterfuck. It would break my heart to see you die because you won't take a chance on something new."

A faint clattering noise overhead distracted my attention. Nerves raw, I stepped out from the shelter of the thatched roof. Rain drizzled on my upturned face.

"You'd like me to believe these amulets of yours would improve my odds," Dorothy said. "Believe me, I'd like that, too. I would dearly like to believe you have good intentions. But I do *not* believe you are so ignorant you don't know that to the old ones, *flexibility* is just another way of saying *six million ways to die*." She held out her hand without looking. One of the nearest vampires gave her a Coke, already opened. She poured it down her throat. "I still can't get used to it myself," she said quietly.

"Haven't you got family back in the States, Ms. Foulkes?" Scott interrupted. "I'm sure they'd be glad to see you."

A movement at one of the windows on the next floor dragged my gaze up. A small object came flying out. I lunged and made the catch. It was good to see my cell phone again. Watching the group inside the grotto, I noted that a connection was already open, and cupped the phone to my ear.

"Nice catch."

Unexpectedly strong relief flooded me at the sound of Keita's voice. "I'm starting to get used to your habit of throwing things out of windows at me."

"It's just my way of showing affection."

"I would have preferred some backup. Dorothy and Jaize just got through trying to kill each other. Where were you?"

"I don't do Speedos. We're in the lounge on the mezzanine. Which do you want first, the good news or the bad news?"

"Good news? That would be a refreshing change."

"Politik thinks he's figured out what's going on with that brand. Uh, based on the biodata we have for Jaize and this guy. He's up here, too, just vegetating. Our guess is that he and Jaize were born at the same time of day, same three-month period, either the same year or twelve years apart. He's Jaize's mirror. Or you might say he's Jaize's conscience." Keita laughed softly.

"And this helps how?" The group in the grotto had begun to file back into the spa. "Listen, maybe we should go to Plan B—"

"Yeah, the quiet academic life is starting to look better to me, too."

"Jaize is *so* fucking dangerous," I whispered. The very sight of his back vanishing into the steam inside the spa gave me the shivers. "He tried to kill Dorothy, and she's just letting it *go*. He has to be – Keita, it seems like we're the only ones he can't get to. We have to – have to eliminate him."

"Maybe later," was Keita's only response. "Ready for the bad news?"

"I thought that was the bad news."

"The *qingshi* are headed this way. Two Hummers full of them. We've still got time to vacate the area, but it's going to be close."

"Christ. The what?"

"The *qingshi*. A private security outfit. From China, or maybe Taiwan. Anyway, they're not Japanese, and they're not affiliated to anyone's household. They usually hang out at Court, but Gore uses them for official jobs. Let me see… you can recognize them by their sunglasses."

"Should we assume that this Prince Chigusa, whoever he is, invited them here?"

"Yeah, well, either Gore convinced him that there are exceptions to every rule," Keita said dryly. "Or else Dorothy has a traitor in her camp. That would explain the attack on Nero's, too… They're still stuck in traffic on Yasukuni-dori," he added as I molded myself to the safety fence, peering down at the rain-soaked streets. "You couldn't see them coming from there, anyway."

At the belated realization that he could see *me*, I clocked the crow circling beyond the safety fence. Then I glared up at the windows.

"We'll be waiting in the lobby," Keita said. "Cute bikini, by the way." He broke the connection.

I hurried back into the spa. In the open area behind the cubicles for pre-bath showers, Dorothy and Jaize were arguing, watched by the others and by several staffers who havered at a distance, plainly working up the courage to intervene.

I saved them the trouble. "May I interrupt this program..." I put on an announcer's tone. "We have an incoming threat identified as *qingshi*." As I spoke, I tried to get a read of each face. Of course, the traitor needn't even be here. But my gaze snagged on Ni-chan, whose faint smile made her look like someone's kindly auntie.

Everyone else started to question me at once.

"No need to hurry or anything," I said pointedly.

In the changing-room, Dorothy kept me explaining while we whipped on our clothes. I didn't even have time to suggest to Ruth that we switch back to our own stuff. She'd probably got used to my nice baggy shorts. As for me, it looked like I was going to be running away from vampires in a micro-mini skirt... *again.* At least I had my gun back. Dorothy slid it to me wrapped in a towel. My holster appeared to have vanished in the chaos between Nero's and here, so I just stuck the Glock in my hoodie pocket.

"Fangs do come in handy sometimes," Dorothy said, biting the pricetag off a black spandex tank top. She followed it with a pair of black short-shorts with cargo pockets that bulged with spare clips. The Colt .38 Special went in a Sam Browne holster on the belt of the shorts, and she threw a black zip-front hoodie on to hide it. I was amused to note that now she and I pretty much matched. Ni-chan wore newly purchased black, too, a sort of loose yoga outfit, probably from the same sporting goods store Dorothy had made a pit stop at.

Two storeys high, the lobby featured an ornamental fountain and promotion booths where clerks demonstrated health and beauty products. Clients lingered over iced drinks in a roped-off café area, or drowsed in electronic massage chairs in front of the vast window that filled the lobby with watery grey light. Scott, Jaize, and the Nero's vampires were waiting for us at the reception desk.

"Well, I tried," Jaize said. He held out his hand. Dorothy merely looked at it.

"You tried, but I don't think I like what you tried to do, Three G. Moreover, I don't see you offering to stick around and demonstrate your shit against the *qingshi*."

"You're a funny lady," Jaize said. "I know my limits. Plus, I have a meeting at the office regarding the rollout of the fashion line." He looked at his watch. "Gotta dash. Make sure and look after my boy Aleksey, OK? " His voice quavered slightly; I felt almost sorry for him. "We can reopen *that* discussion when we're not under so much pressure."

Before Dorothy could answer, Keita and Politik lurched down the open spiral staircase from the mezzanine, followed by another of the young Nero's vampires, dragging Aleksey between them. Aleksey was moving his feet, although his knees buckled at every step. As Ruth had said, his eyes were open. But it wasn't much of an improvement. Shrunk to the size of pixels, his pupils wandered restlessly, and his open lips worked.

Jaize and Scott froze. I inwardly cursed. They hadn't known Aleksey was so close.

Unaware that he'd blown Dorothy's strategy, Keita addressed her directly. "I assume Clare's filled you in. Here's the update: we'll have to leave on foot. They're already in the parking garage, and it looks like it's not just the *qingshi*, it's Zuleiko's personal guard as well. You met some of them at the Princessa Royale," he added to me, and now I understood why he was so worried.

Gore was only after Dorothy. If worst came to worst,

Keita could have blended into the background and saved his own skin. But Zuleiko's people would recognise him. They'd probably do a whole lot more than that.

"Her Prime Numbers?" Dorothy raised an eyebrow. "Well, they do need the combat experience. Shame they ain't gonna get it today." She faced her vampires. "OK, kids, we are gonna deploy a basic tactic, I think I already taught you this one, it's called Run Like Hell. Rendezvous at St. Luke's. Not even Gore would shoot up a fucking hospital," she muttered.

The vampires scattered.

"*You,*" Jaize said. I flinched at the venom in his voice. Even the vampires stopped in their tracks. Jaize's long upper lip curled with hatred and his eyes narrowed to vanishing point. Keita warily stepped back, leaving Politik to stagger under Aleksey's weight. "*You,*" Jaize snarled. "The wannabe magician."

Apparently Keita and Politik hadn't managed to keep their research as much of a secret from Yurika as they'd thought.

"As they say, we meet at last." Keita coughed. "Maybe the dramatic confrontation could wait until we're not about to be surrounded by hostile vampires?"

Regaining control, Jaize turned to Dorothy. "Did you know this guy hangs out with Skriva of Harajuku?" I could see him trembling with the strain of pretending he didn't want to grab Aleksey and run. "Those punks broke into my house once, stole my fucking TV and stereo, and this guy was with them. For Chrissakes, Dorothy! With friends like this, you don't need enemies."

A man in sunglasses stepped out of the elevator, a double-barrelled rifle on his shoulder, and started firing.

My own explosive motion blurred into the deafening vortex of shouts, screams, and gunfire. I cartwheeled through the air, hit the floor in a somersault, and scrabbled on my elbows until I got behind one of the booths that had stood in the center of the lobby. Only three of them were still upright. The others had been knocked every which way as staff and clients dived for cover. Made of chipboard and paper, the booths would hardly stop bullets. Still I shared the angle of shelter with half a dozen people, one woman screaming and several others yelling into their cell phones. No consensus on how to react, no one helping anyone else – was this what war felt like? The rifle roared again. It sounded like the gunman, or a different one, was up on the spiral staircase. Rolling to see out from behind the booths, I confronted the horrible spectacle of three or four very old people stranded in the middle of the carpet, painfully crawling in different directions.

I clapped my arms over my head as another fusillade of shots blatted out from behind the reception desk, the sound cleaner and smaller: a handgun, not a rifle. When I raised my head again, only two of the old people were still moving.

I tensed to rise.

Before I could move, Keita slammed into the carpet beside me. "Now look what you've got us into," he said, shaking with silent laughter. No, not silent – it was just that I could hardly hear over the ringing in my ears.

"Look at those people," I said. "They're old enough to have been in the *last* war. Come on!"

Keita forced me back to the carpet. "Where's your gun? Lost it... *again?*"

I dragged the Glock out of my pocket. God, I wasn't cut out for this. I held the gun out of Keita's reach. "I'm not going to draw their fire. The police should be here any minute. Where are the others?"

Keita was quiet for a moment. The man on my other side wept into his cell phone, telling his wife that he loved her and to look after the children.

"Politik's hurt," Keita said at last. "Not shot. He had some kind of – reaction. He's down there." He gestured vaguely, and I twisted my head. Another drift of terrified people had accumulated on the sunken shelf in front of the window, where the row of massage chairs had stood. Slightly more coordinated than our companions up here, the survivors had tipped some of the massage chairs on their sides and were pushing them into a barrier. I could see one of Politik's knees and what looked like the back of Scott's head. I also saw a crow circling outside the window. "We can't hover," Keita said. "So everything's jumbled up, but I can see Dorothy. She's behind the reception desk. How much ammo does she have? Zuleiko's people are all over the mezzanine, and I think one of the *qingshi* reached the café." Cautiously, he craned his neck. "It's gone kind of quiet, though, hasn't it?"

Apart from the sobs, shouts for help, and the howling of a fire alarm that someone must have hit in panic. "Do you think it was Jaize who ratted us out?" Even as I spoke, I knew that it didn't fit.

"He—" Keita's voice cracked. "Didn't you *see?*"

"It was all a bit of a blur."

"He killed the *qingshi*. Not all of them, but five or six – enough to even the odds. And then he jumped into the elevator. See ya later."

"So those fucking amulets work after all," I said, and strained past Keita, trying to see around the booth again.

"What are you talking about?" He grabbed my face. I struck his hand away.

"The amulets – *sigils* – that Jaize was trying to give Dorothy. Scott called them *Loath Stringless*. They were supposed to turn a person's *qi* on themselves—" I was losing my Japanese. "What *happened?*"

"You didn't see. Well, you were flying through the air. That was Jaize, too. The mastery of air. Has to be. But that still doesn't account for his mind-control trick. And I've never heard of anything like *this*. He just faced them and – a sigil? Could it have been? The *qingshi* stopped and stared at each other, and then they went crazy. One shot the next in the face. I saw another one biting the next guy's throat out."

I was hyperventilating. Trying to calm myself, I inhaled deeply, and almost retched at the smell of gunsmoke and blood.

"You don't understand," Keita said. "Those vamps are mercenaries. Group loyalty, nothing stronger. They'd die for each other. How do you override *that?*"

"You're the one that's been going on about the amazing properties of these sigils," I said.

"I've never heard of a sigil that can manipulate *qi*. It must be a higher iteration... But how come it worked for him, anyway?"

"It didn't really work when he tried it on Dorothy," I said. "He had to cheat with the water to make it look better."

"Well, I guess that was a problem with him, not the sigil. And I guess he's overcome that problem now." Keita giggled, and I could feel him trembling. "That might be my fault."

I would have slapped him, except I was afraid to make a noise. I'd raised my hand all the same, when a motion caught my eye. I went rigid.

A man in a blood-spattered beige suit and sunglasses strode across the lobby. Rifle at the ready, he angled towards the reception desk, looking neither to left nor right.

I shrank against Keita as gunfire erupted in a sickening wave, the noise so overwhelming that I couldn't tell who was shooting at whom from where. Chips of wood jumped from the reception desk. A framed poster ("Ask Us About Family Discounts!") fell from the wall behind the desk, glass splinters showering. The people sheltering beside us clawed at each other as they tried to dig their way into the floor. But when I raised my head, the man in the beige suit – the *qingshi* – was still moving, unharmed.

"That was Zuleiko's boys!" The gunfire had shaken Keita out of his panic. His eyes glowed with mad exhilaration. "They're shooting from the mezzanine. Dorothy's got to be out of ammo —"

The *qingshi* reached the desk, and in one easy motion vaulted over it. I clenched my teeth.

"Oh," Keita said. "I get it."

The *qingshi* flung Dorothy across the desk into the lobby. She landed on the floor and rolled to her feet. "Fucking animals!" she shouted, voice tinny over the ringing in my ears. "You got it, you win, just don't hurt them!" With a last defiant fillip of grace, she stuck out her wrists to the vampires from the Princessa Royale, who were spilling down the spiral staircase to close around her. Muscular thugs, they wore black sweats and white t-shirts with numbers on the back. Not actually the prime numbers, I noted distantly. I guess that would have been asking the late Princess of Shinjuku to make too much sense.

The *qingshi* placed his rifle on the reception desk. He stooped out of sight, then rose again. At arm's length he held the weakly struggling teenage vampire with the cut on his neck. His blank stare stayed on Dorothy for a moment. Then he drew a handgun from the breast of his jacket and shot the teenager in the head.

"Oh God, oh no, motherfucker," Dorothy shouted, struggling against the vampires who now surrounded her. "Animal! You just stole a child's life!"

The *qingshi* spoke for the first time, in English with a strong accent. "You stole it first, Countess."

The Princessa Royale troops hauled the other three Nero's vampires from behind the reception desk. Wounded, barely able to stand, they were nevertheless handcuffed. Dorothy was handcuffed, too. Our companions behind the booths started to give thanks that they were alive. Some of them even stood up to see better.

"They think they're the police!" I suddenly realized.

"Wouldn't you?" Keita whispered. "It's the cuffs that do it. Get *down.*"

The *qingshi* and his allies manhandled Dorothy's group towards the elevators, casually circling the people who lay prone – or dead – on the floor.

"Do something," I begged. "Keita, you've got to do something!"

"Can't."

"You promised —"

"What do you want?" His spittle hit my face. "With all

these people in the way? Do you want an explosion? Or maybe a fire? Would that be a nice finishing touch?"

The group of vampires stopped. Dorothy's captors appeared to argue briefly, the *qingshi* pointing down at something on the floor, the Prime Numbers shaking their heads. The *qingshi* stooped, and rose with Aleksey slung on his back.

I clenched my fists. Aleksey's face rested on the vampire's suited shoulder, awfully still.

The whole group bundled into a waiting elevator. As the doors closed, the last thing I saw was the blank stare of the *qingshi*'s sunglasses.

The man on my other side stepped unceremoniously over us. He cleared the booths, then stopped and vomited on the floor. I guess he'd seen what was left of the other *qingshi*.

I rested my forehead on my knees, gathering strength. I had a horrible sight to face in the next few seconds, and I'd probably have to face a lot worse before we were done. I needed to be resilient. Flexible.

Six million ways to die.

I really was going to have to learn to hold onto my friends better.

Choose one.

Chapter 15.

Four o'clock, according to the torture instrument on the wall with dead flies stuck to the inside of its dirty glass face. Five o'clock. Six o'clock, the hours since Dorothy's capture ticking away... and we were still in jail.

The way this day was going, I wasn't even surprised.

Keita and I hadn't been arrested, but as witnesses to the mayhem at L'Aqua, we'd been "invited" down to the police station in a bleak corner of Bunkyo Ward. The cops had made it pretty clear that if we tried to leave before they had a chance to grill us, we would be arrested. Yet in almost six hours, no one had come to take our statements, and the twitchy young officer at the door refused to say how much longer we might have to wait.

Well, I guess they had other priorities.

We'd arrived in a motley group of thirty or so – all the survivors from the lobby who hadn't been rushed to hospital. They'd stuck us in a conference room with fittings that dated back thirty years. Some time later, they'd brought us a tray of sandwiches and a coffee urn. The sandwiches had gone in approximately five seconds. There was still some coffee left, including an inch in the paper cup that I was distractedly biting.

Keita and I sat on the floor by the wall. Alive to the risk of blowing our cover as innocent bystanders, we couldn't talk about anything that mattered, and neither of us had the heart for chitchat about the weather.

I fingered the weight of my Glock in my hoodie pocket. Since I wasn't a suspect, I hadn't been searched or metal-detectored. That would have been impolite. But it added to my nervous tension to be carrying a concealed, illegal gun in a police station.

Abruptly, Keita stubbed out the cigarette he was smoking. He clicked open his cell phone and hit redial.

"Politik didn't answer the last twenty times you called him, either," I observed, after he'd let it ring for a good forty seconds. "Why do you think he'll pick up now? They probably gave sedatives to everyone who came in from L'Aqua. Knock 'em all out, keep the trauma from spreading through the entire hospital. Or maybe he just lost his cell phone."

"*Maybe* and *probably* aren't good enough for me." Keita stood up and shoved his phone into the back pocket of his jeans. Stepping over people who didn't bother to move their legs, he reached the door and opened it six inches. Our minder blocked the gap. "…might be hurt worse than he looked," Keita said. "I'm worried, OK?"

"I understand, but I'm sure your friend will be fine. There've been no further casualties among the wounded…"

"How do you know that?"

The cop's tired face twitched. "TV."

Openly eavesdropping, some of our fellow victims chuckled at this. Others started asking why we couldn't have a TV in here.

Keita exploded, "At least tell me what hospital he's in, so I can call them directly!"

"I don't have that information," the cop muttered. Then he made a mistake. "I'd have to check with the ops room."

"So let's check," Keita said aggressively.

I cringed. But to my astonishment, the next minute, Keita was following the cop out of the room.

Other people had fairly killed themselves to be polite and got nowhere. Why had Keita's hostile approach succeeded? Left alone amidst the accusing gazes of our fellow victims, I speculated that it was akin to the reason why Dorothy's bruised and bleeding vampires had got into the spa at L'Aqua. This was a country full of people who weren't particularly good at confrontation. As a generalization, when confronted with a nasty attitude, they would cave in. Anyone who stumbled on that core truth at an early age might enjoy a lifetime of getting their own way… if they could deal with the hatred.

No wonder Keita was so worried about Politik, his one and only friend.

I was worried about Politik, too. And that was just the beginning of it.

Keita's company, however silent, had been a necessary distraction. Now that he was gone, my thoughts swirled into a vortex of negativity. I still had tinnitus in my ears. Despite the odor of stale coffee and cigarette smoke in my nostrils, I kept smelling the lobby of L'Aqua.And the shape of the sigil I'd traced in the pool hung in my brain, like a tune that gets stuck in your head.

I was still trying to get rid of the memories when the door opened and Keita came back in. "Get up. We're out of here."

I scrambled to my feet, barely noticing how stiff I was. "Something's wrong," I said, following him down the hall behind the cop who escorted us.

"You're learning the Japanese art of understatement."

I'd been stuck in that room so long I'd almost forgotten there was a whole police station out here, a warren of corridors that echoed with crackling announcements. "Did you find out what hospital Politik is at?"

"Yeah, well. He's not."

"He's not in hospital?"

"Remember another load of people arrived at about three? That's when they got here. Him and Scott."

"Didn't you see them arrive?"

"Wasn't looking," Keita said evenly. "Dropped the ball there, yeah."

"So – are they *suspects?*"

"Not likely. No, Scott gave his statement, and then one of Jaize's minions came to pick him up – in a limo, according to the cops. And… he took Politik with him."

"Oh God," I said softly, stunned. "Instead of Aleksey."

"No," Keita said through his teeth. "No, I don't think that's it at all."

Our cop escort left us in the public foyer. A dispatch radio blared behind the desk and uniformed cops standing guard at the closed and disabled automatic doors. Lights whirled outside the glass.

The two civilians who'd been sitting alone in the waiting area rose and hurried towards us. They were Hiromi and a young man in a grey suit. The strangeness of seeing Hiromi in such normal company added to the shock of seeing her here at all. "Are you here to bail us out?" I bantered lamely.

"I called her when you were in the bathroom," Keita said. "They wouldn't let her in. So she made a call or two of her own." He nodded at the man in the grey suit.

"Hi, Clare." Hiromi briefly forced a smile onto her face, but her attention was already leaving me. "Keita, I really think we should at least stop for a burger. You can eat on the way."

"We're barely going to make it as it is." Heading for the door, Keita didn't break stride.

"Well, they often start late," said the man in the grey suit. Short fangs flashed when he spoke. I did a double take.

"Skriva!" I hadn't recognized him without his tattered black jeans, big hair, and facial jewelry. "What's the occasion?"

He'd jammed one of those collapsible metal headbands over his hair, pressing it flat in front. The grey suit had a cheap, iridescent sheen, and he'd accentuated it with a Nightmare Before Christmas necktie.

"The *kyuudan* of the Countess of Roppongi." Skriva flicked his tie with a fingernail. "Side benefit of the *hakushaku* crap. *Invited;* on a couple of hours' notice. Very subtle."

"Kyuudan?" I said.

"Trial?" Keita said in English. "No, what's the word. *Arraignment.* But it's more like what the Chinese used to call a struggle session. An efficient way of creating complicity."

"In what?" I demanded.

"Depends how it goes," Skriva said. We reached the doors. The cops manually opened one of them, but barred our way while they stepped outside. Flashes of light splintered the twilight, swarming above crowd control barriers that had been erected in front of the station.

One of the cops leaned back through the doors. "Where you parked? We can escort you to your vehicle, if it's close by."

Detecting a certain deference, I looked from the cop to Skriva and back again.

"Fuck," Skriva said. "Don't get me wrong. I'm not shy of publicity." The cops both laughed as if he'd cracked a joke. "But in this gear? I'd never live it down. Isn't there a back door?"

"We don't have time," Keita started.

Putting my doubts aside, I wriggled between them. "Let me handle this." I smoothed down my hair and gave my cheeks a couple of quick slaps, wishing I had a mirror. At least I could play on the superficiality of the camera. I shucked off my hoodie and tossed it at Keita. "Bunch up and stay behind me." Head up, shoulders loose, back straight. "Don't look at them, and don't —"

"They'll recognise me, no matter what I do," Skriva whined.

"Yeah," Hiromi said, giving me an unfriendly look. "Skriva's famous, didn't you know? He's got his own band."

I almost laughed. A minute ago, I'd jumped to the conclusion that Skriva had leveraged some shadowy understanding between the vampire organization and the Metropolitan Police Agency to extract me and Keita from witness processing. It was definitely possible to overthink the significance of this paranormal stuff.

"So you're a celebrity, too, Skriva! All the better." I reached up, dragged the headband off Skriva's head, and used both hands to fluff his hair into the anime-hero glory I remembered from Harajuku. Then I undid the top button of his shirt and slid the knot of his tie down for a dishevelled effect. "Your new look." I offered him my arm. "And your new squeeze."

With my hand resting lightly on Skriva's arm, my face

composed into the solemn expression (for national tragedies, legislative defeats, and the re-election of Republican presidents) that I'd been perfecting since I was twelve, I stepped out of the police station into a storm of flashes. Every TV station on the globe must have had a crew here, not to mention the print media. As Skriva had predicted, some of the reporters knew him by name, and they used it to barb their pointlessly intrusive questions. None of them recognized me. But as a gaijin, I made a conspicuous figure, and I knew that most of the lenses were zooming in on my face. Suddenly, the big news had become me and Skriva, arm in arm. The media really are that shallow.

Skriva restricted his answers to, "No comment," leaving me to express our shock at the L'Aqua tragedy and emphasize that we were united in mourning the loss of life, etc., etc. Keita and Hiromi walked in our shadow, as invisible to the cameras as the cop who paced on my other side.

Finally, we reached the end of the gauntlet. The last paparazzi lost interest and returned to the station to lie in wait for fresh prey.I fell into the middle seat of the van that had pulled up to the curb, a white Toyota people-mover driven by one of Skriva's goth buddies from Harajuku. The air conditioning smelled of old rubber, and an air freshener in the shape of a hemp leaf swung from the mirror. "You need new wheels," I told Skriva. "This is not a rock-star ride."

"That's kind of the point." Skriva leaned back in the front passenger seat. "What a feeding frenzy."

"I think it went well," I said. "We looked fine." I laughed softly, gazing out of the tinted window as the van started to move. The rain had stopped.The trees sparkled wetly in the coronas of the streetlights, every leaf seemingly bejeweled. "Good job, everyone."

And when they reviewed the tapes, or when the footage reached America, someone would recognize me, confident and chic in my little green dress (the lights would bleach out the stains, and they hadn't had room to shoot as far down as my sneakers). Daughter of Nilson Standing and supporter of vampire rights, there I'd be, arm in arm with the Count of Harajuku, using a tragedy as a soapbox. Everyone except Colin, my father, and James would take it for a typical C-list celebrity stunt. And even they would be reassured.

Not bad for five minutes' work.

And now for the real thing, I thought, tuning into Hiromi and Keita's argument. They sat ahead of me.

"You don't feel hungry, right? As a matter of fact, you feel kind of high. Like you could keep going forever. But I know what I'm talking about. If you don't eat, you're just going to crash and be no good for anything. No use to Politik—"

"Lay *off*," Keita said. "We don't have time."

"I'm only trying to look out for you," Hiromi complained.

I leaned forward. "Guys? We're on the way to Dorothy's arraignment and you're discussing whether to stop for a *burger?*"

"Why are we taking her, anyway?" Hiromi said to the men.

Skriva turned around in the front seat. "Listen, I'm not sure I want to take any of you. I'm not even sure *I* want to go. Why don't we stop at Mickey D's and talk it over?"

Keita jerked as if he'd been stabbed. "No, Skriva. We don't have *time*. Politik's hurt, he's scared, they've probably told him I'm dead. And why wouldn't he believe them? It was total carnage. So he's vulnerable. But it could still go either way. We *have* to get to him before Jaize... before he..." Abruptly, his voice faded and his eyes went wide. I shivered, knowing that he wasn't seeing the interior of the van. "They've arrived. I *knew* Jaize would be there. He is the conducator of Shibuya, after all; Gore couldn't *not* invite him... Now they're getting out of the car. Jaize... Scott... some girl... And yeah. Politik." Keita ground his teeth.

"Can you tell?" Hiromi begged. "Can you tell if he's... there of his own free will?"

"No, I can't fucking tell! Even the crows only have two

eyes."

Skriva said sagely, "I always did think there was something a bit off about that kid. Something, I don't know, *sneaky.*"

"You—" Keita started furiously, and then shut his mouth. Hunching to stare out of the window, he said ungraciously, "Please, Skriva. Please."

What could scare Keita enough to beg? Maybe Jaize had filled Politik's head with illusions, as he had mine at our first meeting... but that would wear off. Unlike me, Politik wouldn't be so stupid as to touch one of Jaize's sigil medallions, let alone put one on. The worst possibility I could think of was that Jaize really did mean to make Politik his mortal toy, a substitute for Aleksey. (What was it Keita had said? *His mirror... his conscience.*) But Jaize could hardly tie Politik up and brand him while they were at this arraignment thing...

I said nothing. I wanted to get there as much as Keita did.

Eventually, Skriva said, "Oh, OK."

He fiddled with the dashboard controls. Punk rock burst out of the speakers, the woofers behind the rear seats thumping so loudly that my teeth jarred in my skull.

Ahead of me, Hiromi scooted closer to Keita. They talked quietly, but I couldn't overhear them, and the music made general conversation impossible.

It didn't matter, I told myself. All that mattered was that we were taking the fight to the enemy at last.

The city zipped past in a sparkling blur of shop windows, neon, and Sunday-evening traffic. The sky was a rich shade of violet, steadily deepening into night. Wet asphalt reflected the glow of traffic lights. The rain had soaked off the humidity; people milled outside the clusters of shops and izakayas around each subway station. They seemed to move in sync with the soundtrack of dirty guitar noise that filled the van. Shirtsleeves and black hair, cleavage and miniskirts, blond hair and supertanned limbs – the people of Tokyo were beautiful, and the city itself was beautiful, too, with its futuristic skyscrapers, pocket timewarps, and wall-to-wall advertising. It was worth defending.

I knew my American heritage was taking over when I started getting sentimental.

Unfortunately, I was also half English, and that part of me was muttering: *Are you utterly insane?*

I shifted on the scratchy upholstery as we skimmed past yet another agglomeration of train station, subway station, and department store – *Meguro,* said the roman letters below the kanji on the station entrance, and I finally got a sense of where we were. South of Shibuya, west of Roppongi. We'd driven clear across central Tokyo.

Skriva turned off the CD player. "We're going to be fashionably late."

The shops gave way to hilly streets lined with trees. Another residential district, but neither as posh as Jaize's neighborhood nor as trendy as the Aoyama Gakuin area. Low blocks of condos kept their backs turned to the street. No convenience stores, not so much as a vending machine – "Are we still in Tokyo?" I asked with a laugh that did nothing to dispel my nerves.

Hiromi slewed her eyes around. "People say this part of the city looks like America."

"Oh."

"Lots of gaijin here. You can't even rent in Shiro-Kanedai on less than ten million a year."

We parked at the end of a line of BMWs, Crown Lincolns, and luxury SUVs. "Want me to stay with the van?" the driver said hopefully.

"Oh, all right," Skriva said, glancing at the young vampire's shorts and Che Guevara t-shirt. "You're not dressed for this, anyway."

Sighing in relief, the driver lit a cigarette. The rest of us climbed stiffly out of the van. I inhaled the scent of wet foliage with an appreciation I'd never felt before. It was amazing what the fear of death had done for my perceptions.

"I need the leashes," Skriva said. "I think they're under the passenger seat." He leaned back into the van. The driver poked around amidst the fast food wrappers and beer cans on the floor.

Keita let out a soft hiss of impatience and lit a cigarette, the smoke curdling my appreciation of the night. He'd spent most of the journey on the edge of his seat, mentally ranging out ahead with his crows. The effort had left him looking drained, but if he'd learned anything useful, he hadn't seen fit to share it with anyone except Hiromi.

"Try the glove compartment," Skriva said to the driver.

"We're going to stick out a mile," Hiromi fretted. She tugged at the bulky fanny pack she wore, arranging her loose grey tank top over it. Under the tank, she wore yesterday's cutoffs. Keita was also in yesterday's jeans and t-shirt, impressively the worse for wear. I looked down at myself and giggled. "What's so funny?" Hiromi said.

I shrugged. "I'm finally dressed for the occasion."

Keita abruptly came back to earth. "I've thought about it, and you're staying here." He eyed Skriva. "It's too much of a risk."

Hiromi said, "I thought we decided to take her in with us. You said she might be able to — "

"I've changed my mind."

"Oh, have you?" I said. "Well, let me remind you that the life of one of *my* friends is on the line, too. I may not be able to do anything to help her, but I'm damn well going to be there." I raised my voice as Keita began to object. "Excuse me, Keita, it's not up to you."

Skriva turned from the van. "That's right. It's up to me, and I say she can come if she wants to. Her funeral." He and the driver both laughed. "But seriously, you should all be OK as long as you're with me." His hands dripped with chains. "It's the etiquette." With a slightly apologetic expression, he handed a chain to each of us. They were about four feet long and quite heavy, with miniature skulls on the loops at one end.

"Skriva, you're crazy," Keita said, voice thick with rage.

"Right. I'm crazy just for bringing you guys here. Put the shit on your wrists. You're supposed to use your dominant hand, but we can pretend you're all lefties. Thread one end though the loop." Watching us fumble with the chains, he snapped, "It's just for show, Matsudaira. You can keep hold of the other end for now."

We walked down the hill. Apart from the faint susurration of raindrops falling from the trees, the only sound was the jingle of the chains looped in our left hands. The line of luxury vehicles continued around the curve at the bottom of the hill. Almost all of them had tinted windows.

"Look at this rabble," Skriva said. "Got to be everyone down to *danshaku*. He's doing it by the book. Bit of a gamble!"

"You think?" Keita said.

"No." Skriva sighed. "Not really."

We rounded the curve. Lights blazed from behind the trees in a walled yard. Two long storeys, with a higher circular wing stuck onto the back, the building within looked like some kind of institution. Outside the gates, vehicles idled while their passengers hustled out. The scene reminded me, in a cracked way, of kids getting dropped off at school, late for class. But these "kids" were tall and dressed in elegant evening wear. Hiromi and Keita speculated on their identities. Skriva pronounced that most of them would be of the White Duke's household. It appeared that Shiro-Kanedai lay in the clave of this character, properly known as the Duke of Meguro-Gotanda.

"They had a concert or something scheduled for tonight, according to their website." Skriva chortled. "Wouldn't it be funny if some people showed up without realizing it had been cancelled!"

"We can't see inside," Keita complained. "The auditorium doesn't have any windows."

"It's mostly underground. What were you expecting? This is a school for vampires."

"What kind of school?" I said. "Bloodsucking 101 and

Murder For Beginners?"

"No," Skriva said. "Eternal Family Elementary. What are you looking like that for? Vampires have kids, too."

"Although some say they shouldn't," Keita said.

"Hey, I'm one of them. No rugrats for this vampire, thank you. Still, a lot of the White Duke's crowd are all about being normal, you know, just like humans." Skriva's voice rose slightly. "My point is, if you're going to act like a human, why be a vampire? You're a fucking embarrassment to the *real* vampires. Why don't you just pluck your fangs out and start dying? That's what you really want, anyway. *Eternal Family!*" Skriva jerked his chin at the modest plaque on the gatepost we were now approaching. "That's a fucking contradiction in terms. And so are *they.*"

I said, "It seems like a contradiction in terms to try a supposedly dangerous traitor at an elementary school, too."

"Oh no, *that* makes perfect sense," Skriva said grumpily. "It's Gore's way of telling the White Duke and all his happy little families not to get too comfortable."

The last of the latecomers, we crossed the empty schoolyard. Off to the right, a wooden jungle gym stood beside a slide and a sandbox. That was why the scene outside the gates had reminded me of a school run, I realized: without consciously noting it, I'd seen the top of the jungle gym over the wall. A handful of teenagers were goofing around on the tyre swings. It might have been night outside any school in America. Heart aching, I remembered the boy who'd been killed at L'Aqua today. If only he'd known there was more than one way of being a vampire teenager.

And had I really just learned that vampirism was *inherited?*

God help me, the evidence was piling up in favor of the medical model. But how could vampirism be a genetic disease? The data we had on vampire networks, both here and in America, clearly showed patterns of "contagion" based on social contact. Well, given a viral or bacterial transmission mechanism, there was no obvious reason why parents shouldn't "infect" their children, and in fact we had a few such cases in the USA. But where would that leave the mysterious process of "Turning"?

And hadn't Skriva implied that you could *choose* vampirism? Or was that just his way of expressing his loathing of "happy families"?

" — put in a good word for heraaaah," Keita yelped. I jerked out of my reverie to see Skriva lunging to grab him. Chain jingling, Keita skittered back, but not fast enough to escape Skriva, who bulled after him, backed him around the entrance of the school, and pinned him against the wall. "You are not, repeat *not* going to start anything in here." Balling Keita's t-shirt in his fist, Skriva shook him for emphasis. Keita's head bounced off the pebble-dashed wall. "Sure, I feel bad for Dorothy. But she's just not worth it to me. And if it comes to that, Matsudaira? You're not, either."

"How many times do we have to tell you!" Hiromi danced on her toes in distress. "All we care about is Politik!"

"That's not what he said." Skriva shook Keita again.

"All I said," Keita protested, "was that it doesn't seem fair — "

"You haven't seen unfair yet," Skriva said grimly.

Keita's gaze lurched over Skriva's padded grey shoulder, as if he expected me to explain why he'd spoken up for Dorothy. *Our pact.* Irritation twisted in my stomach. *For God's sake, I'm not going to hold you to it,* I wanted to tell him. *I know things have changed. I know I'm on my own.*

"Basic facts of life," Skriva said softly, his face inches from Keita's. "Gore runs this town. The *kami* regime is totalitarian. It was you who taught me that, Matsudaira. Black is white, allegiance is slavery, freedom is death, taxation is robbery, respect is crawling on your belly... and justice is whatever Gore says it is. Are we going to put up with it forever? Fuck no. But you can't fight the power if you're dead. You taught me that, too." He paused. "There are about four hundred of them in there, and how many of us? Four, counting the chicks. So you know what, I'm going to keep my mouth shut and let whatever happens, happen. And so are you."

"Cool your jets," Keita coughed. Chain jingling, he reached up to loosen Skriva's grip on his t-shirt. "We've got a deal, haven't we?"

"What deal?" I whispered to Hiromi.

"Skriva's supposed to get us in here," she muttered. "And I guess we're going to help him and his friends take Three G down. But that's dependent on getting them organized. They were all hopped up after they heard about what Keita did to Zuleiko, but Skriva was talking about testifying in Dorothy's favor when I met up with him this afternoon, and look how long *that* lasted. Basically, you can't count on them for anything. But it makes me so *mad* – " She raised her voice. "Skriva, you ought to be ashamed of yourself! Politik is your friend, too!"

A shadow blurred the rectangle of light outside the doors of the school. I said, "Uh, I think someone's coming."

"No ruckusing on school grounds!" A stern voice preceded its owner down the steps. Skriva and Keita separated. A heavyset man in a navy suit came around the corner. "Is this how you behave at home?" He checked at the clink of chains.

"At home I behave much worse," Skriva said.

"I'm sorry, I thought it was the kids." Tiny fangs showed when the man spoke. He gestured in the direction of the jungle gym. "We only go up to sixth grade at present, but we can't keep the older kids off the grounds. There are so few places they can go, without... So that's who I thought you were. But hadn't you better go in, if your... er... the testimonies have already begun."

"Good. I can't stand those endless opening formalities," Skriva said. "By the way, what's the royal headcount? I assume the court's sent someone?"

The navy-suited vampire looked more uncomfortable than ever. "Archduke Moritsune is here as observer and enforcer of the auspices – "

"That dinosaur."

"Prince Chigusa is also here, but as an, er, injured party, rather than an observer. Since the latest tragic incident took place in his clave. And the great surprise of the evening, Princess Zuleiko—"

Keita said, "*What?*"

"—must say it's extremely courageous of her to be present in person."

"You mean she's not dead," Skriva stated.

"Not in the least. Undead as ever... Well, not perhaps quite *as ever.*"

"Well, fuck," Skriva said. "Guess that was just a rumor." His jaw worked.

"Greatly exaggerated," the navy-suited vampire said sadly.

Without looking at any of us, Skriva snapped his fingers. Keita moved first, as if in a dream. I understood how he felt. How could Zuleiko have survived the conflagration at the Princessa Royale? She'd gone up in *flames!* And not just any flames, either...

Face blank, Keita placed the end of his wrist chain – his *leash* – in Skriva's hand. Hiromi copied him, and I reluctantly followed suit. Skriva looped the ends of all three chains around his fist, shortening them.

"The auditorium is just down that corridor," the navy-suited vampire said, catching up with us inside the glass doors. "Without intending any offense, I would – I would advise you to preserve due decorum. Er, if your friends—"

"My *slaves,*" Skriva said, "won't cause any trouble. Just got through disciplining them. They'll behave for oh, at least fifteen minutes now."

The man winced. "By the way, I know we've met, but I'm afraid—"

"Skriva."

"Count of Harajuku to you," Hiromi piped up.

"And you are?"

The man reacted to Skriva's title. "I have the honor to be the principal of Eternal Family Elementary School, appointed to my post by His Grace the Duke of Meguro-Gotanda."

Skriva turned down the corridor the principal had indicated. Over his shoulder, he said, "The line of applicants must have been out the door that day."

Science-fair posterboards and children's drawings lined the walls of the corridor. At first glance, the drawings could have adorned any school in the world – but when I looked more closely, most of the colorfully depicted human figures had fangs. I also spotted a vampire Doraemon, a vampire Pikachu, and a vampire Anpanman. Obviously, self-esteem was a major tenet of Eternal Family's educational philosophy.

"I killed her," Keita mumbled. "Goddamn it, I *killed* her!"

Skriva gave him a cold look. "I'm starting to wonder if the rumors about your shit-hot new magical powers were greatly exaggerated, too."

"No rumor could do them justice," I said. "I don't believe she's alive. It's got to be an impersonator. A PR ploy."

"Oh, is that how you think we do it?" Skriva walked faster. "I should have known. That bitch is the next closest thing to immortal."

"I don't believe in immortality," I said. "Not of the body."

"Guess what? No one gives a shit what you believe."

"Fine, but *you* thought she was dead, too. Everyone did. I'm sorry if this is a touchy topic, but it seems that most of you vampires don't believe in immortality, either."

"Whatever," Skriva said.

Outside the double doors at the end of the corridor, a woman with the harried look of a PTA volunteer sat on a folding chair. "ID, please?"

Skriva dragged his wallet out and handed over his driver's license.

"Shintaro Nakamura?"

"Skriva," Skriva corrected her, not looking at the rest of us. "Of Harajuku."

"And three slaves. Will you be testifying, Nakamura-san?"

"Absolutely not," Skriva said.

"Then you may join the spectators' section on the right side of the auditorium."

She ushered us through the doors into darkness. As when arriving at any theater, it was like stepping into an alternate reality. This transition hit extra hard because of the smell. Perfume, aftershave, and cologne, the mix changed with every shift of the air, and underneath it lay a dry stench like a foxhole: the smell of rotten meat caught in decaying molars, bones gnawed and left unburied.

Fighting nausea, I registered the rustling tension of a packed house. A high-pitched voice streamed from the PA system, speaking less-than-fluent Japanese. I knew that intonation from somewhere... But before I could get a proper look at the stage, Skriva dragged on my leash. Following the flashlight of an usher, we stumbled around the back of the auditorium. I fingered the Glock in my pocket. An incredulous sense of relief overpowered my nausea. That was it. That was all. We were in.

"I can't believe we didn't get searched," I whispered to Keita.

"It would be a breach of etiquette," he whispered back. "Insulting to Skriva. And besides, who'd dare to, quote, <u>start anything</u> here? It'd be like shooting up the Oscars. Or Congress."

Skriva jerked our leashes, making me stumble and bump into Keita. At the rattle of chains, people in the back row glanced around crossly.

Our usher led us into a knot of people and turned. He was scarcely over five feet tall, gaunt in a baggy black suit. Silhouetted against the stage, his hair was pulled back into a slick topknot. "Standing room only," he murmured. His breath reeked like a Dumpster. Seeing me involuntarily recoil, he cackled and inverted his flashlight under his chin. Cadaverously bony, his face had the dead pallor of a spook mask. Heavy fangs overlapped his lower lip, making his chin appear to recede. His slightly bulging eyes were a milky brownish-grey. He popped them wide, stuck out his tongue like Gene Simmons, waggled the flashlight to give me the full effect, then cackled again and left us.

"What a clown," I muttered, playing down my shock. "Shame about the halitosis."

"Yeah, well, that was one of Gore's *kenin*. Word is he feeds them on raw meat," Keita said.

"That explains it, then. No omega-3s. Essential for brain function. Also, they've got to be short on vitamin D," I said, and gasped down a giggle. I was starting to feel slightly hysterical.

Down on the stage, a spotlight framed the solitary figure of Dorothy sitting on a straight-backed wooden chair. Staring stonily into the auditorium, she was still clad in her shorts and tank top. At the back of the stage stood eight or nine *kenin* in black suits. Each of them held an assault rifle. Nothing like naked weapons aimed, albeit loosely, at the audience to add an edge of drama to the proceedings.

Gorozaemon Edonokami himself, in a black tailcoat with shoulderpieces that stood out like samurai armor, hulked behind a battered wooden lectern at the front of the stage. Eloise, my red-headed coworker from Exiles, stood at another lectern, monologuing about Dorothy's financial shenanigans.

"...and her employees are allowed to keep their tips! There was nothing I could do about it, but I knew it just wasn't right. So, doing what I could, I make it a rule to donate all my tips to good causes, including regular contributions," Eloise beamed into the audience, "to the scholarship fund of this wonderful school..."

Gore leaned on his lectern, the stiff shoulderpieces of his costume rising. "Thank you," he cut Eloise off. "That was very informative."

Ruth had suspected Eloise of being the one who betrayed Dorothy at Nero's. Most likely, she was right. But I'd had my own suspicions...

"We have heard how the traitor mismanaged the responsibilities that were entrusted to her, how she succumbed to greed, and how she cheated the Emperor of his due," Gore boomed, while Eloise was escorted offstage by half a dozen men and women in loose black boilersuits. "But we are not here to prosecute her for tax evasion. Far more atrocious charges are laid against her."

His dramatic pause turned into a delay. A small girl in a fluffy pink dress ran out, sat down at the upright piano at the back of the stage, and launched into an excruciating arrangement of "Home On The Range." The stagehands darted into the wings, came back, conferred with Gore, ran off again. Sweat trickled down my back. An occasional thread of cool air on my face suggested that the A/C was working, but it couldn't cope with this crowd. To distract myself from the heat and the stench, I studied the other latecomers around us. Presumably, they were all vampires, but they looked like guests at some second-tier benefit in DC: they'd mostly come in couples, and their anxious expressions belied their polished outfits and hairstyles.

Skriva, Keita, and Hiromi stood on tiptoe, scanning the rest of the audience. We had a splendid view of the backs of a couple of hundred heads. But we could also see the faces of the people seated on the far left side of the auditorium. "Are those the witnesses?" I whispered to Keita.

"No. Down front in the middle."

Sure enough, there was Eloise being escorted back to her seat in the second row.

"Over there, that's the observers," Keita whispered. "See the old guy in the first row? That's Archduke Moritsune. Actually, I think most of that whole section is his entourage. They're here to make sure Gore doesn't bend the rules too far." His brow knitted. "You heard Skriva say Gore's doing this by the book. But he didn't have any choice. Dorothy was too hard to kill: she survived the attack on Nero's, and Gore must have realized it was going to be impossible to cover up another operation on that scale. So he fell back on the old 'resisting arrest' scenario. But it *is* a gamble. He can't be sure that this show is going to go his way. It's decided by acclaim… no one has to individually stick their neck out. Skriva's being negative about it, but I think Dorothy may have more supporters here than anyone realizes."

It would be nice to think so. The "arraignment" was obviously a kangaroo court.

"Something's really starting to bother me," I murmured. "Where's the Court in all this?"

"Over there, I told you. The ones who look like they woke up in nineteen-thirty."

"No, I mean, why do they let Gore run this town? Why is he free to terrorize the entire vampire community? Why do they let him get away with murder? He's only a glorified tax collector, according to everyone. Where's the real power? Where's the Emperor?"

"The real power? Gore is it." Keita smiled mirthlessly, still scanning the auditorium.

"So the Emperor's just a figurehead!" Although I'd more or less come to that conclusion myself, it still crushed me. No court of appeal, nowhere to petition for justice. Gore was it.

"The Emperor's the source of legitimacy. There's a difference between power and legitimacy." Keita finally paid attention to me. "How much Japanese history do you know?"

"Tokugawa Ieyasu unified Japan in 1603…"

"That's it right there. The court and the *bakufu*, authority and power. They have an emperor… and they have a shogun." Keita indicated Gore. "I don't know if it's a vampire thing or a Japanese thing, but I lean towards the latter interpretation." He stared bleakly down at the audience. "No one in this country ever takes responsibility for their actions, unless they get caught… and power invariably falls into the hands of the worst hypocrites of all. *That's* why I didn't go the corporate route."

"And there I thought it was because no one would hire you with that attitude," I said.

"No, that was Politik." Keita didn't take offense at my gibe. That in itself was unnerving. "He went through the whole job-search thing, but I guess the recruiters could tell his heart wasn't in it. Six months after graduation, he was back on campus, kind of half-heartedly doing coursework for a master's in sociology. That's when he hooked up with me and Ryu. The funny thing is how completely he... It was like he'd finally found what he was born to do. He's almost more into it than I am. And you know how single-minded some people are. Once they set a goal for themselves, they'd rather die than fail."

"Well, maybe I haven't mentioned this, but I really admire you guys for your persistence," I said awkwardly. *If for nothing else.*

"That's all Politik. He was the one who updated the cycles from my grandfather's notebooks. When something went wrong, he'd stay up all night to redo the calculations. He's done all the same *qi* exercises as me, he did all the drugs when I was doing them... and he's never even *failed* so you'd notice. And I never noticed how tough it was for him. And now, there he is!" Keita pointed at the front rows. "With *him.*"

"Home On The Range" came to an end. The child pianist bowed, to thunderous applause, and ran into the wings. I hoped her parents were there to take her home to bed. What was she doing here in the first place? What was *I* doing here? I spotted Politik at last. Seated in the first row, he was a head taller than his neighbors, two men who I identified as Scott and Jaize 3000. "Why?" I said. "I don't understand. *Why?*"

"Oh, isn't it obvious?" Keita said bitterly. "Jaize has offered him the one thing I couldn't give him. *Power.*"

The stagehands carried a chair onstage and positioned a mic stand in front of it. Gore stepped out from behind his lectern.

"I say we go down there," Hiromi whispered. "While everyone's distracted, we can just creep down there and —"

"And what?"

"Once Politik sees we're alive —"

"And what if it's not that easy?" The words seemed to be torn from Keita. "What if he doesn't want to be rescued?"

301

"Listen." Skriva thrust his head between Keita and Hiromi. "After the testimonies, we all move. The last bit happens outside. It's not as civilized as this. I still think you stand a good chance of getting yourselves killed, but I can see you're not going to walk away and leave him... so I won't stand in your way. Just wait for the grand finale, OK?"

"You mean the trial by water?" Hiromi said. "I thought that was only if she was proved untrue."

"She will be," Skriva said, nodding at the stage.

Leaning on the arms of two burly vampires in tuxedos, a spectral figure hobbled across the stage. Draped from head to foot in a polka-dotted pink and yellow veil, unsteady on jewelled high heels, she allowed Gore to help her into the chair. The audience let out a collective gasp when she flung her veil back.

"The Princess Zuleiko," announced Gore. "Her grievous injuries could not prevail over her desire to see justice done."

"Nor could her vanity," Skriva muttered. "Now *that* tells me she's out for blood."

I swayed, and bumped into Keita. "It's OK," he hissed, steadying me. "We're all the way back here, she can't see us."

"I don't think she can see anything," Hiromi said. "She looks like a baked fish. Her eyes are all white."

I swallowed a fresh wave of nausea. "I'm OK. It's just... kind of gross, isn't it?"

Zuleiko's flesh had been melted down to the tendons, her face reduced to a plasticked anatomical specimen – and yet she'd survived. Maybe she really wasn't human. Certainly, she no longer looked it.

Her voice croaked and crackled over the PA system. "I can't understand a word she's saying," I whispered. "Anyone?"

"She's leaving you guys out of the story to make the Countess look worse," Skriva muttered. "So how is she going to explain...? Oh, I see. Her security crew has flamethrowers. Well, *that's* nice to know. They keep the arsenal locked up, but the Countess managed to get hold of one.

Smuggled it inside her bra, I guess... At the cost of his own life, Zuleiko's Number One saved her from the inferno. Can't you just hear the violins?"

So Ichi was dead. *"He* evidently wasn't immortal," I murmured.

Skriva was too involved in Zuleiko's testimony to bristle. "The older you are, the tougher you are. Zuleiko's supposed to have been born in the eleventh century. But her Number One – wait a minute – he was originally a merchant from, uh, Holland. He was *only* several hundred years old." Skriva laughed. "That's pretty funny! He survives for several hundred years and finally gets his wick scrubbed by fucking Matsudaira."

"Skriva!" I clutched his elbow. "Oh my God. Look – in the second row of this section. I'm sure that's Ni-chan!"

"From Shinjuku? Could be. I've never met her, but I know the name. She was Zuleiko's Number Two, until she decided she couldn't dig the capitalist lifestyle."

"I think she was the one who betrayed Dorothy, for revenge," I said breathlessly. "She is – was – Dutch, too. She and Ichi must have been Turned at the same time. They must have been close..."

"Close? I heard they were married."

"Married!"

"But she left, and he stayed with Zuleiko. They were enemies. So why would she be all hot for revenge now?"

"I just have a hunch about it," was all I could say.

Actually, I was sure I was right. But even if I could get to Ni-chan, what would I do – shoot her? The problem of escalation that I'd confronted in Aoyama Cemetery felt more relevant than ever. When did you abandon reason and resort to bullets? I prayed for God to take the decision away from me, and wondered if I should really be praying to overcome my own cowardice.

Zuleiko rose to her feet and approached the front of the stage. I gathered that she was taking the audience, step by step, through the detective work that had led her to the stunning insight that – wait for it – Dorothy was a traitor. At the climax of this speech, Dorothy herself finally reacted: she affected a yawn. This caused more of a stir in the audience than anything Zuleiko had said. As if in retaliation, the Princess tore off the veil that had hitherto covered her blonde hair. Staring tragically around with her blind white eyes, she tore off her hair. It was a wig. Oozing burns disfigured her scalp.

"Drama queen," Skriva snorted. "It was a wig to begin with."

"She must have third degree burns all over her body," I said.

"Told you the old ones are tough. Next time, Matsudaira, you don't leave the scene until she's *ashes.*"

Abruptly reverting to her role as victim, Zuleiko sank into the arms of her Prime Numbers. Gore thanked her with a deep bow. When she'd been helped offstage, he faced the audience.

"We have heard of the traitor's heinous attack on the Princess of Shinjuku. This was nothing short of attempted murder." His voice boomed through the auditorium. He wasn't using a mic. "How many of you are now convinced that she is not a true vampire?" Or was it *real? Not a real vampire?*

A patter of applause arose. But to my astonishment and delight, the Court party kept their hands in their laps. The vampires around us also remained silent.

Chapter 16.

Gore surveyed the auditorium, his tangled shock of hair sliding over the peaked shoulders of his tailcoat. "So," he rumbled, "we shall continue. Our next testimony comes from one whom many of you were surprised to see here tonight. Others were seen asking him for his autograph."

Laughter rippled through the audience. Gore smirked.

"Yet the adulation of the mortal media has not tainted his vampire virtues: the love of honor, a passion for truth, and loyalty to the Emperor. The conducator of Shibuya, Jaize 3000!"

Around me, people craned their necks. Jaize climbed the steps to the stage, followed by Scott and Politik. He wore white trousers so tight they looked like leggings, white boots laced to the knee, and a ruffled white shirt with cascades of lace at the wrists and throat. On his head perched a white fur top-hat. The effect was horrendously cheesy... or maybe deliberately parodic. Simply by standing on the same stage as Gore, Jaize made the Marquis of Edo look ridiculous.

He coordinated the angle of his bow precisely to match Gore's, then took his time adjusting the mic. Scott and Politik flanked him, in full penguin rig. I half-expected them to start swaying and burst into a chorus of *doo wops*.

Dorothy sat immobile, not deigning even to look at the man she'd once called ally and neighbor.

"Friends, vampires, fellow subjects of the Emperor Underground, may he live forever," Jaize began. "I might as well say at once that I wish I wasn't here. I wish I didn't have to testify against the Countess of Roppongi. I can't count the number of times she's offered me friendly advice, when I felt like I didn't have a friend in the world. She was *neighborly*. You know? But as we say in America, high fences make good neighbors... and I guess the fences between us weren't high enough." He bowed his head for a moment. "Last night, I got a call from her. Well, I already knew there was trouble in Roppongi. On top of that, the rumors that Princess Zuleiko was dead... I was devastated. Anxious. So it was good to get Dorothy's call, and I was flattered that she needed some friendly advice from *me* for a change. I may be the most famous vampire in Japan, but among you, among my people, I know I'm the lowest of the low. So... I met her by appointment at L'Aqua."

God, he was good, I thought, depressed.

"Now, I figure at least some of you have been watching TV today. There's not much I can add. I had another business meeting, so I left before... before the... tragedy. But I've brought two colleagues who saw the whole thing." Jaize turned to nod at Scott and Politik. "They would like to supplement my testimony with their own, if that's acceptable, Marquis."

Hiromi clutched Keita's arm. *"That's* why he brought him!"

"That's a risky assumption," Keita said.

"It makes sense to me," I said. Politik had never given a damn about Dorothy in the first place. To him, her death would simply mean one less vampire.

Jaize launched into an account of how Dorothy had suggested an alliance against Gore, and he'd tried to dissuade her. It was a mixture of truth and self-serving lies, but no stranger to self-serving lies, Gore smiled behind his own lectern, plainly liking what he heard.

"Jaize is going to get exactly what he wants out of this," Skriva muttered, twitching. "The title he thinks ought to be his by right; *and the territory!* But he's not going to keep it long—" His fangs extruded past his lower lip, transforming his face into a boarish mask. His eyes gleamed.. "He's not even going to keep what he's got. He's going to *die.*"

"Yes, but to quote a wise friend of mine," Keita said, "not here."

"No. We're going to pay him another visit, aren't we,

Matsudaira? And this time, we're going to make sure he's home." Skriva's heavy fangs gave his grin a hideous aspect. "*Justice*. For that, I can wait… but not too long."

When I was sure Skriva was no longer listening, I whispered, "Isn't it the *kami* regime he's supposed to be revolting against?"

"He's a bit confused about who his real enemies are," Keita murmured. "It's been a problem."

"Politik was right all along," Hiromi said. "We should just kill them all."

Politik took Jaize's place at the lectern. Without waiting for the applause to end, he began to speak, awkwardly stooping over the mic.

The *qingshi* had approached Dorothy peacefully, he said, to inform her that the Court wished to question her about the attack on Zuleiko. She and her followers had resisted and gone berserk, causing all the deaths that had been reported on TV, including the deaths of six *qingshi*.

"The police are still trying to work out exactly what happened to them." Politik rubbed his mouth and glanced sneakily at the audience. Jaize hadn't flipped him – I knew it for sure. He was still Politik, dwelling with nervous relish on the thought of all those dead vampires. "But first, they'll have a job to match the body parts up."

His testimony garnered far less applause than Jaize's had. Scott took his place at the mic and proceeded to deliver a near-identical account.

Hiromi looked dismayed. "Is that all?"

"No, it doesn't make sense, does it?" Keita said.

I finally had to admit that it didn't. "Maybe," I started, and the truth hit me at the same time as it must have hit Hiromi.

We shared a look of apprehension and horror. Then, as one, we stared down at the stage. Behind the lectern, Jaize stood with his hands folded… but out of Gore's sight, visible only from the extreme right side of the auditorium where we were, his fingers moved, tracing patterns in the air.

"He's going to try something," Hiromi whispered. "He must be crazy."

"Not that crazy, Hiro-chan," Keita murmured back. "You didn't see what he did to the *qingshi* at L'Aqua."

"Loath Stringless," I whispered. "Scott called it *Loath Stringless.*"

"Yeah. I couldn't imagine how he pulled it off at first," Keita whispered. "The sheer amount of energy it should have taken! But I've been thinking about it, and it's got to be because the *qingshi* are undead. They all share the *qi* of their creator. So he only had to cast once… and the effect spread to all of them, like a chain reaction. Highly efficient. It burned itself out before it could reach them all – there are physical limits on these things. Distance limits. But… look where we are now."

"Wait a minute," I said, fighting panic. "Dorothy was standing right there. It didn't affect her. Or her followers."

"Every undead is a vampire, but not every vampire is an undead. Still, this is a glamorous crowd. I'd estimate a lot of undead in here."

"And where does that leave Politik? He's going to be gun fodder," Hiromi answered her own question. "He's just going to use him to distract them while he…" She looked ready to cry. "Why, Politik, *why?*"

"Why, Jaize, why?" Skriva mocked her crossly. "You're getting paranoid. Jaize is the big winner here. Why would he risk it all – for revenge? Because Gore once humiliated him? He's not *that* dumb."

Hiromi shook her head. "Kay, what can we do?"

"Escape?" I suggested, looking around for the emergency exits.

Keita rubbed his free hand over his face. "Clare. I really wanted to address this at a more suitable time. But I need to ask you about what happened at L'Aqua."

"I already told you–"

"But now I need to know what really happened. The pool, uh, malfunctioned. It was pretty impressive. Did you see anything or, uh, do anything that might have caused that?"

He was being so careful with me that I wanted to laugh. I said, "Jaize was cheating. He was drawing a sigil in the water, which suggested that he *wasn't* using the medallion around his neck. So my idea was to cancel out that second sigil. I thought it might work like noise-cancellation technology, where you emit a frequency in opposite phase to the one you want to damp out. But then I decided that wouldn't work. I mean, why would my sigil be in opposite phase to Jaize's? Just because I was on the opposite side of the pool? However these sigils operate, they don't obey the laws of Newtonian space. So I just cast it as hard as I could. Turned up the volume and blew the speaker – in this case, the pool." I waved my free arm around, enjoying the looks on their faces. "It seemed to work."

"Why didn't you tell us you could do magic?" Keita said.

"Because I can't," I said. "Jesus. I'm bullshitting you. Isn't it obvious?" I bit my knuckles. My leash clinked.

"Maybe she *didn't* do it, Kay," Hiromi said. "She's not even Waterborn. How could she have?"

I looked from Hiromi to Keita. "This is more of that astrological crap, isn't it?"

"It's relevant," Keita snapped. "Magical ability correlates to your biodata – the year, time, and date of your birth. That's what the old Taoists, and for that matter the hermeticists in Europe, never figured out. They all started off by trying to master fire, and only a fraction of them ever succeeded... those born under the secret sign of fire. They had all the information they needed, but they never put it together." His voice thickened with pride. "Until my grandfather came along. One revolutionary thinker every thousand years."

"I take it *you're* Fireborn."

"Correct. And so are you. Or so we thought. Are you sure about the exact time you were born? Politik worked it out..."

I gasped. "Did he account for daylight savings?

Keita looked down at the stage. "Politik," he said. "You blessed idiot."

"Speak for yourself," Hiromi said. *"You* should have thought of that."

"So she's Waterborn. It *does* hang together — "

"Not likely," I said. "I'm, uh, kind of phobic about water. I can't even swim."

"People only use ten percent of their brains," Keita said. "Almost everyone has magical potential. But almost no one ever develops it – and Politik has a theory about that." He was talking fast, pelting me with information. "He thinks it's *transmissible*. Exposure to magic can cause latent magical ability to manifest. In other words — "

"It's not who you are, it's who you know." I swallowed. "That makes a scary amount of sense."

"It's who you are, too. You've got to have strong *qi* – one in a hundred, that kind of strong. And there may be some other factors we haven't identified yet. But it's exposure that seems to engage the neural switch. Cumulatively... or instantly. When we were up in the lounge, I told Politik – I described your little tidal wave. I said it looked like Jaize's magic had switched your latent ability on, or somehow enabled you to master a *second* element, because we thought you were Fireborn..." Slowly, Keita shook his head. "I probably should have kept my mouth shut."

Suddenly, I felt cold despite the stuffy heat.

Politik was so full of ideas. And maybe my stunt with Jaize's sigil had given him some new ones.

Maybe that was exactly what Keita was afraid of.

Down on the stage, Scott wrapped up his testimony. The applause was slightly louder this time.

As Jaize returned to the lectern, Hiromi turned to Keita. "What are you waiting for? Fry him!"

"I can't hit him from this distance, Hiro-chan! Politik's too close; I can't see air between them."

"I told you to get your eyes retested," Hiromi said almost tearfully.

310

"Do you wear glasses?" I said.

"Contacts. I need to replace them." Keita forced a wretched smile. "Been putting it off."

Jaize readjusted the mic, brazenly continuing to trace his sigil on its stand. Paralyzed with fear, I thought I knew what was going to happen next.

But I was wrong.

In response to Gore's fulsome thanks, Jaize cleared his throat. "I actually have another testimony to give, regarding the Countess of Roppongi…"

"Excellent," Gore rumbled. "Time, however, is limited —"

"I would also - I would like you to guarantee in the presence of His Grace —" Jaize bowed to the Court section — "that my slave, who was kidnapped by the Countess, will be returned to me. He *is* here?"

"It pains me that you require assurance on that score, but it can be provided."

Gore glanced into the wings. A moment later, two black jumpsuits assisted Aleksey onto the stage. He tottered between them, barely conscious. Several of the vampires around me tutted. I remembered Skriva saying *Freedom is death.*

The stagehands deposited Aleksey on a chair next to Dorothy. When he started to slide off it, Dorothy sprang to catch him. A few days ago, she'd been the queen bee of Exiles, and Aleksey had been the hired help; now they were just two prisoners. She knelt in front of him as if reassuring him. The *kenin* advanced a pace, the muzzles of their guns dropping into firing position. Glaring at them, Dorothy returned to her chair.

"Aleks," Jaize exclaimed. "Oh man, it's good to see you in one piece!"

Aleksey's hand came up and waved. Uneasy laughter rose from the audience. It looked like the motion of a puppet. Little did they know, I thought, that was exactly what it was. The Mastery of Air, Keita had called it.

311

Jaize turned back to the auditorium, and the spotlight on Aleksey dimmed. That was the end of his cameo role.

"Like all of you," Jaize began, "I'm concerned about the *zako*. The rank outsiders are multiplying. It's a major public relations problem. I think we need to show the mortals that we're being proactive on this issue. So, as some of you know, I've implemented a system of volunteer street patrols. The measure has been well received by the mortal authorities. They know all too well that Tokyo is no longer the safest city in the world..."

"No kidding," I muttered.

"...patrolling peacefully, when they met with a vicious attack. The rank outsiders were *provoked!*" Jaize asserted.

Dorothy half-shouted, "My people didn't have nothing to do with it!"

"Silence, traitor," Gore rumbled.

Keita said to Skriva, "So you still don't feel bad about letting her take the rap on this?"

Skriva scowled. "The only thing I feel bad about is that we didn't kill more of them. *And* I wish we'd let them know who was kicking their asses. Yeah, that I feel bad about. I want him to know who's destroyed him and his pansy martial arts freaks."

"Wait a minute," I said. "It was *you?*"

"Course it was. We drove downtown and rolled up on them from the south. Wore masks... Matsudaira, if we ever get out of here, remind me to show you the photos. We looked hilarious, before we got blood all over everything."

"So Zuleiko was half right," I said to Keita. "You *did* coordinate those attacks."

"Didn't do a very good job of it," Skriva said. "He hardly gave us any warning before the *zako* came out of the trees. They'd have eaten *us* if we let them, the hungry little fuckers. Most of them haven't had a taste of vampire blood since they were Turned."

"I was distracted," Keita said defensively. Then he said to me, "And you needn't start! You'd still be at Jaize's place if we hadn't created a diversion."

"No wonder you were right there when we needed you," I said.

"Aren't you even going to thank him?" Hiromi said.

"Right now, I can't find words to express my feelings," I said.

Keita had not only attempted to murder Zuleiko, he'd masterminded the attack at Aoyama Cemetery that triggered the whole mess. And he wanted me to think he'd done it for *my* sake.

Leaning close to him, I whispered, "So you talked me into that depraved little... arrangement, in exchange for your help – to get Dorothy out of a mess that was all *your* fault to begin with?"

"I won't hold you to your word, if that's how you feel."

"How very generous," was all I could say.

Down on the stage, Jaize was explaining the administrative structure of the Human League for Peace. Gore interrupted, "Conducator, this is hardly relevant."

"But... Yes, Marquis. Sorry." Jaize smiled ruefully at the audience. "Well, I guess that's all. Anyone who's interested is welcome to come and talk to me later "

"OK, I think this is it," Keita muttered. "He bought himself enough time with that speech to get his sigil ready to cast. Better get down there. Skriva, you with us?"

The vampire glanced wistfully at the emergency exit. "Oh, dammit. Might as well."

We stumbled after Skriva through the crowd, trying to look as if we weren't hurrying.

Gore had the stage again. "We have now heard ample proof of the traitor's brutality and lack of control. Her violent attacks on Jaize 3000's mortals should serve to condemn her."

"Gore," Dorothy shouted breathlessly. "Believe me. I... had... *nothing*... to do with that!"

With everyone's attention centered on the stage, we sneaked down the side aisle. At the corner of the spectator section, we halted, and Skriva and Keita conferred frantically.

Although we were still in the shadowy margin of the auditorium, I felt horribly exposed. Gore loomed at the front of the stage. Footlights illuminated his face like a pouchy devil mask from hundreds of years ago. "How many of you *now* vote her untrue?" Or was it *unreal?*

Applause filled the auditorium. It sounded lukewarm to me, but Gore smiled.

"The nation has spoken." He turned to Dorothy. "Traitor, the consensus is against you. But in accordance with our laws, you have one last chance to prove yourself a real vampire. We shall proceed to the trial by water."

In the middle of the center section, a man rose to his feet. A spotlight settled on him, and a stagehand darted up the aisle to place a mic in his hand. He was Caucasian, with a round stubbled face and sandy hair that stood on end like a toothbrush.

"The White Duke," Skriva muttered.

In contrast to the formal wear of most of the vampires, the White Duke wore khakis and a short-sleeved green dress shirt. "Edonokami, I think I'm speaking for a majority here." He might not look like David Bowie, but he did have a British accent. "I'm not terribly in love with this blatant rush to justice. You've given us a lot of circumstantial evidence, but I'm not persuaded that it adds up to anything. One has heard rumors against every vampire in this room. It doesn't mean they are all traitors. I'd like to give the nation a chance to find *for* Dorothy Foulkes."

Gore stared at him, but couldn't stare him down. "Very well," he rumbled. With an impatient gesture, he beckoned to the crowd.

The applause half-deafened me. For the first time, the vampires in the spectators' section were clapping. I smiled in delight.

"I ask you to judge the traitor on the basis of her crimes!" Edonokami roared.

"Looks as though the nation prefers to judge on the basis of character," the White Duke drawled. "And where's the evidence that her character hasn't been stainless to date?"

A slight figure leapt up from the first row of the center section: Ruth in a skimpy yellow cocktail dress. Hair flying, heels clattering, she dodged Jaize, Scott, and Politik and ran up the steps of the stage.

Dorothy came upright in her chair. "Girl, you ain't allowed to be here! You better cut out this heroic shit before these animals decide to snack on you —"

"I can tell you about her," Ruth yelped. With a fearful glance at Gore, she darted to the witness's lectern and grabbed the mic. "I've known her for longer than anyone. And she didn't just start being evil and brutal. She's been this way ever since —"

A squeal of feedback interrupted her. Several people in the audience were on their feet.

"Quiet, please," Gore purred. "We will let the mortal speak."

Into the reluctant hush, Ruth said in her fluent Japanese, "I come from Kentucky, that's in America. We've got a big military base in state: Fort Campbell, home of the 101st Airborne. I used to live right near there. My father took off before I was born, and my mom was in and out of lockdown. I lived with my gramma. Trailer trash, they used to call us. The military kids were the worst, so cliquey. *Trailer trash.*"

"Ruth," Dorothy said from her chair. "You don't have to tell them all this."

Ruth flushed. "So I grew up and got my first real boyfriend. Tony. People used to say we looked like brother and sister. His whole family was military, and he was going to enlist as soon as he turned eighteen, never mind that he weighed about ninety pounds soaking wet. But he wasn't like the rest of them. He'd put me on the back of his dirt bike and we'd go down to the roadhouse. We were underage to drink, underage for everything, but Tony's cousin who got discharged for Gulf War syndrome, he worked as the bartender on weekends. So we were cool. Bud for two dollars and Motley Crue on the jukebox. Good old Donnie the

315

Hog's."

Recounting her past, Ruth seemed to have forgotten about her present. But Aleksey hadn't forgotten her. His head had turned towards her. He was still in there.

"I lost my virginity in Tony's cousin's pickup, out in the parking-lot of the Hog."

The silence in the auditorium could have indicated disapproval – or voyeuristic interest. On the plus side, as long as everyone was watching Ruth, they weren't looking at the corner where we were.

"That was a *white* joint. On base, the brothers and the white dudes worked together, but off base, they wouldn't drink together. So everyone was doing double-takes when one night, this was my junior year of high school, this black girl walks in and orders herself a triple Jack on the rocks. What's she, trying to make a statement or something? Well, she is a *walking* statement. What I mean is, she's a knockout. Light-skinned with beaded cornrows down to her ass and legs up to her ears. So it doesn't take long before the dudes start to hit on her. She's playing them all along: she's dancing with this guy, now that one..." Ruth smiled into the darkness. "I bet none of you have ever seen her dance."

Personally, I couldn't picture Dorothy with beaded cornrows. But I couldn't throw stones, either: ten years ago, *my* hair had been blue with green chunks.

"I expect you all know where this story is going. I come back from the restroom and she's dancing with Tony. I got him away from her and made him take me home. He said she was ex-Air Force. She'd done a tour in Germany, a tour in Japan, now she was out and getting her college education. She was down in our neck of the woods to see some old friends. Sure, I said, but you ain't her friend. Are you? He said no. But the next night, he didn't come over, and I heard from my friends that he was down at the Hog, waiting for her to show. He wasn't the only one. But he was the one that she got to the worst. He was, man, he was head-over-heels. That weekend, we had a big fight about it. I found marks on him: *bites*. I didn't know what that meant. Back then, every-one thought vampires only lived in New York and Los An-geles. You'd never meet one in your local juke joint. Besides, they weren't supposed to be able to go out in the sun... But I was mad enough *without* knowing. I sent Tony away. Told him to choose. Me, his future wife? Or this ho? Make up your mind and then come back, I said."

Ruth took a deep breath, amplified into a raw tearing sound. Dorothy buried her head in her hands.

"He never came back. They found his body out in the woods behind the Hog. His throat ripped out so bad, they thought it was a bear kill. My Tony. We parted in anger, and I never got to say 'I love you' to him again." Ruth's voice quivered. "Meanwhile, *she* vanished out of town. I told them she did it. I told them about the... the bites on him. But they wouldn't listen to me."

Gore said, "Beyond the moderating influence of the Em-peror's authority, incidents of this type are unfortunately to be expected. But they must be labelled crimes, for they are the hallmark of a vampire that lacks control, a danger to her-self and others." His voice oozed satisfaction.

Dorothy raised her head. "I was young. I was hungry. I didn't know what I was doing until it was all over. I know that ain't no excuse. But he was so sweet... I cried for him. I covered his body with leaves. I wanted flowers, but I couldn't find none. It was night."

"My whole life was gone," Ruth said. "My future, my dreams. Everything. So I fixed on a new dream. No matter what it took, no matter how long, I was going to find her. Track her down. And make her pay."

She turned and made a short run at Dorothy, stopping a few feet from her.

"How does it feel? How does it feel to have everything taken away?"

"It was her," Keita said. "She was the traitor in Dorothy's camp. Wow."

"She must have been waiting for her chance all these

years." I was shaking. I'd *trusted* Ruth. So much for my instincts.

"It's taken me longer than I thought it would," Ruth said. "But I never gave up. I came halfway around the world to kill you, and you offered me a *job*. Yeah, that took me by surprise. But after a while I understood: To you, it's all a game. Flies with honey. You thought you could stalk me, turn my head, and drink my blood, just like you did to Tony. Wouldn't that have been fun? In your perverse world —"

"It's called making up for things done wrong in the past," Dorothy interrupted her. "It's called atonement."

Anger blazed from Ruth's face. "I don't want to hear your apologies. I told you that before. And now I've got news for you, bitch." She spat. It landed on Dorothy's bare leg. "*I win.*"

She wheeled away from Dorothy with her head high.

"I'm through. She's all yours, big guy. Have a ball."

Keita shoved me. "She's coming down the steps on this side."

I dropped to my haunches. Among the worried faces of the spectators in the first few rows, I saw Ni-chan. She smiled and patted the empty seat next to her. The vampires on her far side were the survivors of her crew from Shinjuku. They shifted over to sit in each other's laps. Skriva, Keita, Hiromi and I squashed gratefully into the row. "I thought it was *you*," I whispered to Ni-chan. I swallowed. "I'm sorry about... Ichi." He, too, must have had a real name once.

"For me, grief is not something to be shared. Nor can it be ameliorated by violence."

Well, here was one person who lacked the revenge instinct.

Unfortunately, Ni-chan was in the minority.

This time, when Gore asked the audience to vote Dorothy "unreal," the applause made my ears ring. Little by little, the center and left sections rose to their feet. I spotted the White Duke among them. Dissatisfaction pursed his lips, but he was clapping with the rest.

318

"It's the random slaying thing," Skriva muttered. "No one dares to be all understanding and tolerant about *that*. I mean, imagine if Ruth gave that testimony on TV. The whole country would be out to lynch every vampire they could find."

I hadn't the heart to tell him that in America, the whole country had been fed a diet of horror stories like Ruth's for years, and vampires were lynched quite regularly.

But for the first time, I had a real sense of the fear that the vamps lived with. Maybe the fear was even more acute in Japan, precisely because they'd gained a foothold here. They had more to lose.

"Very good." Gore smiled widely enough to display the needle-points of his fangs. "The nation has spoken with one voice. We shall proceed."

The house lights came on. I cringed, thankful we'd found seats. But around us, everyone was rising.

"The Countess will be put to trial by water," Ni-chan said sadly. "There is a swimming-pool outside."

Hiromi craned, searching the crowd for Politik. "Maybe we should just grab him," she said frantically.

"No – *no!*" Keita held her back.

"Wait!" It was Dorothy's voice. The auditorium gradually stilled. She said hoarsely, "I claim my last drink. It's the law, Gore. You can't get around that."

Gore's eyes rolled, gauging the mood of the audience. "Very well. If you can find a consenting mortal." He smiled. There were few enough non-vampires here.

Ruth approached the foot of the stage, frail in her little yellow dress. "I'll do it. How about that, Dorothy? You get to taste my blood at last."

Jaize slipped through the crowd of vampires who'd already left their seats. He murmured in Ruth's ear, but the blonde girl merely shrugged.

"I guess I've won, so I can afford to be generous." Her lip curled. "Or maybe I just like the idea that mine will be the last face she ever sees up close."

Dorothy stared down at her and shook her head. "You know what, honey? I wouldn't touch your blood if it came with five stars from Michelin." Ignoring the *kenin* and their guns, she dropped to one knee in front of Aleksey's chair. Whatever she said, I couldn't hear it. But I saw Aleksey nod.

"No!" Jaize bellowed in English. "Jesus, Dorothy, no! You can't do that to me!"

Tenderly, Dorothy eased Aleksey out of his chair and settled him in her lap.

"Poor thing," Ni-chan said. "She'll kill him. Perhaps she means it as an act of mercy, to cheat Jaize of him."

"He hasn't *consented*!" Jaize yelled, earning looks of distaste from the vamps around him.

"It is our law," Gore said, not without a hint of satisfaction: he didn't mind seeing Jaize humiliated, now that he no longer needed him to win his case. "You will get your slave back; that was our bargain. We said nothing about him being alive."

Kneeling on the bare stage, Dorothy lowered her face to Aleksey's neck. With a flash of extruding fangs, she struck.

Some of the vamps close exclaimed in surprise. Onstage, the *kenin* surged towards Dorothy and Aleksey. They stooped, mouths hanging open, and prodded Dorothy with the barrels of their guns. I jumped up on my seat and stood on its arms. I still couldn't see what was happening. Dorothy's back hid Aleksey's upper body from view. His legs drummed on the stage. Across the crowd, Gore glanced my way; his gaze was distracted, pondering. Then his head thrust forward like an animal straining towards its prey.

"There she is!" he shouted. "The daughter of Western nobility! *Take her!*"

"Oh, shit," I said.

I tumbled on top of Keita and Hiromi. Ni-chan's followers drew knives. Skriva dropped our leashes. Three *kenin* leapt off the stage and forced a path after us, jabbing the barrels of their guns at anyone who didn't get out of their way quickly enough.

We bulled up the aisle. But the crowd up ahead was too thick. We couldn't make it. I braced my back against the wall, Glock in one hand, leash bunched up in the other. I might previously have despaired of my own lack of fighting spirit, but now that the moment had come, I knew myself to be incapable of surrendering to these milky-eyed samurai from hell.

The vampires shuffled past me, glancing over their shoulders at the approaching *kenin*. Scattered laughs suggested that they took the scene with a pinch of salt.

A bluish light roared up behind them. In a horribly protracted moment, the orderly egress disintegrated into a stampede. Keita reeled out of the crowd and crashed against the wall next to me, Hiromi behind him. I saw the *kenin* who'd been coming for me. They were on the floor, still crawling jerkily towards us. Spines of wyrdfire reared from their backs, and blue tongues licked over their faces, probing their gasping mouths. Their flesh as it charred gave off a rich porky smell. A fusillade of bangs twisted one of them into the air like a fish. The spare clips in his ammo belt were exploding, I realized, hammering shrapnel into his body. Blood streamed from his mouth and immediately caught on fire. It smoked like burning oil.

"OK, I take back what I said," Skriva shouted. "That's quite a technique... Matsudaira?"

Keita was slumping, sliding to the floor.

"It's the feedback!" Hiromi shouted. "He's not used to it. He'll be OK in a couple of minutes!"

"That may be longer than we have," Skriva said, staring at the smouldering *kenin*. Another vampire reeled backward and trod on them. The wyrdfire leapt up his legs. He barely had time to scream before a third vampire pounced on him and bore him to the floor on top of the burning corpses. My gaze bounced past them, to land on another violent and apparently senseless scuffle. Not all the vampires were running for the exits. In fact, something like half of them had simply risen from their seats... and started fighting. Each other.

Jaize 3000 had cast Loath Stringless.

Chapter 17.

Chaos spread through the auditorium. The *kenin* still on the stage beat Dorothy with the butts of their guns, trying to separate her from Aleksey. One of them grabbed her braid and yanked her head back. Blood spilled down her chin. But as they pulled her away, Aleksey writhed after her, clutching her wrist to his mouth.

"Huh?" Skriva shouted. "She's shared her blood with him. What the hell is that, some kind of noble gesture?"

"I can see where one of them dropped his gun," I said. "I'll be right back."

At the end of the aisle, a male and a female vampire, both in black tie, slapped petulantly at each other. I circled them with extreme care. All at once, with a scream of frustration that froze me in place, the female vampire pulled off one of her shoes. She leapt on the man and plunged the stiletto heel into his eye. Blood gouted from the socket.

He curtailed her screech of victory by driving his stiffened fingers into her throat.

A third vampire ripped the arm off a seat and set about battering the pair, only to lose interest and start whacking the other vampires who were running or trying to sneak past him.

Jaize had improved his command of Loath Stringless – or maybe it was a function of the enclosed space. Either way, the "chain reaction" wasn't burning itself out. It seemed to be escalating.

On the other hand, it seemed like Keita was right about the spell only spreading among the undead. Up near the exits, a scene taken straight from a terrorist attack was unfolding: the still-living vampires screamed and shoved, trampling each other to get to the doors.

I knew how they felt. But before I could think about escaping, I had business to take care of.

I dived for the gun I'd spotted, which had fallen just beyond the spreading slick of flames. It was a serious rifle, an M16 or something like that. My arms shook as I hauled its strap over my head. I'd never fired a rifle, but how difficult could it be?

Onstage, Dorothy lay face down in front of the piano. Had the *kenin* killed her? They were acting very oddly, striding in circles around the stage, bodies listing. When they bumped into each other, they traded blows, wielding their hitech weapons like cudgels. Maybe Gore was dead (I could hope), and that had fried what passed for their brains. But they did seem to be aware of the screams and cries from the top of the auditorium. One by one, they reached the front of the stage. There, they cocked their heads, smiling hellishly.

They were undead, too.

I collapsed to the floor a split second before the rifles roared in unison, obliterating every other sound.

From where I lay, deafened and dazed, I could see Skriva, Keita, and Hiromi taking cover quarter of the way up the side aisle. A berserking undead careened towards them, bleeding from multiple wounds, brandishing a woman's severed arm like a club. The ball joint trailed red scraps of tendon and muscle where it had been ripped out of the shoulder, but the hand still wore a wedding ring and a gold watch. Skriva rolled, stuck out a leg, and tripped the vampire, who toppled and simultaneously burst into flame. My friends scrabbled clear and took cover behind the seats. The vampire lay in the aisle, charbroiling.

Bullets chewed the air into sonic splinters. Seats at the top of the auditorium exploded in puffs of plaid fiber. The *kenin* were aiming at the crowd around the exits. The din drowned out the vampires' cries, but I could see them falling.

I hadn't fired my own scavenged rifle yet, and the *kenin* hadn't noticed me. I crawled towards the stage, pushing the M16 ahead of me. Skriva's leash still trailed from my left wrist. I zigzagged around the charred corpses of the *kenin* who'd tried to arrest me, lying in now-guttering pools of wyrdfire, and at least half a dozen dead vampires who lay still, except for the blood spreading from the wounds they'd inflicted on each other. God, if their blood carried CAIN... I was crawling through puddles of the stuff. I might effectively die of the scrapes on my legs.

But before I started worrying about that, I had to live through this. The *kenin* were firing single rounds now, picking off survivors. Very slowly, so as not to clank, I rose on my knees. I struggled to lift the M16 to my shoulder, then changed my mind. I was close enough to the stage that I hardly needed to aim. Besides, they always fire from the hip in the movies.

What would James think if he could see me now? What about my father?

I pulled the trigger.

The two *kenin* nearest to me collapsed, undramatically. The gun kicked, juddering, the stock sliding between my elbow and my hip. I lurched sideways on my knees, trying to keep the barrel from arcing around. It was too hard to control on automatic. I fumbled for the lever to switch it over to single-shot mode.

Arms snaked around me from behind, and bloodstained paws wrenched the M16 over my head. I screamed and clawed, terror giving me strength. But not strength enough.

Gore whipped my leash around my body, pinning my arms to my sides. Holding the M16 as easily as if it were a plastic toy, he shouted a command. The *kenin* on the stage peered our way. The barrels of their guns wavered, uncertainly homing in on us. Gore shouted again, urgently.

One by one, the *kenin* sat down on the stage and slipped to the floor. They crowded around us, faces creased in suspicion. I kicked out.

"You are mine," Gore crooned hoarsely. "Mine, mine. Remember who created you."

God, I thought. God the father, the almighty, maker of heaven and earth – and of all things that are in the earth? That just didn't seem plausible anymore.

"Remember who made you what you are."

Nilson. James. Mummy.

I spat in the nearest *kenin*'s face and kicked backwards at Gore's shins.

Hopelessly ineffectual, I might as well have been a mosquito. Edonokami delivered a gentle cuff to my head. Ears ringing worse than ever, I stumbled with him as he turned to face the auditorium. The only people left in the seats were dead and draped over them. I couldn't see anyone I knew.

"Rebel!" Gore's voice boomed out. "I have overcome your vile mesmerism."

I thought Loath Stringless had probably just run its course, but I didn't feel like correcting the Marquis.

"You cannot get out. Stand and face me. You cannot get out."

The echoes rolled around the auditorium and died.

Gore pulled me in close to his body. I felt him panting. His fancy costume was a mess, heavy black sash hanging loose from his waist, shoulderguards askew. Never taking his gaze off the auditorium, he dragged me over to the first row of seats in the Court section. Several people were already sprawled there: Aleksey, Ruth, and Scott.

While his followers and subjects were running amok, the *kami* of Edo had been thinking ahead. He'd been collecting hostages.

He plumped me unceremoniously down in the seat between Ruth and Scott. With a couple of quick flicks, he knotted my leash around its arm. I strained to see the stage, but from this angle, the wings hid the piano, and Dorothy – if she was still there.

On my right, Scott slouched with his chin on his chest. The side of his face was a mask of blood, one eye pulped shut. "Oh God," I said. "He needs help."

"Ask me," Ruth said. "See if I care." Head resting on the back of her seat, she seemed to be staring up at the ceiling, but her eyes were closed.

"Yes, Jaize has paid a price for his victory," Aleksey said

from my other side. "But I think it's not yet high enough."

I gaped at him. Trickles of blood had dried below the puncture wounds in the hollow of his throat. More blood stained the colorless stubble that had grown in around his mouth. But that awful slackness had gone out of his face, and his eyelids hung at half-mast over alertly gleaming pupils.

"Aleksey?"

His lips formed the wry little smile I hadn't seen in what felt like months.

Towering above us, Gore trumpeted, "Rebel! I have your slave. I have the Western noblewoman, I have your traitor bitch, and I have your lover. Stand and face me, or they die."

"Murderer," Jaize's voice rang out from behind me. "Monster."

Pot, kettle, black? Anyone? The back of my head felt vulnerable. I scrunched lower.

"The Emperor will have your blood for this, Gorozaemon. Why don't you just commit harakiri and save him the trouble?" Jaize walked out of the center aisle into my field of view. His once-white outfit looked as if he'd wriggled to safety under the seats. His lace cuffs hung in bloody clots. But his battered top-hat still perched on his head. Surveying the corpses in front of the stage, he removed it and held it over his heart for a silent moment. Then he strolled between the puddles of blood and faced Gore at a distance of a few metres. His gaze darted to Scott and Aleksey. He licked his lips. "I challenge you for them. A duel."

"An amusing suggestion," Gore purred. "But a duel requires seconds. Shall I lend you one of my household warriors, since you have none of your own?"

"Not necessary," Jaize said, snarling slightly. "Inobe-kun! A few more to go, here."

Seats *sproinged* a few rows back. Politik strolled down the aisle. His tuxedo jacket gone, shirt torn open to the waist, he cut a grimly dashing figure – until he stopped short and did a double-take. *"Clare?"* He nudged his glasses up his nose. "You're *alive?"*

"At least for now," I said. Then I lost control and started screaming. "Politik, leave him! Get *help!*"

The nearest *kenin* slapped me in the face. I shut up.

His big face sagging miserably, Politik walked to Jaize's side. He put his arm around the vampire's waist.

"Keep your mind on the job, handsome," Jaize laughed, camping it up.

"Your weakness for mortal men is most amusing," Gore rumbled. "A shame that mortal men are so weak in general."

The *kenin* guffawed.

"I know you've got a reputation for wit," Jaize snapped. "But this is no laughing matter. Name your second, and let's decide who this city really belongs to."

"This *country* belongs to the Emperor," Gore answered.

With Keita's historical analogy fresh in my mind, I could tell it was a purely formulaic assertion. The fate of the city, or at least its vampire population, really might be decided right here in the next few minutes.

Gore beckoned his *kenin* forward. "Set a dog to watch a rebellious cur," he mused aloud. "But which one?"

I peered around Scott's slumped form. "Aleksey, I'm so glad you're OK," I whispered.

"Never more so," he whispered back.

"Is – is Dorothy…"

"She bit me. And then she opened her wrist with her own fangs and fed me. I never thought it would feel like *that.*"

"Like what?" I couldn't help asking.

"As if I were being reborn. I saw a light. I was a shadow drifting in the dark, and I was drawn to it from far off. It was like the end of a long, long tunnel. I almost reached it. But then I heard a voice. It was Dorothy. 'Turn around,' and she called me by my name. 'Turn back!' And I did. And here I am."

My fear left me for a minute, replaced with a complex mix of triumph and disappointment. At last, I'd solved the mystery that experts had been arguing over for years, the question of the "transmission mechanism." Or rather, Aleksey had solved it for me. "Turning" was nothing more or less than a classic near-death experience.

"I feel as if I could leap over high buildings. I could compose a symphony. I could —"

"Aleksey." I swallowed. "Not that this is necessarily a bad thing, but I think you may have to prepare yourself for a change of lifestyle."

Watching us narrowly, Jaize drawled, "Marquis, how hard is it to choose among a handful of soulless cannibals? Get on with it, and let's name our weapons."

Gore backed up to regard Jaize with an almost bovine stare.

Voice thrilling with a premonition of victory, Jaize said, "I choose… magic."

"Magic," Gore said. "Is that your little secret? Fascinating. For myself, I prefer human technology."

In a blur of movement, the *kenin* levelled their rifles and fired.

Jaize vanished. His top-hat rocked in the air for a moment, Cheshire cat-like, then fell to the floor. Nothing remained where he'd stood but bloody footprints.

"Oh my God," I said blankly. My ears were ringing all over again. "He teleported."

Baffled, the *kenin* jostled each other and brought their guns to bear on a new target: Politik.

Who was crouching in the aisle, holding up a small copper talisman.

Bullets bounced off the air in front of him. They pinged back and fell harmlessly to the floor, lead gravel rolling down the slope of the aisle.

Politik laughed with the innocent glee of a child, and gestured.

The *kenin*'s rifles all malfunctioned at once. Two of them exploded in the *kenin*'s hands. The surviving *kenin* shook their weapons and tied their barrels in knots. One broke his open, only to have it snap shut on his fingers. Only when I saw Gore fling his own M16 to the floor, its barrel uselessly twisted, did I understand that this was no product quality issue. Politik had gained the Mastery of Metal.

Brandishing their inoperable guns like clubs, the *kenin* rushed Politik.

I expected them to bounce right off his shield. But maybe it only deflected bullets, not vampires. He turned to run – and tripped on a corpse in the aisle and went headlong.

"Somebody do something," I begged, trying to unknot my leash from the arm of my seat.

Staring at the ceiling, Ruth rolled her head from side to side. "They can massacre each other for all I care."

Aleksey leaned around me and Scott. "So you are enjoying the sweet taste of revenge?" Without waiting for Ruth's answer, he darted towards the stage.

Not allowing myself to feel the shock of his abandonment, I pleaded, "Ruth, at least help me get this damn chain off!"

As the *kenin* fell on Politik, Gore stood watching with folded arms. His back looked like a vast black silhouette on a firing range. I still had the Glock, but I couldn't fire it one-handed, not and have any realistic hope of hitting him. I couldn't ask Ruth to shoot him, either; after what she'd done to Dorothy, I had no confidence that she wouldn't shoot *me*.

"What're you doing with a slave leash on, anyway?" Ruth said to me, as if the *kenin* weren't murdering Politik a few yards away.

"Long story," I said between my teeth. *"Please."*

She sighed and picked at the chain. "It's really knotted."

Sweating, I tried not to hear Politik's cries. If four *kenin* pile onto one large but not very muscular graduate student, how long will it take them to tear him to pieces? GMAT Question From Hell number six million and one.

A crash erupted at the top of the auditorium, followed by shouts. I wrenched around, drawing a curse from Ruth. Bulky silhouettes crowded into the auditorium. For a horrible moment my brain struggled to make sense of their heavy carapaces and protuberant snouts, the long axes they wielded... *"Firefighters,"* I exclaimed, almost weeping for joy. "Thank you God, thank you, thank you."

Keita, Skriva, and Hiromi! They must have done the sensible thing for once in their lives, got the hell out of here, and dialed the Japanese equivalent of 911.

"About time," Ruth grumbled.

The firefighters' martial shouts turned into grunts of horror as they found themselves wading through a drift of corpses.

"There!" Ruth said.

I sprang out of my seat, the leash swinging from my wrist. "Down here!" I screamed. They hadn't seen that down here were some lives they could still save. "Officers! We need medical assistance!" The *kenin* had fallen back to Gore's side when the firefighters piled into the auditorium. I darted up the center aisle. If Politik was still alive – if I could keep him alive until they got here —

I fell on my knees. His glasses were gone, his face a lumpy mess, nubbins of flesh hanging loose. They'd taken *bites* out of him. Blood soaked his white shirt and it trickled out from under him, it ran in a little stream down the aisle.

I grabbed his hand in both of my own and squeezed, his blood sealing our skin together. "Hold on," I begged him. "The cops are here. It's going to be all right."

"How many?" he whispered.

"What? How many cops? I don't know. Enough."

"How many... of the bloodsuckers did we kill?"

Despairingly, I glanced towards the back of the auditorium, where the rescue workers were triaging casualties as they moved, filling the air with shouts and radio noise. "About seventy or eighty?"

"Oh... is that all?"

Through tears, I said, "No, I was wrong. You got hundreds of them, Politik. *Thousands.*"

"Thought so." The ragged flap of his upper lip twitched. He was trying to smile. *"Annihilated* them."

"But why, Politik? Why?"

330

"Our world. They want to… take over."

"I know, I mean I get that part, but… oh, Keita felt like you betrayed him for Jaize."

"Kay… indecisive. Supposed to be… making a *plan*. To destroy them. But never got any farther than making… *friends* with them. Likes… hanging out with them. Likes having them… need him. Jaize… not so fucking soft. Take first opportunity… destroy regime. Suited me." Politik fell silent, as if it took all his energy just to breathe. "Poor Kay," he whispered.

"I don't know what they told you, but Keita's not dead," I said, praying it was true. "He's not mad at you, either. He understands—"

Politik blinked angrily. I tried to clear the blood out of his eyelashes with my fingers, only to snatch my hand back when he grunted in pain. "Understand? *Kay?* Never understood… anything." He squeezed my hand, painfully tight. "Clare?"

"I'm here, I'm here—"

"Tell him that Jaize… not a vampire."

"Not a vampire?"

"No. Scott… no bites. He… introduced me to his mother. She… she gave me…" He fumbled weakly at his side. I spotted the copper medallion on the floor and placed it in his hand. "My first sigil. She's going to give me more…"

Jaize's *mother?* Scott's mother? I had to have misheard. "I saw what you did," I said. "It was really incredible. When you're all better, I want another demonstration."

"Sure," he whispered indifferently. Then his eyes came alive again. "We did it, didn't we? Me and Jaize and Scott… we formed a troika. And we *did* it. Didn't we? Destroyed them."

"Yeah," I said. "You wiped them out. Politik? Stay with me! Can you hear me? I need you to stay with me." I shook him. "The cops are *here*, they're just taking forever, but they—"

At a fresh outburst of shouts, I whipped my gaze to the

back of the hall – and froze. The firefighters were pounding down the central aisle, straight towards me. Behind them, someone yelled through a megaphone. Though garbled, the words obviously meant *Freeze! Hands up!* They were going to arrest Gore and the *kenin*, or more likely overreact and kill them.

"Officers!" I shrilled. "We need a stretcher!"

The men in the lead didn't so much as slow down, although Politik and I were blocking the aisle. Fifteen yards and they'd be on top of us.

"Officers!"

At ten yards, I realized they weren't going to stop. From wherever he'd concealed himself, Jaize must have been whispering in their minds, driving them like a weapon at Gore. They could see nothing else.

Sobbing in panic, I tried to drag Politik into the safety of the seats.

Five yards.

My muscles wouldn't obey me, wouldn't lift his weight. "Leave me," he bubbled. I dragged him by one wrist. Fresh blood coursed from the wounds beneath the rags of his shirt.

Two yards.

I howled despairingly and ran. Afraid to look back, blinded by tears, I collapsed in the now-empty front row.

A rough little hand seized mine and yanked me up again. Ruth dragged me to the stage steps and slapped me until I climbed them. On the edge of the stage, I collapsed again. "I couldn't," I sobbed. "Oh God, I couldn't save him."

Ruth administered another round of slaps to my face. I sat up in sheer outrage. She smiled cynically. "Survive first, cry later."

"At least Gore's finally going to get it," I said, sniffling back my tears.

The firefighters mobbed the Marquis of Tokyo. Gorozaemon Edonokami stood proud and scowling, a ragged giant from another era. He had an antiquated sense of honor: he would neither surrender nor try to flee. His *kenin* weren't as tough. They cowered behind him, scowling nervously, as if they hoped they could pretend they'd just been passing by. But it would do them no good. The firefighters' fear was going to get the better of them. I could see it. In this killing zone where bodies littered the floor, Gore, too, was going to die an ugly death, bludgeoned by a mob... and serve him right.

Suddenly Jaize was there, shoving between tarpaulined backs and reflective elbows. Over the blaring loudspeaker, I caught his easy joking tone. He pointed at Gore, shook his head, made calm-down gestures.

After an infinite moment, the tension ebbed, leaving a vague pall of shame. Professional again, the firefighters broke into teams. Half a dozen of them laid hold almost respectfully of Gore and the *kenin*. Gore twitched and rumbled to no avail: he and his warriors were all handcuffed. Jaize looked on, haggard but smiling.

"I thought Three G teleported away or something," Ruth said.

It awed me how she was able to accept impossibilities without even trying to understand them. "I guess he didn't go far," was all I could think of to say.

Maybe Jaize hadn't been *able* to go far. He looked to be completely out of juice. Painfully, he made his way to the corner nearest us, giving me a view of his face, though he never looked up. Lines of weariness marked the chiseled cheeks, and there were greenish hollows beneath his eyes. He was staying on his feet by sheer willpower, I thought, and when he reached the end of the front row, he collapsed on the floor. Someone reached around the last seat. *Scott.* Jaize's head dropped onto the other man's shoulder, and they held each other.

Here and there throughout the auditorium, people were standing up and struggling out to the aisles. Many of the "live" vampires had survived – but scarcely one of them was unhurt. The paramedics were working flat out. That warmed my heart, humans helping vampires, prejudices cast aside, just doing their jobs. But why couldn't they have come in time for Politik?

"Pssst." The hiss came from behind me. "Clare. Girl-friend."

I floundered upright. Every muscle in my body hurt. Concentrating on putting one foot in front of the other, I made it to the piano at the back of the stage, where Aleksey sat on the bench with his head in his hands. Dorothy sat crosslegged at his feet. I knelt to hug her. She patted the back of my neck with a cool hand, then pushed me away. "What were you gonna do, sit there until they decide to take you in custody, too? Get out of here."

"Good idea. Let's go," I said, trying to haul her upright. The inside of her left wrist was all torn up.

"Nope, I'm staying here with Aleks. Got to look after him now. Besides, if Jaize sees me, I'm gonna land in jail right alongside of Gore... so we're gonna chill here until, hopefully, that magic-using mofo bails. Then we'll sneak away. You go now. Just don't catch the eye of them cops."

"There must be another way out," I said, looking into the darkness of the wings.

"Elevator. But the goddamn stagehands, after they escaped, they left it up there on ground level. And it's one of those that you need the key to operate."

"Hey," Ruth said, jabbing me in the ribs. "Isn't that your friend Matsudaira?"

A flicker of movement at the top of the auditorium resolved into two people: Hiromi, pattering down the central aisle, and Keita, stumbling after her, almost falling, catching himself on the seats.

It's the feedback, Hiromi had said. How much of a hit had Keita taken with his repeated castings of wyrdfire?

They reached Politik's trampled body, which no one had yet got around to moving. They dropped to their knees in the aisle. They shook him.

Hiromi gave up first. Crying hard, she lunged the rest of the way down the aisle. I saw her get a distracted lecture from one of the cops. Brushing him off, she darted straight at the corner where I'd last seen Jaize and Scott. She danced in and out of my sight, reaching into her fanny pack and throwing things on the ground.

Dorothy shook her head in admiration. "I don't know that girl, but I want to."

"She's got strong *qi*," I said.

Hiromi reeled backwards and sat down hard. Keita helped her to her feet. They moved towards the stage. I couldn't tell who was dragging who.

The floor behind them rippled, heaving upward.

Jaize and Scott stumbled into view. Thin green snakes whipped around their legs, coiling up their bodies. The cops who'd gathered around Gore sprang towards them, drawing their guns, but then fell back, gaping at the snakes – no, *vines*: I could see blood where thorns dug into flesh. And I could smell them all the way up here, a fresh scent like grass after rain. Livid green, they curled around Scott's chest. Jaize was struggling to hold one clear of his neck.

If the police did nothing, they'd both be dead in a couple of minutes.

I had a flash of inspiration. "Play something!" I yelled at Aleksey. "Distract the cops!"

Aleksey shook his head and held up his hands. They trembled visibly.

"To hell with your hands!" I screamed. "Just play!"

With a despairing sigh, Aleksey bowed his head. Then he swung around on the piano bench and lowered his hands to the keyboard. A tune thundered out, musical shock-and-awe with the rhythm of a military march. If I'd had the breath to spare, I would have laughed.

Debout, les damnes de la terre!
Debout, les forcats de la faim!
La raison tonne en son cratere
C'est l'eruption de la fin!
Du passe faisons table rase
Foules, esclaves, debout, debout!

As one, every person in the auditorium turned to stare at the stage. Forgotten, Jaize and Scott fought Hiromi's vines with their bare hands. *The essence of wood,* I thought, making a private bet that those particular vines wouldn't be found in any botanical encyclopedia. *Die,* I thought, *die!* I wanted to clap and cheer Hiromi's vines as if they could hear me.

Unfortunately, the police had also forgotten Gore. He gathered his massive shoulders and jerked his arms forward. The handcuffs on his wrists snapped like cheap plastic. His battle roar split the air, and he charged forward with the *ken-in* at his heels.

"Traitor!" he bawled, vaulting onto the stage. "Now I see it all, Countess. You schemed with Jaize to commit this slaughter, all to save your paltry life. But you shall not prevail!"

Blankly, I drew the Glock and fired. I missed Gore. I might have winged a firefighter. Talk about making a bad situation worse.

"You still got your nines? Give me that!"

Dorothy seized the Glock from me. She flowed into a two-handed shooting stance and fired. Her first shot opened a hole in Gore's broad pale forehead. Her second shot dropped him on the stage. She kept on firing, the hammer clicking on empty, until I pried the gun from her. Hands shaking, I wiped it on my hoodie and hurled it into the wings. I might be a failure as a bad-ass gunslinging bitch, but hey, I knew the protocol for dealing with murder weapons.

"My lord, would you look at that!" Dorothy kicked Gore's corpse. "Dead as a fucking doorknob. What kind of ammo you had in that, silver?"

I gasped. "Oh my God, I think it *was.*"

Dorothy laughed out loud. She gave Gore's body another kick, and then spat on his face. "Damn, I can't tell you how long I have been waiting to do that."

Below the stage, a group of rescue workers hacked frantically at the vines strangling Jaize and Scott. Our distraction had failed, yet Aleksey continued to play, ornamenting the

Internationale with wild swirls in the bass.

Busy rescuing Jaize and Scott, the cops were too late to stop Gore's *kenin* from scrambling up to the stage. Dorothy whirled to face them. "What, y'all want some of what he got?"

Belatedly, the firefighters rushed the stage and seized the *kenin*. The little vampires fought their captors ferociously, snarling and biting. I circled the conflict and helped Hiromi drag Keita onto the stage, past Gore's body. Keita was drenched in sweat, wobbling on his feet. Yet he muled against us, stooped, and scribbled with one finger on the black tailcoat. Wyrdfire flared up, momentarily etching the sigil in white flame. Then it caught Gore's hair.

Shocked, the firefighters lost hold of one *kenin*. He pounced on us, jaws stretching wide. I remembered the bites on Politik's face, and swung my leash. It hit the *kenin*'s cheekbone with a crack that knocked him backwards.

Aleksey played louder. The *Internationale* segued into a tune I didn't know. Wild and joyous, it sounded like Cossacks dancing on a table, smashing all the glasses. "Go!" he shouted. "I'll be all right. The nice cops will look after me."

Dorothy dragged him off the piano bench. "You're an illegal overstayer, son. As far as they're concerned, that's over and above everything else."

"I'm a defector–"

"Bullshit, you're just a common criminal. What was it, selling cell phone jammers?"

"Hey, you lot!" a firefighter yelled desperately. "Don't go anywhere. We need to ask you some questions."

"I've heard that one before," I muttered. The *kenin* who'd broken free was tottering after us again. I whirled my leash and hit him in the face again. "That's my statement," I shouted. "And for the love of God, remember handcuffs don't hold them." I threw the leash down and ran.

Backstage, I caught up with the others. The lights were out, and we tripped over furniture and boxes at every step. At least we weren't tripping over bodies anymore. "The elevator," I panted.

"Around here," Dorothy called. We traced her voice to a storage bay with a service elevator. "Got to be some way to call the shit," she began, then blinked. The elevator doors stood open.

"Politik did it," Hiromi choked. "It was the last thing he... Save yourselves, he said."

"He was still *alive?*" I said. "After all that?"

"Was," Hiromi whispered.

"Stayed alive just long enough to say sorry," Keita rasped. "Sorry! What the fuck? What's the point of saying sorry, and then *dying?*"

The elevator spat us out in the staff garage. Out on the street, whirling lights flung arcs of red and blue on the trees, illuminating a crowd of media and the cops who were holding them back. Radios squawked in patrol cars. We ducked under the crime-scene tape and walked away. Some escapes are easier than others.

The residential tower at Roppongi Hills had metal detectors and security guards who knew Dorothy by name, among other signs that they actually did their job. That didn't explain how the two *qingshi* standing outside Dorothy's apartment on the thirty-sixth floor had got there. But it did explain why a couple with small children passed the vampires without any sign of alarm as we approached. Their young daughter cheerfully greeted Dorothy and told her that her visitors had been waiting for ages.

I didn't quite see how Dorothy got rid of the *qingshi.* Maybe she just told them to go away.

Beyond a door fitted with a chain and an internal security camera, the apartment had fluffy white carpets, a sink full of dirty dishes in a blinding white all-electronic kitchen, and a living-room furnished with a fawn leather three-piece suite. The air freshener fetish was the only clue that a vampire lived here.

Ruth clicked on the TV and flopped down on the sofa, while Aleksey made a beeline for the pine hatch set into the wall, which turned out to be a wet bar. I almost smiled. No catastrophe was big enough to stop these two chronic free-loaders from taking what they could get, whenever they could get it.

For a few minutes we all watched live coverage of the outside of Eternal Family Elementary School, a reporter blathering against a backdrop of ambulances. Then Ruth switched over to CNN. Iraq, Iran, Paris Hilton, and the sudden death of a senator – *what?* The *suicide* of Senator Charles Blumfeldt, Illinois Democrat and my father's biggest supporter on the Judiciary Committee. "Shit," I said aloud. He'd stuck a .44 in his mouth and pulled the trigger... Senator Blumfeldt? The idealistic gun-control advocate? "The senator is said to have been depressed over his wife's threat to file for divorce," Linda Stouffer said solemnly, and Ruth changed the channel to a baseball game.

"You got satellite. Living large, Dor," she said, and looked at me. "Her old place was about a third the size of this. She used to live down in Nishi-Azabu. Until I broke in one day. I was going to kill her with my bare hands... but she woke up."

"That was when you still thought we die at sunrise," Dorothy said. "You didn't even bother to be quiet. Course, you'd know better now, wouldn't you?" With a close-lipped smile, she left the room.

After everything I'd been through, the only, pathetically inadequate thing I could think of to do now was take a shower. Undressing in Dorothy's deluxe bathroom, I relived the nightmare at Eternal Family. Dread, horror, confusion, denial, and frantic curiosity: I'd done all these emotions a dozen times in the last few days. I did them again. But after the cycle had worn itself out, while the hot water pounded on my body, a new, colder emotion settled at my core. Politik was dead. And he wasn't the only one. Somewhere between fifty and a hundred people had been gunned down in cold blood. Under the influence of Loath Stringless, others had murdered their own friends, their own husbands and wives.

It didn't matter that they'd all been vampires. It mattered that they'd been innocent. God! They'd been the good citizens who showed up for jury duty.

I'd escaped. They hadn't, Politik hadn't, and there was nothing I, or anyone, could do about that.

But as they say: pay it forward.

You don't need to be a bad-ass gunslinging bitch, I told myself (already regretting that I'd thrown the Glock away). You just need to work the probabilities. *Agency; agency.*

Dorothy had enough bath products to stock a spa. I shampooed my hair and washed all over, resisting the impulse to scrub and scrape the places that hurt, as if I could decontaminate myself that way. When I got out of the shower, the mirror was fogged over. I swiped it with a towel and glanced at my pale, shell-shocked face. There was a splatter of pink marks on my left cheekbone and temple. Burns from the wyrdfire? I was losing track of all the things that had hurt me. The mirror fogged over again, and I let it.

Chapter 18.

"**M**y turn for the shower," said Aleksey. He drained his drink and brushed past me.

Fingercombing my wet hair, I took stock of Hiromi and Ruth, slouched at opposite ends of the sofa. "Where's Dorothy?" I said.

"In there." Ruth nodded at a door on the other side of the room.

I knocked – drawing a scornful laugh from Ruth – and entered a small home office. Dorothy stood behind a glass-topped desk, cordless phone to her ear. The Roppongi skyline scintillated outside the window.

"Just listening to my messages." Dorothy smiled tiredly. Hitching one hip on the desk, she returned the phone to its base and switched it to speaker mode.

"...not yet confirmed, but if it is the truth, may I have the privilege of being the first to convey my congratulations..."

Dorothy hit fast-forward. "Message seventeen, received at eleven... oh four... pm." I glanced at the digital wall clock. Less than an hour ago.

"Congratulations! My dear Countess. Or should I say my dear *kami?* Ha, ha. I hope that I'm not being overly hasty in tendering my respects, and may I say the *gratitude* of all of us here..."

Message eighteen, received at 11:06.

"You traitorous gaijin whore! Don't you try to put it about that Gorozaemon started it. There are plenty of us who know that you tricked him into your trap. No matter what the Court says, we'll never accept you as *kami!*" Click.

"Gotta trace that one," said Dorothy, making a note.

Message nineteen, received at 11:07.

"Congratulations!"

"Are they all like that?" I said.

"Ninety percent kissing my ass. Nine percent telling me

to die, nigger bitch." Dorothy pressed fast-forward again.

"And the one percent?"

"That was the hospital, saying another of my boys died. Oh, now this I want to hear. Let me rewind."

Message twenty, received thirty-seven minutes ago, started with a few seconds of crackling and a distant announcement summoning Yamada-sensei to the cardiac section. Then a male voice said in Japanese, away from the telephone, "Is he? Damn. Right, I'll be there in a sec," before switching into English. "Well, Dorothy, I suppose I ought to join the rest of the world in congratulating you. Forgive me if I find that rather difficult. I'm presently at the hospital where twenty-five of my people are in emergency surgery, and I've just come from talking to the police... there wasn't enough room in the morgue. Not enough *room* in the fucking *morgue*. They had to ship the corpses out as far as Tachikawa. All right... I'm all right. Just rather upset. I'm sure you can appreciate that." The White Duke took an audible breath, composing himself. "I thought it was all over for you, so I left immediately after the verdict. How on earth did you manage it? Reports conflict. Most of the witnesses were terribly wounded, you see... Several people have you in cahoots with that ghastly half-caste pansy. I'm going to go out on a limb here and say that I'm prepared to lay the massacre at his door, but I do *not* believe you knowingly helped him. If you did, of course, I should have to do everything in my power to bury you." Click.

"Oh, Marty," Dorothy whispered. "Have a bit of faith."

Message twenty-one. "Bloody machine cut me off. As I was saying, I want to hear the whole story. On your honor, Dorothy. But in the meantime, you... you have my support. There'll certainly be some awkwardness about the Archduke. Fortunately, or not, I have an eyewitness who saw him go mad and bite his favorite concubine's throat out. We won't let them pin *that* on you. And basically, whatever else you may or may not have done, my eyewitnesses say that you did slay the Elephant. Silver bullets, they say." The White

Duke paused. "Really, I'm most awfully proud of you. Not to mention grateful. I would have done it myself years ago, only I couldn't bear the thought of getting lumbered with the job... And if it's true that you went to Jaize for help? I only ask that next time, you come to your real allies first. You and I may have our differences of opinion, but I've always had faith in you, Dorothy, and I would hope that you have at least a fraction as much faith in me."

The machine clicked off again. This time Dorothy pushed the stop button. "That's Martin," she said. "The White Duke, as they call him." She gazed out the window. Her eyes were shining suspiciously. "Good to know I've still got some friends."

"He was the one who swung the crowd over to you," I recalled.

"Yeah. He's right. I should have had more faith in him."

"He seems like a nice guy."

"Don't let him fool you," Dorothy said instantly. "He's all smooth on the surface, with that sexy accent, but—" She checked, shaking her head. "And there I go, mistrusting my friends again."

I impulsively stepped forward, holding out my arms. "Oh, Dorothy."

She slid off the desktop and retreated to the window. "Clare, I need to be alone right now, OK? I... I got to listen to the rest of these messages. They're still coming in, and I got it set to go straight to the machine, but there's one call I can't afford to miss. That's from the Court. All these fools wishing me well, it don't mean shit on a shingle without the imprimatur of the Blood Imperial, may he live forever and ever, amen."

I swallowed. "'The Elephant'?" Gore lying on the stage, his tusks shattered by Dorothy's bullets, his heavy clothing in disarray. "It certainly fits... *did* fit. But is it a real vampiric title?"

Dorothy laughed without energy. "Just a joke between Martin and me. People complain about Gore in public now, I mean they did, but there was a time when nobody dared to even whisper behind his back. That's when Marty started calling him 'the elephant in the living-room.' I can see you ain't laughing, but we had to take our jokes where we could find them."

"Well, I'll let you get on with it," I said, moving to the door.

"You do that. Tell Ruth and them I'll be with y'all shortly." She picked up the phone. As I closed the door, I thought I heard her whisper to herself: "Wonder what they'll call *me*."

Back in the living-room, I demanded, "Is it true that Dorothy's going to be the next *kami*?"

"That's how it works," Ruth said, blinking coldly at me. "You kill someone, you get their job. So yeah, she'll be Dorothy Edonokami the Forty-Ninth. *If* the Court decides the slaying was on the level. And that's a pretty big *if*, wouldn't you say?"

"But what does that mean? When is a... a slaying *ever* on the level?"

"Beats me. Mind moving? You're blocking the screen."

I circled around the back of the sofa. Hiromi was eating her way through a bowl of instant udon. "That looks yums," I said, desperately trying to sound bright. In fact, the noodles looked revolting, like a bowl of innards in blood, but I was hoping that my faintness stemmed from hunger, and was ready to force some food down my own throat. "Where'd you get it?"

Hiromi waved her chopsticks at the kitchen. "Keita'll show you. He wants to talk to you, anyway."

"Good," I said. "I have to talk to him, too."

Hiromi looked up and made a face. Through the savory steam from her bowl, she whispered, "He's in one of his giving-up moods. Normally, he gets over it if you leave him alone for a while. But now..." Her upper lip trembled. She inhaled steadily. "You heard him say that one of his crows saw Jaize going home? With a police escort?"

"Yes."

"We're going to avenge Politik. That's settled. But the way Keita is now, he just might get himself killed, instead. So see if you can snap him out of it. And see if you can get him to *eat*. It's not a perfect solution, but I've been doing this for years, and I know. It lets you absorb that much more feedback before you crash." She ploughed her chopsticks through her noodles. I straightened up. "Protein is best, but this stuff will do." With tears in her eyes, she started eating again.

"Well, I'll see what I can find. I'm sure Dorothy won't mind if we ransack her kitchen," I said in a normal voice.

It was petty, but I caught myself thinking that Hiromi had changed her tactics. Since there was no point treating me as a rival anymore, she'd decided to enlist me in her attempts to "manage" Keita. But as far as I was concerned, Keita didn't need to be managed like some spoilt young prince. He needed what my mother had called "a smack on the botty."

Or maybe...

Entering the kitchen, I saw him sitting on a stool at the island with his head in his hands. Beside him on the counter lay Politik's pitiful little sigil, its copper dull with dried blood.

I bit my lip. "Stiff drinks called for, I think." I returned to the wet bar, where I mixed two doubles of Jack Daniels. "Here." I placed one in front of Keita. "And now what about some solid food?"

Silence. I started opening cabinets, and soon hit the jackpot: a survivalist's supply of instant ramen and udon.

"Seafood or beef?"

After a minute Keita said, "Any Spicy Szechuan Pork flavor?"

"I don't – ah. Yes, actually." I switched on the electric kettle."I'm sorry about Politik," I said with my back to Keita. "I tried to save him, but—" My throat tightened. I changed the subject. "He gave me a message for you."

"That Jaize isn't a vampire? Whatever that means. He told me that, too. It was the last thing he said. " Keita

345

laughed hollowly. "Apart from *sorry*."

"He must have thought it was important."

"What was important was that he didn't want me to think he'd betrayed us. He *did* betray us, and he knew that I knew it... but at least I got to forgive him. I just wish he could have forgiven *me*."

"What for?" I managed.

"Oh, for not understanding! For not understanding that he felt so strongly about our project that he'd have *had* to betray me, sooner or later, just so as not to betray *himself*. My alliance with Dorothy was the last straw, I think. Of course, I didn't tell him what was in it for me. Ha! So now do you believe I'm honorable?"

Shoulders hunching miserably, I poured hot water into the noodles.

"See this?"

I turned. Keita was holding Politik's copper medallion. With a rictus grin, he swung it against the side of the island. "The First Sigil of Metal."

"He said it was the first. And they'd promised him more."

"Bullshit." Clink, clink. "This is the only Metal sigil they've got. If they had any others, Scott would be doing more than making magical trinkets. No, they lied to him, and he fell for it." Keita tossed it back on the counter. It fell to the floor. He swung sideways off his stool to retrieve it. "I can't win," he cried, grabbing the edge of the counter to haul himself back up, face red. "All I have to offer is truth and hard work. Jaize has the connections, the looks, and the ability to lie his face off and make people believe him. Of course, you have to *want* to believe... But Politik always was a bit too reverential about angels and that kind of thing. Angels, my ass! *Qliphothic entities!* Let's at least be accurate."

"Sorry," I said. "What's a qliphothic entity?"

Keita beckoned to me, palm down. His eyes were bulging. "A demon," he hissed. "Qliphothics are the worst kind. There are others: fiends, infernals, imps..."

"Like your crows?"

"They're different." His lips twisted self-mockingly. "Then again, maybe I'm just saying that because part of them is inside me... But yeah, them too. They're *all* demons. That's what I learned when I astral-travelled to their plane, and it's probably the most important thing you'll ever hear, so don't forget it. Everyone... everything in that realm. They'll pretend to be gods, angels, your dear dead mother, whatever it takes to get across the divide. But they're all demons. *All* of them."

I crossed myself.

Keita laughed. Lighting a cigarette, he said, "Superstitious."

I took a gulp of whiskey, then put the glass down to hide the fact that my hands were shaking. I'd learned in the past that when magicians clashed, more or less the first thing they accused each other of was summoning demons. It was the magical equivalent of a political smear. Meanwhile, the truth went missing in action.

And so did people.

"I'm trying to stay focused on the facts here," I said. "I've seen so much shit tonight that I never even used to believe in. I've *done* things that I never used to believe in. To tell you the truth, I'm losing my sense of the rights and wrongs of it all..." But no, I thought, recalling the look of childish rapture on Politik's face as bullets bounced off the air around him. That was a wrong against nature, against the fragile capacity of that poor boy's heart. "We have to make Jaize pay," I burst out.

"Yeah." Keita sighed. "Well, I've already called Skriva. He's picking us up here in an hour."

I blinked. "Does Hiromi know?"

Cigarette clamped in his lips, Keita got up and opened drawers in search of chopsticks.

"Ah," I said. "I see. You're planning to leave her behind. Well, you're not leaving *me* behind. Just letting you know. We'll have no more of that 'It's too much of a risk' —"

"And how exactly are you going to help? Are you finally

going to get around to using your sigil? Or are you going to blow them all away with your high moral principles?"

"I don't have a sigil. I can't do magic. What the hell?" I meant to sound outraged, but I only sounded pitiful.

"You can. You *did*. At L'Aqua."

"I just copied Jaize's sigil and rechanneled his *qi*." That was the best way I could explain it to myself.

"For fuck's sake, he's Airborn! He couldn't have done what you did."

"He was doing it!"

For a moment Keita looked uncertain, almost frightened. Then he shot back, "Well, he didn't do it as well as you did!"

"I don't even know *what* I did!"

Keita paced between the fridge and the sink, trailing smoke from his cigarette. "The sigils are shortcuts. They give you powers that would have taken our ancestors decades to achieve. Listen! Politik and I worked on *qi* craft for a while. But we were wasting our time. To get anywhere with that, you need to train intensively, like the Shoto people – and it just doesn't repay the effort. Levitation? Ninja stunts? Big deal. On the other hand, the sigils put real power at your fingertips. All you have to do is let them work for you."

"Which would be why it took you two decades to get yours to work for *you?*"

"Maybe what I'm saying is you need faith."

"And maybe that's my problem. I don't believe I can do this shit. Therefore, I can't."

"You can. You did."

"But I can't do it again." I grabbed a pair of chopsticks and started eating. "I mean, I don't even know *how!*"

"You focus your *qi*. Rain, blood, wine – anything with a reasonable percentage of water in it should work as a link between the cognitive and material planes. If you had a sigil made of your metal, you could try to cast the essence of water... but I don't know what *that* would look like, and I'm not sure I want to know. So just do what you did at L'Aqua. "

I put down my chopsticks, rubbed my finger on the nozzle of the faucet, and drew "my" sigil on the counter. It was clear as ever in my mind. "I don't remember what I did at L'Aqua. I was panicking."

"Just articulate a command. But—"

Water hit my face. I reeled back, eyes popping open. Torrents streamed from both faucets, rebounding from the sink and spattering noisily to the floor.

Keita sprang past me and shut the faucets off.

I took a dishtowel from its hook and wiped my arms. The front of my dress was soaked. Watery soup overflowed my bowl of ramen. I could still hear running water.

"The bathroom," I said, at the same time as Ruth whisked past the open door of the kitchen.

She banged the bathroom door and rattled the knob. "Aleksey? Aleksey, what are you doing in there?"

"It's not him," I said, feeling sick. "It was me."

"He's been in there for ages. And now it sounds like he's running the shower *and* the faucets—" She skipped back. Water had started to spread out from under the bathroom door.

"Let me try," Keita said. He crouched and fiddled with the doorknob.

Dorothy hurried down the hall. "What you all fussing about? OK, we got a flood... Shit, Ruth, where's your head at? You shouldn't have let him go in the shower by himself!"

Ruth flushed. "Out of my way," she said to Keita. Shifting her balance, she drove a yoko-geri kick into the door just above the knob. It popped open. She, Dorothy, and Hiromi piled into the bathroom and yanked the shower curtain aside. Aleksey lay in several inches of water, his face drenched in the spray that pounded from the showerhead.

"Just in time," Keita said.

Squelching, Ruth and Dorothy dragged Aleksey out of the bathroom. Hiromi lingered to turn off the shower and the faucets in the sink. Aleksey was naked, and I reflexively grabbed one of the less wet towels off the rack, but he wouldn't let me tie it on him. He was muttering in Russian and rolling his head around as if he couldn't lift it all the way. Dorothy's fang marks glowed an ugly red on his neck.

"Help me get him into my room. He needs to lay flat." Dorothy hiked Aleksey's arm around her neck.

"He's not gonna make it." Tears thickened Ruth's voice.

"Yes, he is." I glimpsed Dorothy's profile: caring, tender. "He's just hungry."

We all trailed down the hall after them. Dorothy kicked open a door and Ruth hit a light switch with her elbow. Had I not been so dazed, I would have smiled. Dorothy's bedroom was the dream room of a Cinderella fan, all frilly pastels with a skirted dressing-table, pink cushions heaped on the window-seat, and net curtains tied back from the four-poster bed. Yet the musky perfume in the air was anything but childlike.

Ruth and Dorothy schlepped Aleksey onto the bed and struggled to put his t-shirt and boxer shorts on him. He resisted, hunching into a fetal ball. His wet body left dark blotches on the coverlet. The brand on his flank was less eyecatching than before; it might almost have started to fade. I gave Dorothy the towel I still held. Tucking one long bare leg under her, she sat beside Aleksey and started to pat him dry. "Go on, all of y'all, out. I need to see to him now."

"What are you going to do?" I felt dizzy and achy all over.

"I'm going to feed him. He's a vampire now... or he's gonna be, if we can get him over this hump. But it'll be OK. I got enough experience doing this by now."

While we spoke, Ruth had been rummaging in the drawers of the dressing-table. Now she turned around with a smothered cry. Blood streamed from her left wrist. Dropping Dorothy's nail scissors, she clambered onto the bed.

"Damn, girl, I just had this shit drycleaned last week!" Dorothy's hand shook as she pointed at the drops of blood falling on the coverlet. "Y'all are *destroying* my fucking crib. And can I ask what the fuck you're trying to do?"

"I want to feed him."

"Well, that's a change of heart from the girl who swore she'd never let anyone sink fang into her," Dorothy muttered. Louder, she added, "And you know perfectly well you can't do that, unless you want him put down. It's vampire blood he needs, and that's all he's gonna get, until he peps up."

Competent in a crisis, Hiromi pulled a handful of Kleenex from the porcelain box on the dressing-table. I swayed. In the instant that she leaned over the dressing-table, I'd seen her reflection in the oval mirror behind it. The mirror showed a bloated old hag, mouth pursed with chronic frustration and hate, wispy black hair thin on her skull. "Here you go," she said softly, passing the Kleenex to Ruth. Eyes worried but forehead smooth, she folded her plump, firm arms.

"So am I hearing this right? Turning causes a physiological crisis?" Keita said. *He* hadn't forgotten the objectives of our study. I wanted to hug him for it. "Newly Turned vampires need the blood of another vampire to... to stabilize their body chemistry. And if they don't get it?"

"Hello, mister or miss *zako*," Dorothy said. "Sssh now." She slid her arm under Aleksey's head. He turned to her like a child seeking its mother's breast. "Pretty, pretty." She stroked his forehead. "Oh, you're burning up... Tell you what you can do for me, Ruth. Go in the living-room and look in the corner table. There should be a scalpel in the sterile pack."

Ruth didn't move. Hiromi left the room. Ruth knelt on the bed, holding the wad of Kleenex to her bleeding wrist. "So you're going to feed him. And who's going to feed you?"

"I had some from him back there. I'll be all right."

"But you didn't take as much as you needed. You were putting him first. And if you're going to donate again tonight, you need to replenish your energy."

"I said I'll be fine, Ruth." Taking the scalpel that Hiromi passed to her, Dorothy shook her head decisively. "You spent so much effort keeping your veins to yourself over all these years. Stick to your guns, girl. Be a shame if you cave in now."

"But you said my blood was so sweet you could smell it. You said if you could just have one little sip —"

Dorothy interrupted her, voice rising. "Forget it. I don't want your blood, I don't want your help, I don't want anything except for all of you lookyloos to get the fuck *out!*" She glared at us. "Besides, I think I heard someone at the intercom. Make yourselves useful, tell them to fuck off, too. If the phone rings, I'll take it in here."

Keita and Hiromi backed to the door, but I took a step towards the bed. "I can feed you, Dorothy." Her perfume gathered around me. "I don't mind. I haven't got any issues around – around sharing…"

Dorothy seemed about to retort crossly, but then her face softened. "Just look at you. You ain't in no shape… Turn her around, Crow Boy, have her to look at herself in that mirror over there. The paleness of her. Poor little thing, she's just about dead on her feet."

Her voice seemed to come from a long way behind me. Keita turned me by the shoulders to face the dressing-table. I saw his haggard "mirror face," with the discolored bags under the eyes, the pencil moustache and drooping mouth. And I saw my own face. As Dorothy had pointed out, I was pale. But apart from that… "Holding up pretty well," Keita said. He smiled. The mirror turned it into a grisly leer. But I barely noticed. My gaze zeroed in on those pink marks on my cheekbone and temple, like a spatter of raspberry-colored freckles. They were more noticeable than before. They might be burns, or they might be…

"Oh God," I said, and turned my back on the mirror. "Please," I said, not knowing who I was addressing.

"No, Clare," Dorothy said. "It has been a long night, and the answer is no."

"Keita?" Hiromi called from the hall. "I just talked to security downstairs. Skriva's here. I don't know what he wants, but should I get them to let him in?"

Keita grimaced. "No, just tell him to wait! We'll be right

down."

"It sounds like they're trying to kick him out. I'm going down." The front door slammed.

"Y'all gearing to bounce?" Dorothy said distractedly. "Take care then. If you need anything, get at me." Aleksey was reaching for her wrist, as if even in his delirious state, new instincts drove him. Dorothy tutted. With a movement so quick I barely saw it, she jerked the scalpel across her own wrist, slicing open the scabbed wound that she'd made earlier with her fangs. Blood welled up.

I said, "You aren't a real vampire, are you, Dorothy? You're not immortal. None of them are. It's all fake."

"It ain't that black and white," she said, looking up at me. "And it ain't fake, but it ain't about the blood, really. It's about the love."

"So, we'll be going," Keita said, trundling me towards the door.

"Then it has to be me," Ruth said. "I'm the only one you can trust. I know you think I'll regret it, but I can guarantee you…"

"Oh Ruth. Just hush. We can discuss it later. Matter of fact, I think we got a lot to discuss, you and me." She offered her bleeding wrist to Aleksey. "Here you go, pretty."

Aleksey latched onto the wound with a crowing exclamation in Russian. Through gritted teeth, Dorothy whispered four-letter words. Ruth moved around and gave her her hand to hold onto. Aleksey slurped and champed at Dorothy's wrist.

Keita and I backed out of the room. He shut the door and fell against it with exaggerated limpness.

"What a mess," I said, looking at the wet trample marks on the hall carpet. "What a mess."

"Well, there's no way I'm leaving you here after *that*." Keita herded me down the hall towards the living-room. "But I think we can spare a couple of minutes to raid the bar."

The little sink in the wet bar had flooded, too. The faucet was still trickling. Keita turned it off and sorted through the bottles.

"Absolut Plasma," he pretended to read. "Bloody Mary mixture with genuine T-cells... just kidding. Or maybe prophesying. It's a fast-growing niche market." He swept several bottles into the crook of his arm and paused, gazing out at the stunning thirty-sixth-floor view. "Someday I'm going to have a lifestyle like this. Until then, I guess I'm stuck with doing the right thing."

I said, "Sometimes, I'm almost convinced you have a sense of humor."

Skriva's vampires fell on our booty with approval. Initially subdued by the news of Politik's death, the atmosphere in the back of the van soon grew boisterous. It was a different van from this afternoon, with the back seats stripped out to accommodate a dozen vamps, plus Keita, Hiromi, and me. The air-conditioning labored to disperse the reek of cologne and the foxy stench of vampire.

Sporting messy warpaint, trading crude banter and opaque slang, the Harajuku vamps reminded me of a rock band – which made sense, since at least some of them were in one. Undead Cancer, Skriva's band, took their punk heritage seriously. Leering, they showed us their arsenal of knives, tyre irons, cudgels studded with broken glass, and bike chains with links sharpened to razor edges.

"But do they know what they're getting into?" I whispered to Keita.

"I told them Loath Stringless only works on the undead." Keita grimaced. "If that turns out not to be true... But I'm pretty sure. And they're such outsiders, they'll be more or less immune to Jaize's mind-control games, like we are."

"And we definitely have conventional superiority," Hiromi said, watching the vampires whet their knives.

I wished I shared her confidence. Back at Eternal Family, fear had been a luxury I'd sacrificed in favor of survival. Now, my adrenaline was at a low ebb, and I was frankly terrified of facing Jaize again. I wanted to avenge Politik, but sheer willpower had its limits. Where did the others get their physical courage?

As if answering my unspoken question, Keita passed me the bottle of Remy Martin.

"Liquid courage." I took a gulp. "Although I feel like we should really be swigging forties of malt liquor."

"Is that like happo-shu?" said the nearest vampire. "We got happo-shu. You want?"

"I want," I said recklessly.

He opened the bottle with his fangs and presented it to me. "Special for the Water Witch!"

The worst of it was that Keita and Hiromi had blabbed about my alleged powers, and now the vampires seemed to think of me as their secret weapon.

"Watchoutyou'regonnahitthem!" Skriva yelled.

The driver slammed on the brakes. I tumbled into a heap of vampires, then picked myself up and goggled over Skriva's shoulder.

The van had come to a standstill on a shadowy street lined with trees. In the skirt of light from the headlights, nothing moved.

"They were *there*," the driver said. "A whole family. Just crossing the street."

"How likely is that at two a.m.?" Keita said. *"Drive!"*

The vampire put the van in gear. Skriva grunted and shot out a hand to hold him back.

I saw them. A family of four, taking their time to cross the street at the furthest reach of the headlights. Now Dad was stopping to lift the little girl onto his shoulders. The little boy rode a kickboard scooter. Cleancut, clad in crisp summer outfits, they were a preppie stereotype, the face of 21st-century Asia, everything the Human League for Peace purported to defend. Heading for the park, or the store, or the baseball field...

...at two in the morning.

Something splosh-thumped into the back of the van,

hard and wet.

The nearest vampires tried to open the rear door. Hiromi screamed, *"Don't open it!"*

The driver stepped on the accelerator.

The family turned to face the van, not even trying to get out of the way. "Oh hell," the driver moaned, swerving.

The little boy glided on his scooter across our path. In the full glare of the headlights, his eyes shone bright yellow, like the eyes of a sheep that wanders onto the road at night.

The fender grazed him. Without a jolt.

"Drive," Skriva shouted, picking up Keita's refrain. "Drive, drive, drive —"

The vampires piled to the rear of the van. "There's something in the road!" – "You hit him, Jorrick, you hit him!" – "It's not the right shape —" "Where'd the rest of them go?"

"We just met a few of Jaize's allies," Keita said loudly. The van rounded a curve. "They were – don't worry. They weren't real."

"No wonder this fucking neighborhood always gave me the creeps," Skriva said. "Allies? OK. Be more specific." He wasn't all that drunk.

"Gods," I said, shivering. Fog sliding through the trees, mistletoe bulging like goiters from the branches. The patch of dank Irish woodland couldn't have covered more than half an acre, but I couldn't seem to find my way out. On and on I'd blundered, with the faint sound of singing now in front of me, now behind me. "Old gods. Feed them and they wake up."

"Not gods," Keita shouted. "Demons."

Skriva gave him a flat stare. Slowly, his lip curled, and he said, "Yee-haw."

The other vampires burst into laughter, relieving the tension.

"Thanks for warning us," Skriva added.

"I didn't think Jaize was that stupid," Keita said angrily. "Look, I've suspected for a while that he might be dabbling in summoning... demons. There's stuff he knows that he couldn't know any other way, and, well. But..."

I gave him a gentle kick. He hit out at my foot without looking. Guilty, I thought. Guilty, guilty.

"So those things are dangerous?" a vampire said suspiciously.

"Are they dangerous!" Keita exclaimed. "If Jaize is controlling them, hell yeah, they're dangerous. If he's *not* controlling them... I don't even want to think about it."

High beams glanced into the van from behind. The driver, Jorrick, slowed down, but instead of passing us, the other vehicle loomed closer, its four headlights blazing. The lower pair rode so high off the ground that the vehicle had to be an SUV or a Hummer.

"Fuck him," the vampires said. "He's not real. Ghost car."

"I don't think so." Keita's voice rose. "Step on it before they ram us, you dumb vampire!"

We careened along the dead lanes, straight through blinking amber lights. The SUV clung to our tail with annoying ease, its headlights filling the interior of the van. My instincts yammered at me to get down on the floor, but I couldn't act like a coward in front of the vampires. At last Jorrick braked in front of Jaize's front gate. The Jeep, the Beemer, and the Ferrari were in the garage, but the house was dark.

The SUV stopped behind the van.

Knives in hand, the vampires poured out into the SUV's headlights. Their shadows crisscrossed as they split up and encircled the SUV. Jorrick darted to the gate and went to work on the lock with a bolt-cutter.

The SUV just stood there, its headlights blazing. The vampires crouched at a distance, knives ready. Behind them, fireflies bobbed in the overhanging trees.

"I don't like this," I said loudly.

"I don't, either. Out, out." Keita slid out of the van and ran to join Jorrick in the shadow of the gateposts. Hiromi and I followed. Keita gripped the lock and bowed his head. The stench of burning plastic rose. I turned to look at the ring of vampires around the SUV.

In the shadows behind them, the fireflies had stopped fluttering about. They hovered in pairs, a clear eight feet off the ground.

"Guys!" I screamed. *"Behind you!"*

The shadows converged on the vampires behind the SUV. The points of yellow fire no longer looked like fireflies.

"Get into the light, into the light!" Keita yelled. "They can't stand the light!"

Most of the vamps tumbled around to the front of the SUV, but one stood his ground. Flickering limbs of shadow reached for him, dark on dark. His knife cut straight through them. He staggered. Then he jerked rigid, eyes rolling white, teeth clacking. He moved toward his friends with a bizarre stiff-legged gait.

"All they have to do is t-t-touch you." Hiromi – brave, competent Hiromi – was in tears.

The vampires bunched up in the headlights of the SUV, back to back, all except Jorrick, who cursed and ran for our van. He switched on the engine, illuminating the slope of the street to the next curve.

The SUV's headlights went off.

In the darkness between the two vehicles, the vampires howled despairingly.

Cold blue light blossomed beside me. For an instant, I saw the vampires fighting in a mêlée, overtopped by tall shadows with fiery yellow eyes. Then the shadows simply disintegrated, melted by the wintry glare that pulsated from the globe of werelight in Keita's hand.

Jorrick backed the van around, spraying gravel, and shone the headlights on the fight.

With a metallic boom, the SUV's doors slid back and half a dozen men jumped out. The Human League vigilantes fought with their bare hands, downing one vampire after another with clinically placed blows – not all of which actually connected: they were using their *qi* craft. I noted that they were careful to stay in the light. Some of the vampires hit back, but others just flailed mechanically at whoever they could reach, including their friends.

I wrapped my sleeve around my hand and jerked at the lock of the gate. Its casing snapped, bits of frizzled circuitry spinning loose, and the gate rattled back.

Keita knelt beside me. The globe of werelight in his hand pulsed like a frightened heart, its light strobing wildly over the trees. "There's a back way in," he said, voice strained. "Skriva and I found it when we were here before. A cave in the garden. It goes down into a kind of basement storage area, then back up into the house."

"The vamps are fighting each other," I informed him. "It's Loath Stringless. It *does* work on them."

"No, it's not. Those elementals have possessed half of them. But I can exorcise them if I get up close. That's what this is for." He walked the globe of werelight over his knuckles. "My grandfather told me. I'd forgotten. Everything has two sides, yin and yang. Fire destroys, but light chases back the dark."

"Don't get hurt," Hiromi sobbed.

"*You* be careful. You hear me, Hiro-chan? Clare? If it's too dangerous, get out. Do *not* take any risks —"

Without waiting for him to finish, I ran into the garden. Hiromi followed me.

The cicadas screeched in the trees, drowning out the noise behind us. Beneath their foliage, the shadows lay black and deep. Thank God, I could see no fireflies. Pale blossoms soaked the air with fragrance. We slowed to a walk. I yipped when something fluttered through the dark in front of us: a bat.

Hiromi touched my arm. "Sorry I lost it back there," she whispered. "It's just... the demons. They freak me out."

"Understandable," I murmured, although her reaction puzzled me. As Keita and Politik's lab assistant, she should have been relatively acclimatized, shouldn't she? Then again, maybe that's *why* she was terrified: she knew more about demons than I did.

359

"They're OK as long as they're in a circle, or bound some other way," she whispered. "That means you can send them back any time. But they don't want to go back. They want to stay here. And the only way they can stay is *inside people...*"

I felt rather than saw her start to shiver again. Worry muted my adrenaline. Over the drone of the cicadas, I heard the burbling of water somewhere in the garden.

Chapter 19.

Almost unconsciously, I angled towards the sound of water, and Hiromi followed me. We stopped short at the edge of an ornamental pool fed by a trickle from a crevice in the rock behind it. Waterlilies glowed in the dark. And on a bench beneath an overhanging willow tree sat a woman, fair hair trailing over the shoulders of her dark pantsuit. The amulets on her breast clattered softly as she rose and came around the pond.

Hiromi and I backed against each other. I wanted to turn and run. But *Politik, Politik,* I thought, and all the innocents at Eternal Family – I couldn't let them down –

The branches of the willow brushed the woman's hair. They descended all at once, with a hissing of leaves, and long tendrils lashed at her throat. Then they danced in an absurd flurry, and then dangled limp.

Hiromi moaned and fumbled in her fanny pack.

The woman smiled, eyes crinkling. "Don't, my dear," she said. "I felt you coming. You both stand out quite brightly, you know."

I said nothing. I was staring at the shadows that writhed at the woman's heels, dark on dark, gelatinous.

Hiromi croaked unintelligibly, then managed, "You're a demon."

"My dear! Not at all. Oh, I did summon those lippit-yslickeree liyeroilers –" Those *what?* It sounded as if the woman had slipped for an instant into gibberish. "But they are not dangerous, you know, as long as you don't cross them. And although your friends have foolishly done just that, there is no need to fear." Her tone momentarily darkened. "That warlock out there appears to have the better of them. I do *not* think it fair to begrudge my lickitorshy lowslayers their spree, but I shall not hold it against *you.*"

"You've got them all around you," Hiromi cried.

"They're coiling around your ankles like cats. Oh Clare, if you could only see—"

In the act of turning, the woman froze and frowned for an instant. "There. Is that better?"

The shadows dispersed, fleeing for the trees. Some of them had legs.

"Y-yes," Hiromi muttered. "Thank you."

"Good. Then let us go in."

Moving in a trance, Hiromi and I followed the woman around the rock behind the pool. Its rear side bore a stone plaque with a haut-relief bodhisattva four feet tall, one hand raised in blessing. Effortlessly, the woman pushed the plaque aside, exposing a hole ribbed like a dark throat. I didn't have the courage to go down there. But it seemed I had no choice. Following the woman down uneven stone steps in the dark, I knew I was half-hypnotized, but I couldn't pierce my fog of bemused acceptance. I did manage to say: "Who are you?"

Warm laughter threaded up from the dark. "My name is Eva."

"You speak English?" I said idiotically.

"Yes, indeed. I lived for a good many years in the United States."

"Whereabouts?" My repartee was getting more and more brilliant.

"San Jose. Have you ever been there?"

"No – only to LA…."

"Oh, what a pity you didn't have a chance to talk to Jaize about Hollywood. He adores the glamor of the movies." A slim hand waved deprecatingly. There was light at the bottom of the stairs. I followed the woman – Eva – towards its source.

We arrived in a cavern with a ceiling half stone, half earth, shored up by age-blackened beams. On the bare rock floor, a circle three meters in diameter had been outlined in fresh red paint. Inside the circle was painted a pentacle bordered with runic markings. A fat black candle burned at each point of the pentacle. Its center formed another, smaller circle, but the paint of that one looked scorched, and the markings inside it were obscured by a dark stain.

Rugs and curtains decorated the walls, a jumble of ethnic patterns. Furniture – a desk and office chair, a divan, several chests – had been pushed back into a corner. We kept following Eva, shuffling around the outside of the circle. At last she stopped and turned to face us. She was Caucasian, with deep-set eyes, a straight nose, and a jawline that made her slightly resemble Claudia Schiffer… in another thirty years. Her hair wasn't blond, but white. The candlelight revealed slackness at the corners of her mouth, a collapsed look about her eye sockets.

She was the right age to be Jaize's (probably apocryphal) mother, but the wrong race. Still, I said, "Are you related to Jaize? I mean—" I laughed apologetically.

"Not at all. I am his adoptive mother." She went to one of the divans along the wall of the cavern and felt among the velour blankets heaped on it. Politik had brought similar blankets out of the *oshiire* closet the first night I stayed at their apartment, I remembered, velour with splashy floral prints. Oh, Politik… Jaize had taken advantage of his idealism, used and discarded him with utter selfishness. This had gone beyond turning the other cheek. I would… What was that tail of hair peeking out of the blanket? A wig, or part of a traditional festival mask…

"I found him playing by himself," Eva explained chattily. "He was just two or three. All alone! Clearly, his parents had abandoned him, so I took him home with me, and we've been together ever since. I saw at once that he was special, you see. My first husband would have called him a Void child. My second husband, I am afraid, called him a cuckoo, and other things that were not very nice. That is why I divorced him and moved back to Japan."

She was working away at something beneath the blankets, trying to hide it from our sight.

"Scott, however – Scott is my natural son – he has never harbored any animosity. Jaize is the stronger of them. It could not be otherwise, since he was born in the moment before the sun reaches its zenith, when the Void reigns. The Void dominates all other elements, and contains them within itself. But it warms my heart to see how close they are. I do believe that no resonance, neither sexual nor comradely, is as powerful as that between brothers..."

The shock of the revelation cleared my head. Goddamn Ruth and her dirty mind! Well, it was my own fault for having believed her without proof. If I'd only used my eyes, I'd have seen that Scott and Jaize never had acted like lovers, when they weren't deliberately camping it up for someone else's benefit. They acted like... well, like brothers.

Hiromi raised a shaking hand and pointed at Eva's back.

As I followed her gaze, a human leg slid out of the blankets, a livid mark on its ankle, only to be swiftly covered up again. And now, at the other end of the heap, I saw a trailing swathe of black hair.

It seemed to me that our silence must betray what we'd seen. I said in an artificial tone, like an eager student, "Eva, I thought one had to know a person's date of birth to ascertain their element? If Jaize was already two or three when you – adopted him..." Kidnapped him, more likely, while his mother's back was turned, I thought.

"To be sure, one has only to look at them. Perhaps not you, little blonde witch, but I think your friend has the third eye... don't you, my dear?" As she spoke, Eva casually rearranged the blankets to hide the corpse on the divan. She strode back towards us, long legs, broad shoulders, a Valkyrie unbowed by old age.

"I don't know what you think the third eye is," Hiromi said, her voice strangled. "I can't see anyone's element. But I can see the spirits of trees and plants – and I can see demons. And I can see that you're a bad, bad woman!"

"Well, perhaps I am," Eva said, her laugh low. She flickered at Hiromi and scooped her off her feet. Slinging her over her shoulders in a fireman's carry, she snapped plastic ties onto her wrists and ankles and yanked them as tight as they would go. Hunched beneath Hiromi's screaming, thrashing weight, she lurched into the center of the circle and bent to dump her over her head. The candles flung their shadows over the wall. Hiromi's skull hit the rock floor with a nauseating crack. Her screams stopped as if someone had hit a switch.

Eva straightened up, smiling, and between her lips gleamed the points of fangs.

I hadn't screamed. I hadn't even moved.

"What do you think, little blonde witch? Am I a bad, bad woman?"

The flames of the candles didn't return to the upright. They leaned towards me, slightly to my left. I held my breath, and felt the gentlest of draughts.

"You're performing human sacrifices to summon demons," I said. "You tell me."

"How naïve you are." She touched the toe of her pump to Hiromi's mouth and worked it around on the girl's teeth. "Naïve and – pitiable. Magic is all that we have to defend ourselves against the powers of this world. It is the only tool of the weak. This—" she scraped her shoe lightly over Hiromi's face— "is nothing to what *they* do every day: your presidents, your kings, your ministers of state. They oppress their enemies in secret, and in secret we defend ourselves the only way we can... But you know nothing of that, nor do you need to. Know only that I pity you. Nowhere to belong – here you are at the end of the world, seeking something, you scarcely know what... Why, you remind me of my younger self."

"Insult to injury," I said, trembling.

Eva simply smiled. "Shall I save you the agonies of self-doubt I endured – shall I tell you what you seek? Yes. You seek a master."

"Behind every strong woman," I sighed. "Who's your master, then?"

"He is dead. As am I." Her smile faded. "Oh yes, that is what it is, though I breathe and move. I did not choose to become a vampire, you know… But who has the good fortune to choose his allegiance?"

"I happen to believe in free will," I said. "And I believe there's no sin God won't forgive, if you ask. So let her go!"

Eva's mouth twisted, making her momentarily look older. "Oh, sit down and shut up," she said, and gestured.

An invisible blow swung into my face, knocking me backwards. I staggered – caught myself – lurched sideways towards the nearest divan. Then I leaped diagonally downwind into an ukemi flip that carried me head over heels without touching the floor. My legs punched through the wall hangings. I hurtled into a dim corridor and landed at a run.

The corridor led to a staircase of plain wooden planks that I climbed on hands and knees, inching upward while the wind tore at my clothes and tried to yank me backwards into thin air. It weakened as I climbed. Either Eva's range was limited, or she couldn't cast effectively out of eyesight, or she'd decided not to bother with me anymore. Maybe she thought I couldn't get out.

And maybe she was right.

Halfway to the bare bulb that hung at the head of the stairs, it occurred to me that I'd climbed further up than we'd come down. And when I cautiously opened the door beneath the lightbulb, I found myself at the end of a paneled hall that I recognized. I was on the second floor of the house.

I had to fetch help. I knew enough about black magic to know that Eva couldn't sacrifice Hiromi immediately. Whether she was using *jajutsu* or hermetic magic, she had incantations to utter, circles to walk, salt to scatter, and a bunch of other ceremonial crap to get through first. I said a quick prayer, reached into my pocket, and yes! I still had my phone. Nervously watching the hall, I dialed.

"This is Keita Matsudaira. Leave a message."

All right, so I was on my own. I hit disconnect and began to inch down the hall.

The floor creaked. I froze.

Not a sound came from the doors on either side of me. I relaxed incrementally. Then I heard a rustle overhead, and footsteps moving rapidly across the ceiling.

Old clothes and books – magical implements. Jaize and Scott looking for something Eva needs for her ritual —

In a blind panic, I skittered down the hall and tried the first door I reached. To my astonishment, it offered no resistance.

The footsteps rattled on the stairs.

I slipped through the door into darkness and flattened myself to the wall. I'd wait until they went back to the attic, or if worst came to worst, surprise them when they came in…

Light flooded the room. I flinched away from the wall. My shoulder had hit the switch.

On the great circular bed in the middle of the room, Jaize and Scott sat up and stared.

I wheeled, heard the lock snick shut, and shook the doorknob anyway. Giving up, I turned to see Scott pointing a small black object at me. I took it for a gun and flinched before I saw that it was just the remote control for the lock.

"Why bother with a remote control when you're doing it by magic?" I said.

"It's just an empty case." Scott tossed it aside. "But you get in the habit."

Behind me, the doorknob turned futilely, and a volley of blows rained on the outside of the door, which didn't even shiver in its frame.

"Well, Clare," Jaize said. "We've really got to stop meeting like this." He palmed something from a niche in the headboard, then slowly swung his legs off the bed. He wore only sweatpants. Scott wore a pair of tartan boxer shorts and a gauze pad taped over his eye. Both of them bore puncture wounds and weals from Hiromi's vines. Jaize limped over to one of the chairs by the window. Without looking around at me, he said, "What are you doing here?"

"I came to kill you," I said. "I think. I'm not really sure

anymore."

"I'm not fucking with your head, you know."

"I know."

"All right," Scott said. "She's a witch, bro. She knows."

"I got the picture," Jaize said wearily. "You'd think the Court would have sent someone better, is all."

"I'm not here from the Court," I said.

"You sure? Don't you work for Dorothy?"

"Not anymore. Anyway, she didn't send us. A lot of other people are out for your blood, too." Outside the room, all was silent. I said helplessly, "What are *you* doing here? Shouldn't you be running away or something?"

Jaize's laugh was tired. "You run, you lose. Tomorrow, the Court is gonna be on our asses like hemorrhoids. So tonight, we're resting. Hell, I couldn't run anywhere right now even if I wanted to."

I glanced at the mirrored wall and knew he was telling the truth. His reflection looked hollowed out, almost translucent. Scott's mirror face was dark, his skin rusty, blotchy.

Jaize caught my eye in the mirror and nodded. "I am so wiped. After we lost Aleks..." He shrugged.

Feedback, I thought, and finally understood what Aleksey had been to Jaize, before he died to him.

"You lost Politik, too," I reminded him, and had to add, when he looked blank: "Inobe-kun. Seiji."

"Oh, him. Good kid. Pity, yeah."

"We didn't have time to get to know him real well," Scott said.

"Why did you do it?"

Scott's chuckle turned into a cough that sounded painful, but there was real amusement in his voice. "Check it out, bro, this is where we run down our fiendish plan to take over the world." He tiredly tilted his head towards me. "Your friend – Inobe – had some crazy fixation on destroying the *kami* regime. We're not that ambitious."

"So what was the fiendish plan?"

"Oh, kill Gore," Jaize said. "Become *kami*. Intimidate the

fuck out of the rest of them."

"You nailed that last bit," I said.

"Yeah, but I lost Aleks." Jaize suddenly brought his fist down on the arm of the chair, but said no more.

"Vampire society is hierarchical, ya know?" Scott said to me. "Vampires are bound to the one who makes them. Can't be bound to anyone else."

"I think I've found out how vampires are made... Turned," I said. "Some people say it's a retrovirus, and I think now that's probably true. The ingestion of vampire blood must cause changes at the DNA level. But that's not the whole story, or even most of it. I think it's also a question of mind over matter." I hesitated. "Was it your mother who Turned you?"

Jaize laughed.

"So you've met her," Scott said. "She finished with Naomi yet?"

"Yes," I said baldly. "And my friend Hiromi is next. I got away... I don't seem to have got very far. But I think I may have come to the right place." I walked across the room, expecting to be flung backwards by a special-delivery gust of wind. Nothing happened. I stood over Jaize. "I need your help."

"Your friend who?" Scott said behind me.

I bit my lip. "The girl... the wood witch who was at Eternal Family."

"Ho! Skriva's pet witch. Hey bro, there's some good news, huh? With a sacrifice like that, Mom might even be able to summon her prince." Scott's voice dropped to a contemplative croon. "So Mom's got Skriva's little witch, and we've got Dorothy's."

I started, my heart racing afresh.

"Chill," Jaize said, with a shadow of his old smile. "We won't let her sacrifice you if it's not necessary. And it won't be, I'm pretty sure. I should be able to back the Court's minions down by myself once I get my energy back... Depends who the new *kami* sends, of course."

I drew a deep breath, and felt something shift inside me like a weight, as if I'd been standing with one foot on solid ground, and now braced to hurl myself beyond all reckoning of safety. I knelt in front of Jaize. Trembling, I fumbled my hair back to expose one side of my neck."Feed from me. That'll give you your energy back."

Jaize flinched. I looked up at him, challenging him, and understood something new about the relationship between vampire and victim: it wasn't all one way.

"Keep that pretty white neck to yourself, honey," Scott said, approaching behind me. "His bite is mine."

His camp act wasn't convincing. I glanced around at him, and confirmed what I'd noticed subconsciously: he had plenty of thorn-stabs and other superficial wounds on his chest and belly, even some on his neck... but a man who'd been donating for years ought to have scars on both sides of his neck. Scott had none. Formerly, I might have concluded that Jaize drank from his inner thighs. But now I knew they were brothers, that would be pushing the limits of credibility.

"You don't feed on him at all, do you?" I said, sitting back on my heels. "You know what it does to people, and you care about him too much. It's just a convenient explanation for why you guys are so close."

Jaize's eyes glittered with fear and anger. His left fist worked on his knee, and I remembered that I'd seen him grab something from the headboard of the bed. A sigil?

"You can't help being a vampire," I pressed. "But you're ambivalent about it, because you grew up with it. Your mom getting older and weirder. Getting so she couldn't go out in the sun anymore. Getting so she didn't mind killing people —"

"Naw, she was always pretty weird," Scott said. "She gave birth to me when she was eighty-four. How normal is that?"

"Shut up, Scotty. This is so wrong." Jaize glared at me. His jaw clenched. I had to force myself to stay put in my submissive posture. "My whole – my whole *life* is about defending the vampire nation. You want to get through this century without some fucking terrorist blowing us all into outer space? Then we need a global government that works, and the vampires are the only way we're going to get one. That's why I have to be *kami*. I have to get closer to the top, get to the Emperor—"

"So stop your mom from killing my friends! We want to get to the Emperor, too! Feed from me, and Christ, let's do this together!"

Jaize let out a miserable little cry. He raised his left fist towards his mouth.

I caught his hand. Though he could easily have resisted, he let me pry his fist open. In his palm lay two tiny white objects.

I rocked back and bumped the coffee table. "Ow," I said, laughing in disbelief. "Ow, ow. Oh my God."

Jaize 3000 wore fake fangs. Politik had been right. He wasn't a vampire at all.

Pacing up and down the room, Jaize cursed me, Scott, Gore, Dorothy, the Human League for Peace, Eva, the government, and the media. Scott was trying to reason with him, which only drew out his anger. I crouched on the carpet, imagining Hiromi's pain and fear, and knew I'd have to make a move soon.

The windows exploded.

Before the last splinters of glass fell to the carpet, I sprinted for the door. But Jaize and Scott turned to face the intruders leaping in from the balcony.

The qingshi.

Training handguns on us, they fanned out, low and fluid in their movements, every sunglassed face a blank insectile visage. They wore black suits, and I had time to notice that their cheeks and foreheads looked oddly furry. Then Scott sketched a gesture, and every gun in the room blew up. A constellation of flashes spat bullets into the floor and walls.

Coughing on the stink of gunpowder, we ducked out of the room.

In the hall, Scott stumbled, and then Jaize and I were dragging him, half-falling down the stairs to the basement. I understood: as Jaize's acolyte, Scott must have shared in the metaphysical bond that made Aleksey the dump for Jaize's magical feedback. Now he, too, had lost the power to use his sigil with impunity.

Eva's high, wavering chant greeted us as we pushed through the hangings into the crypt. Behind us, I could hear someone trying to be quiet on the stairs. But I couldn't move, staring at Hiromi, who lay where she'd been before, on the stained rock in the center of the circle, except now she was naked. Eva stood on the far side of the circle, a white robe over her pantsuit. In one hand she held a censer and in the other a long knife. Greenish aromatic smoke filled the air.

So, not *jajutsu*, said the professional in me. Black magic, straight down the line, or rather widdershins around the circle.

I scuffled clockwise, kicking at the salt scattered over the painted lines, whirling my arms to break up any enclosure of what the Neo-Druidae in Ireland called spirit energy, but Eva probably called odic force. But as I neared her, I slowed. My limbs felt leaden and my ears hurt.

"They've sent the *qingshi*. Came in the fucking window," Jaize was saying. His voice sounded thin and far away. "It's too late, Mom. Help me get Scotty out of here."

"Not so downhearted, *liebling*," Eva said, faintly to my ears. "I have summoned my prince, promising him not only this delicate morsel, but a surfeit of coarser prey."

I fell back, realizing that the outer circle must have done its job already. The smaller circle that held Hiromi was the one that mattered now. The candlelight seemed to be shimmering over her body like heat rising off asphalt at noon.

The harsh voice of a *qingshi* rang from the corridor, "You have five seconds to surrender! Drop your weapons and come out with your hands on your heads!"

"You damn fool, if I know Three G there's gonna be a back door," came a familiar voice. Dorothy slid into the room, clad in her shorts and a black nylon bulletproof vest, a Kalashnikov clamped to her shoulder. She fired a burst. In the enclosed space it sounded like a landslide. Scott crumpled to the floor. Dirt and chips of stone showered down from the ceiling.

The chips that fell towards Hiromi slowed in mid-air and fell sideways.

"Christ on a fucking pogo stick," Dorothy said thinly. "Who the fuck is you? What you doing with my girls here?" Catching sight of Jaize, who was trying to drag Scott towards the other exit, she shouted, "And you, Three G, just stay where you're at. Messing with magic on the downlow, playing like you're psychic and shit. You deserve to have your fangs took off. I *might* let you live after that, depends how I'm feeling."

Half a dozen *qingshi* piled into the cavern around her, some of them sooty and bleeding, all of them armed or re-armed, and there were way too many guns pointing in my direction. I fought for breath. "It's not Jaize!" I screamed. "Eva! *Her!* She's the one who's doing it!"

But my warning came too late. During the shouting and the shooting, Eva had stood calmly, her lips moving. Now the shimmer over the center of the circle had taken on a transparent coloration like stained glass. It glowed the purple of twilight, then the mauve of some expensive orchid, then the blue of frostbitten fingers, and with every shift down the spectrum, the pressure on my ears grew worse. I was now completely deaf, but inside my head I began to hear distant singing, a chorus thundering a chant of joy. A wind from nowhere gusted through the cavern, and long gasoline-colored curves appeared in the air over the circle, belling and flexing like the sides of some giant jellyfish. Hiromi struggled to a sitting position. I was glad I couldn't hear her scream.

The *qingshi* shot at the fast-coalescing apparition. I couldn't hear that, either, but I could feel the shockwaves in my chest, and see the holes appearing in the far wall. Their bullets were passing straight through the… *thing* in the air.

Jaize jerked, staggered, and fell.

Instantly, Eva darted to him and lifted him in her arms like a child. Blood dripped from his dangling fingertips. It was a mother at bay who faced us now, and her eyes blazed defiance for a split second before Dorothy's fire cut her off at the knees. She toppled gracelessly, still managing to break Jaize's fall with her body. Suddenly, I could hear myself screaming hysterically. Her legs, God, her *legs*, and the blood gushing, soaking the hem of her white robe —

Dorothy frantically jacked the lever of her Kalashnikov. It must have jammed. "Fuck, fuck, fuck." But she was staring not at Eva, but at the apparition that floated over Hiromi, now a seven-foot man with wings of iridescent feathers that thrilled gently in the air. His skin was golden, his face a poem with bones like carved stone, and I wanted to go on my knees to his beauty. Inside the circle with him, Hiromi stopped crying. Naked, she knelt up and held out her arms.

The apparition –the angel – settled lightly to the floor of the cavern. Tenderly, it raised Hiromi to her feet.

Dorothy passed a hand over her face. "Gotta kill her the rest of the way," she muttered. She strode towards Eva, slinging the Kalashnikov back, drawing her .38 Special.

"No!" I screamed. "Dorothy, she summoned it, we've got to make her send it back!"

"You can do that, can't you?"

"No! Don't kill her yet!" The shout expressed my own sense of urgency, but it came from behind me.

Keita plunged between the *qingshi*. Hair wild, t-shirt patched with sweat, he overtook Dorothy and skidded to his knees beside Eva. Thinking it extraordinary that he ignored the angel, I ran after him. He was shaking Eva, speaking through gritted teeth. "Where. Are my. Books?" Dust bunnies clung in his hair. It must have been him I'd heard up in the attic. "Bitch! *Where are my fucking books?*"

Crimson pumped sluggishly from the wreckage of Eva's legs. Any human would already have been dead of blood loss and shock. Eva's head jounced back and forth as Keita shook her, and her voice shook too, but it held an unmistakable tinge of satisfaction. "Where you'll never find them, mortal."

Keita let out a sob of rage and despair. "You betrayed my grandfather. Shopped him to the *kempetai*, then stole his books. Where are they?"

Words bubbled hoarsely between Eva's fangs. "So that is who you are. Horibe's line. You remind me of him... the same... foolhardy persistence. But your revenge comes too late. I have been... dead for years."

And then she died. I saw the life, or the unlife, going out of her, a subtle slackening of her body, a drooping of the facial muscles.

Jaize feebly tried to rise. "Mom. Mom! Oh God, don't do this to me!"

So he was still alive. So what? In the shadows shuddering around the two remaining candles, I faced the angel. Too late. It had enfolded Hiromi in its wings and fastened its face to hers. Its shoulders hunched and its throat worked. It was feeding. On Hiromi's soul.

"I never wanted to see one of these again," Keita groaned. His Zippo flashed in his hand. A thin vapor rose from the angel's golden back, and it shrugged itself more firmly about Hiromi. "Fucker won't burn!" Keita gestured in a rage at the divan, and the blankets burst into flame. He dragged at them, perhaps intending to fling them on the angel. Then he recoiled as he uncovered Naomi's corpse. It started to burn, too.

"Ain't no one got any spare ammo?" Dorothy yelled. "That thing ain't gonna sit there like a duck forever!"

She was right about that, I thought. As soon as it got through eating Hiromi's soul, the angel – no, the angel-like *thing* – would presumably gain the power to escape the summoning circle, and the only woman who could control it was dead. Think, Clare, *think*. It had a physical body. What was it made of? Ectoplasm, at a guess. And what was the chemical composition of ectoplasm? Heaven only knew, but I could guess at one element that went into it, one the angel-like thing could have sucked out of the very air as it coalesced.

My eyes were watering from the smoke in the air. I moistened my fingers with my own tears and swept my sigil through the smoke at arm's length. "Cry! *Cry!*"

Behind me, I heard Jaize burst into horrible wrenching sobs.

"Not you!" I screeched. "Cry, motherfucker! I banish you! In the name of the Father, Son, and Holy Ghost, *cry!*"

A long shiver rolled through the angel-thing. Its wings flapped. Its beautiful head flinched back from Hiromi's face, jaws gaping wide. Then its body started to *shrivel* like a balloon withering on fast-forward. Hiromi fell back. The angel-thing vomited cloudy liquid over her and collapsed, feathers and flesh melting to swamp the whole pentacle in an oily-sheened puddle that gave off a stench of rotten eggs and bile.

The last candle went out.

For several instants the cavern was a Boschean hell – wyrdfire eating its way through the furniture, Naomi's skull grinning amidst the flames, panicked vampires shouting, Jaize sobbing like a lost soul. I bent my mind up through the earth, visualizing the ornamental pool and the little spring that fed it. *Flow!* I mentally commanded it. *Wash all of this away!*

Exhausted, I sank to the floor – and immediately jumped upright again. I'd sat in the liquefied body of the angel-thing. It was faintly warm, and God, it reeked. Hiromi sat on her heels, hair over her face. I took off my hoodie and draped it around her shoulders. She fumbled to get her arms into the sleeves. "I'm so glad you're all right," I gasped, giving her an awkward hug.

She clawed her hair out of her face. "Ha! That big sack of devil-spit lost the game the minute it glommed onto me. I bet you were scared, weren't you? But it was never going to get out of that circle."

"Oh," I said blankly.

Hiromi cackled as I helped her up. "It might have thought twice about trying to snack on me – and I guess *she'd* have thought twice about trying to sacrifice me – if they knew I've been possessed before!"

"You've… what?"

"Been possessed before, I said. It was two years ago. Ryu and Politik – well, and Keita, but he was just following Ryu's lead – they tried to sacrifice me to a demon. I was a runaway, sleeping on the street. No one was going to miss me, right? Well, the ritual went wrong. Ryu had the power, but he'd never been taught how to use it. They summoned the demon all right, but they couldn't command it. So it didn't eat my soul. It possessed me." She shivered. "It only lasted a few minutes, I guess. Ryu managed to exorcise it. But it felt like forever. And while I was inside my head with the demon, just the two of us all crammed up in there, I learned – well, I *absorbed* a lot of stuff…"

"Oh my God, Hiromi. You poor thing. I can't believe – " What? I didn't believe Keita would do something like that?

"Save your pity," Hiromi snapped. "That's how I got to master my element, after all. And I dealt with that demon prince just now, didn't I? It would be out of the circle by now if I hadn't, and you'd all be dead, so how about 'You saved our lives, Hiromi,' instead of 'You poor thing'? Thanks for the sweatshirt, anyway."

The *qingshi* were trying to beat out the fire with their jackets, displaying an excess of military discipline as if to make up for the way they'd cringed from the angel-thing. One of them reeled back, flames leaping from his shirtsleeves. He rolled on the floor. The flames hissed and went out, and I realized that the floor was a couple of centimeters deep in water. I could hear it trickling down the stairs and spreading through the cavern, pooling in the unevennesses of the stone.

Dizzily, I knelt in the wet at Dorothy's side. She was supporting Jaize with an arm around his shoulders. Pain contorted his face.

"You had us all fooled, Three G," Dorothy said grimly. "Funny thing is, though? Even looking back, you were a better vampire than the real vampires. I don't mean *better*, but you were damn convincing."

"I'm not sure there's any difference," I said weakly. "I mean, where does the performance stop and the reality start? To millions of people, Jaize *was* a real vampire... he still is."

"I guess your mom coached you, huh?"

"I asked her to Turn me," Jaize croaked. "I *begged* her. She never would. Oh, Mom..."

"Huh. Well, I've met a few old ones like that. Think it's their duty *not* to Turn anyone. I know where they're coming from, too."

"Mom didn't want me to be a vamp. But she wanted me... and Scott..."

"She wanted you to get into Court," Dorothy finished for him. "With that mind-control power of yours."

"Scott!" Jaize called. "Scotty! You OK, dude?"

"He's dead," Dorothy said brutally. "I got him already."

Jaize began to snivel again.

"Don't worry. You'll be seeing him again real soon." She paused. "As you may know, Three G, I'm *kami* now."

"Y-yes."

"And I am sorry, but that means I got both the right and the duty to punish you for what you done, and for what you were going to do."

"Hell, Dorothy, you of all people – you've got to understand! If we don't drag them into the twenty-first century, there'll be no future for any of us! It was all for the nation!"

"And this is for Marty's people," Dorothy said, and shot him in the head.

"And this is for Politik," Keita said. He kicked Jaize's still-twitching corpse. Then he yanked off his amulet and pocketed it.

Dully, I watched the *qingshi* collect Eva's severed lower legs, replace them beneath the gore-soaked hem of her robe, and fold her arms on her chest. Her eyes seemed to open, slivers of white showing. I shuddered.

"Believe we'd better put a stake in that," Dorothy said thoughtfully. "I'd ask Crow Boy to cremate her for us, but it's too damn wet down here. By the way, Clare, you wanna turn off the water now?"

"Might as well just flood the place," Keita said gloomily. "Nothing to find here."

I tried to concentrate on the flow of water into the cavern, but I couldn't *grasp* it the way I had earlier. I felt nauseated and sleepy at the same time. *Feedback.*

"Hola!" Skriva appeared with several of his minions, who were lugging computer and stereo components.

"You missed the fight," Dorothy said beadily. "You ain't got no right to that shit... But, who the fuck cares. Here, you can do the honors." She handed Skriva a leg off Eva's desk, splintered off sharp, blackened by the fire.

"With pleasure, *kami,*" Skriva grinned. He drove the desk-leg into Eva's corpse with revolting enthusiasm. Her ribs cracked audibly.

By now, the water was almost knee deep. The body drifted away to bob against the far wall, the stake sticking out of its bosom like a parody of a mast. Keita's gaze followed it with regret, and Skriva teased him that he was sorry he hadn't killed her himself. But more likely, I thought, he regretted the secrets that had died with her.

I hadn't killed anyone, either. We'd avenged Politik without bloodying our hands. So why did I feel so damn tainted?

Feedback, my brain whispered again. It ain't about the blood, it's about the love.

On our way out, I found the faucet that fed the ornamental pool and shut it off by hand.

Chapter 20.

"**W**hen did you guess she was Eva Stauffenberg?" I said.

"When I saw her." Keita upended another drawer. "If you find any blueprints, can you toss them over here? Thanks."

We were ransacking Scott's workshop. We'd ended up spending the night here, secure in the knowledge that Skriva's vampires were standing guard to show the remaining members of the Human League for Peace that there'd been a change of management. I'd had trouble getting to sleep, but once I did drop off I'd slept dreamlessly until eleven, when Keita had rousted me out to help him search for sigils. He'd already gone through the wreckage of the crypt with the Harajuku vampires, as evinced by the tidemarks on his jeans and the smears of soot on his arms. Now he was systematically emptying the tiny drawers of the carrel that stood on Scott's workbench, while I sorted through the desk on the other side of the room.

Glass-roofed, the workshop adjoined the back of the house like a conservatory. The noon sun glared down on us – we'd turned on the air-conditioning, but we couldn't operate the blinds for the skylights. Scott had probably worked them by magic. Outside, cicadas chirped in the shade of the trees, and Keita's three crows – I assumed – sat on upper branches, lazily preening.

"I had another look in the attic this morning before I woke you up," Keita said. "Turned it upside-down. No luck – but I did find some letters. From Wilfred Hauptmann, from some people in Paris, even a few old love letters from Fritz. They're all in German and French. We'll have to get someone to translate them…"

"But what was it you found up there last night?"

"Another bunch of old letters. From a lawyer acting for

my grandfather. Dated 1937 and 1938. Ordering Eva to turn over the property she'd stolen from the estate of Wilfred Hauptmann, which had been legally willed to my grandfather. By that time, of course, Hauptmann had been dead fifteen years... I guess the legal owership of his books didn't become an issue until Fritz died, and Eva and my grandfather quarrelled over who was going to lead the Atelier. It looks like Grandpops may have taken her to court, but who knows whether he ever got the Sigilaries back? My guess is he didn't. That's why he told me they'd been destroyed in the war – because they were gone, anyway. What was it she said? *Where no one could ever find them...*"

"I suppose they're lost forever, then."

"I'm not giving up that easily. This trail isn't cold yet. The next thing to do is to find out who Turned her, and when." Keita emptied another drawer into his palm. "Huh, gold wire. Might come in handy." He stashed it in one of the Tupperware containers he'd requisitioned from the kitchen.

"I think," I started. In the early morning quiet, before I could get to sleep, I'd found myself pondering Eva Stauffenberg's life and death. I suspected she would haunt me for quite some time. "I think she was Turned during the war. She'd have been stuck in Japan. A citizen of neutral Switzerland. Not interned, but all alone. She got her revenge on your grandfather and his buddies, according to you: she had them arrested for practising magic. But that would have left her friendless. Revenge has a way of backfiring," I added bleakly. "She'd have had to use her own magic to make a living, and that would have forced her into the black economy... and I think that's how the vampires found her. Maybe back then, they didn't distrust magicians as much as they seem to now... But she must have escaped to America after the war. Remarried, eventually. Settled down in California with her family."

But then she'd come back here. Unspoken in my mind was the conjecture that Eva's return to Japan had coincided with, or closely followed, the date when she would have died, had she not been a vampire... when she crossed over from life to undeath. Could there have been some metaphysical compulsion at work there? Something to do with the theory that the undead shared the *qi* of their maker?

"And all the time, she was teaching the sigils to her sons," Keita said. "But not *all* the sigils." He held up a Tupperware container of sigil medallions: silver and gold, bronze and copper, and one in a dull grey alloy. "There's a couple here that I haven't seen in the Dracula's Crypt shops, but most of those are fake. Total, five proven sigils. *Five.*" He picked out a copper medallion identical to the one Politik had used at Eternal family. "This is the First Sigil of Metal. Scott relied on it pretty heavily. Have you noticed something about this workshop? No forge, anvil, whatever jewellers normally use… nothing except a vise and a few hand tools. He must have done it all by magic. It's fucking pre-technological."

"Like the way the Human League for Peace fought with only their *qi* craft," I said. "You're right, it really is weird how magicians seem to deliberately reject technology. I've seen it over and over."

"Pride," Keita said grimly. "Sheer pride. Anyway, so then here we have the First Sigil of Water. Only one. I guess Jaize didn't have occasion to use it very often." He tossed it across the workshop to me.I caught it by the chain. It was the grey one.

"I'm allergic to nickel," I said. "But thanks anyway."

"It's mercury. That's your element. He must have blended it into an alloy."

"Better and better. Or didn't you get the memo about mercury poisoning?" I stuck the sigil in my pocket. I'd finally changed my clothes, having found some things to wear in Jaize's closet: a pair of black bell-bottoms and a baby tee with *Just A Little Bit* printed on the chest in gothic script. It was one of the worst puns I'd ever heard, but everything else was emblazoned with the Dracula's Crypt logo… aka the sigil that Keita was holding up now.

"The First Sigil of the Void." He swung it on its chain at

eye level. "You find me strangely attractive," he intoned. "You want my body. You'd do anything for me…"

"Shut up!" Giggling, I threw Scott's bright pink hand-exercise ball at him. He ducked, and it bounced to the floor.

"Forgot, it doesn't work on you." He dropped the sigil back in the container.

"Nope, sorry, I'm not quite that easy."

Keita's smirk faded. He said brusquely, "It worked on a lot of other people, anyway. That mind-control shit is worth all the rest of the elements put together. *And* he could use all the other elements, just with this one sigil…" He shook his head. "I feel so stupid. The Void isn't *in* the secret element tables that Politik and I put together. The Year of the Void comes around five times in every sexagenary cycle, and the Month of the Void is intercalcated once every six years, but we don't have a Void hour: just Fire, Water, Air, Metal, and Wood. There's no *room* for the Void!"

"Yes, there is," I said. "The planet moves around the sun while it spins on its axis. So the solar day is twenty-four hours, but the – sorry, I don't know the Japanese – the sidereal day is a bit shorter. To be precise, three minutes and fifty-six seconds shorter. That's your 'Hour' of the Void, counting back from noon."

Keita stared at me. "Did Eva tell you that?"

"She hinted at it."

Brow furrowed, Keita turned back to the workbench. "No wonder there are so few of them, then," he muttered.

We worked for a couple of minutes in silence. "So what other sigils have you found?" I said at last.

"Huh? Oh, well, I'm assuming *this* is the First Sigil of Air. I got it off Eva's body. All the rest of her amulets were just black-magical crap, ankhs and pentacles and so on… And this one here is the sigil they called Loath Stringless. I got it off Jaize. I think it's a higher iteration of the Void. See, this part is the same on both of them? The Void governs thought, volition, loyalty…"

"And all the others are fake?"

"All I know for sure is none of them are Fire, and Hiromi says none of them are Wood. You could test them, too, if you like. But look, it's like code-breaking. The basic sigils are the key. Any higher iterations are going to incorporate parts of the basic ones. That's why I think the rest of these are fake."

"Well, that seems to prove Eva lost the Sigilaries, or disposed of them, a long time ago," I said. "She only taught Jaize and Scott the sigils she could remember."

"All five or six of them?" Keita scoffed. "My grandfather had hundreds of them memorized. He just wouldn't teach them to me."

"Yeah, well, for one thing, these sigils are constructed like Chinese ideograms," I said tartly. "I still think they may *be* ideograms that have fallen out of use. And in case you haven't noticed, Westerners don't take naturally to radicals and stroke counts. Hell, I can still only write about fifty kanji without a computer. So it would have been much easier for your grandfather to memorize the sigils than it was for Eva. And here's something else: I don't think elemental sorcery was even her main thing. Before she came to Japan, she studied hermetic magic with Wilfred Hauptmann's Paris circle. And I bet even after Hauptmann and your grandfather discovered the sigils, she still stuck to what she knew best." I looked levelly at Keita, remembering what Hiromi had told me last night. "Plain old black magic. It works pretty well for summoning demons, doesn't it?"

"Don't remind me," Keita said with an affected shudder. "How're you coming with those binders?"

I fanned out the handful of design sketches I'd found. "This is all. Most of the binders are correspondence and accounting stuff. Scott seems to have been the one who actually ran the business on a day-to-day basis."

"Ha! Dorothy's going to wish she hadn't killed *him.*" Keita stood up and began to pack his loot into a paper carrier bag with the Dracula's Crypt logo. "Did you hear about the party?" The harsh sunlight suited his face. His dark complexion seemed to glow, and his strong nose and heavy brows

384

looked ethnic, almost Indian.

"No," I said. "What party?"

"Aleksey's re-birthday party. Skriva usually just takes his new vampires out drinking. And I don't mean beer. But Dorothy's apparently planning a traditional-style bash for Aleksey... I'm going to try to be there, if only to see who the main course is." He snickered. "It's on Friday night."

I had to think to figure out that today was Monday. So much had happened in a single weekend. "That's almost a week off."

"Yeah. Well, I guess I'll see you then."

I jumped to my feet. I couldn't help it. "Where are you going?"

"Out of town."

"Uh... are you going far?"

"Sendai. An hour and a half by shinkansen. That's where Politik's family lives..." Keita grimaced. "Someone's got to break the news to them."

Which left me, I realized, to break the news to Professor Kamikawa.

The professor took the news of Politik's death in stride. I knew of the old-school Japanese cultural reluctance to show emotion in public, but this was something else. He ordered me to write up a report of the débâcle at Eternal Family, using his computer, not one of those in the department office. When he found me sponging my eyes over the keyboard, he took my place and read what I'd typed so far. At last he looked up, face wrinkled with compassion. "Such things happen," he said. "You understand? Such things happen."

The words brought home to me the depth of experience he'd amassed in his long life – a life that, after all, included childhood experience of war. If this was a fight we were engaged in, a fight for truth and objectivity, Professor Kamikawa had been on the front lines far longer than I. *Such things happen.* People die. You keep on.

He took me for a coffee, and then I finished my report.

The next day, he returned it to me covered in red ink. The final version we submitted to the dean's office ran to half a page.

I spent the rest of the week preparing my progress report for James. I was tempted to include the whole story of the Atelier de la Science Odique and the sigils, but I limited myself to what I'd learned about vampires. That contained quite enough shocks for him. Describing the political structure of the vampire *kuni*, or nation, I was forced to make the radical claim that vampires were at least partially immune to the aging process. *It's looking like the CAIN hypothesis is partially correct,* I wrote. *Brent et al. are still treating it as a disease. IMO it's more likely to be a mutagen bundled in a virus. But isn't there someone else out West analyzing vampire DNA? That's where the breakthrough's going to come from. And I hate this, James, but I think we need to retract our position* before *they publish their results. We need to be the first to say there's nothing supernatural about it.*

I mailed this to James on Friday, but took the risk of phoning him the night before. I ended up bewailing the imminent triumph of the medical model to him, at the same time as I recalled the evidence *against* CAIN: Skriva's *Just pluck out your fangs and start dying,* and Dorothy's *It ain't about the blood, it's about the love.*

In some sense, I thought, vampirism was a continuum – and even a fake vamp like Jaize 3000 had a place on it. There was so much more I could have shared with James, if not for my own need for proof.

James said immediately, "But what is supernatural and what isn't? We can't fall back on a 'supernatural of the gaps,' Clare. And we mustn't slip into thinking that the province of paranormal studies is the unproven. We study that which is *not normal,* regardless of whether the hard sciences can explain how it works. We ask *why.* Our business is the believe-it-or-not, the stranger-than-fiction, the billion-to-one chances, the miracles... the keys to Jung's theater of archetypes, Frazier's gallery of myths, that obstinate strand of the numinous in the human cultural enterprise. The vampires, the witches, the ghosts… and us. That's Tsuyoshi's line, of course," James added parenthetically. "He's convinced that paranormal phenomena exist as responses to emergent metasocial needs."

It sounded like James had got more out of Professor Kamikawa's writings than I had, if he was suggesting that the professor endorsed the idea of some kind of emergent group or species mind. I kept quiet, and James grew a touch sarcastic.

"Good gracious, Clare, have you ever looked through my file of faerie sightings? I'm sure science could explain them all, given world enough and time. But that wouldn't explain why people see faeries in the first place. And no DNA analysis can explain *why* there are vampires, let alone why Tokyo seems to be their stronghold, and why they cling to the bizarrely antiquated power structure you describe. An Emperor, for the love of Dog, my dear! Without having read your full report, I'd say that's your line of investigation. Leave CAIN to the men in white coats, get in there, and *keep an open mind.*"

"I already had this pep talk from Kamikawa-sensei," I said grumpily. "Of course I'm going to get in there, but…" I trailed off, wishing I'd given more emphasis to my hypothesis that Turning was a near-death experience. The men in white coats weren't going to pursue *that* line of investigation, and my hunch told me it was central to the answers we all sought. As was the concept of *qi*, which science had debunked already, only millions of martial arts practitioners, including the Human League for Peace, hadn't noticed… And if the truth about *qi* was to be found anywhere, it was in the Japanese traditions of *jujutsu*, *onmyodo*, and *ninjutsu*… Now I wished I *had* told James about my recent experiences with magic. "Oh, it's all such a tangle," I said. "But I know one thing, at least: truth doesn't live in a laboratory. It's wild. So I'm going to get off the phone and go hunting."

"Excellent. Make sure you make full use of your resources there. When I spoke to Tsuyoshi a couple of days ago, he sounded confident that he can get our funding renewed on that side, after the tragedy at the vampire school. It really is an ill wind!" James laughed. "Speaking of which, don't let those adventuresome students of his convince you to take unnecessary risks. In fact, I forbid you to get killed, maimed, or traumatized in any way, is that quite clear?"

"Yes," I muttered, grateful for the concern in his humorous "order." "Sloppy kisses to Aaliyah, and say hello to Yurika for me."

I hung up, knowing that James's warning came too late: I was already pretty traumatized. I sat on the balcony of Yurika's apartment, among pot plants withered brown – I hadn't watered them, after all. Emotionally numb, check, body aches, check, brain fog, check. I knew the signs of PTSD as well as anyone.

But I had another call I couldn't put off any longer. I dialed Nilson, glumly foreseeing that by the time I got through justifying myself to him and Colin, I'd be even more depressed.

The crows wakened me at dawn. I'd been sleeping only lightly – my conversation with Nilson had left me unsettled. I got up and went out to the balcony, flinching when a black shape thudded onto the rail. Sheeny pinions folded, and the bird – or demon, or whatever it was – gave me that jewel-hard sideways stare.

"Hey, Keita," I said, staring right back at it. "If you're spying on me, I don't appreciate it. If you want to talk, come to Exiles tonight. If you don't, then find something better for your birds to do... You heard me." I clapped my hands. "Scram!"

The crow cawed once and flapped into the air. Heart beating hard, I watched it soar away into the dawn. I felt properly alive for the first time all week – and then the crow was a black dot against the lemon-gray fire of the Tokyo sunrise, and then it was gone.

388

A banner over the door of Exiles said in English, *HAPPY RE-BIRTHDAY ALEKSEY!!* More banners hung above the heads of the crowd inside, and black and silver balloons festooned the ceiling. Clad in black hot-pants and silver bustiers, the hostesses circulated with trays of drinks and hors-d'oeuvres. I'd expected to have to break the news to Dorothy that I wasn't working here anymore, but since she hadn't tapped me for waitress duties, it looked like she'd already written me out of the schedule. Perversely, that depressed me further.

A quick circuit of the room confirmed that Keita wasn't here, and my mood continued to deteriorate.

Ruth wore white hot-pants instead of black. I snagged a cocktail off her tray. "How's it going?" I shouted over the music.

She shrugged, avoiding my gaze. "All right."

"How's Aleksey?"

"See for yourself later. He's in the show. He did the music for it, too."

Unusually, Ruth was wearing her hair down. She turned her head, and I saw a Power Puff Girls Band-Aid on her neck.

She caught me looking. "Yeah! I'm sharing with him, now get over it."

I said deliberately, "So is it this big special experience? Inquiring minds want to know."

"Inquiring minds can find out for their goddamn selves," she muttered. Then she looked me in the eye. "Not really. What I'm told is, Aleksey's just a new vamp, so he doesn't have the power to make it really special. But you know what? I'm going to be there for him, anyway."

Having only half listened to her last words, I said, "But I thought you – Dorothy – "

"No. Oh, that one time? She cut me. And I'm here to tell you *that's* just about as special as a root canal with no novocaine."

My gaze slipped past her, roving the crowd as I mentally reconfigured the story I'd been telling myself all week.

"She's over there," Ruth said. "Now let me get back to

work before she catches me slacking. It's been fun." She shimmied away.

Dorothy was holding court in a group that included half of a famous manzai comedy duo and a couple of B-list taren-tos. I hadn't the energy to deal with that kind of thing right now. I found an unoccupied banquette and sank down to nurse my cocktail, a raspberry-flavored highball with a swizzle stick topped by a silver plastic spider.

When Angela appeared in front of the curtain and start-ed to sing to a recorded accompaniment, the crowd quieted and dutifully faced the stage. Seeing Dorothy alone at the corner of the bar, I planted myself in front of her. She wore a clingy black spaghetti-strapped dress that flared above the knee, ending in a see-through flounce. In ankle-breaking black patent leather sandals, she towered over me. I drew inner strength from my own outfit: a long evening gown with a handkerchief-pointed hem, off one shoulder, in a red so dark it was *almost* black. I'd bought it for a few thousand yen in 109, the Shibuya shopping mall.

"Love your hair," Dorothy said.

I touched my updo, into which I'd been shoving the swizzle sticks out of my drinks as I finished them. "Did you get these made specially for tonight?"

"Yeah, but we're gonna use them in here from now on, and in the other clubs. I designed the spider logo myself. I'm gonna get it trademarked."

"Sounds like a page out of Jaize's book."

"'Cept my little Incey Wincey only has one kind of pow-er, and that's the power of branding." She laughed loudly. "We're gonna make him into a pendant and sell him through Dracula's Crypt. I'm taking that over, too."

"I thought being *kami* was a full-time job," I said.

"Oh, yeah. Well, that's all in how you interpret it. Old Gore wasn't never happy unless he was out on the street, putting the fear into anyone that looked at him crossways. But when you boil down the basics, the organization is a business, just like any other. And I'm seeing a lot of potential synergies."

As she pronounced these words with vigor, I felt an intangible veil coming down between us. My sense of an unspoken understanding faded.

"Why you so down-mouthed?" Dorothy said suddenly. "Didn't you get enough observations recently to write a whole passel of books? Mind you, you better had make them fiction, cause ain't no one going to believe it's the truth." She laughed softly.

I said defensively, "It's just that I've had some bad news from the States. It isn't official yet, but – my father is a senator, as you know. As a matter of fact, he's the ranking Democrat on the Judiciary Committee, which is the committee that—"

"I know what it is."

"OK. Then maybe you also know that they've been considering a proposal to reauthorize the Citizenship Act. And when I talked to him this week, he said that they've almost reached a compromise on the vampirism issue: they won't define vampirism as a cause for detention. Instead, they'll just make blood-drinking 'an activity dangerous to human life that is intended to intimidate or coerce the civilian population'..." I sighed. Behind me, people were applauding. "In other words, don't ask, don't tell."

Dorothy snorted. "If that ain't just like Ameri-K-K-K-A. No offense to your dad. But hey, I can't say I'm surprised. I told Leon just today, if we're going to get anywhere in the States, we're gonna have to go covert."

"Leon?" I started to say. "Is Leon here?" and then Dorothy took my elbow and turned me to face the stage. The little hairs on my forearm prickled at her touch. I saw that the applause hadn't been for Angela, or not only for her. Aleksey had joined her on stage. So had Leon Foulkes, The Vampire Of The East.

The two men wore black jeans and t-shirts – Leon's hip-hop-styled, Aleksey's tight to his body. Aleksey lay flat on the stage, eyes closed, while Leon strolled back and forth in front of him. The speakers poured forth a throbbing, sinister piano melody. Leon pantomimed daily activities: reading a newspaper, eating, talking on the phone. A natural performer, he gave a little something extra to each dumbshow, as when he banged an invisible payphone, trying to get his money back. The audience chuckled.

"He flew out on Tuesday," Dorothy shouted in my ear. "Oh, you should have saw him. My heart almost broke. But look how he's perked up now, ain't it something?"

I nodded. Now Leon was miming going down stairs, sinking to his knees, then to hands and knees. Rolling his eyes and biting his knuckles to show fear, he crawled slowly towards Aleksey.

Aleksey sprang. With a turn of speed I'd never imagined him capable of, he bounced upright, carrying Leon with him, and they danced a struggle. "This part is traditional," Dorothy said in my ear. "We changed all the first part, to update it. You supposed to use these funny little gestures that don't mean nothing unless you seen a lot of Noh plays. So we made that more realistic. And we changed the music. Originally, they would use just drums and that wooden flute, the shakuhachi, and maybe a shamisen. But I like Aleksey's music for this part, especially, don't you?"

"Am I getting the right idea – this is a traditional performance?" A kind of passion play, I thought. The interaction between vamp and mortal, archetypified. "What's it called?"

"Oh, Hatsuin. The First Bite, what else?"

The dance reached its climax. Aleksey fastened on Leon and mimed a strike at his neck. To an endless high note from Angela, they stood frozen. Then Leon went limp and tumbled to the stage. Aleksey raised his arms, triumphant. The music ended on an unresolved chord, dying away into the bass. Leon leapt to his feet, Aleksey relaxed, Angela left the mic, and they all bowed.

"Now comes the bit you ain't gonna like," Dorothy murmured in my ear. She stood very close behind me.

Where my dress laid my back bare, I could feel heat coming off her body.

As if at an unspoken signal, the audience pressed forward. Several people started to climb up on the stage, but Ogino the maître-d' sprang forward and stopped all but two: Ruth, and a white man with sandy hair that stuck up on end. "The White Duke," I said in surprise.

"Yeah, that's Marty. He did me the honor of coming here for Leon. He's older than I am, he can give him more time. He's incognito, though... Ruth, she just insisted."

While the speakers played on, Leon advanced behind the White Duke. Hamming it up, Martin pretended not to know there was a vampire behind him, and then pretended to struggle when Leon captured him, in a comic parody of *The First Bite*. Laughter mingled with the sighs and gasps from the audience when Leon finally struck.

"Good thing we ain't got don't ask, don't tell here, huh?" Dorothy chuckled.

I swallowed. The sight of Leon's fineboned face buried in the White Duke's neck aroused me unexpectedly.

"Now look at the audience."

Throughout the club, vampires and humans were pairing off. Some of them just exchanged kisses, handshakes, smiles. Other vampires began to feed... passionately. I shivered.

"You see," Dorothy whispered, "a re-birthday party, for a vampire, is more like when people renew their vows..." A note of irony entered her voice. "Of course, some people just come to hook up."

Ravel's *Bolero* oozed from the sound system. Ruth stood before Aleksey, looking less comfortable than ever in her little silver-and-white outfit. After a moment Aleksey pulled a face, and they hugged awkwardly.

Dorothy's hands slid down my arms, barely touching. The zippers on her dress brushed my shoulderblades. "Ain't no compulsion, of course. Everything's voluntary, now that I'm running this town."

I swayed back so that our bodies touched. Her breasts squashed against my shoulders, mindspinningly soft. "I don't want to... hook up," I said thickly.

"I don't, neither. You know what? I came to get you out of trouble last week, not because I'm *kami*, although that was part of it... but I said to myself: Girl, you just let someone go into danger that's special to you. What was you *thinking?* And so I rounded up the *qingshi* and I went."

"And now we're going," Keita said, shoving through the crowd to reach us. He gave Dorothy a hard stare, then took my arm and eased me away from her. "Sorry, Countess. Next time I'll be more punctual."

We walked up Gaien-higashi-dori and went into McDonald's. Neither of us spoke until we'd bought coffees and found seats on the third floor. Keita lit a cigarette. "Did you know what you were letting yourself in for back there?"

I shook my head. "Nice suit, by the way." It was plain black, off the rack for sure, and his white shirt was open at the collar. But it still made an impression, since I'd never before seen him in anything but jeans.

"Politik's funeral was this morning. I got back from Sendai around three. Stopped in to see Kamikawa-sensei, and ended up staying to dinner."

"Did you talk about where we're going with the study now? In light of... of the fact that there are only two of us left?"

"I told him I can't go on at my current pay rate." Keita sat forward, animated. "I mean, we're risking our lives here. We deserve hazard pay! And more to the point, I'm going to have to find a new apartment, and that means paying a deposit and key money – buying new furniture – paying *rent*... Well, Kamikawa-sensei agreed in principle, for what that's worth. And he also agreed that we need more help, considering how the scope of the study has expanded. We thought we were only going to be diagramming vampire social networks. I could have fudged that," Keita said, with a blithe disregard for truth and objectivity. "But now, thanks to your report, he's had evidence shoved in his face that he can't ignore... evidence that we've just been looking at the tip of the iceberg. So now we've got to do an analysis of the whole *kami* regime. We aren't even qualified – have *you* studied socioeconomic theory? Didn't think so. Trouble is, Kamikawa-sensei wants to keep it in the department..." He slurped his coffee and brooded.

"Well, I know how you can solve at least one of those problems," I said. I'd forgotten to pick up a stirrer, so I took a swizzle stick out of my hair and used it to mix creamer into my coffee. "Dorothy would find you somewhere to live. She still wants you on her side. And if you were under her protection, now that she's *kami*, Zuleiko wouldn't dare to come after you. I suppose that's what you're worried about."

"Among other things. But no thanks, I'm not squatting in a vamp building again, even if it is rent-free. And I'm afraid I still don't trust Dorothy as much as you seem to."

"Well, considering she's the best source we've got for the study, I think you could try a bit harder not to alienate her," I snapped.

Keita stared at me. A faint smile tugged at his lips. He leaned further forward and said in a low voice, "Clare, she's stalking you."

"Excuse me?" I felt a starburst of panic in my gut. "That's ludicrous."

"Is it? What would have happened if I hadn't arrived when I did?"

"I don't know." I lowered my head. To my horror, tears prickled my nose. "Oh, why don't you just let me be?"

"Friends don't let friends get bitten."

"Oh, so now we're *friends*," I said, staring at the table.

His chair scraped. "I'm sorry I wasn't around this week, OK? I had stuff to take care of. Apart from the funeral, I mean. I can't count on that pay raise, and even if Kamikawa-sensei can swing it, it won't happen until the beginning of the next academic year. I'm so broke it's not funny. So I—"

He sighed. "Politik and I – we were registered with this dispatch agency. We never got many jobs, since we didn't have a track record, but now – now… well, I thought it would be worth giving it another try. So I had to go over to their office and take some tests. But the good news is, I passed. So now I'm a Gold level staffer, and I've already got some appointments scheduled. I could have worked tonight if I wanted. I said no because I was worried about you," he finished virtuously.

I stared at him. "What kind of jobs, specifically?"

"Freelance." Keita coughed. "The agency's called Occultra. They provide, uh, magical services. Lost items found, love charms, curses lifted, fortunes told, that kind of thing."

Yurika's words echoed in my head: …*they join a bad agency to get money for their work*… I smiled sadly. At last that particular mystery was solved.

"I found some books at Jaize's place," Keita added. "Some grimoires I've never seen before, notebooks dating back to the Paris Circle. The stuff Aleister Crowley edited out of Hauptmann's manuscripts! Seriously exciting. I copied a few useful spells into my laptop and sent the file to my cell phone… that's how I passed the Occultra tests. I guess you could call it cheating." He laughed uneasily.

"Well," I said, keeping my emotions in check, "it looks like you're all set then, doesn't it?" I pushed my chair back and stood up. Angry that I couldn't even think of an original exit line, I said, "It's been fun." I pushed between the tables and clattered downstairs.

Keita caught up with me outside the restaurant. "Clare," he wheedled. I ignored him, walking fast with no destination in mind. "Clare."

At Roppongi Crossing, I crossed the street and randomly turned right, heading down the hill. Keita kept pace with me.

"You can't just walk out on me like that. We're colleagues! We have to work together…"

"Exactly what I said when I first got here," I said, biting off the words. "But every time I think we've finally resolved our differences, you turn out to be hiding something from me. You didn't even care about avenging Politik. You just wanted to find your goddamn Sigilaries! We could have all been killed! People *were* killed! And as if we hadn't had enough black magic to last us the rest of our lives, now you go and sign up at a bloody freelance magicians' registry! Well, I've had enough. I'm sick of being manipulated. Sick of your lies and your justifications. Sick of…" I waved my arms. We'd left the neon behind. On either side, dark buildings crouched in the shadow of the expressway that roofed Roppongi-dori. "Sick of this city," I shouted over the surf-like roar of traffic from overhead.

"You aren't thinking of leaving yet. You can't!" Keita grabbed my arm.

I shook him off. To our left, the buildings opened up on a pocket-sized park, ginkgos sheltering split concrete levels. I climbed up to the top level, a little plaza with a fountain in the middle, now just a nozzle sticking out of the water. I sat down on a bench. Keita sat at the other end. I stared at the water, hugging my bare arms. I'd left my wrap at Exiles, and the night was cool. I felt a sudden piercing longing to be back in Washington Square Park, eating icecream and watching the chess-players… back in the days before my life got so complicated.

"I've seen too many people die," I said, shivering. "I've *killed* people."

"You mean at Eternal Family? Shit, they were only *kenin*—"

"Only *kenin!* That's what I told myself, too. Unfortunately, I don't believe that vampires don't have souls."

"Well, it was us or them. Don't beat yourself up—"

"Oh, so it's all right because *everyone's doing it?*"

Keita was silent for a minute. Then he pointed to the building on the other side of the plaza. "That's your religion, isn't it?"

I squinted, and almost smiled. One of the things I'd found most estranging about Tokyo was the absence of churches. No spires on the skyline, no Gothic steeples huddled at the feet of the skyscrapers. Now I'd finally stumbled on a church, and it was just a low building with a cross over the door. Spotting a couple of stained-glass windows – a Catholic giveaway – I nodded. "Probably."

"Well, isn't God supposed to forgive all sins? Aren't you supposed to just go to confession and be – what's it called – absolved?"

I swallowed. "Yeah." Then I said more strongly, "But the most important part of that is *go and sin no more.* And I... I feel like if I stay here, I'm almost guaranteed to sin again."

"So your solution is to run away," Keita muttered. Then he shifted a couple of inches towards me. "Don't leave. I – all right. Don't leave. Please. I need you."

"Now you've lost your loyal sidekick, I suppose you do," I said dryly. That sounded crueler than I'd intended. "Sorry."

Keita winced. "That's not why. I – oh, why can't you just trust me?"

Without giving me time to answer, he scooted along the bench. His arm went around my shoulders and his mouth found mine. Involuntarily, I tipped my head back to meet his kiss. His tongue searched my mouth, thick, powerful. At the same time he stroked my bare shoulders with a feather-light touch. He smelled salty, yet milky: slugs and snails and puppy-dogs' tails, I thought with an inward giggle of sheer pleasure. I put my hand on his thigh, feeling the warm hardness of muscle through the cheap fabric of his suit. The surge of desire in my body astonished me, and I felt a grateful sense of wonder. I broke off the kiss and pulled back. "I'm still not convinced you held up your end of our bargain," I laughed breathlessly.

"Our bargain? Oh yeah." Keita made a noise like a little whine of pain, and dropped his head into his hands. "That was wrong. Sorry."

"There's nothing wrong with a few kisses," I said uncertainly.

"What? Yes, there is. If I kiss you, I'll just want to go further. And that's not happening, is it?"

"N... no. That's definitely not happening." I tried to sound decisive. In reality, I was unsure how I felt. How my body felt, well, that was a different story.

Keita rubbed his hands over his face. "We need to manage this relationship carefully," he said, voice strained. "We're double semblables. That means we have natal resonance – both born in the year of Wood Rabbit. And we have inner resonance – both of our inner elements are Fire. You triggered my magical potential, and then I triggered yours—"

"I thought Jaize triggered my potential," I objected, somewhat dizzied by the change of subject.

"That's what I thought, too, but it couldn't have been. You didn't have any resonance with him or Scott. If you did, they'd have reeled you in, like they did Politik." He nodded sharply. "I used to think the transmissibility theory was separate from the elemental resonance theory, but of course, it all fits together. That's the only possible reason why Ryu and I never triggered Politik's potential—"

"So let me put this together." I was feeling cold again. "Resonance is a kind of connection that boosts the magical ability of everyone involved."

"Boosts their *qi*, to be precise, but yeah."

"OK. And for it to work, you need at least natal resonance. Born in the same year, or twelve years apart."

"And preferably inner resonance as well. Born in the same set of months."

"So what happens if you have secret resonance, too – all three elements the same?"

Keita grimaced. "You get a mirror semblable. That's—"

"Like Jaize and Aleksey." I pressed my knees together to stop them from shaking. "That's why Aleksey was so important to Jaize. Born in the Three and a Half Minutes of the Void... finding him must have been like finding a needle in a haystack. And he must have had strong *qi* to begin with. He's a talented pianist. But Jaize is more than talented, he's a magician. So he bound Aleksey in some way. Turned him into his mirror. *His conscience.*"

Keita stared at the ground.

"So he could go on TV, preen in dressing-rooms, and use his sigils whenever he liked... while Aleksey *lived* his feedback for him. His portrait of Dorian Grey, up in the attic. Slowly dying."

"That word, *feedback,*" Keita said. "Politik came up with it. I'd rather call it what it is. Karma."

"What goes around comes around? OK. But here's what I'm wondering now." The sheer normality of my own voice amazed me. "*How* did Jaize bind Aleksey to him? What would that ritual have consisted of?"

"There are many possible types of magical bonds," Keita said. "The most common is friendship. How do you build that, well, by working together, eating together, facing danger together. The usual. Apart from that, you've got family bonds, like Jaize and Scott. They weren't genetic brothers, but it's the closeness from childhood... But there's always another type of closeness. For Jaize to activate a mirror semblable relationship with Aleksey, it would definitely have been, uh, sex." He managed a snigger. "Lucky for Jaize he swung both ways. Not so lucky for Aleks."

"Gotcha," I said. "Thanks for confirming that."

Sleep with me. Just once... it's just a little thing...

I stood up and walked over to the fountain. Without turning around, I said, "Well, now I know where you got the idea for that pact."

"We'd only just met," Keita said from the bench, hopelessly. "Once I got to know you, and I realized what – what a cool person you are, I knew I couldn't go through with it."

"Correction. You decided not to go through with it after you realized you'd calculated my birth hour wrong, and I wasn't your mirror semblable, after all."

"Fine!" Anger as well as embarrassment colored his voice. Nervously, I turned around. He spread his hands and let them drop. "I guess we'll never know if I would have gone through with it or not. But the point is, we can still work together, can't we? We're double semblables, that's pretty special —"

"Ah, I get it," I said, not letting up on him. "You want me to register with you at your bloody rent-a-wizard agency. You're afraid your magic won't work unless I'm around, and you *need the money!*"

"It's not like that," Keita said despairingly. "Once it's been triggered, it won't go away again. Well, it does seem to work better with you around. But I need you *anyway!*"

He crushed me into his arms. No feather-light caresses this time. He clutched me so tightly it hurt, bruising my lips with his mouth, grinding his pelvis against mine. Unnerved, I wriggled. He pinned my arms behind my back, and his mouth left my lips and roamed over my face. He kissed my cheeks, my eyes, my nose, as if to suffocate or bury me. My alarm escalated into panic. I held still, clearing my mind, and then sent a sharp thought at the pool behind me.

Splash and slop, the water gathered itself into a wave – *I* gathered it, raised it up, and let it go above Keita's head, a chilly deluge that drenched us both in an instant and poured away, running down from level to level.

Driven to my knees, I scrabbled back over the wet concrete. I had to wipe my eyes to see. Even before I opened them, I heard Keita laughing.

"Talk about a cold shower!"

He gave me a hand up. Soaked to the skin, suit dripping, curly hair plastered to his forehead, he grinned. His eyes glinted dangerously.

"Remind me, the next time I molest you, to pick someplace further from the water!"

"Next time? There better not be a next time," I warned.

"Kidding, Clare, just kidding."

I smiled grudgingly and squeezed the water out of my hair. "Just out of curiosity, what would happen if we did sleep together?"

"Ah. Well, since your secret element is Water, and mine's Fire, it would give you power over me. I'd be your acolyte, like Scott was to Jaize." Keita wrung out his jacket and added ruefully, "So you see, I have a pretty good incentive to control myself."

"As do I," I said, glancing at the church on the far side of the park. My conscience was in a parlous enough state already without adding unchastity to the mix. Experience had taught me that that seemingly trivial sin was often, in fact, the straw that broke the camel's back. Making a mental vow to recommit to my principles, I shivered and swayed on my feet. "I'm not feeling so hot," I confessed.

"Don't." Keita steered me away from the pool into which I'd begun to peer, looking for my reflection in what was left of the water. "I'll take you home. You need to eat, get into some dry clothes, rest..."

"But you don't have any clothes at my place. You'll have to stay until yours are dry..."

"Or I could just go home like this." Keita scanned the street for a taxi.

"Where are you staying, anyway?"

"With Ni-chan's people. What's left of them. At Skriva's."

"I think you'd better stay with me." I might regret it later, but right now I just didn't want to be alone.

"I can't think of anything Yurika would hate more..." He sighed. "Or anything I'd like more."

"Then it's settled. As long as..."

"Nothing's going to happen," Keita said. A taxi pulled over. He smoothed his hair back and gave me a brilliant smile. "I promise."

Tokyo, June 2009

Exclusive Extra!

Read on for an excerpt from Rose Nanashima's first novel, *Music to Die By*, a thriller set in the Japanese indie rock scene.

Rose Nanashima

Music to Die By

Part I: Unfair Game

"**L**et's talk about you," I snarled. "It must've been the first time. So did it excite you?"

Gen stood on my left, hunched over his Ibanez as if he were trying to protect it from the crowd. He wore his uniform of jeans and a plain black t-shirt. Sweat fell sparkling from his curls. When I tore into the chorus, he raised his head and bellowed the harmony into his own mic. He had the best voice of any of the boys, a raspy tenor that harmonized nicely with my own voice. I was more of a shouter than a singer, and inevitably got Janis Joplin comparisons, although I preferred to think of myself as the female Layne Staley, without the heroin problem. I had enough problems as it was.

Our faithful supporters swayed an arm's length in front of me, chaotically out of step. About three-quarters of our guest list had showed up by the time we went on stage. It does mean something to be headlining. And it didn't hurt, either, that Ace's High was so small that this modest crowd was a capacity one. We couldn't take all the credit: Dew Over, Bloodthirsty Fakers, and Vanilla Camp had left a residue of punters who were determined to get full value for money, curious about a band with two gaijins in it, or simply willing to give us a try. Some of them had trickled away during our first number, but others lingered. They even clapped.

Unlike Gen, I didn't just stand there. I covered the whole stage – which wasn't difficult: I could only take two paces before I bumped into Gen or Tad, our bassist. I struck poses, touched myself, danced with the mic stand, and interacted with the boys. My bottle-green top hat shadowed my face in the hot, shifting spotlights. When I finally doffed it, applause went up. I mugged, did a clownish shuffle, then hooked the hat on my mic stand and started dancing in earnest. I wore my cowboy boots, my lucky talismans, harness brown with turquoise, gold, and white flames. Their heels made me tall enough to see four or five deep into the crowd.

"Let's talk about you," I ranted, "and the little places you call home."

Tad planted his left foot on a wedge speaker and banged his head as he churned out the bass solo. A pair of black cat ears poked out of his flying hair. At home he also had floppy white bunny ears, tall grey donkey ears, and a magician's hat with stars and moons on it. He liked to wear that one with a gold kimono.

"It was the only thing you've ever done! I hope, oh yeah, I hope it was a good one."

I extended the end of the phrase into a melodic scream, jammed my mic onto the stand, and let my head fall forward as Gen took over for the outro. Through the curtain of hair that slid in front of my face, I saw constellations of cigarette ends explode in the outer darkness as the technique freaks applauded. I straightened up and gestured broadly, helping the spotlight on Gen to make its point.

Joaquin crashed both hands down on the keyboard of his Korg. An instant of silence, and then the applause kicked in. I stepped back to the mic and thanked the crowd.

"For those of you that we haven't got to know yet, Joaquin's the tunesmith." In his place behind the Korg, Joaquin bowed. "I write the lyrics. They let me do that because I can't play an instrument."

Tad grabbed my mic and said, "I've got an idea, Shanti. You can have my job and I'll have yours."

I grinned and said over the catcalls, "Shut up, Tad, I'm busy showing off my Japanese."

This got a huge laugh, as usual. To the extent I spoke

Japanese, I spoke it like a native. For that I could thank my sense of pitch, but more to the point, as Joaquin could have explained, once you have a second language, it's no big deal to acquire a third one. As a kid in Paris, I'd gone from zero to fluent in French in a year, and as an adult in Tokyo, it had taken me only slightly longer than that to learn Japanese. I still had plenty of holes in my vocabulary, but they didn't show onstage.

"Now guess what, you lucky people, we're going to do a song off the new album. U-Turn Day, out next Saturday from Cold Coeur Records. Available from your local clued-up independent music store, or buy it on our website, where we're streaming select tracks for your listening pleasure. Now here's another dirty little sample." I leaned into the mic. "When I first started writing lyrics for Gorot, I didn't want to write about the same old thing. You know. Lurrrve."

Nina, Joaquin's wife and our recording angel, dodged across the Bermuda Crescent in front of the stage with her digital camera. Our Shimokitazawa gigs rarely got rowdy enough for the crowd to venture into that buffer zone between us and them. Even when they did, they retreated when the music stopped.

"But I've learned a lot since I've been in this band," I said. "I've realized that I have more to say about life in general than I ever knew."

I saw him.

His blond hair shone in the dark. He was leaning against the wall about three people behind Nina. At this distance I couldn't see his eyes.

"A lot to say," I repeated. "A lot to say."

I had nothing to say to Ned Gallant, now or ever.

But maybe it wasn't him. Maybe it was just some coworker of Nina's who hadn't been on the guest list, or one of the European drifters Joaquin collected.

Tad glanced sharply at me. I couldn't tell if he was alarmed, or just trying to prompt me, but it reminded me why I was here, why I'd written the song I was currently supposed to be introducing, and how I'd felt while I was writing it, in my tiny studio apartment with my headphones on, pushing rewind over and over again on the rough mix: as far from Ireland as I would ever get.

"Recently," I said, "I realized that I even have something to say about love. And this is it. 'Heartbreak.'"

I signaled to Joaquin with one hand behind my back. The silence lengthened: one, two, three, and the first plaintive piano notes floated out over Tad's bass line. Shingo tapped on the rim of the snare, a sinister rhythm like a clock ticking. Until its closing seconds, this song required no more of Gen than filler duties. "Heartbreak" was that rare thing in our repertoire, a slow burner designed to prove that I could actually sing, and that was appropriate, because it was my song of liberation.

"Struck dumb by a closing door," I sang, cupping my mic in both hands for a bit of distortion, "face down on the bathroom floor. Here's a dirty little sample, better keep it to yourself. I've lived, I've been, I've seen…"

Joaquin's line swelled, surging towards maximum volume.

"I've sunk, I've swum, I've fallen in between…"

Someone whistled deafeningly.

"And you, you think that you'll remain in my memory like a stain, but you'll fade like everyone! You were never here!"

Sweet, languid Jonathan had been the lead guitarist of the first band I was ever in, back in New York, and I'd thought he was the love of my life, until he turned out to be a cheater and a liar. When he cheated on me, I hadn't just dumped him, I'd left the country. Top that, asshole. I'd won, but it had taken me another four years to write him, literally, out of my heart.

And in the meantime, I'd discovered something strange and surprising, better than sex and almost as good as music.

Friendship.

I'd once had a boyfriend. Now I had four boy friends

who meant more to me than Jonathan ever had.

I'd written "Heartbreak" for them, and if the lyrics didn't really reflect that... well, my lyrics always turned out kind of dark.

I couldn't lose them. I couldn't, but my own words sounded like a dire prophecy as I sobbed, "Stupid enough to not quite see the temporary nature of everything behind your eyes!"

It was Gen's moment. Unexpectedly, he launched a gargoyle of a riff that climbed on the back of Joaquin's piano line and reached for the stratosphere. We'd heard this variation in rehearsal, but never live. I signaled to Tad and went for a repeat of the chorus. Gen's riff toyed with my voice, then folded up and flatlined into a distorted hum that grew louder and louder until it swallowed Joaquin's last notes.

After that, our last number was an anticlimax. I thrashed around the stage, but I couldn't stop looking at that spot over by the wall. In a montage of underexposed stills, I saw him draining a can of beer, taking off his knit cap, and putting two fingers in his mouth and whistling. So it had been him.

"Encore! Encore!"

For once I wished our supporters weren't quite so faithful.

"Encore!"

I bowed for the third time. Behind me, Joaquin hissed, "What are you waiting for?"

"No encore," I said through my smile.

"Fuck off. What's wrong?"

With the show officially over, we could take a minute to confer. I went back to Joaquin, mic in hand. His face was scarlet and his hands hovered on the keyboard. "OK," I told him, "I'll do an encore. But not 'You're No Fun.'"

"Don't give me this shit. If you don't want to do it, why did you want it on the set list?"

"Joaquin, I can't fucking do it!"

Joaquin's jaw tightened. He seized the mic from my hand and plunged around the Korg, shaking the cord clear.

"OK, we'll do another track from Xenophobia," he said out of the side of his mouth. "They've heard the whole album many times, but what the hell."

He arrived at the front of the stage in a single stride with his smile on full. A storm of clapping greeted him. Everyone knew he was the brains of the band, and although he seldom took a producer's bow, they felt he deserved it. He thanked them in English, Japanese, and French, and waited for the applause to subside. I hovered at his side, trying to look supportive rather than apprehensive. He said in Japanese, "We are delighted that you come all the way to Shimokitazawa to see us. I mean, it's the middle of nowhere, eh?"

Laughter.

"We hope you will come all the way to Hokkaido to see us, too! We can't reimburse you for the airfare, but we think it will be worth it. They say that Sapporo is a beautiful city. Myself, I've never been there, but I'm looking forward to it. Yes, ladies and gentlemen, Goro is going on tour!"

I did what I had to do, which was lead the applause. When we were debating whether to tour for U-Turn Day, I'd been anti. I didn't know why I even bothered, since Joaquin always got his way in the end.

"Some of you are familiar with Kinderbox," continued Joaquin, naming another of the acts he produced for our label, Cold Coeur Records, which he also owned. "We tour together. We will look for you next week in Sapporo! Hakodate! Aomori! Morioka! Yamagata! Sendai! Fukushima! And Utsunomiya! But if we don't see you there, we hope to meet on Tuesday the twelfth of March at Oasis in Shinjuku, where we plan a party for our homecoming. It is also the release party for U-Turn Day! Yoroshiku onegai shimasu. Also," Joaquin added rapidly, "we have gigs upcoming throughout March, please check out the information on the flyers. We're running late, but we will do one more song for you tonight. 'Dreamstomper.'" Throwing me a look of triumph mixed with a challenge, he hopped back behind the Korg.

Numbly, I waited for the piano loop to roll out of the speakers. In the interval of rustling silence I cleared my throat. "This one's for everyone who got lost along the way," I said, wishing Ned Gallant had.

Backstage, Nina handed out bottles of Crystal Geyser. Joaquin upended his over his head, splashing everyone. "To Cold Coeur Family Volume I!" This, unbelievably, was what our tour had come to be called. Infected by his mood, the other boys slavishly acted like they'd all been excited about it from the start. The manager played along, too, opining that it would be just the ticket to launch us into the big time. Joaquin followed him into his office to sort out our cut of the door. After retrieving our kit from the stage, Gen, Tad, and Shingo piled into the cruddy little restroom down the hall and jostled for access to the tap.

I gulped water. As soon as Joaquin squared the manager, we were due to join up with our faithful supporters and head to an izakaya. Ned might turn out to be someone else, and it wouldn't be the first time. My fight-or-flight reflex often went off at the sight of a blond head and a pair of blue eyes. But if it had been him…

Pushing a hand through my damp, tangled hair, I went out the side door and said hello to my friends. There were about two dozen people left in the house, and I didn't know all their faces, let alone their names. Back in Gorot's early days, the same people had come to all our gigs and we'd gone to all their gigs; now we had friends and fans, and it was getting harder to tell which were which. I clocked the blond guy hovering near the exit.

I went back through the grey room, past the manager's office and the restroom, looking for another way out. There was an emergency exit, but it was padlocked.

I retrieved my shoulderbag, threw on my coat, and ducked back through the side door. I didn't have a plan. All I knew was that I had to keep Ned away from the band. I couldn't be sure that he wouldn't approach me in front of them, and I was even less sure of my own ability to deny to his face that we'd ever met. I wasn't even sure that would be the best line to take. He might react unpredictably.

"Shanti, you're not skipping out?" Nina said in astonishment.

"You're on PR duty, gorgeous," I said. "Oh, I left my hatbox back there. Could you take it home with you? I'll come over and pick it up tomorrow or sometime."

I beelined to the exit, calling goodnight to the technicians who were shutting down the equipment onstage. As I passed the blond guy, he took an abortive step towards me. I pushed through the door into February. His footsteps echoed mine on the stairs. Out on the street, the rest of our supporters were hanging around in groups, smoking and chatting. I shouted to them that I had an early start tomorrow and inconsistently turned left, away from the station. He caught up with me. I kept walking. At the 7-11 on the corner I turned again. He matched my strides. A cold, dusty wind blew around us.

"Fuck, this feels weird." His voice was deep. I'd subconsciously been expecting him to sound like a child. "But it feels kind of natural, too, doesn't it?"

"Well, it's been a while," I said, head ringing.

"A while?" He laughed. He looked like none of the men I'd mistaken for him over the years. He was still blond, and his eyes were still that eerie blue – but he was no longer small or pale or skinny. His skin had seen a lot of sun, and he hulked over me with shoulders as broad as the axle of a small car. He'd turned out as big as Nigel. But his accent no longer sounded like Nigel's. It had softened dramatically. "I guess you've added the art of understatement to your repertoire. It's been half our lives. No, more. I was twelve, and your birthday is before mine, so you'd have been thirteen."

He spoke as if he didn't remember exactly. This confused me.

"So how's Alastair doing these days?"

411

We were turning corners at random, and although I couldn't remember crossing the railway tracks, we must have done, because we were now descending the gentle hill on the far side of Shimokitazawa station. Shuttered boutiques lined the narrow street. Here and there, golden light from the windows of a restaurant shone through a screen of trees. The wind numbed my face; it seemed to have penetrated to my bones and slowed down my brain. Ned and I were talking. How had this happened?

"Alastair lives in the States," I said. My brother had spent his early twenties trying to be an artist; now he was the assistant manager of Windrose & Sons, a 150-year-old gallery in Boston's Back Bay that sold objets d'art and antiques from all over the world, true to its origins as a clearing-house for plunder from the Orient. He and his girlfriend Maisie lived together in Somerville with her second-hand Volvo, his BMW 6-series, and two Weimaraners, and he seemed happy. "He's doing OK, I guess."

"Figures. He was bound to land on his feet. And June? Still painting, is she?"

"She moved back to France years ago," I said. Our mother had nothing to do with it. Ned would have no reason to track her down, nor could he learn anything from her he didn't already know. "She lives near Bordeaux now. It's la France profonde, the true France. She keeps chickens and goats. And yeah, she's still painting her heart out."

Ned laughed. "You know something funny? All this time I thought your family was still in Thailand."

"You're kidding! We only stayed there for six months."

I remembered promising Ned that he could come with us. Promising it would be all right. But I was only thirteen and it wasn't my decision to make.

Ned would probably have hated Thailand, though. We did. After Ireland, it had been so hot that I felt like I'd stepped onto another planet. I remembered the energy draining from my thirteen-year-old body, the sunlight so bright that my eyes hurt, and a hundred and one permutations of boredom and anxiety. That was nothing to how June must have felt. She'd dragged us halfway around the world to the one man who had to take us in: our father. Malcolm Ogilvie had settled in Phuket. He was a poet – we'd owned an actual book of poetry by him at one point – but he subsisted on the generosity of hotel and bar managers who gave him odd jobs. From his point of view, having the three of us descend on him must have been the worst trip of his life, especially since he had a live-in Thai girlfriend.

Somehow, we all managed to cohabit in his disgusting bungalow for five or six months. That was how long it took June to accept that she'd made a mistake. She fell back on her brother Red, my corporate lawyer uncle in Philadelphia. And just like that, as if the first thirteen years of my life had been a dream, I'd suddenly had the life of a privileged American teenager.

Not for long, though. Unlike Alastair, I hadn't been able to keep it up.

"As for our father," I said, "he's dead."

It was Ned's turn to exclaim, "You're kidding!" And in his smile I saw a hint of schadenfreude that chilled me to the bone.

"He hanged himself about ten years ago," according to the letter that the Thai girlfriend had sent June. It had been wrapped around a small teak box that contained Malcolm's ashes. "He left a typical, self-pitying note. Saying he'd failed everyone and he was sorry. Talk about wasted sentiments. *We* weren't."

Ned hissed between his teeth. I thought I'd succeeded in shocking him. But he said in the same easy tone as before, "Funny thing is, *I* live in Thailand now. On Koh Samui. I go across to Phuket all the time, and I used to ask around for you, but no one's ever heard of you or your father."

Shit.

"Ned, how on earth did you end up in Thailand?"

"I'm an architect," he said, and went on expansively, in the strange nonaccent he'd acquired. "Koh Samui is booming.

The tsunami created a lot of opportunities. New regulations, new land up for sale. I've got my own business, building villas. Referrals from all over. The clients appreciate having someone on the ground to see their projects through to completion: they don't want to deal with the Thais themselves. They're racist fuckers, as a rule. But I believe in doing the best work possible."

"Wow."

"I'm building my own house, too. It's still under construction. I've been working on it on and off for the last four years. But it's going to be fucking stunning. I can show you some photos if you're interested."

Laughter bubbled up in my chest. Ned was a *builder*. I didn't know why this struck me as so funny. I said, "Cool. Did you study architecture at school?" I wanted to find out where he'd spent the twelve years that were still unaccounted for. Why couldn't I just ask?

"Sure, I learned on the job. That's the best way. Hands-on experience. You've got to be focused, though. Thailand is full of Westerners who just drift from beach to beach..." Ned shook his head.

"Oh, we've got them here, too, except they don't come for the beaches. They come for the jobs."

"Still, I can't criticize that lifestyle. I lived on Bali for a while. Bummed around Indonesia, Malaysia, India." We reached the level crossing at the bottom of the hill. The barrier was down, the warning bell pinging. "I guess I was looking for something, but I didn't know what it was," Ned shouted as a train rushed past. "Maybe it was just a decent living," he added, laughing.

"Look," I said, pointing to a record shop on a side street. "They sell our albums. We've got our own label, and we're hooked up with an independent distributor."

"Oh yeah? Way to go!"

"Jesus, Ned, what *has* happened to your accent? You sound almost American."

"You sound fairly American yourself, Shanti."

"Well, I went to school on the East Coast. High school in Philly, and then NYU." No need to mention that I hadn't graduated, committing myself to rock 'n' roll instead of to the library.

"Get a load of you. I didn't go to university at all. After you left, my grandmother showed up and took me back to Denmark with her."

"Denmark!" That was it, of course. He didn't sound American. He sounded ever so slightly Scandinavian. The legend came back to me all at once: the mother who did a runner when Ned was three, leaving Nigel to raise him whilst making a go of his business, Allihies Ceramics. I even remembered Ned telling me where she'd come from. Somewhere like Norway, but without the funky mythic associations. *Denmark.* "I didn't know you even *had* a grandmother!" I said.

"Neither did I, until she walked in and told me to pack my stuff. I had a terrible time adjusting in Copenhagen. Couldn't get my tongue around the language. I used to think about you and Alastair jabbering away to each other in French. How did you do it? I picked up enough Danish in the end to get by, but as soon as I got out of school I buggered off. I used to go back as often as possible to see my grandmother, though. I owed her, didn't I?"

"She must be an amazing lady," to have put up with you, I added to myself.

"She was. She died last year."

"Oh Ned, I'm so sorry."

I caught his flickering glance of contempt. He didn't believe I was sorry, although when I said it, I *had* been.

We rounded the corner onto the plaza. I veered towards the station entrance and started up the stairs. Ned climbed beside me. He was explaining how it was that he could jaunt off to Japan at his pleasure, with zero hardship or sacrifice, but I wasn't really listening, because I knew it was just a bunch of excuses. I was wondering if I could lose him in Tokyo's fiendishly complicated rail system. "Have you got a ticket?"

"I need to buy one, do I? Where to?"

I thought quickly. "To Shibuya, but the tickets are priced by distance. It's a hundred and twenty yen."

I watched him shoulder through the milling crowd to the ticket machines, scoop change out of his pocket, and examine every coin before putting one into the slot. I had a prepaid Passnet card. I thought about dashing through the wickets while his back was turned. But there was only one platform. I'd have much better odds of losing him in Shibuya, where the JR, Tokyu, and Keio Inogashira train lines and the Ginza, Hanzomon, and Denentoshi subway lines all looped around each other in a multistorey knot.

As we came out of the wickets at Shibuya, I plunged ahead of Ned into the horde pouring down into the Mark City building. He seized the shoulder strap of my bag. "You don't mind if I hang onto you? This is fucking mad. I've never seen anything like it in my life. Feel like I'm about to be swept off my feet."

"Yeah, it's crazy, isn't it," I said, teeth gritted in frustration.

But then again, if I'd cut and run I would have looked guilty. And he'd just turn up again at our next gig, wouldn't he? My only hope was to brazen it out and get rid of him by some means as yet beyond the reach of my imagination. Leave him as completely as possible in the dark.

Yet every minute he was finding out more about my new life. I showed him how to buy a JR ticket and we rode the Yamanote line south, squashed shoulder to shoulder between drowsy drunks and noisy ones. At Gotanda I got off. He got off. We left the station and walked along a dark street, embroidered on one side with snack bar signs, which led back along the foot of the Yamanote line embankment. There was no traffic. Gotanda was an undercover town, buttoned up during the day and sleazy by night, with the highest concentration of love hotels south of Shibuya. You never bumped

416

into anyone you knew here, which was why it suited me.

Among the office buildings on this side of the station towered a few elderly apartment blocks. I came to the dinged elevator doors at the foot of my building and turned to face Ned, feeling panicky. "Well, now you know where I live."

"Pretty ritzy." He craned his neck to look up at eight floors of concrete balconies.

"At least it's supposed to be earthquake-proof," I said.

"Oh sure, that would be a concern in this country."

We stood between the morgue-like walls of mailboxes. Was he waiting for me to invite him in? Did he plan on crashing *at my place?* No. No. No. This was not happening.

"Whereabouts are you staying, Ned?" I said bluntly.

"I've a couple of mates living in the city." He looked away from me. There was a trace of anger in his voice. "They came to Japan to work and save money, and they're spending it as fast as they make it, but they're good lads. I'll introduce you at some point. Mike's got a job in the public school system; Gavin works for one of these English conversation schools, same as you. They're raking it in. So they've a house, not just a crappy little apartment, in Nakano. You know where that is?"

Five minutes west on the Chuo line from Shinjuku. A goodly haul from here. But nowhere would be far enough.

"I can stay with them as long as I want. It's party central, but I'm not fussy. You've no need to worry about me on that score!" Ned chuckled, an unamused masculine sound that reminded me of Nigel.

"Ned, how did you find me?" I blurted. Immediately, I had a sensation of having taken a misstep. "I've often thought about *you*, but I had no way of knowing where you were."

He looked at me for a long minute. I concentrated on not letting a muscle of my face twitch. At last he said, "I searched for your name on the internet. Googled you, and up you popped. Your band's website. Pictures and everything."

I'd known it. I'd *known* it.

"So I knew it was you. Of course, it had to be you; there can't be two people in the world named Shanti Hazard."

Oh God. To hell with staying true to myself. I should have changed my name.

"That was about eighteen months ago."

So I'd been living in jeopardy, my illusion of safety hanging by a thread, for more than a year.

But how could I have talked the boys out of putting up a website? How could I have forced them to leave me off it? I was the face of Gorot, literally – Tad had used a picture of me for our logo, and they were always pushing for more pictures: pictures of me walking on the beach, drinking coffee, laughing out loud – pictures that would make me seem like someone you knew. I vetoed all but the blurriest live shots. That had made me feel better about the website, as did the fact that not much of the information on it was in English. But what difference did that make when my *name* was out there?

"I thought about getting in touch there and then, but you know how it is. Life gets in the way. By the time I finally got around to it, I thought I might as well just pop over and see you. So I got a Japanese mate to translate the squiggly bits for me, and here I am!"

"And how do you like it so far?" I keened softly through my chattering teeth.

"Well, I'll tell you. It's bloody confusing and it's bloody cold." Ned lowered his voice conspiratorially. "And do you get the feeling that these people don't know how to relax? This is according to my Japanese mate at home, but the culture here is fucking totalitarian. The level of social control is such that the people can't make their own choices. If they could, maybe they'd choose to be a bit more free!"

"I like it here because I fit in," I said, provoking a cry of disbelief from him. I explained, though it felt futile: "I didn't do very well as an American. It's much easier to be a foreigner."

"Well, in that case, then, I know what you mean! It was a

nightmare living in Denmark, as I said. Looking like them but not speaking their language, not knowing their TV shows or their songs, not knowing shit about their fucking history and not caring. But when you're a Westerner out East, no one cares where you supposedly come from. No one asks why you've got a funny accent. You don't have to pretend to be something you're not. You can be yourself, can't you?"

Ned's face lit up as the words tumbled out. I didn't want to agree with him about anything, so I said nothing.

"Shanti, this is the kind of conversation I want to have with you! It's not everyone who understands, is it? But you're on my wavelength. You've had the same life experiences. You were *there.*"

Feeling dizzy, I steadied myself on the mailboxes.

"I just want to talk. No games, no bullshit." He looked eagerly into my face. "I just want us to be open with each other."

"Yeah, OK," I said faintly, "but can we do it some other time? I'm dead on my feet, and if I don't get indoors, I'm going to die of hypothermia."

"Oh well, then, I won't keep you," he said, drawing back with unsettling rapidity. "We couldn't have *that,* could we?"

END OF EXCERPT

Music to Die By is now available for purchase from your preferred online book retailer in print and ebook editions. Learn more about the book and the author at www.knightshillpublishing.com